Mayhem

Visit Paul Henke on his website
for current titles and future novels at:

www.henke.co.uk

or email Paul at

henke@sol.co.uk

Mayhem

Paul Henke

To Anna,

Many thanks!

Paul Henke.

GOOD READ PUBLISHING

First published in 2000 by Good Read Publishing
A Good Read Publishing paperback

10 9 8 7 6 5 4 3 2 1

A CIP catalogue record for this title is available
from the British Library

ISBN 1-902483-02-2

Typeset by Palimpsest Book Production Limited,
Polmont, Stirlingshire
Printed and bound in Great Britain by
Omnia Book Limited, Glasgow

Good Read Publishing Ltd
Auchleshie House
Kelty Bridge
Callander FK17 8LS

This book is dedicated to my wife Dorothy without whose help I couldn't succeed.

Acknowledgements

I would like to thank the editors who have done such a fine job, in particular Anne Buhrmann of Falkirk, Les Stevenson of Burton-on-Trent and Mary Young of Balfron.

Prologue

In their own country the two girls were denied any semblance of childhood. In spite of the fact that neither had yet reached puberty, they wore the chador whenever they appeared in public. Even then they were constantly surrounded by an army of guards and a platoon of chaperones. They did not attend school like other children but had private tutors. In their own country they lived like prisoners, albeit prisoners kept in a gilded cage. Tragically their fate was linked not to their own identity, but to their grandfather's. It was unfair. They had no say in the matter. It was only on those rare occasions when they were abroad that the door to the cage was opened and they could step outside and taste freedom. Even then it was highly restricted. Being virtually unknown outside their own country, they were able to dress like ordinary children and do things that other kids took for granted. Like go to the zoo or walk in the park. Or go to the cinema and have a Big Mac afterwards. Which was what they were doing that wet and rainy afternoon in Paris.

It was a persistent rain that dragged an early dusk with it. The traffic was chaotic, bumper to bumper and, at the end of the working day, Parisians' tempers were frayed. The two children had been to see a Disney feature-length cartoon and were now running, along the pavement to a Macdonald's less than fifty metres away. A nanny and a bodyguard ran with them. They all had their coat collars turned up, their heads bent. The car with the diplomatic number plates was trapped outside the cinema, the driver swearing profusely. He had insisted they climb into the car and he would drive them. The two girls had objected and disobeyed him. They had resolutely walked away dragging the nanny with them. The bodyguard had shrugged and followed them. The driver of the car was now trying to pull into the traffic. To most Parisians a diplomatic number plate meant nothing. To others it was a red rag to a bull. It represented parking tickets not paid, speed limits not obeyed, driving in a manner even a Parisian wouldn't countenance. In a word, many Parisians were jealous. Irate drivers eloquently raised their middle fingers so often that he finally bulldozed his way into the slowly moving stream of traffic.

He had his window open and could see the bodyguard catch up with the other three. He recognised the sound of a gunshot and watched in horror as the bodyguard stumbled and fell. The nanny stood in shock and began backing away, pulling the children with her. Hiding them behind her. The driver swore, stopped the car and climbed out reaching for his gun. Immediately the air was filled with a cacophony of horns as infuriated Parisians vented their anger on somebody stupid enough to stop in the middle of a busy thoroughfare in rush hour. Those who saw the man with the gun quickly stopped blowing their horns. The driver committed a brave but senseless act as there was nothing he could do to save the children. As the bullets hit him and he died, his uppermost thought was one of thankfulness. It was better to die than to face the wrath of the children's grandfather.

1

Hunter was sitting in the comfortable living room of his parents house, enjoying a Speyside malt whisky with a dash of soda. The room was large, wood-lined in light oak and one wall was filled with books. A fire burnt low in the grate and although it was the beginning of June, there was a distinct chill in the Scottish air.

'Cheers, Dad.' He raised his glass to the man sitting opposite him and took an appreciative sip.

His father smiled, raised his own glass and said, 'Good health.' The years had treated Tim Hunter kindly. A tall, spare man with a shock of grey hair, he still looked fit for his age. He had been a reporter when he had met his wife. Soon after their marriage he had been offered a job by the family firm to manage a Scottish fishing fleet. It had been made clear that it was no sinecure and that results were expected. His father had been a deep sea fisherman off the eastern coast of Newfoundland. Tim Hunter had spent his childhood working on fishing boats of all descriptions. He knew and understood the men who worked the dangerous seas around the British Isles and he had worked hard for the company and for his men. He had built the fleet into one of the biggest and most successful in Europe. Somehow he had even managed to weather the storms that devastated the fishing industry of Britain when it was sold out to Europe by Margaret Thatcher in the early eighties. By adding fish processing, farming and distribution to the portfolio, he had created one of the most profitable and important divisions in the company. His reward had been a seat on the board, share options and, as he put it, more money that he could reasonably spend. After retirement he had turned his hand to writing novels. His training as a newspaper reporter in his early twenties stood him in good stead and he enjoyed researching the information he needed to ensure his stories were written with complete authenticity. 'Well son, are you going to tell me all about it?'

Hunter nodded. 'I've written a lot of it down. It's for your archives only, Dad, don't forget. You can publish it after my death.'

'Dear God, I hope I'll be gone a long time before you. However,' aware of what his son did and the dangers he often faced, Tim Hunter nodded, 'should something happen I'll make sure the records are kept straight. So what happened?'

Hunter related to his father the rescue of the hostages and the death of Habib. When he was finished, he went into the hallway where the drinks cupboard was to be found and replenished the contents of his glass. He walked back to the fireplace, and added some more logs. His father sat pensively watching the flames, thinking about the parachute jump and how close his son had come to being killed. The other officer with him had died, shot when landing on the roof of a building in an attempt to capture one of the most wanted terrorists in the world – Aziz Habib. That had been his son's first operation working for the new, anti-terrorist organisation, The International Force Against Terrorism, acronym TIFAT.

'Nick, don't you think,' he paused, cleared his throat and continued. 'Don't you think it's time to quit? After all, you've made lieutenant commander. Prospects in a shrinking Royal Navy aren't that great and there are companies to run. You know the firm could use you.'

The firm was the sprawling empire carved out by the Griffiths family during the last hundred years. They were involved in all the world's major industries from banking to airlines to insurance. One day, a small percentage of the company – perhaps three to four percent of the family's holdings – would pass to Hunter. When it did, he would be rich beyond words. Although he was in no hurry to collect.

He shook his head. 'I'm not ready, yet. I have,' he shrugged, 'let me say, rivers to cross and mountains to climb, before settling down to a life in business.'

'If you live that long,' his father replied, dryly.

Hunter grinned. 'Well, it means Louise will get that much more. Anyway, I don't intend to die. Not for a long time. You know, Dad, it's not like the bad old days. "Over the top and charge" went out of modern warfare a long time ago. Now it's all carefully planned, over planned, if the truth were known. And the reality is we won't be fighting nation on nation. We'll be fighting with overwhelming technology against tribes who are barely out of the stone-age.'

Tim Hunter took a sip of whisky, unadulterated by either ice or soda and said, 'Son, you can't kid me. I may be retired but I still know what's going on. The Middle East has more weapons than they know what to do with. The Soviet Union is in pieces, there's more hardware sloshing around the world than ever and the result is more localised wars than in the history of mankind.'

'Who says?'

'*Time Magazine* is who. They listed them. Sixty-four conflicts of one sort or another are presently being fought. Northern Ireland is not a thing of the past in spite of the Good Friday agreement. So if we start there and look around the world we have strife in Europe, Africa, Asia and America. In fact, across the world. And you're right in the middle of it with Macnair.' His father was talking about General Malcolm Macnair, the officer commanding TIFAT.

Hunter smiled at his father. 'I wouldn't want it any other way. And don't forget, now that we've moved to *Cochrane*, I'll see a lot more of you and Mum.' Hunter was referring to the shore establishment at Rosyth in Scotland. TIFAT had spent the last few weeks transferring equipment and personnel from Plymouth. 'Dad, somebody has to fight these people. Terrorism has been described as the twenty first century's war and it's true. If we don't stop them, wipe them out at every opportunity, the world will go to hell in a basket.'

'If it hasn't already. Okay, okay,' his father held up his hand,

3

'I won't argue. I know they have to be stopped.' He forced a smile, looking his son in the eyes. 'I only wish that somebody else could do it.'

'Do what?' The door had opened and an attractive woman stood there, taking off her gloves, unbuttoning her coat. Only the grey streaks in her hair gave a true indication of her age; as Sian Hunter said of herself, nearer sixty than fifty.

'Hi, Mum,' Hunter crossed the room and kissed his mother's cheek. 'Can I help you?'

'Please, Nick. Empty the car so that I can get dinner. What were you two talking about? As if I couldn't guess.'

'Nothing much, Mum,' said Hunter, looking uncomfortable, not wishing to upset her.

'It's all right,' she touched her son's cheek, 'I know. Well, I agree with your father but I won't try and persuade you otherwise. Get me a sherry, will you?'

While her son poured her a drink she stood in front of the fire, warming herself. 'You know, your father has never come to terms with the idea that the women of the family are as tough as the men. And that's in spite of the fact that he wrote the definitive history of the family and nearly won the Pulitzer for it. Thank you, darling,' she took the proffered glass and sipped. 'Just be careful, that's all I ask.'

'I'm always careful,' Hunter replied, but then spoilt it, by adding "usually" under his breath, as he walked out of the door. At the back of the house he happily unloaded the groceries from the car, enjoying the humdrum nature of the task.

Later they sat in the kitchen while his mother prepared their meal, chatting about the village, family and friends. Over dinner, which they ate in the dining area of the kitchen, his father asked, 'What's next? Are you up to anything?'

Hunter shook his head. 'Nope. We've been training for the last week or two, waiting for something to happen. We spend a great deal of time accumulating and sifting through data that comes in from all over the world. Some of it is useful but a lot of it is complete dross. The useful stuff we either use or pass on to relevant governments or agencies. You're right about what you

4

said. There's a hell of a lot of conflict going on and nobody seems to be too bothered by most of it. As long as it's contained within borders and doesn't affect us or ours then we let them get on with it. It's a sad state of affairs, of that there's no doubt.'

'What about the latest in the Middle East?' his mother asked. 'Will there be war?'

'Between Israel and the Arabs? I doubt it. Israel has a nuclear capability and has made it clear that should they ever be threatened with an overwhelming force then they would use it. No, the Arabs will continue to fund the Palestinians who will continue to die in the service of their country and religion. A few Israelis will be killed and the Arab world will say, "Look, we're doing everything in our power to beat the Jews and give the Palestinians their own, independent country. We can't do any more". Stupid really, but I think it will continue like that for a long time to come. Unless something happens to upset the political balance in the region. Should fundamentalists on either side get too strong then all hell could break loose. It's one of the strategic games we play on the computer. It's called Operation Slaughter,' Hunter paused and took a sip of wine. 'Anyway, enough of that. How's Sis?'

'Louise? She's fine. Sends her love and hopes to be here tomorrow,' his mother replied.

'Where's she coming in from?'

'Los Angeles,' Tim Hunter answered. 'It's her first trip as Captain.'

Hunter smiled. 'Good for her. What's she flying? A 757?'

'No, a European Airbus,' said his mother. 'She did well to get the job she did.'

'Mother!' Hunter spoke in exasperation. 'Seeing as the Firm owns the company it was hardly going to be difficult for her to get the job.'

'No, you're wrong there,' his father said, sharply. 'It was more difficult. Not only did she have one of the best records of anybody interviewed but she had to prove herself time and again in the simulator. She handled more incidents better than any of the other twenty-eight pilots who were applying.'

'How do you know?' Hunter asked.

'Because I told your uncle James to make it difficult,' replied Tim Hunter.

'Why on earth did you do that?'

His father grinned, 'Because I then made sure the results were leaked and everyone knew just how hard it had been for her. Otherwise there could have been cries of nepotism.'

Hunter roared with laughter. 'Good for you, Dad. Does Louise know?'

His mother, Sian, shook her head. 'And we'd rather you kept it that way.'

'Sure. I won't say a word. Is there any cheese?'

'There's some Stilton in the fridge,' said his mother. 'I'll get it while you find the port.'

They spent an enjoyable evening, chatting and playing Scrabble. Towards midnight Hunter stood, stretched and said, 'I'll take Winston for a walk before I turn in.' At the mention of his name the dog, a golden Labrador, perked up from his comfortable position in front of the fire. 'Come on, boy,' said Hunter. As they went out through the front door Hunter picked up the dog's lead, though he rarely ever had to use it.

The two of them stepped out into the street and wandered down the hill towards the river Endrick. The longest day of the year was only three weeks away and there was a glow in the sky. It came partly from the orange lights of Glasgow showing over the top of the Campsie Hills and reflected in the scattered clouds and partly from the quarter moon rising behind them.

It was a still night, with only the slightest rustling in the leaves from a light breeze. At the river they crossed the bridge and turned right along the track. Tall trees lined both sides and the gurgle of water could be clearly heard rushing over the stones. Hunter enjoyed the stroll, the night air clearing the fugue of alcohol from his brain. Winston, although nearly ten years old, was darting back and forth like a puppy, happy to be with his master once again. Suddenly the dog stopped and crouched, his tail low and flat, swishing slowly back and forth. Hunter made a low hissing sound and the dog slinked silently to his side. Hunter reached down and stroked the dog's head.

'Let's take a look, old boy,' he whispered. They moved stealthily nearer the river. Hunter sniffed the air. 'Cigarette smoke,' he said softly. 'Was that what you smelt? Come on, quiet now.' They stepped off the track and down to the river. Stealthily they walked downstream, Hunter carefully scrutinising the dark shadows. It could be another person walking their dog or it could be poachers. His father had told him that there had been quite a spate of poaching incidents recently and that the bailiffs were desperate to stop it.

After a few minutes Hunter halted and knelt beside Winston. His instincts told him that they were close to whoever was there. He was also sure that whoever it was, was up to no good. He heard a splash and a loud voice yelled, 'Got it!'

'Quiet, you fool. Not so loud!' Another voice whispered fiercely. Twenty metres away three men materialised out of a copse and stood next to the water.

'Hurry up,' one of them hissed. 'Afore the bloody bailiffs get here.'

Suddenly there was a loud commotion and a whistle blew. Yells of "Stop!" and "Hey, You!" filled the air. The three men froze, looked about them and then started running towards Hunter.

'Quiet, boy,' he said. 'Let them come here.'

There were more yells and curses. One of the men tripped, falling flat on his face. The other two poachers kept running. Hunter saw the prostrate man being pounced on by his pursuers before turning his attention to the two running towards him.

'Oot o' the way,' the accent was harsh Glaswegian, the burly man threatening Hunter with a raised stave.

Hunter stepped to one side and said, 'Pass.' As the man came alongside, Hunter put out his foot and barged into him. The man gave a shriek and went flying into the river. The second man, a slight figure, tried to dodge past but Hunter grabbed his arm, spun him around and flung him after his friend. He landed with a loud splash and many curses.

Three other figures came running up, panting. 'Thanks,' gasped one of them. 'We can take it from here.'

7

'Want a hand, John?' Hunter asked.

'Nick! I hadn't realised it was you.' Warm handshakes were exchanged. 'What are you doing here?'

'Visiting the folks and right now, walking the dog. I came out for some peace and quiet. The last thing I expected was to get caught up in catching poachers. At least, I assume that's what's going on.'

'Aye, it is. I've been after them for some time, so I appreciate your help. I estimate they've taken about a thousand pounds worth of salmon from the river in the last six weeks.' As head gamekeeper for one of the local landowners, John Meredith was responsible for the hunting and fishing that went on over an area of more than forty thousand acres.

While they had been talking the two poachers had been helped out of the river and were now standing, dripping and bedraggled, surrounded by John's men.

'The police are coming,' said one of the men. 'The van will meet us at the bridge.'

'Come on, you three. I don't want you catching pneumonia and dying on me before I can get you to court.' He turned to Hunter and said, 'Thanks again, Nick. How about a pint?'

'Sure, why not? Tomorrow up the Pirn suit you?'

'Eight o'clock,' said John.

The burly poacher turned to Hunter and said, 'I'll know you. I'll git you for this, you bloody interfering . . .'

The poacher stopped when John and his men burst out laughing and started hustling the offenders away. Hunter heard John say, 'Don't even think about it. You were lucky he only shoved you in the river. Last year I saw Nick take on six . . .' the voices faded into the distance.

Hunter smiled. The story got better with the telling. Actually there had only been four of them and they had been drunk. He recollected that it had been pretty disappointing, as fights go. He sighed and turned to continue his walk. 'Come on, Winston. Let's go and find a few rabbits for you to chase.'

The remainder of their walk was peaceful and soon Hunter found himself at the road that led up to the crossroads and back to the house. A short while later he arrived home, showered and turned in.

Early the following morning his sat-nav telephone warbled softly. Hunter was awake immediately and flipped it open. 'Hunter.'

'Macnair. I need you.'

'General, it's,' he looked at the clock, 'zero, six hundred hours and I'm on a long weekend. Can't it wait?'

'Sorry, my boy, it can't. I've been up all night. All hell is breaking loose.'

'Where?'

'In France and the Middle East.'

'I'll be there in a couple of hours.' He severed the connection and climbed out of bed. As he shaved and showered wondering what on earth could have happened to have Macnair so fired up.

Hunter sped along the A811, enjoying the feel of his MGB Roadster on the straight road through the beautiful Stirlingshire countryside. In the morning mist he could see the castle in the distance and, to the left of it, Wallace's tower pointed at the sky, a reminder of the Scots' battle against the English in the thirteenth century. Hunter grinned. With the Scottish Assembly now in existence, independence might yet become a reality. The thought intruded and he contemplated where his loyalties lay. If the truth were told, he was saddened by the idea. The strength of the United Kingdom was precisely because it was united. Even if Scotland did become independent, Brussels was proving to be the real power in Europe, where the meaningful laws were passed. Sovereign parliaments were little more than rubber stamping, talking shops, fiddling with tax laws and excise and duty rates. I'm becoming a cynic, he thought and then corrected himself – too late – I am one.

Under the sheer cliff face and walls of the castle he turned right for Stirling town centre. Once through the town he drove along more beautiful countryside until he reached and crossed the bridge over the River Forth and drove through the village of Kincardine. Turning right for Westfield and the power station, he sped towards Dunfermline. Twenty minutes later he pulled up outside the gates to HMS *Cochrane*, with its new sign, The International Force Against Terrorism. It had taken a month to find a set of initials that did not spell out a rude or insulting name in one language or another and after numerous efforts Macnair had settled on TIFAT. Hunter showed his identity card to the sentry at the gate and was waved through. Out of the corner of his eye Hunter could see David Hughes inside the gatehouse. The NCO in charge of security was putting away his gun and noting Hunter's time of arrival. The clock on the dashboard showed 07:45.

He parked outside the administration block and went inside. Unlike other naval shore establishments HMS *Cochrane* had no history and no splendid public rooms to awe visitors, having been built in the utilitarian sixties. With the cutbacks it had been easily mothballed but now had a new lease of life. Hunter pushed through the swing doors and took the stairs facing him two at a time. He found General Macnair in his office, with TIFAT's computer expert, Isobel Sweeney.

'Morning,' Hunter greeted them both, wandering across the room to the coffee percolator. He held it up, offering them both a refill but they shook their heads. He added milk and sat down opposite his boss. 'So what's happened?'

'Thanks for coming in so quickly, Nick,' Macnair said, 'but the proverbial has hit the fan in a big way.' The General paused, collecting his thoughts. 'Yesterday morning two children were kidnapped in Paris.' Before Hunter could do more than raise an eyebrow in query the General continued. 'They were Saddam Hussein's granddaughters. He has been ranting and raving all night and has threatened to wipe Israel off the face of the earth if he doesn't get them back.'

Hunter frowned, sipping his coffee. 'That doesn't make any sense. Why would the Israelis take two kids? They don't make war on children, no matter whose they are.'

'Agreed,' said Isobel. 'Our Foreign Office has pointed this out to the Iraqis in no uncertain terms. So have the Americans. The Israelis deny all knowledge of it and have asked for calm and good sense.'

10

'Calm and good sense are contradictions in terms when it comes to the President of Iraq,' said Hunter, dryly. 'It still doesn't make any sense. Why should Saddam think that the Israelis are behind the abduction?'

Suddenly General Macnair let lose his thunderbolt. 'Because they are.'

'What?' Hunter sat up straight, almost spilling his coffee. 'The Israelis? I don't believe it. They just wouldn't do such a thing.'

'I would have defended them with every breath in my body,' said the General, 'except that late last night I had a telephone call from David Golightly.'

'The deputy prime minister we rescued from Habib?' Hunter looked puzzled.

'The same. He has confided in me a great deal of disturbing news. It appears that there is a group of right-wing fanatics in Israel who believe that it is their duty to secure a Greater Israel as an Orthodox Jewish State. For them any means justifies the ends.'

'So what has that to do with Saddam's grandchildren?' Hunter frowned, sipping his coffee.

'This group is trying to provoke the Arab world into lashing out at Israel. If Israel is forced to defend itself against an overwhelming enemy it will have to resort to nuclear weapons. They believe that if they use nuclear bombs and fight to the end the Arabs will lose the war, agree a peace and leave them alone inside their expanded borders. All Arabs and in particular the Palestinians will be forced to leave. Israel will become a Jewish state for Jews only.'

'That's nonsense,' said Hunter. 'The West won't let it come to that. We'll stop things getting out of hand.'

Macnair tilted back his chair and put his hands on his head, a thoughtful look on his face. 'I'm not so sure. If the Israelis provoke a fight by committing acts of terrorism against innocent men, women and children, where will our sympathies lie? I don't think it will be with the Israelis. So matters escalate to the point of no return. If the Israelis find themselves alone and the Arabs *think* they're alone, then the Arabs could mobilise a massive

11

force against Israel. There would be a nasty brutal war and if the Israelis use nuclear weapons the Arabs would use chemical and biological weapons in retaliation.'

'Hell, General, the land would be returned to desert if that happens. It will be unusable for decades, maybe hundreds of years. You've seen the results of Operation Slaughter on the simulations. No matter how we play it, it seems to end up in a no win situation. Hell's teeth, I was talking to my father about this only last night. I just don't believe it.'

Isobel butted in. 'I've spent some of the night looking at other scenarios into the game and none of it is encouraging. Even if we came in at the last minute and forced the Arabs to pull back, our tenuous relationships in the area will be irrevocably damaged. If Israel is proven to be sponsoring terrorism then . . .'

'Hang on a moment,' Hunter interrupted her. 'I thought you said,' he looked at the General, 'that it was a faction within Israel who were responsible? Not the whole Government. Can't they deal with a few fanatics themselves?'

'I suggested the same thing to Golightly. He tells me that it isn't as simple as that. First of all they're a democracy and they have to obey the law. There's no proof that the people he believes are responsible actually carried out the kidnapping. Secondly, even if there was proof, what good would it do? If Saddam doesn't get the children back safely he'll say, with justification, that it's the fault of the Israelis. You know as well as I do that Saddam is very good at rhetorical speech making and there are a lot of countries in the Middle East who will back him. But it's worse than that.'

'Worse? What can be worse?' Hunter asked.

'According to David Golightly other atrocities are planned which are designed to provoke the Arab world. He says that there's a small group in the Knesset who are defending these people, arguing that the safety of Israel can be assured once and for all.'

'They're mad. Stark, staring bonkers,' said Hunter.

'Probably,' said Macnair. 'Be that as it may, Golightly phoned asking for our help to find the children. He says that he will be doing everything in his power, albeit within the law, to stop the trouble makers. In the meantime, we need to rescue the children and prevent any other atrocities.'

'General, such a statement from anybody else would result in me sending for the men in white coats. How are we going to rescue two small children who were kidnapped in France and then gallop to the rescue of other people in situations we know nothing about? It's ludicrous.'

Macnair sat forward in his chair and pointed a finger at Hunter. 'I agree but that's not the end of it either.'

'There's more?' Hunter frowned.

'The French have been on the telephone already. Golightly had asked them to send for us. They told him, and phoned me to reinforce the message, that we weren't needed. They said the crime took place on French soil and France would solve it. They also pointed out that thanks to their special relationship with Iraq they may be able to persuade Saddam to give them more time to find the children. Before the Iraqis invade Israel, that is.'

Hunter leaned back in his chair, his legs stretched out, his hands behind his head. 'Even if they find them, what good will it do? This isn't a hostage situation that's negotiable. It seems to me that there's nothing to be lost by killing the children and letting the bodies be found. In fact, quite the reverse. There's a lot to be gained if they are killed.'

Macnair nodded. 'I agree. The problem is the French don't have the big picture. David Golightly told me everything in strictest confidence. It's as important to keep this quiet as it is to prevent it happening. At the moment, the Israelis can keep denying any involvement and blaming everybody else. If there's no ransom demand then that may have to change. What they cannot do is admit to any involvement by any individual within Israel.'

'Do we know who the leader of this Jewish sect is?'

Macnair nodded. 'More bad news, I'm afraid. David Golightly named Samuel Dayan as the leader.'

'The industrialist?' Hunter queried.

'The same,' answered Isobel. 'I've been trying to get as much

13

information about him as I can.' She waved a floppy disk in the air. 'It's all here. Or at least, as much as I could find.' She shrugged, 'It's still early days yet so I expect to get a lot more.'

'Are we sure he's the man?' Hunter asked.

'We can only go by what David Golightly said. I can tell you, Nick, he is a very worried man. He's spent months putting together the information he e-mailed to Isobel last night. It's pretty damning, although I'll be the first to admit that there's no proof as far as a court is concerned. It's mainly innuendo and rumours but when added up it's a pretty strong case. However, with the money Dayan has and the power he wields, the Israelis would have the devil's own job even getting him into a court, never mind convicting him.' Macnair got to his feet and wandered over to the window, looking down on the quadrangle, watching some of his men go about their business. In the distance he could see the dockyard cranes and the gleam of water that was the Forth Estuary. 'Besides, there's another problem.'

'Another one?' Hunter was incredulous. 'Don't tell me, nobody knows where Dayan is.'

'How on earth did you know that?' Isobel asked.

2

'I didn't know, I guessed,' was the laconic reply. 'So what do we do now?'

'Officially, nothing,' said the General. 'The French don't want us and neither do the Israelis.'

'But I thought David Golightly . . .' Hunter began, but was interrupted.

'He isn't the Israeli Government. He phoned me because of what happened with Habib. He's terrified about the consequences if we don't stop Dayan.'

Hunter looked perplexed. 'General, I don't understand. First you tell me Dayan has to be stopped, then you tell me we can't do it.'

'I didn't say that,' Macnair turned from the window and smiled. It reminded Hunter of years ago at Edinburgh Zoo when he had watched a wolf about to be fed. Macnair had the same predatory look. 'I said *officially* we can't do anything. If we leave it to the politicians it'll be too late. By the time we're called for, God alone knows what will have happened. The French are a stiff-necked bunch who will never countenance asking us for help no matter what goes down. I tried persuading them otherwise but they were adamant.'

'So what do you propose?'

'I propose we act unofficially. We use our resources here, masking any operation as an exercise but use some of our ill-gotten gains to finance a few of our activities.'

Hunter sat in stunned silence, the enormity of the proposal

washing over him. He did not need to ask where he would fit into the equation. Suddenly he smiled and nodded. 'What do you propose?'

'Are you positive?' Macnair sounded unsure himself for the first time that morning. 'I'll cover for you in every way I can. The buck will stop with me but make no mistake about it, our necks will be well and truly in a noose. The problem as I see it, though, is if we don't act then it could be too late to save possibly millions of lives. Somehow we have to contain the situation in Israel.'

Hunter nodded. 'If we're seen to be running wild, being gung-ho, it could jeopardise TIFAT's very existence. The politicians will disband us with alacrity.'

'Some of them will, that's for sure,' Macnair agreed. 'Others will fight our corner and say that we did the right thing. However, in a democracy, we have to be ruled by the politicians. We can't have the military running about, taking the law into their own hands.'

'But that's precisely what you're planning to do,' Isobel protested.

Macnair grinned, 'I know. But then I believe that in this one instance we have right on our side. If Dayan provokes a bloody conflict in the Middle East then we'll still be pilloried. Why hadn't we stopped him? Why didn't we find the man and his organisation and kill or imprison him or them? The call for us to be disbanded will be just as great but based upon the fact that we didn't act. It's a no win situation. At least if we try and stop him we can say we acted in good faith.'

'We need to find him first,' Hunter pointed out.

'Leave that to us,' Macnair said. 'Golightly has sent us a lot of information and Isobel has found out a great deal more. Governments aren't co-operating but individuals are. Golightly has a friend in the Mossad,' Macnair was referring to the Israeli secret service, considered one of the best in the world, 'who's passed everything they have on Dayan to Golightly, who forwarded it to us. Dayan's tentacles reach everywhere. He's an American by birth, born into an ultra-orthodox Jewish sect in New York. Made a fortune in computers in the sixties and now

16

has interests in major building projects, ship-building, software houses and mobile phones. Plus real estate all over the world. Isobel can give you all the details. Let me get on the phone and chase up a few of my contacts and see if I can shake anything loose. Nick, time is of the essence. We need to find those children and find them fast. Then we need to be ready for anything else Dayan chucks out. Think about how you'll deploy and who's to make up the teams. Secrecy is vital so think about how you'll handle it and what you'll tell the lads.'

'My instinct, sir,' Hunter replied, 'is to tell them the truth. If we trust each other with our lives I don't think it's a good idea not to trust each other with the real agenda.'

Macnair nodded. 'That's my gut instinct as well. However, if anything goes wrong and we're called to account for operating without authority they won't be able to claim that they were only following orders. If we tell them that we're mounting a black operation they won't have that protection.'

Hunter nodded. 'I see your point. Let me think about it. For now I'll work on the basis that this is another training exercise. How's Major Carter getting on with fitting out the shooting range?'

Hunter was referring to TIFAT's quartermaster. Major James Carter had proven to be an expert at finding and acquiring all sorts of useful equipment, much of it non-military.

Isobel replied, 'He told me yesterday that it's just about finished.'

'Good. I think we need to practice at shooting bad guys and not hostages. There's a lot of skills we need to brush up on that are decidedly lacking right now.'

'Oh? I wasn't aware of that,' Macnair spoke coolly.

'I've been giving it a lot of thought, General. We're all specialists in something with one common thread running through us. We're military up and at 'em types. Give us another Habib situation and we'll sort it out. Give us a delicate position where negotiation and finesse are needed and we'll have a problem. We need lectures on hostage taking and rescue missions. We need more in-depth training on a raft of subjects. We won't be going to war, we'll be engaging in isolated skirmishes. Deadly, no doubt, but where stealth and cunning are as important as an overwhelming superiority in numbers and fire power.'

Macnair looked through Hunter, deep in thought, and then nodded, 'Yes, you're right. I hadn't realised it myself. I saw our role with a military mind-set and that's wrong. Let me think about it. I know somebody at the FBI who may be able to help us out. Right,' Macnair sat down heavily behind his desk, 'I've a thousand and one things to do and so do you. Be ready to move as soon as I know where to send you. Isobel, let's get back to work. I want to try and identify any of Dayan's companies with property in Europe.'

Hunter walked along the corridor to his own office. He sat with his feet on his desk, pensively tapping his finger tips together. Would he really be operating outside the law if they were to go after Dayan? If they rescued the two children then who was to say that they were in the wrong? As he thought about achieving some sort of rescue he remembered the opening words of Mrs. Beeton's recipe for jugged hare. "First catch your hare". In this case, first find the children. Standing up, he opened a wall safe and withdrew a Beretta 92C, the compact version of the gun, only 197mm long. Hunter depressed the magazine catch on the left side of the butt, behind the trigger, slid out the magazine and pulled back the slide to eject any round in the chamber. He inspected the chamber through the ejection port, released the slide and pulled the trigger. After the ominous click, he slid the magazine of fifteen rounds of 9mm Parabellum home and reset the safety catch. Putting the straps of the holster over his shoulders, he tucked the holster into his left side. He placed the gun in the holster and put on his jacket. Checking himself in a mirror, he made sure that no bulge showed and satisfied, he left the room. He felt self-conscious carrying a gun, something he would never do normally on the streets of Britain.

Hunter walked away from the buildings towards the furthest corner of the establishment, near the waters of the Forth. Years before, when HMS *Cochrane* had been a thriving naval base, the area he was now in had held metal structures that were meant to represent parts of a ship. Inside, oily fires were lit, and the men would practise fighting fires, wearing breathing apparatus and jetting foam or water at the danger. It had been stressed time and again, that fires at sea were the navy's nightmare. Luckily he had never had to use the training.

'Why are you grinning like a Cheshire ape?' Carter asked him, stepping out of the doorway of a new building and wiping his hands on a wet rag.

'Hello, Jim. I think you're mixing your metaphors but actually I was remembering this place when we used to practise fire fighting. Are you finished?'

'Just about. Let me show you.' Major Jim Carter walked along the middle of what could have a been a street in a provincial town anywhere in Britain. 'I've copied the set-up the SAS have at Hereford, with one or two minor alterations. Once the timer starts, you walk along here and targets will appear. Some you shoot, some you don't.'

'I've done Hereford a couple of times. What changes have you made?'

'We're able to alter the targets to be . . . what shall I say? More ethnically correct. By that I mean, if we think the targets are Chinese, we make them Chinese. If Pakistani, we make them Pakistani. It could help in certain circumstances.'

Hunter nodded. 'Good idea. What about a variation of the situation?'

Carter shrugged. 'Not a great deal we can do except to change the good guys for the bad guys and so have a fair number of targeted situations. The only thing I can guarantee is that a shoot-out will not take place on a straight road with you playing Wyatt Earp. All we can hope for is that we hone your skills so that when it comes to making a decision you each make the right one.'

There were ten fake buildings on either side of the road. Each had a different style of door and windows. Some were only single storey, others two storey. At the end of the street was a new brick building, towards which they were walking. Carter opened the door and led the way in.

19

'This place has been sound-proofed so the noise we make on the simulators won't frighten the local wild-life. We get four complete systems next week which will enable us to practise various routines without having to resort to the use of bullets and explosives. It's much like a child's computer game, except that we are able to scan in live photographs and film of actual targets to get a better idea of what we're doing. It's not ideal but it's the best we can come up with right now.'

'How on earth did we afford this lot?' Hunter asked.

'Courtesy of Habib,' was the reply.

Hunter nodded. 'Good. Somehow that fills me with a great deal of satisfaction.' Carter was referring to the fact that when Hunter and his men had killed the terrorist Aziz Habib they had used Isobel's computer skills to, as Macnair put it, liberate the banks and institutions of the money Habib had amassed over the years. TIFAT had salted away over four hundred million pounds into accounts and investments that only TIFAT knew about. The money was intended for use by TIFAT to purchase equipment that was not normally available to the military. And, as the General pointed out, to be used to pay for things that were impossible to account for – like bribery and corruption.

'What else are you thinking of buying?'

Carter smiled. 'Whatever we might need. If you have any ideas let me know. I can tell you, it won't be like the Bond films, with esoteric gadgets at our finger tips, but there are a few useful things we're working on. The idea you had about the underwater chariots is a good one and the modifications should be finished in a few days. And we've altered the parachutes you used with Pierre and will be trying them out tomorrow. All being well we'll have them in use by the end of the week.'

Hunter nodded, remembering his jump. Pierre Flambert had been the only man killed when they had stormed Habib's hideout. It was little consolation to know that Pierre's parents had received a cheque for one million pounds, paid by the General, out of the money taken from Habib's estate. Still, should something happen to any of them, it was comforting to know that their immediate family would not suffer financial hardship.

'When can we start on the roadway?' Hunter asked.

'Will Monday do you?'

'No. Today or tomorrow will, though.'

'What's the rush?'

'We could have a job on soon. I need to get the lads working on their hostage awareness skills as well as their snap-shooting decision making abilities. The General says he's got somebody at the FBI who might be able to help. Still, we need to get started sooner rather than later.'

'Okay, in that case we can be ready this afternoon. I'll leave you to arrange the teams. I presume you're going through as well?'

'Sure, I can't lead from behind. I need to be as good as anybody else in the teams. Ergo, I need all the practice I can get.' On that note Hunter strolled back to his office. When he arrived, he pensively put the kettle on, spooned some instant coffee into a mug and picked up a box of dried milk. As he poured the white granules onto the coffee he pondered his dilemma. If he left the service tomorrow it wouldn't matter. Assuming he survived the next few months and whatever they might bring, virtually nothing could prevent him from living a comfortable life. For the others in TIFAT there was no such luxury. They were all career men and women who depended on their salaries and promotion for their quality of life. He did not have that problem. Did that make him a better officer? It did mean that he didn't make a decision based on whether it was good for his career or not. He did what he thought was right. It was as simple as that. Pouring the boiling water into the mug, he stirred the muddy-coloured liquid and sat down at his desk. Making up his mind, he slouched down in his chair and put his feet on the windowsill, reached for the telephone and dialled Sergeant David Hughes. He told him what he wanted.

'I don't have a problem with it, boss, but it's a Saturday and I don't know where everybody is.'

'I take it nobody's left their sat-nav phones behind so you ought to be able to track people down. Taff, I know it's the weekend but this is important. We could be on an op sooner rather than later and we need to brush up on a few things. I'll brief everybody later on what's happening.'

'Okay, boss, leave it to me. Where can I get you when I've finished?'

'In the computer room. I need to see Isobel.' He broke off the connection, dropped his feet to the floor, stood up and walked along the corridor to the vast office that filled the end of the building. Inside there were banks of computers, nearly all of which were switched off in deference to the weekend. A map of the world filled one wall. It was a replica of the one at GCHQ, the government eavesdropping establishment at Cheltenham, and displayed the location of some of the satellites currently orbiting the earth. Only GCHQ had the full picture.

'Is that working?' he greeted Isobel, nodding at the wall.

'Yes, finally. Thanks to Sarah, we now have a pretty good copy of what she sees, albeit with some exceptions. Apparently there are some secrets even we aren't privy to. However, what we've got could be a big help.'

'Have you found out anything useful yet?'

Normally there would have been at least six operators in the room but everybody was away for the weekend and only Isobel was available to run the computers.

'I think so. Let me show you something.' Her fingers flashed across the keyboard and after a few moments the screen in front of her changed. She pointed at the information now displayed. 'We've programmed the computer to cross-match all his business interests. We then asked it to look for property. There have been a number found in France and other parts of Europe but all in populated areas. And then we found this.' She tapped the screen with a pencil. 'I'm pretty certain that's a dummy company. It has shares in this trust which in turn holds shares here, here and here. None of it means anything except when we get to here.' She tapped the screen with her pencil and said, 'That company, registered in Liechtenstein, owns property. To be specific, one single property in the Alps.'

'French Alps?' Hunter queried.

'No. Swiss. On the border with France at a place called Aig du Tour.'

'Never heard of it. Where's it near?'

'Chamonix. It's about twenty kilometres further into the mountains. Let me show you.' Again her fingers flew across the keyboard and this time a map of France and Switzerland appeared on the screen. She said, 'Look at the wall screen and I'll get the area as tight as I can.'

Hunter looked at the wall and watched as the relief map turned from a hundred kilometres a metre to one kilometre a metre. He studied the picture for a few minutes. 'It looks promising,' he said, finally. 'But it's not enough to go on.'

3

Hunter looked at the screen and said, 'Give me a chart any day. What does this mean?' He walked across to the wall and ran his finger along a dotted line.

'I think that's the border. The property is there.' She used a laser pointer and the red dot hit the screen. 'You see that line,' she shifted her pointer. 'I think that's the perimeter of the estate.'

'How big is it?'

'According to the information I have, about ten thousand hectares.'

'How big is that in real size?' Hunter asked with a smile.

'In real size it's about twenty-four thousand, seven hundred and nine and a bit acres, approximately,' she added, returning his smile. 'It consists mainly of this mountain and some of this valley so it's not exactly what you'd call prime or even useful land.'

'But it is isolated. And somebody has taken a great deal of trouble to hide the name of the owner,' said Hunter.

'And it is close to France and I don't suppose there are any border checks. Once past Chamonix there's nowhere to go. You can't cross into Switzerland because there are no roads. It's a dead end. An ideal place to hide two kidnapped children.'

'Any chance of a look at the place?' Hunter asked.

Isobel nodded. 'Possibly. I telephoned Sarah at GCHQ and she's looking into it for me now. Even if she can get a satellite to pass it doesn't mean to say we'll be able to see much, because of the terrain.'

'What's the weather like right now?'

'I've checked. It's clear but not very warm. You must remember that the area here,' she waggled her laser pointer, 'is all glacier. The house is situated nearly three thousand metres above sea level. That's nearly ten thousand feet.'

'That's ludicrous. Whoever would have built a house there? Who'd want to live in such an isolated place?'

'I can't help you,' said Isobel. 'Right now I can only give you what information I've got.' The phone interrupted her and she lifted the receiver. She listened for a few moments and finally said, 'Thanks, Sarah.' Mischievously she added, 'Nick sends his love,' and hung up.

'No, I don't. What did she say?'

'She sent you her love in return.'

'Very funny. I hardly know the woman. And that's not what I meant.'

'No, I know it isn't. There'll be a satellite moving in the right direction in twenty minutes. We might see something then.'

She moved to another console and spent a few minutes on the keyboard. The screen lit up and they watched the earth revolving before them. She magnified the picture tens of thousands of times and the perspective changed from global to individual towns and villages. She then put another programme into the computer and the picture magnified further until they could see individual houses.

'That's too close. Back off until we know where we're looking.'

Isobel gave Hunter a pitying look.

'What did I say?' Hunter asked.

'Nick, you need to spend a little more time in here. I've programmed in the co-ordinates of the property which have been supplied by satellite and told this one where to look. It'll show up when it gets there. I've set a timer so that when the picture is within a kilometre of the place it will record and retain. We can then look at it to our heart's content.'

Hunter nodded. 'Clever. Any other leads from your magical box of tricks?'

'There are a few things I'm following up on, but quite frankly nothing as promising as this. I can't find anything else connected to France although there is something in Italy.'

'What?' Hunter wandered over to the coffee machine to pour them both fresh mugs of coffee.

'I don't know yet. It could be anything from a dummy company to a shirt factory. I need to do more research but it won't take long.' Just then a buzzer sounded briefly and she added, 'That's it. Let's take a look.'

The picture on the wall screen changed and they were now looking down on an alpine scene. It unfolded rapidly, peaks of mountains showing in the distance, the valley turning from white and green patches to icy white. A building came into the picture, isolated, sitting on a flat expanse of ground that appeared to have been cut out of the hillside. There was ice in every direction except around the house, where it was obvious that they were looking at solid rock. The house flashed across the screen and vanished into the left hand corner. The satellite continued filming, showing more of the Alps. Isobel altered the magnification and the panorama changed to a far larger picture. Individual objects could no longer be distinguished but towns and villages became identifiable. Then the picture went blank.

'I've turned it off. Let's re-work the film and we can take another look.' At that moment her telephone went and she lifted the receiver. 'Hi, Sarah. Yes, we got it. Okay, thanks. Speak to you later.' She hung up. 'Sarah said the satellite will make two more passes today, each from slightly different angles to give us a more detailed perspective. Once we get them, we should have a better idea of the size of the place. Right now it looks as though the building covers an area of two thousand square metres and is possibly two stories high. The flat rock around it is about seven or eight thousand square metres, which is quite a size.'

Hunter nodded. 'Why clear the ice? Any ideas?'

Isobel shook her head. 'Unless it was to give them firm foundations for the house.'

'They could have done that by drilling into the rock and putting in steel stilts to build on,' Hunter replied. He shrugged, 'What the hell, it doesn't matter. What we need are more details on the place. See if you can trace any plans, architects drawings, planning permission applications and so on.'

Isobel nodded. 'I'll try, though I haven't a clue where to start. Any ideas?'

'Can you find out what region the place comes under? If it's Switzerland it'll be the Canton of Valais, possibly the town of Martigny, and if it's France we can start with Chamonix.'

'How do you know that?' Isobel looked at Hunter, questioningly.

He grinned. 'A lot of my youth was misspent in the area. I was a ski-bum for a chunk of my teenage years. I knew the whole area at one time, though I dare say a lot of it has changed in the last fifteen or twenty years, what with new developments and new lifts and so on. I tell you what. Concoct a letter saying that you have seen the property and are interested in buying it if you can trace the owner. No,' Hunter snapped his fingers, 'better still, you represent a client who is interested.'

'Also,' Isobel added, 'if it's not for sale, did they know who built it? I'll tell them my client would commission something similar in another part of the Alps. We might be able to find something out but, to be honest, Nick, I can't see us getting the information in a hurry. I can contact every lawyer's office in the region. I can get onto what passes as the local authority that gave the planning permission but it'll take until the middle of next week if we're lucky.'

Hunter nodded. 'I agree. Let me talk to the General. Perhaps he can find a way to hurry things along.'

'Hurry what along?' Macnair asked, standing in the doorway.

Hunter explained the situation. While he did so Isobel re-ran the film, this time in slow motion, to give them more time to study the picture.

When Hunter finished speaking Macnair thought for a moment. 'I'm not sure I can help. Not with the French wishing to solve the kidnapping themselves and bearing in mind the phone call I had. No,' he shook his head, 'I like your thinking, but we need to go it alone. We daren't risk warning the French that we're interested in anything in or near France in case they smell a rat. Once you've found out all that you can we'll evaluate what we've got and make decisions. Like you, I think the Alps looks like our best lead yet.'

'I know sir, but it's not enough to go in heavy handed.'

'I agree. However I have just been speaking to David Golightly. He has told me that a source within Dayan's organisation has sent word that cold weather gear of significant amounts was purchased recently. It included skis as well as alpine clothing.'

'How good is the source?'

'I asked David the same question and he told me it was impeccable. He would stake his life on it.'

'Good enough, sir. I've asked Sarah to see if there are any heat sources. She's working on it now and will get back to us in an hour,' said Isobel.

'Good. I gather,' Macnair turned to Hunter, 'that you're going to use the new street Jim's made. I'll come with you. I want to see the team in action.'

The two men left Isobel with her computers. Outside the day was turning blustery with a hint of rain in the air. A number of other men were walking in the same direction, making for the target range. Some had changed into battle fatigues, "can't-see-me suits" as the camouflaged clothing was referred to, and others, like Hunter, wore civilian clothes.

At the range, Jim Carter said, 'Right, I've drawn two teams, port and starboard. Lieutenant Commander Hunter will take the port team and Captain Clements the starboard. You will draw your weapon and walk down the middle of the street. As you go a figure may appear on either side. Shoot if you decide it's an enemy but don't shoot if you think it's an innocent civilian. I must warn you that you'll see both. You get ten points for a clean kill, nothing for wounding and minus ten if you injure an innocent bystander or a hostage. I've programmed in ten different scenarios for each team so you can't give any hints as to which targets to shoot and which ones to miss. You go in at three minute intervals, as that's the time you have to walk the street.'

'How will we know if we're going too fast or too slow?'

Joshua Clements, an American on secondment from Delta Force, demanded.

'I'll be following your progress. You'll be in communications with me and I'll tell you whether or not to speed up or slow down. I will also tell you what you've hit with each shot.'

'How can you do that, sir?' Sergeant Hughes from the SAS asked.

'You've done this at Hereford often enough,' said Carter, 'so you should have an advantage. However, in answer to your question, I've built in a refinement that Hereford doesn't have. I can read on the computer what damage the bullet has done. It means we don't have to stop and examine the street after each walk through. Remember,' he spoke loudly to them all, 'it is one shot per target only. There are a possible fifteen targets so those of you using guns holding fewer rounds than fifteen had better be ready to reload p.d.q. Right, let's get started. You first, Lieutenant Commander,' he said to Hunter.

Hunter walked down the street, gun butt held in his right hand, the weapon cradled across his chest, supported with his left. He looked left and right, observing the doorways, windows, roofs and alleys.

'Slow down, Nick,' Carter spoke in his right ear. 'It's not a race.'

Hunter slowed his pace. His heart was racing and his hands beginning to sweat. He willed himself to calm down. Suddenly a figure materialised in a window in a house on his right. He saw a gun pointing at him and smoothly dropped to one knee, aimed his own gun and fired.

'Nice one, Nick. Clean head shot. Keep going.'

After the first shot Hunter settled down. From then on the silhouettes came thick and fast. He killed eleven bad guys, wounded two and critically shot three bystanders. When he finished, Hunter found he was bathed in sweat, his heart was pounding like he had run a marathon and he felt absurdly upset that he had "injured" three civilians.

At the end of the afternoon both teams had been put through their paces. Major Carter declared a draw but then announced,

'Right, we now need to analyse exactly what we did. We need to know how you each feel, how we can help you to improve your performance and, very importantly, how do we reduce the likelihood of shooting an innocent hostage or bystander.' There were groans from the men. 'However, that'll wait until tomorrow.' At which they cheered up and drifted away to clean their guns.

Hunter was sitting at his desk pulling a piece of four by two, as the rag was called, through the barrel, when Macnair entered his office. Hunter used the small piece of oily rag to wipe down the magazine before he reassembled and reloaded the gun.

The General stood there watching for a few moments before he said, 'Isobel has those additional pictures. According to Sarah there are people in residence but she can't tell how many. At any one time, the most that have been outside the house is four. Three are obviously patrolling the perimeter while the fourth seems to approach each in turn as though checking up on them. On the face of it, it looks good and I think we should take a much closer look at the place.'

Hunter nodded. 'So do I, sir. Let me finish up here and I'll go and look at the pictures with Isobel. I need to phone a few people and cancel my arrangements for tonight. If what you say is true then we need to be on our way shortly.'

The problem of travelling across Europe with various types of military hardware was solved by Carter. Three of the team flew from Edinburgh, laden down with ski-gear. If anybody had bothered to ask they would have learnt that the three were going glacier skiing; flying to Geneva and hiring a car. The military equipment they needed was to be parachuted to them. Carter had arranged with his contacts to use the plane that ferried men to Bosnia for the United Nations peace keeping force. He had passed it off as an important NATO exercise, dropping two parachutists and their equipment into the Alps. Carter's explanation had been accepted without question.

The skiing team consisted of Jan Badonovich, a Russian Spetsnaz NCO, Clements and Lieutenant Sam McReady, Royal

Marines, Special Boats Service. It was their task to reconnoitre the house and grounds. The parachutists were Hunter and David Hughes who flew out of Brize Norton at 22:00 hours on Sunday. Every bit of information Isobel could amass indicated that the kidnappers were at the house in the Alps. Macnair decided to gamble that they had made the right choice and send in his first team. Other teams were ready for deployment elsewhere, should Isobel be proven wrong with her first guess, but so far nothing appeared as promising. Even so, she continued to look for other possibilities, but so far had drawn a blank.

On board the Hercules C130 Hunter and Hughes carried two large, white, reinforced plastic cases. They were shaped like elongated eggs, aerodynamic and specially constructed to withstand a heavy impact in the event of a parachute failure. The plane was less than a third full, ferrying men, women and stores to Bosnia. They were of all ranks from major to private, a glum lot, each aware that they faced a thankless task and all wishing that they were going somewhere else. Hunter and Hughes sat at the rear of the plane, next to the huge cargo doors, separated from the remainder by the mounds of gear stacked in the hold. They both preferred it that way, hidden from prying eyes and gossiping tongues.

Both men settled down in the uncomfortable canvas seats and, as if they hadn't a care in the world, went to sleep. Twenty minutes before the jump the Sergeant Loadmaster came aft from the cockpit. He found Hunter and Hughes checking their equipment, ready to go.

He nodded his appreciation of their professionalism and helped to complete their preparations. Both men looked like spacemen. "Jumping High and Landing Low" was a dangerous way to get to work, as their instructor had told them when they learnt the art over the Arizona Desert a few years earlier. Luckily, modern technology now made it a lot safer than even a year or two earlier. Under normal circumstances it would have been suicidal to jump into the Alps from over twenty thousand feet and to open a parachute at seven hundred. In this instance they carried a homing device locked on to a beacon planted by the advance

31

party which they would aim at as they "flew" free through the freezing air. By changing their aerodynamic profile when they fell, they could manoeuvre themselves a long distance, easily as far as five or six kilometres.

The red light over the rear doors turned to amber, the Loadmaster spoke in his headphones to the pilot and yelled. 'Ten minutes, gentlemen. You two first and then the containers. Let's run through the checklist.'

They did so, methodically and slowly, double checking everything. Once they jumped, it would be too late to correct mistakes. Finally they used their throat-mikes to speak to each other and went on oxygen. Their masks fitted snugly, the mouthpieces clamped tightly between their teeth. As both men were highly trained divers, they were used to using throat microphones and understanding each other's restricted speech. Their jump-suits were specially insulated and heated from a small battery carried in their harnesses. Although there was little likelihood of them dying from hypothermia during such a short jump, too much cold could be a serious impediment and could leave them disabled.

The Loadmaster held his thumb up and received the same signal from both jumpers. The Loadmaster checked his own harness and then walked over to the control console for the doors. The rear ramp dropped open, the backdraft dragging the warm air out of the aircraft. The light turned green and Hunter and Hughes threw themselves out left and right.

Dropping through space was exhilarating. In the warm cocoon of their suits, breathing oxygen, the false sense of security left them with a feeling that was indescribable. There was no fear, no thought as to what might happen if their parachutes failed. Just an adrenaline rush that was completely intoxicating. In the moonlight they could see lights scattered for miles across the country, some isolated, others showing villages and towns. There was an odd contrast between the dark of the valleys and the gleaming, ice and snow covered mountains that were rushing to meet them.

'Boss, do you read? Over?'

Hunter's earphones burst into life. 'Roger, Taff, loud and clear. We are three hundred metres to the right.'

'Agreed, boss. Moving now.'

Both men changed their body positions and slowly edged back on track helped by their wrist indicators receiving the signal from the beacon on the ground. Rapidly their field of vision narrowed until it consisted only of the peaks around them and the light of the single house below. All too soon, Hunter said, 'Heads up. Here we go.' Normally a barometric switch was used for such jumps. It knew the height of the parachutist above sea level and opened the parachute. Unfortunately, in alpine terrain, its accuracy was suspect to a degree that could mean death to the jumper. The problem was solved by the signal from the beacon, which gave an exact readout of the jumper's height above the ground. Hunter came up with a jerk, his feet pointing at the ground, the aerofoil an open canopy above his head. There was nothing further he needed to do to steer towards the beacon, now less than five hundred feet below. The parachute was controlled by the signals it was receiving and he moved gently towards the target. He looked about him and saw Taff Hughes less than fifty feet to his right. Their foils were programmed to land in intervals of twenty feet. He could see nobody else as the aerofoil flared a few inches above the ice and then he was down. His feet gently touched the ground and the foil collapsed quickly around him. The white patches that detached themselves from the ground were the team wearing camouflaged gear and they helped him to fold the foil. Within moments he had stripped off his oxygen gear and was checking to see that Hughes had landed safely.

'No problems?' Joshua Clements asked.

'None,' Hunter replied. 'Everything go smoothly your end?'

'As far as we can tell. Nobody knows we're here. We've set up camp in a hollow above the house. We've been watching all day and there's no doubt something odd is going on.' A warning bleep sounded on the beacon and the men looked upwards, eyes straining in the thin, clear night air.

At a thousand meters it was not difficult to make out the aerofoils holding the cases of equipment. Each case was two metres long and one metre in diameter. Each was slung under a single aerofoil that had opened at three thousand feet above the beacon. Due to the weight of the containers, they had plunged nearly a thousand feet, before the falling cases came under aerofoil control. Then the foils read the signals and made the necessary alterations to their shape as they changed direction, aiming at the landing site.

A hydrostatic switch opened small, pressurised bottles of helium sewn into the leading edge of the foil. The sudden extra lift operated like air brakes, the foils flared, and the cases landed nearby with hardly a bump. So far the operation had been text-book perfect.

They broke open the canisters and distributed the gear. Hunter and Hughes changed into ski-boots and strapped on extra wide, deep-snow skis, ideal for glacier skiing. Then, in single file, with Clements leading, the five men trundled across the glacier and up to their base camp. Once they were settled in, Hunter used his sat-nav phone to call Macnair and report their progress.

'Glad to hear it,' the General replied. 'Isobel still hasn't found any other target as tempting as the one there, although she has found out some interesting things about Dayan which I'll tell you later. The French have no leads that I know of but they have said that Saddam has given them an extra day to find his grandchildren, which,' the General's voice became sardonic, 'is very thoughtful of him. He says that he's preparing for all out war with Israel and is currently mobilising his forces. My informants in Iraq tell me that the people have no stomach for a battle in spite of the propaganda Saddam is circulating.'

'What about the Israelis?'

'The Knesset have been in session all day. David Golightly says that there's uproar. The hard-line right want a pre-emptive strike and the left don't know what to do. The men in the middle, which includes Golightly, want to prepare for war and recommend mobilisation in three days' time. Commander, the bad news is that they are secretly preparing to use nuclear weapons. They know that they can't hold out against the Iraqis if they attack in force.'

'What are the Americans saying?'

'Publicly, they're telling Saddam to back off and warning the rest of the Arab world not to get involved. Privately, they are admitting that they cannot claim the moral high ground if it's true that the Israelis took the girls. For the first time in six years I see their President dithering. The American press is beginning to turn on the Israelis, which has never happened before. I've had copies of their weekend newspapers faxed here and they're seriously anti-Jewish and anti-Israel. As it is, I think the Middle East is on a knife edge and it won't take much to tip the scales into a holocaust. If those children are there, get them out fast and get them to Italy.'

'Roger that, sir. We'll do our best.' He slid shut the mouthpiece, cutting the connection. He repeated what Macnair had said. 'I think we should go in tonight. It's now zero one twenty-seven. Lowest ebb is around zero three to zero four. That's when we'll attack. Okay, Josh, what have you got for me?'

'There's three guards on at any one time,' Josh Clements replied. 'If you look through the nightscope for long enough you'll see them walking the three sides of the perimeter. The fourth is the mountain. We took a look earlier on and on the face of it there's no way in that way. So we need to take the guards,' Clements nodded at the Spetsnaz, one of the best trained soldiers in the world when it came to Arctic or winter warfare. 'Jan got within ten metres and watched and listened. According to him they're in radio contact with each other but he couldn't tell if that also means they're communicating with somebody in the house.'

'It's safest to assume they are,' Hunter said. 'What language were they using?'

'He doesn't know. He didn't recognise it. I'm not very impressed by their procedures,' Clement's laconic American drawl hid a first class, tactical mind. 'They're sloppy. As if they feel,' he shrugged, '. . . invincible here. Nobody knows they're here and nobody's going to attack them.'

'Or they're innocent guards keeping the place private and not breaking any laws,' Hunter responded.

'That's what I thought. Except they're carrying Uzis, have hand-grenades hanging on their webbing and Jan says there

35

are cameras all over the place. There could be fixed sensors, anti-personnel traps, machine gun pills and God alone knows what else.' Machine gun pills were pillars of steel, with an automatic weapon inside, capable of being aimed by the sensors. They fired without warning at any target they found. The guards would have set paths, safe to traverse and known only to them.

'Are pills likely? After all, if walkers or skiers found themselves wandering around here it would be better to warn them off than to kill them.'

'I agree. Except the General has said war is imminent. If this has all been about starting a war then within days this place becomes obsolete.'

'True. The thought was beginning to occur to me. By the same token, there's no point in keeping the children alive. It's easier to have them killed and dispose of the bodies . . .' Hunter trailed off, deep in thought. 'No! They'll still be alive. If a war is provoked and the children returned unharmed, the Israelis could claim it hadn't been them. That they'd been blamed for something they hadn't done. That they'd been forced to defend themselves. They would be in a position to demand support from their American and Western friends. My God, this is deeper than I thought. It's not Israelis we'll find down there. It's a bunch of thugs, hired by Dayan and completely expendable. That makes more sense than Dayan being found responsible. After all, he wants to be in the real world once it's all over.' The thoughts and ideas tumbled through Hunter's brain. The more he thought about it, the more sense it made.

'So what do we do?' Clements asked, reasonably.

'I think we're expecting too much opposition. All we'll find is a few guards. Armed and dangerous, yes, but not with any of the sophisticated back-up you'd normally expect from a professional organisation.'

'Are you going to bet our lives on that?' Clements asked.

Hunter grinned. 'Nope. I've got another idea.'

4

Para-gliders are double winged with tubes of the same material holding the wings together like an old-fashioned bi-plane. The flyer throws him or herself off a cliff or the side of a mountain and floats gently down. If they find an up-draft, they can bounce higher on the air and stay aloft longer. Sometimes they are able to launch themselves off a cliff, hit an up-draft and turn into it, staying in the air for hours at a time, albeit virtually stationary in their position relative to the ground. The new TIFAT wing carried compressed helium cylinders and had clever pockets sewn into the wing to give additional lift and a larger trailing edge when needed. The helium was also used to fill the connecting tubes. The uplift with the wing was considerable and very little wind was needed.

Hunter had a para-glider unfolded and ready to go just as the moon vanished behind a mountain peak. Hughes and Badonovitch lifted the end of the wings and Hunter stepped into the harness. He teetered on the edge of the slope next to their hideout and then rushed down the hill. After four paces he was airborne, the helium helping to lift him into the air. Using the right-hand release button he squirted more helium into the wing and the ground fell away rapidly as he soared silently upwards. Jim Carter's modifications to the original design were paying off.

It was true that there was no way to reach the heights behind the house unless a climber went for a very long and tiring detour, followed by a dangerous and time-consuming sheer mountain climb. Using the glider Hunter expected to be in position within ten or fifteen minutes.Under different circumstances he would have been enjoying every second of the flight. But for now he needed to concentrate on staying away from the house, out of sight, even when he landed on the flat plateau above the property.

'Boss,' Clements broke into his thoughts, 'we're moving out now. Over.'

'Roger that, Josh. As soon as I've landed I'll call in. Out.'

This time it was colder than the earlier flight. He was wearing his white ski-suit, well insulated but without the built in heater of the drop-suit, and he was not using the oxygen and mask, having thought them unnecessary. He had his hood up and drawn tightly across his face but even so he could feel the cold on his exposed nose and cheeks not protected by his goggles or the ski-mask.

Already he was above the target and about half a kilometre beyond. He turned and headed back the way he had come, angling to the right of his original path. The mountain top was coming towards him too fast, the wind threatening to take him beyond the plateau and even past the house. If he was seen it would be fatal. Quickly he turned again, further right, sliding across the sky like a yacht without a keel, in the grip of the wind. He was still a hundred metres or more above his chosen landing site when the house came into view. If he could see it then the guards could see him. Desperately he dumped the helium by pressing the button in the left handle-bar and aimed sharply down at the ice covered rocks below. He was swooping down from the sky at a speed which could kill him if he landed. Or, he thought, at best break his legs and possibly other parts of him. Glancing back he saw that the house was out of sight. He pressed down hard on the right hand-button, injecting volumes of helium into the wing bags. His headlong plummet slowed but now the plateau was only a few metres beneath him. There was still the danger of a nasty landing which could break his ankles. Even a sprain would be a disaster so he needed a controlled landing. He kept his finger on the button injecting the wing with the lift he needed and tucked his legs behind him in a desperate gamble. The additional helium would either stop him or he would land on his knees with God alone knowing what consequences.

The massive volume of helium he injected suddenly started to lift him away, inches above the ground, threatening to take him soaring up and away, back over the house. Hunter hit the quick release gear on his chest and slipped out of the glider. At the same time the aerodynamic container that held his equipment also dropped free. He landed on his feet with a hard thump and rolled over to take the force out of the fall. For a few seconds he lay winded, catching his breath, wondering if he had broken anything. He vowed to himself to have more practice with the para-gliders.

'Are you all right, boss?' Clements' anxious voice whispered in his earpiece.

'I think so, Josh,' Hunter panted. 'Give me a second to come to my senses.' He sat up, tentatively feeling his arms and legs, flexing his fingers. 'Yes, I'm fine. Landed a bit heavily, that's all. I had to eject at the last second. The wing's flown away.' He looked above about him and to the north he could dimly see the wing as it sliced across the stars in the sky, like a giant bat in a horror story.

He climbed awkwardly to his feet, shook the cramp out of his legs, flexed his whole body and said, 'I'm fine. Definitely. I'm going to the edge.' Hunter opened the container and took out a long length of thin, nylon rope. With a breaking strain of over 1,000 lbs, it was ideal for his purposes. He scouted around the edge of the plateau, looking down, comparing his position to that of the house, seeking a compromise between a suitable anchor for his rope and the place he wanted to land.

Millions of years ago, when the ice had retreated to the north and carved up the land, forming the mountains and valleys that were the Alps, different sized boulders had been left behind, dotting the landscape, disfiguring the smooth sides and tops of the mountains. Hunter searched, his light intensifier goggles giving the landscape a faint bluish tinge. Unlike the old-fashioned goggles that stuck out inches from the eyes and gave the world an odd greenish hue, these looked like diving goggles, compact, weightless and comfortable. If a bright light hit the wearer of the old goggles he would be blinded but with the new ones a micro-chip acted instantly, compensated for the light, and left the wearer unaffected. It took only moments to realise that there were no suitable boulders in the vicinity.

'Listen up,' he spoke softly to the four men now stealthily nearing the grounds around the house. 'There's no anchor point. I need to rig a line. I'll be a few minutes.' He looked at his watch, surprised to find that so little time had elapsed since he had taken off. It was 03:24 hours.

'Roger that, Nick,' the American Delta Force Captain spoke. 'I'm in position with Sam.'

'In position,' said the Russian.

'In position,' repeated the Welshman.

Hunter approached a large boulder half embedded into the mountain and tied one end of a rope around it. He scrambled across the gentle slope for sixty or seventy metres to another boulder where he pulled the rope tight, tied it off and cut it. Darting halfway back, he used a bowline to tie the end of the rope onto the line he had stretched between the boulders. Pushing the knot to the middle of the rope he then walked back to the edge of the mountain. Looking down he saw that he was about fifteen metres out, and so he returned to the line, moved the knotted end and returned to the edge. Now he was close enough to his target. He collected his gear from the container and distributed it about his person. With the abseiling rope over his shoulder he said into his throat-mike, 'Ready. Going down now.'

Hunter leant back into the rope, his feet out before him and ran backwards down the face of the mountain. He had about four hundred metres to go and, he estimated, about three hundred and ninety metres of rope. The line he had stretched between the two boulders bowed under his weight, giving him the additional distance he needed. He landed on the ground, in the metre wide gap between the mountain and the house, with half a metre of rope to spare.

'Landed,' he whispered. The night was utterly silent. The wind had dropped away and Hunter could distinctly hear the guards patrolling on either side of the house. Searching the expanse of wall, looking for a window, he saw nothing. All that was visible was bare cement, smooth and unbroken. He walked quietly along, continuing to search. A rustling of cloth, a hint of movement in front of him and he stopped. In the light created by his goggles, from the corner of the house only a few metres away, a guard appeared. The man walked up to the face of the cliff and was evidently beginning to undo his flies. Hunter drew a syringe from a sheath at his side, stepped up behind the man, clamped his gloved hand firmly over the guard's mouth and plunged the needle into his neck. The fast acting liquid hit the guard's senses like a sledge hammer and he was unconscious before he knew what had happened. The drug would last at least twenty-four hours.

'Got the man on the west side,' he whispered.

'Thanks, boss,' Badonovitch acknowledged, as the guard had been his target.

David Hughes' voice came through their earpieces, 'Mine's down. He walked right up to me.'

The team had spent a slow hour crawling unobtrusively to their targets, moving only when the guards' backs had been turned, closing in on their prey with the patience of leopards.

'Standing up,' McReady said, and suddenly stood in front of the last guard who was five metres away and not likely to come any nearer.

The startled guard gave an oath as McReady suddenly materialised in front of him, his hands in the air, saying, 'Help. *Pardon. Por favor. S'il vous plaît.*'

The guard had taken two steps towards McReady even as he was unslinging his machine gun from his shoulder. He was so intent on watching McReady that he did not notice Clements stand up next to him, clamp his hand on the gun and plunge a needle into his neck. The man collapsed without a sound.

Hunter edged along the western wall of the house. The first window he came to was heavily curtained. He took out a microphone, less than a centimetre in diameter and stuck it onto the bottom left hand corner of the glass. The team listened intently for any sound from within.

'Nothing,' Hunter whispered. There was a murmur of agreement from the others. He continued his careful progress along the wall, hidden from the cameras that dotted the steeply sloping roof, well inside their arc of cover. He continued around the house, sticking a microphone onto each window. Each was on a different frequency. If they heard anything they could switch dials and know immediately which room the sound was coming from. Hunter worked quickly and was soon back where he had started. Nothing had been heard. That left only the upper floor where presumably the bedrooms were to be found.

'What do you think?' Hunter asked softly into his throat mike. 'Are they all asleep? Is anybody monitoring the cameras?'

'Don't know, Nick,' said Clements. 'Can't tell. It looks like a sloppy operation but there are no guarantees in this business.'

'Are there ever?' Hughes asked.

'There's too much at stake, so we'll tread carefully,' said Hunter. 'I'll go back round and do the upstairs.' So saying, he unslung the folded ladder from his back and slotted it into place. The rungs were ten centimetres wide, twenty centimetres apart and each section one metre long. Made from reinforced aluminium, it weighed only six pounds and could take the weight of three men when placed horizontally. Hunter leant it against the wall, quickly climbed up and placed another bug. He continued working his way around. In one room there was the unmistakable sound of snoring, in another what sounded like sobbing. At the last window they heard voices.

It came as a shock, having heard so little throughout the rest of the house. Hunter made his way back down the ladder and placed it on the ground, along the wall. He listened intently to the voices and finally said, 'I give up. Anybody recognise that language?'

The replies were negative. There was laughter and the clear clinking of glasses. Hunter grinned. 'Sounds like a party. We should join them. Make up the numbers.'

'I hate gate-crashing,' Taff Hughes said, unable to hide the glee in his voice.

'Boss, this is Jan.'

'Yes, I know. Go ahead, Jan,' said Hunter. He grinned. Badonovitch always announced himself in spite of the fact that his voice was unmistakable.

'I think they are speaking Albanian. I was there a few times as a child, for holidays. But it's not quite as I remember it. There is a difference.'

'Could it be an Albanian from Kosovo?' Clements suggested. 'After all, they're the new gangsters of Europe.'

'Could be. I've sent a recording to the General,' said Hunter. 'He can tell us later. Isobel will crack it within seconds.' Hunter voiced the faith they all had in Isobel and her computers. 'Okay, it's an amateur operation,' said Hunter. 'Let's get moving. No risks, mind. I'll set a heavy charge on the window, in case we hear anything or something goes wrong.'

'Roger that,' said Clements.

Hunter replaced the ladder and quickly climbed it. He took out a wedge of plastic explosive and ran it like toothpaste, down the side of the window and along as far as he could reach. Stepping down, he moved the ladder, and re-climbed. Another move and he had placed plastic explosive around the perimeter of the window. Placing a detonator in one corner, he dropped the end of the detonating cord to the ground and climbed down. 'Ready. Move now!'

The four men moved to the side of the house and joined Hunter. There was no alarm; the noise of the party continued. Hunter gave his instructions and they moved away. Hunter stayed where he was. He felt around the edge of the window, seeking a means to force his way in but having no luck.

'Boss,' McReady spoke in his earpiece, 'the windows are reinforced glass.'

Damnation! Now what could they do? 'What about the front door?'

'I'm there, boss,' said Hughes. 'I can't tell. I've tapped and prodded and I think it's wood veneer over a steel door. This place has been built like a fortress.'

'Okay, we go through the roof,' said Hunter. 'Sam, run PE

along all the windows on the ground floor. Josh, you take care of the upper floor where we heard the snoring. Get it all together to one det. Taff, Jan, we go up the side and in through the roof.'

Hunter sidled alongside the wall, back to the mountain face where the other two joined him. 'Right. Throw a grapple up to the gutter and see if it'll take the weight,' he ordered Hughes.

Taff Hughes swung the tiny grapple around and around, faster and faster. The prongs were two inches in diameter, made of high tensile steel and coated with rubber. Hughes let go at the right moment and the grapple flew into the air. He tweaked the rope and the grapple fell onto the roof almost soundlessly. The hook caught. Hughes tugged hard and made sure it was securely wedged.

'It feels all right,' he said. 'Whether the gutter will hold or not I can't tell.'

'Up you go, Taff, quiet as you can.'

Hughes braced his feet against the wall and walked up as easily as a stroll in a park. The gutter held, he reached the top, and climbed silently onto the roof. The pitch was exceptionally steep and he sat down, his feet in the gutter.

'Boss, it's thick tiles.' He pushed his knife under a tile and levered it up. Half a dozen interlocking tiles lifted at the same time but he was able to take hold of one and rip it out. 'Got one,' he reported.

'Good work, Taff. What's underneath?'

'Solid wood.' Hughes removed more tiles, sliding them down to the gutter. It did not take long to make a hole big enough to climb through. 'Boss, I need the saw.'

Hunter appeared over the side of the roof, 'I know. I've brought it with me.' He took out a battery operated tool, very much like an electric toothbrush, and slotted a circular saw into the end. The high pitched whine was barely audible three metres away. Hunter sawed into the wood and cut out a finger hole. It fell into the attic with hardly a sound. He then began to cut round the section Hughes had exposed. 'Hold it,' he ordered as he reached the end.

The Sergeant put his finger into the hole. Hunter finished

44

cutting and Hughes lifted the large section of wood clear. Hunter climbed down, his feet searching for a beam to rest on. A few seconds later Badonovitch and Hughes joined him.

'Okay, Josh, we're in. I've found a trap door. Lifting it now. Standby.'

Cautiously he raised a corner of the door and pushed a pencil thin telescope through. By manipulating a bevelled screw he was able to turn the end of the telescope through three hundred and sixty degrees. He was peering into a well-appointed bathroom. The lights were out so he pulled the trap door fully open and dropped onto the tiled floor. The other two followed as quietly. At that moment their luck ran out.

5

Hunter had his hand on the doorknob when he felt it turn. He snatched his hand away as though scalded and stepped back. The figure silhouetted in the lit doorway took half a pace and stopped in shock. Hunter sprang forward but slipped on a rug, giving the man standing in front of him enough time to let out a yell and dart back into the corridor.

As the man shouted a warning, Badonovitch stepped around Hunter and threw a hand grenade as hard and true as a baseball player. The heavy grenade smashed into the back of the fleeing man's head and he crumpled to the floor, his cries extinguished. The Spetsnaz rushed forward and scooped up the grenade and replaced it in his pouch. Hughes was at his heels, while Hunter went in the other direction. Doors were opening and Hunter said into his radio, 'Josh, hit it!'

The men stumbling into the corridor were dazed with sleep, the yelling had stopped and they were fumbling with their wits as well as their clothes.

The plastic explosive shook the building, sending glass flying into the room, shredding curtains and blinds, cutting some of the occupants, although none fatally. Hunter smashed his fist into the face of one guard and threw two "flash-bang" grenades into the rooms on either side of him. The grenades exploded with a devastating noise and bright light, disorientating those in the rooms. The special earpieces and goggles protected Hunter and his team from the grenades while the enemy tottered, screaming and holding their hands to their heads, their eyes shut from the pain of the intense light.

Using hypodermic darts Hunter and his team quickly subdued the men. Joshua Clements rushed into the room where they thought the two girls were probably located and stopped dead. One man held a knife to the throat of a young girl who hung limp in his hands. Clements stood still, taking in the room and the situation. Lying on the lower of two bunks another youngster was staring, wide-eyed, her hand clamped in her mouth, sobs shaking her body.

The man with the knife spoke and Clements replied, 'I don't understand.'

'Move,' he jerked his hand to one side, making a huge error. He used the hand holding the knife.

Clements had been holding his dart gun in his right hand. He used his left hand to draw and fire a Smith & Wesson 625 which fired a rimless .45 pistol cartridge through the man's head. His hostage collapsed in fear, shaking, sobbing, urinating.

Clements spoke on his voice net. 'Sorry, Nick. I had to shoot one.'

Hunter appeared on the scene, his gun ready.

'He had a knife to her throat. I saw an opportunity and took it.'

'That's okay,' said Hunter. 'You took the right decision. I'd have done the same myself. Let's get these girls sedated and dressed and get the hell out of here.'

Hunter smiled at the girl on the bunk and said, 'It's all right. Take it easy. We aren't going to hurt you. Do you understand?'

She nodded.

'We've come to take you home. Where are your clothes?'

She shook her head, fear etched in her face, her eyes wide and staring.

'Sam, is everything secured?' Hunter asked into his microphone.

'Yes, boss. I found a cellar. We dragged them down and locked them in. I also found a pretty sophisticated communications room. We've searched everywhere, but can't find anybody else.'

As he was speaking Hunter had been opening drawers and cupboards. In the last one he found some warm clothes and handed them to the girl. 'Please, put them on,' he said but she ignored him and tears welled up in her eyes.

'Put them on,' he said, more harshly. 'We've got to get out of here.'

Slowly the girl reached for the clothes. 'Now please hurry up,' he said more kindly. 'We want to get you home. Are you Sobia?'

There was silence for a moment or two and then a quiet voice said, 'Yes.' Then, more strongly, 'Yes, I am.'

'Good. Then your sister must be Nadia. Please help her when you're ready.' Hunter knew that at ten she was the older of the two. Her younger sister was only eight. Looking at the fear in the eyes of the two children he was beginning to regret using darts instead of bullets.

Sobia had pulled on the warm trousers and jacket. She stood with her head bowed, her hands held in front of her. Hunter admired her pluck. He knelt by her side and said gently, 'It's all right. Nobody will hurt you.' While he distracted her Badonovitch slid a hypodermic needle into her arm and as shock registered on her face she slid into unconsciousness. In the meantime Clements had carefully injected her sister and awkwardly put on similar warm clothes.

Hunter and Clements each picked up a girl and walked out of the room. The other three led the way, examining each bend, corner and possible ambush site. Nothing happened and the team was soon outside. Silently they trundled back to their campsite. There, sledges and skis were ready. It took only moments to pack up the remainder of the gear in preparation to move away. Faintly but rapidly growing in strength, in the still night air, came the unmistakable whacking noise of two, possibly more, helicopters.

The men froze, knowing that they couldn't be seen and prepared to fight. They watched as three helicopters approached from the south.

'Pumas,' said Hughes. 'But that's strange.'

'What is?' asked Hunter.

'They're white and painted with a red cross but I know that

the Red Cross don't have Pumas, they're too expensive. They use old Wessex helos given to them at the end of their service life. I think we're in trouble.'

As if to prove how prophetic the sergeant's words were, as the helicopters landed, armed men leapt out and opened out into a ragged line, converging on the house.

'Goodies or baddies?' Hunter asked.

'Can't tell,' said Clements, 'but I sure as hell don't like the look of things. If they were French forces come to rescue the girls they wouldn't be using helicopters disguised as the Red Cross.'

'That's what I thought. Hush, someone is shouting,' Hunter said. They distinctly heard the men calling to one another. 'That sounds like two different languages to me. Any ideas?'

'Ja,' said Badonovitch. 'One is Albanian, I am sure.'

'The other is Ivrit,' said Clements, a frown on his face.

'Are you sure?' Hunter asked. Clement's reply was unintelligible.

'What did you say?'

'I said, of course I am. It was my first language a lifetime ago.'

'You Jewish?' Hughes asked.

'Sort of. Lapsed is a better description,' Clements grinned.

'What are they saying?' Hunter asked.

Clements listened intently, catching only some of the words as they drifted across the still air.

'They don't like what they see. Damnation! They've noticed the windows. Now we're in real trouble. They can easily follow our tracks once they get started.'

'Right, time to go. You four head straight down the valley for the Range Rover. Take the sledges. I'll cover and take them away from here,' Hunter ordered.

'But, boss . . .' began Hughes.

'Never mind but, boss. Go! That's an order. I'll go down the other side towards Martigny.' While he was talking, Hunter was lifting gear, sorting weapons and getting ready.

'Phone the General. Tell him code red. The helicopter at Geneva will come straight down for you. There's a flight plan and escape route already prepared. I'll sort myself out.' They heard more yells and watched as men ran towards the helicopters. 'Now go.'

Hunter moved quickly down the slope and when he was sure he couldn't miss, aimed a heat seeking stinger missile at the nearest helicopter. He fired, dropped the launcher and started to langlauf towards the summit three hundred metres away. Barely had he started when there was a huge explosion and he looked back. His target had erupted in flames and much to his satisfaction he saw the next helicopter explode as well. The men had thrown themselves onto the ground as burning fuel and debris rained down. There were more yells. Looking back, Hunter saw them pointing his way. Suddenly the night erupted with the sound of gun fire. His steady, long sliding strides had taken him rapidly along the slope and he was now close to the summit. As the ice and snow burst about him he threw himself over the edge and out of sight.

In a flurry of dry powdered ice he stopped and cautiously peered back. The men were beginning to get organised and Hunter could see skis being passed out from the surviving helicopter. He unslung a SIG SSG-3000 sniper's rifle from his shoulder and prepared to discourage his attackers. The Swiss-made gun was the best in the world. It weighed only 5.8kg when fitted with a NATO STANAG telescopic sight and carried five rounds in the magazine. The third helicopter was masked from him by the burning skeletons of the other two but he still fired five rounds rapidly at where he thought it might be. He slipped the catch behind the magazine, extracted the old one and slammed in a new one. Wrapping the sling around his left arm, he used his elbow as the third leg of a tripod. The other two legs consisted of his right arm and the sling. Now he switched targets. The gun was rock steady and he held his breath as the first man came into sight. He fired and saw the man fling up his arms and fall backwards. He swung the gun a few degrees, took aim and fired again. Repeating the performance five times he was gratified to hit four targets. When he changed the magazine there was nothing more to aim at.

Suddenly, the air was filled with the sound of a helicopter starting up and the ice and snow around him erupted in small explosions as a hail of gunfire was directed at him. Hunter ducked down, cursing. He had hoped to stop the helicopter but already it was moving away, out of range. The firing stopped and he looked carefully back over the ridge. The helicopter was a dot on the horizon, clear against the backdrop of a dawn sky.

By now his night goggles were useless. In the time between dark and full light they were more of a hindrance than a help and he discarded them. Even as he searched for more targets, shots were fired at him and it was more by luck than judgement that they missed. Time to move, he thought.

Hunter slid along the ice, keeping below the ridge-line. He stopped, inched his way upwards and took another look. In the strengthening light he could see a number of shapes moving in his direction. He guessed there were twenty or so men still left on the ground, all wanting to kill him. Readying the rifle, he took aim and fired five rounds rapidly, smoothly moving from target to target. He was sure he had hit at least two, perhaps three. He ducked back as chips of rock and ice flew up around him. One grazed his cheek, blood oozing from a shallow cut. As the sun came over the mountains he heard the helicopter returning and looking up, he saw it approaching, masked by the halo of sunlight. He emptied his magazine at it, slipped the rifle over his shoulder and launched himself down the slope.

Hunter had learned to ski at the age of four on the slopes of the Scottish Mountains. He maintained that if you could ski there, you could ski anywhere. In European terms, Scottish skiing was, at best, fourth or fifth rate, but the result was a greater proficiency when skiing on poor terrain than most holiday skiers achieved on the superior slopes of the Alps. By the time he was fourteen and travelled abroad he could ski just about anywhere under any conditions. When he joined the Royal Navy he was good enough to be selected for the inter-services biathlon competition. The first year they lost to the Army but in the second year the Navy won, mainly thanks to Hunter. Biathlon was a combination of cross-country skiing and target shooting and deemed to be one of the toughest alpine sports imaginable, combining terrific exertion immediately followed by steady, accurate shooting.

His skis were locked together as though welded and he hurled down the mountain with incredible speed. The sun was over his right shoulder, casting long shadows across the ice and snow. He darted between boulders, needing all his skill and strength. The noise of the helicopter's blades warned him of danger and he slewed hard right, stopping in a flurry of ice. He threw the rifle off his shoulder, aimed at the helicopter and fired all in one smooth motion. He saw the bullets hit just as the helicopter swung to port and a man appeared in the doorway. Bullets slammed into the ground near Hunter's feet as he fired the last round in the magazine. The man in the doorway fell back but was instantly replaced by another. Hunter turned and almost flew down the slope, fingers busily changing the magazine, ski-poles dangling from his wrists.

He dodged left and right in short, controlled turns, thankful for the warmth of the white balaclava covering his head and face. The helicopter came nearer and above the noise of the rotors he heard the unmistakable sound of a machine gun. Throwing himself down and to the side, his body bumping over the hard packed ice, out of control, he tried to stop himself smashing into a huge boulder looming at the periphery of his vision. Desperately he pulled the ski pole off his left wrist, grabbed the pole just behind the basket, and jammed it into the ice, slowing him down, turning him around until his skis pointed downhill. He hit the boulder with a force that stunned him. For a few seconds he lay there, partially hidden from the helicopter, taking stock, ensuring his arms and legs still worked.

His vision cleared, he got his breath back and the telephone in his pocket rang. Fumbling in his pocket, he withdrew the phone and flipped it open. Carefully he edged around the rock, keeping out of sight of the helicopter. Shots were fired and chips of rock above his head flew dangerously close to his face. It was bizarre, he thought, to be answering a phone in this situation.

'Nick? It's Macnair. What's happening?'

'Sir, I can't talk. I'm a decoy. Hopefully, the others reached the car and are high-tailing it out of here. Damn,' he said, as he dived around again. 'Sir, I need to go.' He disconnected, stood up suddenly and fired five shots at the helicopter. At least two bullets found their mark and the helicopter careered across the sky in a crabbing motion, rapidly losing height down the mountain. Hunter reloaded and looked up the slope. Strung out across the mountain were at least fifteen skiers, all heading towards him.

Hunter kneeled, took careful aim and fired. One skier went down and he was shooting at a second before the remainder realised what was happening. They skidded to a halt and began to unsling their own weapons. Hunter turned and schussed downhill. He followed the fall line, straight down the mountain. He heard the sound of shots and started a series of short zigzag turns known as *wedeln*. Suddenly he was amongst a patch of moguls, small mounds of compacted snow and ice. Instead of following a safe path around them he adopted the poise for a series of *Gelände-sprunge*, jumps launched from a crouching position during a downhill run.

His speed accelerated dangerously and it took all his skill and concentration to stay upright. The sound of the helicopter broke into his consciousness and he swung right. He knew that the high-speed turn, with the skis kept parallel, should only by attempted by an expert and, more by luck than judgement, Hunter kept his balance. His sudden shift in direction surprised the helicopter and the sound of the rotor-blades faded for a few seconds but quickly returned. Spurts of ice shot up in front of him and he swung to the left, schussing once again. By now his legs were aching, his concentration slipping and he knew that he was in danger of falling. At that speed he would be lucky to walk away.

Ahead he saw that the ice was thinning rapidly and he would soon be on solid earth and rock. Using a series of turns he slowed down, reached a massive rock as big as a small house and stopped. He pressed his pole tip on the release catch at the back of his boots and shucked off the skis. He looked up the mountain, gratified to see the men chasing him were now some way behind, skiing cautiously around the moguls. Even as he watched, one man took a heavy fall and failed to rise. Hunter undid the catches on his boots, pulled them off, and replaced them with his combat boots which he was carrying on his webbing belt. The helicopter was coming back and Hunter settled himself beside the rock. This time he changed the magazine for explosive tip, armour piercing rounds and waited. The helicopter was three hundred metres away when, from the doorway, a man opened fire with a high-calibre machine-gun. Hunter rolled out of the way just in time and took aim. His first shot went through the door and out the other side without causing any damage or injury. The second pierced the tail near the rotor and the helicopter spun around, the pilot nearly losing control. Yet again, the helicopter turned away and moved out of range.

Hunter delved into his knapsack and removed small explosive devices. He looked up the slope making his calculations and set the timers, three, four, five and six minutes. Two devices for each timing. He scattered them across the slope and began to move out. The enemy were at least a kilometre behind him but, now that he was on foot and they were skiing, they closed in quickly.

He moved from cover to cover, aware that he could be shot any time, the feeling creating an uncomfortable itch between his shoulders. Now he had left the snow and ice behind him. Another few hundred metres and he would be on the grassy slopes of the mountains. Still steep but with little cover and, from his point of view, very dangerous territory. In the distance, far down the mountain, he could see a number of villages, one of which he guessed was Trient. Unslinging his rifle he slid behind a small boulder and settled down to some fast shooting. He identified three targets, took aim at the first and fired. Smoothly he changed targets and fired again. His third shot was wasted as no further targets presented themselves. However, he had achieved his objective. They had gone to ground near the explosives.

The first two erupted and Hunter heard a scream. A fusillade of shots was fired in his direction but few came dangerously close to him. He held his fire, looking for a target. Suddenly a man stood up and yelled, pointing at the ground near to his hiding-place. Hunter guessed he had just seen another explosive device. Before the man could move, Hunter shot him in the head. When another two of the devices blew there were more yells and suddenly the men were kicking off their skis and up and running back the way they had come. Hunter loosed off a few more shots but was sure that he hadn't hit anybody. It was now time to move – and move fast.

Instead of heading straight down the mountain, Hunter followed the slope and stayed above the grass and amongst the rocks. He moved quickly, aware that the helicopter could return at any second and the men chasing him would soon be on his heels again. In the meantime the other explosive devices went off harmlessly, creating a lot of noise and no damage. Looking over his shoulder he saw that they were chasing him already. The only consolation he had lay with the thought that there was no sign of the helicopter.

Shots rang out and he saw the rocks downhill of him being hit by bullets. He angled up the slope, ran faster than was safe on the loose scree and dived behind a low wall built to trap snow and help the formation of the piste. Pausing, he sucked in lungfuls of air, as he tried to get his breath under control before he fired back. By this time the sun was well over the horizon and Hunter was sweating profusely. Taking a few mouthfuls of water from his canteen he popped a handful of high protein, high vitamin chews into his mouth. He took aim at his closest pursuer still nearly five hundred metres away and fired. The man reeled backwards, hit the ground and rolled down the slope. The others vanished from sight like a puff of smoke.

Hoping they would stay low for a while, Hunter took time to set a series of explosive traps. Not on timers this time but using trips and plungers. He covered a distance of almost a hundred metres behind the wall and out of sight. From time to time he fired a shot to discourage his pursuers, aware that he was now very low on ammunition. Once his traps were set Hunter discarded the remainder of his kit, apart from the small backpack he lifted from the bottom of the bag, his telephone and his gun. Checking the digital read-out pressure gauges on the sides of the two small bottles attached to the backpack, he grunted to himself with satisfaction and fitted the backpack over his shoulders. The two nylon shoulder straps he connected using two horizontal straps across his chest, holding the pack snugly in place.

The gun was properly knows as a SIG-Sauer pistol, designed by SIG of Switzerland and manufactured by JP Sauer of Germany. The Swiss did not allow pistols manufactured in Switzerland to be sold to the rest of the world. The gun was considered to be one of the finest ever made and was popular with serious competition shooters. Thanks to its high price, few armies and fewer police forces had taken up the weapon. In production since 1975, the magazine held 9 Parabellum cartridges of 9mm, weighed 750g and had an overall length of 198mm.

Taking his fill of water, he emptied his rifle at the enemy and ran as quickly as he dared down the side of the mountain. He held an exact image of the terrain in his head after studying the maps and satellite pictures of the area. Suddenly the slope dropped away and Hunter went head long over a sheer cliff, the tall pine trees far below looking like twigs. Opening his arms and legs wide he controlled the plunge. Death was only seconds away.

6

With the money that Macnair had "liberated" from Habib, TIFAT had gone on a spending spree. Jim Carter, the Quartermaster for the outfit, had spent millions purchasing odd pieces of equipment that could be useful. Even as Hunter launched himself over the cliff, his arms and legs outspread, his fall controlled, Hunter prayed the sail on his back worked. He pulled the handle and the aerofoil opened over his head.

It was made from ultra-light, ultra-thin material, that opened like a wing, six feet long, three feet wide in the middle and eight inches thick when the two small aluminium gas bottles inflated the wing. The material had been developed by NASA for use in the space program and had been a closely guarded secret for years. Gradually, details of its manufacture leaked out and a small firm in America used it to design and make aerofoils. Strictly speaking, an aerofoil was an aircraft's wing, tailplane, flap or other surface that affected the lift or stability of an aircraft in flight. However, to call the wing that opened above Hunter's head a parachute was too simplistic. For that reason the company in America designated it a "para-foil". The helium/xenon mixture of gases gave the wing added lift which allowed the para-foil to be far smaller than normal. It had been available on the open market for less than a month and this was the first time that Hunter had used one. He was relieved when his free-fall towards the valley floor came to an abrupt halt and he found himself sailing gently through the air, eating up the lateral distance while dropping very slowly downwards.

He reached above his head and grabbed the two handles, one in each hand. When he pulled down on the right one the foil moved right and he turned to head straight towards Martigny, its northern edge visible beyond Col de la Forclaz. The remainder of the town was tucked out of sight, in the valley, but represented his best hope of escape. Behind him he heard the sound of explosions and grinned. His booby-traps seemed to have worked.

He had travelled about three kilometres and, according to the altimeter on the small instrument panel that dangled on a cable in front of his face, had dropped from 2,100m to 1,350m. It was looking good for him to pass to the east of Col de la Forclaz and to land near Martigny.

At that moment a helicopter suddenly reared up from the south and opened fire on him.

Cursing himself for not being more vigilant Hunter pulled hard on both handles, virtually collapsing the wing. He dropped from the sky, plummeting like a stone. The helicopter missed him and over-shot to the north. Even as he was tumbling from the sky, in danger of losing control, Hunter saw the helicopter turn tightly and fly back towards him. His fall was too rapid for the machine to keep up and it flew away to the south again, immediately turning to come back. According to the altimeter he was less than a hundred metres above the ground. From the briefing he had received from Carter, Hunter realised that he risked failing to stop in time before he did himself a serious injury. However, he was counting on the fact that a civilian company, selling a product such as the para-sail, would err on the side of caution when sending out safety information. At fifty metres he let go the handles and the wing snapped fully open. It was like applying air-brakes and his headlong fall suddenly ceased. The ground was five metres away and the helicopter was turning towards him when shots were fired. They missed him but ripped open the foil and he was falling once again. Not quite as dangerously out of control as previously but fast enough to do himself serious damage should he land on rough ground or rocks. Luckily, by now he was over pasture and above the noise of the helicopter and the shooting Hunter was aware of the gentle sound of cow-bells.

Just before his feet touched the ground Hunter hit the quick release, landed and rolled away from the para-sail which suddenly lifted into the air, now that it was free of his weight. He rolled onto his back, drew his SIG-Sauer revolver and loosed off all nine rounds at the helicopter. In reality, the bullets were about as effective as gnats around an elephant but at least it was enough to make the helicopter pilot veer away. Hunter climbed to his feet and staggered into the trees, the huge alpine firs hiding him from sight.

Throwing himself down behind a fallen tree trunk, he pressed the magazine release at the heel of the butt. The magazine fell out and he slammed in another. Two more magazines and he would be defenceless. He watched the helicopter land about four hundred metres away and five men leapt out, quickly hiding themselves in the terrain. The helicopter lifted off and Hunter assumed it was going back up the mountain to get backup. I am, he thought, up the creek without a paddle.

Although extremely fit, Hunter was aware that he could not go on forever. He needed food and rest. He had been awake for over twenty-four hours and knew that he was now living on his reserves, with a dose of adrenaline thrown in for good measure. He wormed his way backwards and, when he was confident that he could not be seen, stood up and moved as quickly as he could through the forest, heading down the slope, towards civilisation.

Coming to a fast flowing stream he stopped and took his fill of water, popped the last of his chews, and was soon on the move again. In the distance he heard the sound of more cow-bells and worked his way towards them. Soon he came upon a clearing in the middle of which was a typical alpine hut. It was used for storing hay for the cows, in case the weather suddenly turned bad and they were unable to feed off the grass. Cautiously he skirted the clearing, keeping to the trees, moving as quietly as he knew how. He saw an old Swiss peasant appear on the other side of the clearing and walk towards one of the cows, patting her nose. The farmer turned and spoke to somebody nearby. A young boy appeared and said something, too far away for Hunter to hear. The old man replied and the boy ran off, heading down the hill.

A figure in combat fatigues and carrying a rifle appeared and approached the old man. There was shouting and cursing. A second figure appeared, who listened for a few seconds and then drew his handgun. He shot the old man through the head and gestured towards the path Hunter had seen the young boy take.

Nick Hunter's anger built up like an overwhelming tidal wave, which he had to control before he did something stupid. To shoot a defenceless person was beyond comprehension. He knew that at nearly two hundred metres it was an almost impossible shot for a revolver but he steadied the gun in both hands and rested the barrel on a branch at head height. He aimed carefully about two inches above the head of the man who had fired the fatal bullet and pulled the trigger three times. Hunter was gratified to see the killer throw his arms into the air, stagger backwards like a marionette and then collapse to the ground. The other men around him had vanished. Hunter turned and ran, dodging the trees and fallen logs, ignoring the branches whipping back at his face and hands. That was when his telephone rang again.

Hunter drew it from his pocket and, not slowing down, put it to his ear.

'Hunter,' he gasped.

'Nick, it's Macnair. Are you all right?'

'For the moment. I'm heading for Martigny but the enemy are right behind me.'

'All right. Listen carefully. We got the two girls to the helicopter and into Italy. I've been in contact with a friend of mine in the Italian Army. He has agreed to help and is taking the girls into protective custody while at the same time contacting the Iraqis and telling them that the girls are safe. Josh and the team are heading your way as fast as they can. I've also spoken to the Foreign Office and asked them to get clearance from the French and Swiss to either send in their own men or to let us carry out our own rescue.' Macnair paused.

'And?' Hunter gasped the word, aware that he could not stay on the phone much longer as he needed his concentration to stay alive, not to listen to the General.

'Waste of time. They said it would take days not minutes to get any sort of agreement and anyway, we shouldn't have been there in the first place.'

'Thanks, General. Look, I need to go.'

'Nick, wait. We have you on the sat-locator. Clements is coming in for you, so keep the phone safe. That's what I called to say.'

'What about the Swiss and the French?'

Macnair's response was as expected and in spite of his precarious position Hunter could not stop himself from grinning.

Macnair added, 'They'll be with you in approximately thirty five minutes. Take care.' He broke the connection, leaving Hunter feeling oddly bereft, doubts beginning to gnaw at him now that salvation was near at hand.

What were his options? He could keep going or he could find somewhere to hide and wait for Josh and the others. He slowed down, casting about him for the first time to see if there was somewhere to hole up. Nothing he saw gave him cause for any optimism so he kept moving. Suddenly he was out of the tree-line and stepping into the open. This time it was not a clearing but the end of the forest and stretching out before him were the gentle slopes of an alpine meadow.

Hunter stopped to listen. Nothing could be heard except the melodious sound of cow-bells and, not far away, the bleating of sheep. Looking back at the towering trees and forward across the grassy slope, he made up his mind to run. This was no longer a marathon, but a sprint. Help was not far away and he could utilise his reserves of energy to distance himself from his pursuers.

He was running fast when he heard voices ahead. Coming round a bend on the track was a small group of hikers. Slowing down, he shoved his gun into his pocket, out of sight. He realised that he looked odd wearing his combat gear and did not want to draw even more attention to himself by running. There were only three people, two men and a woman. The few words he heard them speak sounded like Swiss German. As he stepped past the woman he felt a sting in the side of his arm and as the world went hazy he realised that it was not Swiss German he had heard but the German derivative, Yiddish. No, he was wrong! It was Ivrit! The language of modern Israel, an up-dated version of Hebrew, the original language of the bible.

The helicopter hovered a foot above the grassy slope and four men leapt out. Clements led the way, and the other three fanned out to cover his flanks. The signal from Hunter's telephone showed him to be nearby, probably behind the low wall a hundred metres away.

They approached cautiously, guns at the ready. Clements looked over the wall and saw the body. He quickly scanned the area and then slithered over the wall, keeping as low a profile as possible. The headless torso brought bile to his throat. He reached for the arm and pulled it over. The grass stuffed into the coat and trousers rustled reassuringly, a flood of relief washing through him. He checked the pockets and found the telephone which he used to call the General.

'Sir, we've found Nick's gear but there's no sign of him.'

'Has he escaped, do you think?'

'No, sir. I can't see it. Why would he leave all his gear behind? He's been taken.'

'What are you going to do?'

'We'll fly up to the house and take a look. If we see nothing we'll get the hell out of here and think again.'

'Roger that. Call me as soon as you finish. Captain Clements, be careful.'

Clements grabbed Hunter's clothes and climbed back over the wall. As he did so Badonovitch pointed behind the wall. Looking down, he found Hunter's shoes and socks. A further search yielded nothing else and the team returned to the helicopter. They clambered aboard and soon they were nearing the very house which hours before they had fought so hard to escape.

The place appeared deserted. However, the Puma helicopter

hovered above the ground a few hundred metres from the building and the team leapt out. They carefully approached the house while the helicopter went into a hover, twenty metres above the ground, and lined up its weaponry. The helicopter carried enough missiles and fire power to raze the building to the ground.

The men approached slowly. It was deathly still and nothing could be heard. Badonovitch and McReady stood either side of the doorway. The Spetsnaz went low, the Special Boats Sergeant went high and they looked into the building. Nothing.

'Clear,' said McReady.

The others joined them and slowly they advanced into the house.

'All stop,' Clements said softly into his throat mike. He pointed around the room and carefully they retraced their footsteps.

Once clear of the building Hughes gave a sigh of relief. 'Jeez, that was close. What do we do now?'

Clements shrugged. 'Let's move further away and call the General. If they're on a time switch then the whole lot could go at any time. If it's a trap then we could set it off.'

In the house they had seen slab after slab of plastic explosive, primed and ready to go. The only question was, what would set it off? At that moment they got their answer. Luckily, they were nearly four hundred metres away when the explosion erupted. The house was blown to smithereens, rock and debris raining down across a wide area, though none as far as where they stood. The blast made them stagger and the helicopter veered away, the pilot momentarily losing control.

Flames licked hungrily into the air and they realised that the actual brick was on fire. 'Napalm,' said Clements and the others nodded. 'Let's get the hell out of here.'

The helicopter touched down and they scrambled aboard. Once they were airborne, Clements telephoned the General for further instructions.

'Was Nick in there, do you think?' Macnair asked.

'Can't tell, sir, but I doubt it. It doesn't make sense. I think they stripped him to remove any likelihood of him carrying any sensors. Unfortunately, there was only the one in the phone.'

'Okay, we'll work this end to find out what happened to

him. In the meantime get out of there and into Italy. The French are going to come charging in any minute and I want you long gone.'

'Roger, sir. We'll be over the Alps and into Italy within the hour. In the meantime, if you can work out anything about Nick, we can respond p.d.q.'

Macnair hung up the telephone thoughtfully. Isobel was watching him and he shrugged. 'Nick's gone missing and there's no sign of him. Can you see if we've got any satellite coverage for the area and take a look?'

She shook her head. 'No point in even trying. The last pictures were specially arranged as we don't normally cover the area. Nothing ever happens there.' Her eyes moistened and she bit her lower lip, fighting back the tears, 'Until now.'

Macnair nodded and put his hand reassuringly on her shoulder. 'He's a survivor. If anybody can escape he can.' He did not add, assuming Hunter was still alive or uninjured. 'Right, let's get started looking for him. Isobel, phone Sarah and see if she's got any ideas.'

Isobel nodded. It was better than nothing and usually GCHQ had something up their sleeve. Sarah Fleeting was a senior manager at the top secret listening base near Cheltenham and if anybody could find an answer, she could.

'Sarah? It's Isobel.' Telephoning the direct line Isobel had been saved herself the trouble of going through successive layers of operators as she worked her way into the inner-sanctum of GCHQ. Their friendship had been forged during TIFAT's previous – and highly successful – operation. Together they had been pivotal in tracking down the terrorist, Aziz Habib. 'How's the attempt to stop smoking going?'

Isobel heard the smile in her friend's voice when she replied. 'Wonderful. I no longer think about having a cigarette for as long as ten, even twelve minutes at a time. At this rate, by the time I'm eighty I'll have no cravings whatsoever.'

'At least you'll live to be eighty,' Isobel replied.

Sarah laughed. 'True. What can I do for you? I take it this isn't a social call?'

'I'm afraid not. We've got a problem which I doubt you'll be able to help me with, but I thought I'd try it anyway.'

'Go ahead. If I can help I will.'

Briefly and succinctly Isobel told Sarah what had happened in Switzerland.

'Normally, that would be a problem,' said Sarah. 'However, I may be able to help you.'

'How?' Isobel leaned forward eagerly, the telephone suddenly slippery in her hand.

'We have been dabbling with a system code named KEY-HOLE. We use our computers to amass and sort data from aircraft and satellites from all over the world. It's stored until we want it. The photographs are real-time and we use literally everything from sat-nav to reconnaissance and intelligence gatherers. I've been dabbling with it for about a month now and we've had some useful stuff.'

'How will that help? I phoned in desperation, as to be honest, I didn't think we had much in that area.'

'We don't as a rule,' came the reply. 'However, with the unrest we've had all over Europe, what with the Kurds as well as the Serbs, we've begun to take an interest in our own backyards for a change.' In a mass protest at the Turkish Special Forces seizing their leader, Abdullah Ocalan from the Greek embassy in Nairobi, the Kurds had protested across Europe. In the Netherlands they had taken the Greek ambassador's wife, eight year old child and a servant hostage. In Austria, the Greek ambassador, his wife and three workers had been seized. In Switzerland, protesters broke into the Greek embassy in Bern and laid siege to the Greek consulate in Zurich, taking a policeman and two others as hostages. Other protests took place in London, Germany, Denmark, Bulgaria, Belgium and Italy. A concerted effort to bring to the world's attention the plight of the Kurds and the illegal seizure of their leader. The problem was, as far as Turkey, America and most of Europe was concerned, Ocalan was a ruthless terrorist who had murdered thousands of innocent people. It was true what they said – one man's terrorist was another man's freedom fighter. In Germany, when the Kurds had attempted to storm the Israeli embassy the Israelis had opened fire and killed three of the protesters.

'We're now down-loading information to all NATO countries regardless of its potential interest to them.'

'What's the point in that?' asked Isobel.

'We aren't equipped to review it all. Due to the cut-backs, we just don't have the man power. And in any event how can we look at something that's happening say in Bonn or Rome, and assess whether it's important or not? So we just send the lot to the various agencies. We're still acknowledged as a world-leader in this type of work, you know.'

'Switzerland isn't in Nato,' Isobel stated the obvious.

'I know, but it's surrounded by Nato countries. And being so small there's no point in leaving Switzerland uncovered. Besides, they pay us handsomely to keep an eye on things for them.'

'Ah, I see. Trust the Swiss to pay money rather than take part.'

'True, but they can continue to plead neutrality whenever it suits them. Which is very useful sometimes.'

'So can you help?'

'Leave it with me. If I have anything I'll send it to you on the optic fibre lines.'

'Thanks. Oh, and Sarah, please hurry.'

'I'll get right onto it. How's sunny Scotland?'

'Raining, as usual,' was the reply as Isobel hung up.

Briefly she filled in the details of her conversation to Macnair. As she was finishing the telephone rang and Macnair picked it up, frowning. He listened for a few seconds and then said, 'Fax all the information you have and I'll get onto it right away.' He hung up, looked at Isobel and said, 'Trouble.'

He pressed an intercom button and said, 'Jim, come here please, we're needed.'

Major James Carter entered the room. He was nearly fifty, five feet five tall and weighed less than nine stone. He could still run marathons in record time and taught karate at black belt level.

'Is Hiram back?'

'Yes, sir. He's getting changed. What's up?'

'The proverbial has hit the fan. We've incidents in London, Athens and Madrid.'

Carter looked shocked. 'What? That can't be! And what about Nick?'

Macnair shook his head. 'Nothing, I'm afraid. Until we learn more there's nothing we can do about it, either. In the meantime, we've got to sort out these incidents.'

'You mean all three? And what are they?'

'A plane hijack at Heathrow. In Madrid, the Israeli embassy has been attacked and taken and in Athens a huge explosion has demolished an area near the Cathedral.'

'The Cathedral?'

Macnair shrugged. 'We'll get photographs as quickly as possible. In the meantime, we'll watch CNN for any information,' he said dryly. He switched on the television, left it muted and went to stand behind Isobel. 'Can you get us pictures of all three, as quickly as you can?'

'Yes, General, it won't take long. Leave me to get on with this.' She picked up a phone. 'I'll try and find Leo and Gareth.' As her assistants they were both experts on satellites and their use.

'Ah, Hiram,' Macnair greeted his second-in-command as the tall Colonel from the American Delta force strode into the room, 'we've got trouble.'

Macnair filled Walsh in on Hunter's disappearance and the terrible events in London, Greece and Madrid.

'What in hell's going on?' Walsh ran his fingers through his sparse blonde hair, frowning. 'Do we know who's responsible for all this?'

'No idea, as yet,' replied Macnair, sitting behind his desk and waving the other two to be seated opposite him. 'This fax only gives the barest of information. I've a call in to a man named Meadows, who is Head of Security at Heathrow.' The phone rang and he picked it up. 'Macnair,' he said, then listened. 'Thanks.' He hung up, his expression bleak. 'The explosion in Athens was an accident. By that I mean, when it went off it blew at least four bombers to Kingdom Come. It also killed fifty or more passers-by. There's no indication yet as to who was responsible.' He got up, walked across to the coffee machine and refilled his mug. 'This is orchestrated. I don't know yet by whom, but I'll find out.' He returned to his desk and sat down heavily. 'I want the men at Heathrow and Madrid taken alive. Hiram, you take charge at Heathrow, Jim, I want Clements in Madrid. Tell him not to bother coming back but to go straight there.'

'Whose plane has been hijacked?' Walsh asked.

The answer surprised him. 'Saudi Arabia's,' Macnair said.

'What about Nick?' Carter asked frowning.

'Nothing we can do,' was the short reply. 'Tell Clements it's an order. He's to deal with the Israeli Embassy attack and not to look for Nick. We'll see what we can do from this end.' He paused and looked out of the window at the river Forth glinting in the distance. His thoughts were with Hunter, beyond doubt his most valuable asset. It was then that the idea came to him. He turned from the vista and said, irritably, 'Get on with it.' When the two men had left the room he picked up the telephone, checked his private phone book and dialled.

'Mr. Hunter? This is General Macnair. I need your help.'

Tim Hunter hung up the receiver, thought for a few moments and then telephoned the Chairman of the Board. 'Sion, it's Tim. Nick's gone missing and I need your help,' he repeated Macnair's words, explaining the situation and asked, 'Any ideas?'

'Leave it with me, Tim. If anybody can find him, we can. I'll start the ball rolling right away. And don't worry. He's one of the most resourceful men I know.'

Sion Griffiths leant back in his chair, his tall slim frame stretched out in a straight line, deep in thought. Named after his grandfather he looked up at the portrait of his namesake, seeking inspiration as he so often did. 'Well, Gramps, what shall I do?' The smiling, roguish face of the aviator gazed back serenely, the faraway look held a steely gaze of determination and courage. Painted in 1920, it depicted his grandfather in his leather flying jacket, standing on a runway, a Griffin II aircraft in the background. 'Precious few rivers to cross and mountains to climb nowadays Gramps, but the world's a deadly place for all that.' He seemed to draw inspiration from the painting for he suddenly leaned forward and pressed a button on an intercom. 'Dorothy, get me Stuart Wodehouse. I want to see him, urgently.' He severed the connection, stood up and paced his office, deep in thought. A plan took shape in his head and after a few minutes he sat down, satisfied.

At forty-five he was young to be the Chairman but he had mustered sufficient votes to fight the bruising take-over battle of the previous year. The voting of the shares held in trust by the Hunters had tipped the scale in his balance and the company had been saved, once more, by the family. Since then a concerted effort had been made to buy up as many shares as possible, to consolidate the family's position. Finally, family members they could trust held 51% of the shares which effectively brought control back to the founding families. He looked at the portrait on the other wall. His great uncle David, Sir David Griffiths, gazed fiercely down. The artist had somehow exaggerated the predatory glint of Sir David's eyes, giving him a hawkish look, like a pirate contemplating his next raid on a rich merchantman. Sion drew a great deal of inspiration and help from looking at the paintings of the men who had helped establish the family's fortune.

He knew that within twenty-four hours he would have hundreds of men and women all over the world looking for Nick. Their network of spies was legendary, as great as the network run by the Rothschilds in the eighteenth and nineteenth centuries. If anybody could find out where Nick had been taken, they could.

Macnair made more telephone calls. He spoke to contacts all over Europe. From security service chiefs to senior military officers he related to each the same story. There was a reward of one million pounds for information leading to the safe rescue of Nick Hunter. When asked where the money was coming from, he lied. He said it came from Hunter's wealthy family when in fact it would come from TIFAT's own resources – the money they had lifted from Aziz Habib.

He had done all he could for Hunter. Now he needed to concentrate on what was happening at Heathrow and Madrid. His teams needed his help and support.

7

Hunter was unaware of his surroundings. His only cogent thought was that he could not move his hands or feet. Even that was only a dim glimmer of an idea at the back of his mind. He was lost in his dreams, held back by treacle, trying to run from ogres. He knew that he was dreaming and desperately wanted to wake up but he could not get past the fog that surrounded his mind. He only knew that he had to keep trying.

The transition to full awareness came gradually, the treacle became easier to run across, the ogres less threatening. Finally he had his wits about him and stifled a groan as memory flooded back. He was aware of being tied, that the gentle movement beneath him could only be from a ship and that the impenetrable darkness surrounding him probably meant that he was in a hold somewhere in the lowest reaches of the hull. His hands were tied behind his back and his legs tied securely from his feet to his knees. He could feel the rough, cold metal deck on his back and he became aware that he was naked. No, not quite. He still had on his boxer shorts.

His memory came back by degrees. The Alps, his mad-dash escape, those tourists – and then – nothing! Yes, there was something. A jab in the arm and then oblivion. In spite of the waves of nausea that washed over him, he managed to get himself to a sitting position. He closed his eyes for a few seconds and when he opened them again the darkness was as Stygian as before. Slowly, painfully, he inched his way forward across the deck, feeling for anything that could help him to cut his bonds.

In only a few moments he came up against the bulkhead and he moved around to lean back, with relief, against the metal wall. After a few minutes he inched his back slowly up the wall, but even so he still hit the overhead bulkhead with a nasty, jarring thump. He sat down, now painfully aware that the ceiling was less than five feet above his head. He began to move forward again, inch by inch, and quickly reached the opposite bulkhead. He lay down and swung his feet first one way and then the other. It took only moments for him to realise that he was in a compartment about seven feet by six feet and five feet high, and that there was nothing to help him to undo the ropes that were cutting into his hands and legs.

He composed himself calmly for a long wait. He would waste neither energy nor thought on his plight. There was nothing he could do about it and he was sure that he would need all of his strength for whatever lay ahead. Years earlier he had learnt to meditate. After a few months of practice he had lapsed into meditating only occasionally as he could not afford the time to sit quietly for twenty or thirty minutes, twice a day. Now he put his mind to it and quickly established his mantra in his head. He repeated the sound continuously to himself, letting his mind wander and letting the thoughts that bubbled to the surface dissipate. After a while he was lost inside his head, the discomfort of the ropes and his surroundings receded and he fell into a fitful doze. Whether it was the result of the meditation or the residue of the drugs sloshing about in his system he neither knew nor cared. He only knew that the aching stopped and that time passed.

Sometime later he came back to full consciousness, the cramp in his arms and legs attacking him with a vengeance and he became aware of a raging thirst along with an urgent need to empty his bladder. It was a toss-up which became the most over-riding urge that made Hunter move around, feeling with his feet for any sign of a door. After trying for what seemed to him to be ages, he gave up, perplexed. There appeared to be no means of opening the compartment he was in. For a few seconds panic flared as the thought of being left there to die flashed across his mind, but then reason prevailed. If he was to die they would have put a bullet into him long before now and left him in the Alps. No, for some reason or other he was wanted. He tried again. This time he lay on his back and stretched his feet to the top of the bulkhead, moving them up and down, feeling nothing but the rounded heads of riveting bolts. After he had finished the bulkheads he stood up carefully, and straightened his body until his head touched the overhead bulkhead. He moved it slowly back and forth, near to one of the sides. A few seconds later his head hit something and by moving his forehead over it he knew it was a handle of a type used for securing watertight hatches. He took a few minutes to work out in which direction the handle needed to move to open the hatch and then put his forehead against it. He pushed until his head ached and stars floated in front of his eyes. He yelled but got no response. Finally, he edged his way to a corner of the compartment and urinated. The relief was enormous and, for the first time since he became aware of his predicament, he was glad that he wore nothing but cotton shorts.

He noticed that the slight rocking motion of the ship was becoming more pronounced and the direction was gradually changing. After a short while the ship began to pitch and Hunter had no doubt that the weather was deteriorating. Manoeuvring himself into a corner of the compartment, he settled back. He tried once again to lose himself in meditation but this time he found it of little help. Instead he replayed all that he knew of the operation he had been on, looking for a clue. Nothing, so he started again, slowly, remembering every incident, everything he had seen and heard. There was a clue there, he knew, if only he could find it. No good. But something was nudging the edge of his memory. That was it! The prick in the arm. The voices immediately before. Swiss German . . . no! Ivrit! Yes, got it. They had been speaking Ivrit. He shook his head, trying to clear his thoughts. Trying to ignore his thirst. He analysed the few words he had heard and was sure he heard the girl say, *'That's him. I'll take him.'* He knew it was Ivrit because he had once had an Israeli girlfriend and had spent a few months listening to the language. Not learning it exactly but picking up a few useful phrases and sayings. He grinned. Like being able to say "I love you" in fifteen different languages including Japanese.

If the Israelis were involved then whose side were they on? Were the people who had kidnapped him effectively on the side of the good guys? In that case why had they taken him? Did they think he was part of the kidnap gang? Or were they on the side of the kidnappers of the children? Nothing made sense. Then he remembered the old man they had shot. Good guys did not do things like that. Time passed slowly.

It was with a shock that Hunter realised that he should not be sitting quietly. It had been like the unveiling of thin gossamer from his brain, layer by layer. Something had been nagging at him and he knew what it was. Suddenly he was wide awake with every faculty working. Finally the effect of the drugs had worn off and he was, at last, fully aware. Escape was important in the early hours of capture if it was to be successful. His powers and strength, in theory, should be at their peak before sleep, food, drink and sense deprivation took their toll. Hunter tried everything in his power to ignore the tingling in his fingers, the cramp in his feet and the discomfort and numbness in his buttocks and back. He could stay still no longer and he got to his knees, sitting down on his hands, the weight on the backs of his legs. Relief flooded up his back but soon his knees were aching like the devil. He moved slightly and now his hands were on a rough part of the rope. His weary mind took a few seconds to realise that he was sitting on the knot that tied his hands together. Carefully he felt around it and almost instantly found the end of the rope. Picking at the knot, he found it resisted his efforts, his fingers too numb to get a proper grip. He concentrated on what he was doing, feeling the knot, trying to identify it. If he could do that he might have a chance to undo it. If it was a granny knot and effectively a bunch of unscientific spaghetti then there was little hope of him achieving anything. On the other hand, a properly tied knot was clever in that it secured tightly but could be undone easily – usually.

He took his time feeling the rope and when he was finished he decided that he was tied with a reef knot with the ends tucked away in half-hitches, two each end. He moved again, easing the cramp, standing to let the circulation flow before he began work. Eventually he knelt back, found the knot and worked on one end of the rope. He took the rope between his thumb and forefinger and wiggled it back and forth, trying to loosen the half-hitch. He pushed at the rope and thought that it moved a fraction. He moved his fingers a thumbnail thickness back and did the same again. He felt it move and then followed the knot until he could hook his thumbnail into the slight opening he had created. He pulled and it moved. Slipping his thumb in he undid the first half-hitch.

The tension eased out of him and he hung his head, recovering from the sheer concentration it had taken to achieve so little. He did the same again, carefully and slowly. The half-hitch opened far enough to allow him to hook his thumb in the loop and pull it open. Letting out a long sigh he rested his fingers and hands. He did his best to ignore the pain, the discomfort, the pins and needles. He flexed his fingers, told himself to stop being a wimp and attacked the first half-hitch on the other end of the knot. It seemed to take an eternity of slipping fingers, sweat dripping into his eyes, stinging as he blinked them clear, and total concentration before the first half-hitch moved sufficiently for him to hook a thumb in and draw it open. The last half-hitch unknotted easily and he relaxed his aching body, his head hanging down, his strength and determination once more beginning to flood back.

He took hold of each end of the rope between a thumb and forefinger and gently pushed them together. The reef knot slid open and he quickly untied the first tuck of the knot. The second tuck fell open and his arms were free. They fell apart, pain searing across his shoulders as the muscles moved properly for the first time in hours. He moved his arms, luxuriating in their freedom. Already the pins and needles were wearing away, the tingling abating, his strength returning. It took only a few minutes to undo the ropes from around his legs and he was free. He grinned mirthlessly. "Free", he thought, was a relative term. He still had to get out of the hold, off the ship and back to land.

He did a few cursory bending exercises, got the circulation flowing once more and finally felt around his head for the handle to the hatch. Grabbing it, he shoved it over and cracked open the hatch. Listening intently, he heard nothing. He swung the hatch fully open into more darkness, felt above his head, found only emptiness and hoisted himself up. Closing the hatch he pushed the handle tightly locked. He realised that it was not pitch dark as he could make out faint outlines of shelves and items around him and he saw a faint slither of light showing near the deck. Stepping across to it he ran his hand down one side and found an ordinary doorknob. He twisted it slowly and cracked open the door. Although he heard nothing, he went no further as he sniffed the air. Tantalisingly he identified the pungent aroma of cigarette smoke and cooking. More specifically, the sharp smell of garlic reminded his stomach that he had not eaten for an age.

He opened the door another inch and put an eye to the crack. Empty. He was looking into a dimly lit corridor and as far as he could see there were two doors opposite. He knelt down before he put his head out any further, knowing that should anyone be in the corridor they were less likely to notice him at deck level. Cautiously he opened the door further and glanced up and down the corridor. The glance had been enough to show that there was nobody there, and that there were four doors on the other side of the corridor and a further three his side. The doors had all been closed, but a door at the end of the tiled corridor had a black port-hole at head height and there were four dim lights on, imbedded into the overhead bulkhead. The dim lights allowed anyone to see where they were going without casting strong white light into the darkness when a door or hatch was opened. That, coupled with the black porthole, told Hunter that it was night time.

He searched the storeroom, looking for a weapon or clothes to wear. The bulkheads were lined with shelves, some empty, others with a variety of useless items connected with the running of a ship. He ignored the cleaning gear, mops and brushes and finally, in a cupboard in the back, he found a box of overalls. Quickly he found a pair that fitted him and slipped them on. They were dark green and he realised that they were the type worn by fighter aircraft crews. Curiouser and curiouser, he thought. Another box yielded green canvas shoes, the sort that were calf length with thick, black soles. Again he recognised them – they were worn by armies all over the world for desert and jungle fighting. He found a pair that fitted and quickly laced them up. All he needed now was a weapon or two and he would feel a lot better.

Opening the door to the corridor he looked and listened. All was quiet. Walking to the door with the black porthole he opened it and stepped outside. He was on the starboard side of the ship and was surprised at the warmth of the breeze blowing across the deck. In the distance he could see lights on land though they gave no clue as to where he was. Prowling the deck like a panther he moved silently from shadow to shadow. He estimated the ship to be about 220 feet long and a cargo carrier of about 1200 tonnes. As he neared the stern the smell of cigarette smoke warned him of someone's presence.

Hunter stood under the davits of a lifeboat and considered his options. He thought quickly, analysing and discarding schemes almost as soon as they entered his head. Finally he knew that he had no choice. The death of the old man on the mountain convinced Hunter that whoever he was up against was ruthless and deadly. In the moonlight he could just discern the outline of a man standing at the stern rail, looking at the wake, puffing contentedly on a cigarette. Hunter moved silently towards him, pausing often, listening for any others. Standing three feet behind the man, who was wearing an Arab kaffiyeh, he waited for the right moment. As the man flicked the end of his cigarette at the wake, watching the glowing sparks fall away, Hunter struck. A smash across the back of the neck with the leading edge of his hand and before the man collapsed a heave over the stern sent the lookout silently to a watery grave. One down, many more to go, he thought.

If the man had been the lifebuoy sentry, on watch in case of a man overboard, then somebody could come looking for him at any time. He now needed to move fast. The lookout being there also suggested to Hunter that he was on an efficient ship, one that played by the rules of the sea. But he was also puzzled; he had heard Ivrit back on the mountain but the sentry had been wearing an Arab headress. The flag on the stern was white with two horizontal blue stripes and the Star of David in between – the national flag of Israel.

So far luck had been on his side but he knew that it would only be a matter of time before he was seen or someone checked up on him and found him missing. He looked up at the lifeboat and across the water to the lights on the shore. It was his best option but first he needed to check out his escape route. Then he needed a diversion.

He removed the quick-release gear that held the boat tightly against the davits, found the handle that operated them and moved it a few millimetres. The davits shuddered before smoothly swinging away from the ship. He stopped them, reversed the direction of the handle and settled the boat back in its cradle. Next he climbed up into the lifeboat, unhooked the canvas cover, throwing it clear into the sea and checked the boat over. It was a type he had last seen in the early years of his naval career and known as a whaler. An excellent sea-boat, it was used by ships to ferry people back and forth when at anchor but, more importantly, for launching should somebody accidentally fall overboard. Checking the bow he found the launch rope attached and ready to be used. When the boat slipped from the davits it needed to be towed by the ship until it had veered away from the hull and the rope could then be slipped. Otherwise there was a serious danger of the lifeboat smashing into the hull and turning turtle. Launching was usually at speeds between two and three knots; Hunter would be attempting it at a speed closer to fifteen. He tried not to dwell on what could go wrong.

In the lockers under the seats he found the same paraphernalia as he could expect to find in a Royal Naval ship, including a spare jerry can of fuel, another of water and a sealed pack of hard-tack rations. It all went to reinforce his impression of a well organised ship, certainly superior to many merchant vessels and comparable to a military set-up. He needed some answers but where to start looking? Glancing up at the sky he saw that it was a clear night with many stars and a half-moon. He could see that he was still in the northern hemisphere and began to look for certain stars. The pole star was obvious. It was low over the stern which meant the ship was heading in a southerly direction. To the west he found Arcturus in the constellation Boötes, to the east Altair in the constellation Aquila and to the right of that was Jupiter. Hunter was confident that he was in the Mediterranean.

To port were more lights and they seemed to be getting infinitesimally brighter. His instincts told him he was in the Adriatic and Italy was to starboard and Yugoslavia or Albania to port. He climbed back down to the deck of the ship and moved quickly forward. He guessed that the superstructure ahead contained the living quarters of the crew and that he would find the way down to the engine room there. If he was caught trying to launch the boat or even if he escaped but was seen then he would not stand a chance. He wanted to even the odds a little first. He gripped the handle of the door and was about to swing it open when he felt the handle move. There was nowhere to hide so he stepped back and to one side, hidden behind the door. As it opened he got ready to pounce, sure that he would be spotted the instant the door was closed again.

There was a jostling, a rustling of clothes, iron striking iron and a voice said, 'Be careful, fool.' The English was heavily accented and difficult to place but that was not Hunter's main concern. What was more important was how many men had stepped through the door?

8

Colonel Hiram B. Walsh sat in the co-pilot's seat of the giant European Helicopter Industries EH 101 Merlin, ZH821. He knew that they had been lucky to acquire what was recognised as a state of the art helicopter built as a result of a joint venture between the British and Italian Governments. After eight years of collaboration Westland and Agusta launched their first helicopter on 9th. October 1987. The helicopter TIFAT was using was the maritime utility transport with a folding tail and rear loading ramp. The helicopter could carry 30 passengers or the equivalent pay-load, was fast and reliable and already proving to be an asset to Macnair and his team. At that moment they were flying south of Manchester with a priority over-ride by air traffic control to Heathrow. All aircraft were ordered out of their way, civilian jet-liners were being diverted from Heathrow to Gatwick, Stanstead or Luton while others, particularly from the States were being diverted to Schipol and Prestwick. In the skies over the United Kingdom chaos reigned supreme.

'We'll be on the ground in forty minutes, sir,' said the pilot.

'Thanks, Burg. I'll go back and see how the men are doing.'

He undid his seat belt, stretched as he stood up and exited the cockpit door, stepping over the legs of the flight engineer as he did so. He was gratified to see that his team were busy preparing their weapons, checking their gear and generally getting ready to carry out an assault on a civilian aircraft. Don Masters and Peter Weir were poring over plans of a Boeing 757, looking at their options for effecting a way in.

Unlike on earlier helicopters, the sound proofing on the ultra-modern EH 101 was such that they could speak to each other in normal tones.

'Any more information, sir?' Masters asked. He was a sergeant in the Royal Engineers and an acknowledged expert when it came to I.E.D's – impromptu explosive devices often made from ordinary household and industrial materials.

Walsh shook his head. 'No change. No passengers released and no demands made, so far. We're none the wiser now than when we took off. The only difference is that the plane has taxied off the runways to the maintenance area. Let me show you.' He took a map of Heathrow Airport from a satchel and opened it out. 'The aircraft is now parked here,' he pointed at the map. 'They seem to be waiting for something but God alone knows what,' he shrugged. 'Perhaps we'll have a better idea when we land.'

The pilot announced that they were approaching Heathrow and the team of eight men settled into their seats and fastened their seat-belts. The Colonel went back to the cockpit.

'Heathrow coming up now, sir,' said Burg Schwarzkopf, a German aviator who had been working with the Federal hostage release and anti-terrorist force GSG9 based on the Border Police, prior to joining TIFAT. Not only was he a skilled helicopter pilot but he was also a member of the team and could fight along with the best of them.

Walsh strapped himself in, aware that he was the only man there who had ever attempted to re-take an aircraft and release hostages without anyone being injured. And that had only been during exercises, never for real. However, he had seen plenty of action during his career. In 1977, after the successes in Europe of the German GSG9 Group against terrorism, Colonel Charles 'Charging Charlie' Beckwith, convinced the American Army that there was a requirement for a counter-terrorist and hostage release force. Beckwith had been seconded to 22 SAS in the early sixties and had been impressed by the way the Regiment selected and trained its men. Mirroring 22 SAS, Operational Detachment Delta was formed. In time it became known as Delta Force and latterly just Delta. Delta was 400 strong, composed of two squadrons and had its own headquarters and training areas. The squadrons were broken down into four-man teams and were amongst the most skilled fighters in the American Army. Those selected to join Delta were carefully chosen for their stability but also for their speed of action. They trained on timed route marches, had to do 37 sit-ups and 33 press-ups in less than a minute and could fire a variety of weapons needing 100 percent scores at 600 metres and 90 percent scores at 1000 metres. Delta's "killing house" was similar to the one at Hereford. It consisted of four huge rooms, one of which was laid out like the inside of an airliner – that was where Walsh had exercised. However, he had also seen plenty of live action in Grenada, Panama and the Gulf. He had been a raw lieutenant when Delta made its operational debut during Operation Eagle Claw, the abortive mission to rescue the US Embassy staff held hostage in Tehran in 1980. They had learned a great deal from that fiasco. Since then, Walsh had been in and out of Delta as he gained promotion, for no officer spent the whole of his career with Special Forces; it was too restricting promotion-wise. However, Walsh loved the challenge of Delta and when the opportunity came to return to the force he did so with alacrity. When TIFAT was formed the Americans had wanted operational command but NATO had decreed that it should go to a British General, Macnair, and that the Americans could have a Colonel, preferably seeped in the traditions of clandestine operations, as second-in-command. Hiram B. Walsh had been the obvious choice.

They landed out of sight of the Boeing 757 and were welcomed by Paul Meadows, the competent ex-Superintendent, Head of Security at the airport. The two men shook hands and Walsh joined Meadows in the offices of a maintenance hangar which over-looked the parked aircraft. In the meantime the team were busy preparing their gear and setting up observation posts around the plane.

'As you can see,' said Meadows, 'we have armed police surrounding the aircraft. The terrorists have stated that should an armed man come within 50 metres of the plane they will kill a hostage.'

'Nothing else from them?' Walsh asked.

Meadows shook his head in frustration. 'Nothing. It's as if they're waiting for something, but I've no idea what it might be.' Meadows was a trained negotiator and had worked on dozens of siege and hostage situations in his long career with the London Metropolitan Police Force, known colloquially as "the Met". 'Usually we would have received all sorts of demands by now, after all,' he looked at his watch, 'it's been six hours since the plane was taken.'

'What have the Saudis said?' Walsh asked.

'There, I'm afraid, we have serious problems. One of the Princes of the Saudi Royal family is onboard, together with his wife and three children.'

'Hell! I take it we have to negotiate to a safe, happy conclusion when all will be love and light,' Walsh said, harshly.

'That's about it. I received this fax a few minutes ago.' He took out a sheet of paper and handed it to Walsh. It was from the Foreign Office, ordering him that under no circumstances whatsoever was he to try and rescue the hostages but to negotiate for their release. 'The only problem is, no one is talking to us.'

'How many of them are there?'

Meadows knew he was referring to the terrorists. 'Five.'

'How can you be so sure?'

'We now have certain questions we can ask the pilot and get answers. Innocuous enough in themselves but they give us information that is otherwise not forthcoming. Some pilots bother to know the procedures, others don't. In this case we appear to have a switched on Saudi who knows his stuff.'

'What about offering them food and drink?'

'We tried that but were told to stay away. They've warned us that the plane is booby-trapped and can be blown up by any one of them. They also said that we couldn't possibly kill all of them should we attack.'

'Well, we aren't going to do that, that's for certain,' said Walsh. 'Do you have plans of the plane?'

Meadows shook his head. 'We do have Boeing 757 plans but not for that specific aircraft. The layout inside could easily have been modified. You know, the usual thing, a larger first class section for Royalty, different seats, fewer passengers and so on.'

Walsh nodded. 'That's what I was hoping for. Have you sent for details?' He caught the look from Meadows and before he answered, Walsh added, 'Sorry, a stupid question, of course you have.' He frowned, thought about telephoning the General, but then thought better of it. This was his call and it was time to act. 'If I approach from the tail, I can get right under the plane without being seen. If I open this hatch,' he pointed to the baggage handling hatch, 'I can get inside with my men. We go here,' he traced his finger along the baggage hold, 'and get in up this ladder here.'

'In theory, but you'll be heard. The hatch cover opens up the way.' Before he could say more there was a yell and both men looked out through the window. Something was happening. The door to the aircraft was opening and the stairs were sliding into place. A small head appeared, it looked back and then a child walked down the steps, followed by other children. They walked in a crocodile line across the tarmac towards the doors of the maintenance hangar. Even as the last child touched the ground the stairs were retracting and the door was closed. Just then the radio came to life.

'Heathrow this is Saudi Royal Airlines SR 3479, stand by for a transmission.' It was the pilot of the aircraft.

A new voice came over the radio. 'This is the Army for the Protection of Israel. If all hostilities do not cease against Israel and if we are not allowed to live in peace then we will continue our war against our enemies. We will annihilate them like this.'

The transmission ended and Walsh frowned at Meadows. 'What the . . . It doesn't make sense.' He got no further. There was an enormous explosion and the plane was blown to smithereens. One hundred and forty eight men and women died in the blast, including the terrorists. Fire engines appeared from around corners and fought the fire as it spread across the tarmac, the aviation fuel threatening buildings and aircraft alike. Soon, over a hundred men and women were fighting the blaze as they tried to keep it under control. Buildings had been damaged, glass shattered for hundreds of metres and many people had suffered injuries. For many the injuries ranged from slight to serious, for a few they were fatal. The TV cameras set up all over the airport, watching the scene, recorded the devastation and reported it to a shocked nation.

Walsh's phone rang. Dazedly, he flicked it on. 'Walsh.'

'What in hell happened?' Macnair greeted his second-in-command.

'We don't know, General. You saw the kids come out and the next thing we know the plane exploded.'

'No warning? No explanation?'

'Well, sort of. Listen to this.' Walsh played back the tape of the announcement from the hijackers.

'It makes no sense,' was Macnair's response. 'Who on earth are the Army for the Protection of Israel? I've never heard of them.'

'Nor me, sir. But that doesn't mean much. These groups come and go as regularly as ticks on the back of a mangy cur. But we need some answers and fast. All hell is going to break loose in the Middle East unless we can find out what's going on.'

'I concur. There's nothing more you can do there. Get back here while we try and find some answers.' Macnair broke the connection and leaned back in his chair, frowning. He just hoped that Clements would have better results in Madrid. He checked the time. It was just after 19:00 hours. The team would just about be arriving.

Joshua Clements was also Delta Force and had known action in the Gulf and in the former Yugoslavia. He had been with Nick Hunter when they had rescued the VIPs off the ship in Scotland and later when they had killed Habib, the terrorist responsible for the atrocity. He had a good team with him, although there were only five of them. The helicopter landed at the airport near Madrid and they quickly disembarked with their equipment. They were met by the Chief of Police, Colonel Manuel Amado, who spoke little English. Clements replied to the policeman's greeting in fluent Spanish.

It was evident from the relief in the man's voice that he was happy to hand over the problem of the Israeli Embassy to the team from TIFAT. They climbed into police vans and, with sirens blaring and lights flashing, raced out of the airport.

'Captain Clements,' said the Police Chief, 'it is a very unusual situation. We have had no demands, nothing. They have asked for nothing, demanded nothing.'

'How did they get in? The Israelis have about the best security of any embassy in the world.'

The reply was a Spanish shrug, eloquent and meaningful. 'We have learned nothing.' He looked at his watch. Spain was an hour ahead of Britain, and he said, 'It is now nineteen thirty hours which means that they have been in the building for some six hours. It is very strange.'

'Have you learned anything at all?' Clements asked.

'We have caught glimpses of the men as they wander back and forth. They appear to be Arabic, but we cannot be certain.' He caught the quizzical glance thrown at him by Clements and added, 'From the way that they dress. The headscarf and caftan are very distinctive.'

'Perhaps too distinctive?' Clements suggested but the comment passed by the policeman. Looking out of the windows of the van he could see that night was falling fast, which suited him. 'Do you have a plan of the embassy?'

'Here.'

It was handed over and Clements spread it across his knees. The building naturally enough stood in its own grounds and was surrounded by a high stone wall. The gate was guarded by bullet-proof sentry boxes on either side. Moreover there was only room for one person at a time to walk through the entrance. A massive gate in the rear wall could be opened for bulk deliveries, the vehicle being allowed to draw up next to the back door. The grounds were covered with paving slabs, Spanish stone that was pleasing to look at but prevented any trees or bushes from growing. There was no hiding place in the grounds. He stared out of the window, deep in thought. He knew Madrid reasonably well and recognised the Calle De Alcala at the approach to the Place de la Independenca. He knew that it was not much further to the embassy when he would have to start making decisions. What the hell was he to do?

The cars and vans screeched to a halt two hundred metres from the Israeli embassy and men disgorged from the vehicles, guns drawn, looking as though they meant business. Clements and his team took their time, aware that the show by the Spanish forces was for consumption by the world's press. Cameras flashed, television lenses zoomed in and questions were called from the reporters a further hundred metres away. It was already growing dark and so Clements had no hesitation in approaching the embassy, but at fifty metres, opposite the front gates, he stopped. If he went any further the close-surveillance cameras which covered the area would record him for the benefit of the occupants of the embassy. He stood and looked past the gates, at the building. The curtains were now drawn closed and whatever was going on inside was veiled from view.

He noticed Colonel Amato waving and he joined him by the control van. 'A man from the embassy is on the telephone. He wishes to speak to whoever is in charge.'

'I think that should be you for now,' said Clements. 'I'll take responsibility for the operational side of it. You deal with the rest.'

The policeman looked unhappy, nodded and said, 'I have just received this from my Department of the Interior.'

He handed a fax to Clements, it read: Under no circumstances are you to give in to the terrorists or their demands. Israeli special forces are en-route and they will take over the operation. TIFAT is to give all help required but not, repeat not, instigate any action. Estabel Cavvarrio, Minister of the Interior.

'What do we do?' asked Sam McReady when Clements told the remainder of the team about the fax.

'As we're told,' said Clements, phlegmatically. 'But we can help. We need information. I have an idea which I think we'd better work on.'

At that moment Colonel Amado joined them. 'There are five children inside and they are being sent out in two minutes. If we make a move they say that they will blow up the embassy.'

87

'Nothing else?' Clements asked.

'No, nothing. It is very strange.'

'When will the Israelis get here?' McReady asked Clements.

Clements translated the question to the Colonel who replied, 'In about an hour. But I do not see what they can do. The place is virtually impregnable.'

Following a brief conversation in Spanish, Clements turned to McReady. 'Sam, if we're going to get into the building we need to be able to approach it without being filmed.'

'How?'

'We need to identify the underground electric cables to the embassy and when we're ready, cut them.'

'Are you suggesting a full-scale assault? Like at the Iranian Embassy at Princess Gate?' McReady asked. He was referring to the SAS storming of the Iranian Embassy in London on the 30th April 1980. Six Iraqi-sponsored terrorists who claimed to be members of the Democratic Revolutionary Front for the Liberation of Arabistan had entered the Iranian Embassy and taken 26 hostages from the embassy staff, a BBC journalist and a policeman from Scotland Yard's Diplomatic Protection Group. Operation Nimrod was the SAS assault on the embassy. The operation was deemed a success. Five terrorists were killed and one captured. Unfortunately one of the hostages also perished. However, there were a number of significant differences between then and now. First, there had been nearly six days of surveillance, using heat seeking and listening devices which identified the whereabouts of the hostages and terrorists. Second, the building was not an impregnable fortress like the Israeli embassies world-wide where the fear of attack by Arab Nationalists was always a consideration and third, the resources available to the SAS were practically unlimited as the operation took place on British soil. In Spain, Clements and his men were out on a limb. He just hoped the Israelis would bring the sort of equipment they needed.

'The other option is that we negotiate, but according to the Colonel nobody in the Embassy wants to talk to us. If nobody is talking, then there's no negotiating.' He stated the obvious.

'What about finding a way in through the sewers?' Jan Badonovitch asked.

'It's an option and one we can pursue. I'll ask the Colonel for plans of the sewage outlets, and water and electricity supplies.' At that moment David Hughes appeared. 'Finished?'

Hughes shrugged. 'I've set up four listening and heat seeking devices but they don't tell us much. We need to track movement as well as voices so that we can build up a picture and identify the terrorists. It'll take time, boss, as you know.'

Clements nodded. He knew the problems but he wanted to give the Israelis all the help he could when they arrived.

'Boss.' Sam McReady pointed.

The door of the embassy was opening. Five confused and hesitant children walked out and the door immediately closed. The children, two boys and three girls, ranging from a toddler to a young teenager, stood in a cluster, not moving. The door opened again and a harsh voice said something and the children began to walk towards the street. As they came through the gate a burly policeman picked each child up and darted down the street to the control van. Two of the youngest began to cry while the eldest, a pretty teenage girl, tried to get them to stop. The other two stoically kept silent, fear etched in their faces.

'We won't hurt you,' said Colonel Amato when the children had been deposited by the control van. 'But we need to know what is happening. What is your name?' he asked the girl.

She hesitated a second before replying. 'Miriam.'

'You speak Spanish? Good,' said the Colonel.

'Only a little,' was the reply. 'I learn in school. I speak English and Ivrit,' she added.

Clements stepped forward. 'Speak to me then. I speak English,' he smiled reassuringly at her. 'We need to know how many men are in there, how many hostages? What do they want? Why haven't they made demands? What did they say?'

'Hang on, boss,' said McReady. 'Let her answer. You'll confuse her otherwise.'

At that moment the telephone rang and clearly, over the

recorded loud-speaker, came the announcement. 'This is the League for the Elimination of Israel. Death to all Jews.'

The explosion rocked the area for hundreds of square metres. Glass shattered in dozens of building, walls fell down injuring many people. The embassy building was turned to rubble. Nobody was left alive. Dazedly, Clements reached into his pocket to telephone Macnair. What in hell was going on?

9

Macnair voiced exactly the same words to Jim Carter. 'What's going on? First we have Saddam's grandchildren kidnapped, then we have the Army for the Protection of Israel and now we get the League for the Elimination of Israel. Neither organisation has ever been heard of before now. I get a phone call from the Prime Minister telling me that there is unrest fermenting across the Middle East and what do we know about it? And where on earth is Hunter? You'd think that with such a high reward on offer somebody would come forward.'

'There's more,' said Carter. He sat down opposite the General and took out a signal flimsy. The sheet of paper was specially printed to make it easier to understand and clearer to read. 'This is from Mod. We are at Bikini State Red across the Middle East and Amber in Europe.' He was referring to the states of readiness and vigilance required by the governments and military forces throughout NATO as the possibility of terrorist activity increased. 'It goes on to say that there are threats to every country in Europe but nothing specific. Hence Bikini Amber. In Saudi, Iraq and Syria the threats are more specific and we're at Bikini Red for all embassies. The bomb that exploded in Turkey has been claimed as the work of the Army for the Protection of Israel. The target was a mosque in Istanbul. We've just received another report of an explosion in Israel itself, at Haifa. A military barracks has been bombed.'

'Any casualties?'

'Yes. But we don't know precisely how many. However,' he

added, heavily, 'it is reckoned to be in the hundreds.'

'Hell, the Israelis aren't going to sit around for that,' said Macnair.

Carter nodded. 'We know that, but there's more.'

'More? What more can there be?' Isobel asked as she handed out mugs of freshly made coffee.

'It appears that the whole of the area is mobilising,' Carter said.

'Why did this suddenly happen?' Isobel asked. 'I mean, there was no indication of anything like this anywhere. And you know that we would have been the first to discover something with the assets we have at our disposal. It doesn't make any sense.'

Macnair, frowning, nodded agreement. 'I need to speak to David Golightly. Surely Dayan can't be behind all this?' It was a rhetorical question which neither bothered answering. 'He may be able to shed some light on what's going on.'

'You'll be lucky,' said Carter. 'CNN have just reported that the Israeli Knesset are in emergency session. The hawks and doves are yelling abuse at each other.'

'Who's winning?' Macnair asked.

'The hawks,' was the sobering reply.

'As usual,' said Isobel. 'Can I say something?'

'Since when have we been able to stop you?' Macnair smiled tiredly.

'Can all this be orchestrated by Dayan? I mean, think about it. Suddenly we have a crisis. No warning, no warm up. Just a fully blown, mega-crisis. Where did it come from? Why has it happened?'

'I agree with you, Isobel. The objective appears to be all out war. Right now our only lead is Dayan according to David. If he's wrong then who and why are the questions we need answered.'

'Find one and we might find the other,' said Carter.

'Isobel, speak to GCHQ and get everything we can on what's happening. Ask Sarah to concentrate on Israel for the next few hours. Please get me an up-to-date weather forecast.'

Isobel looked out of the window at the unusually clear sky and warm sunshine.

'Not here,' Macnair pre-empted her. 'In the Middle East. I want to know if we can use our KH-12s as well as the Lacrosse satellites.' The General was referring to the Keyhole KH-12 satellites that flew through space, sucking up radio and phone signals as well as photographing and identifying targets. Unfortunately cloud cover made them useless. However, the Lacrosse imaging satellites used radar to penetrate the clouds and gave a picture as clear as the view from your front window. The downside was that the pictures and information came only once every 180 minutes. Furthermore, the satellites were in heavy use over the former Yugoslavia, particularly in Kosovo.

Macnair began to pace his office, deep in thought. 'Isobel, I've no doubt you're right. Is there any chance of us using Mercury, Mentor or Trumpet over the area?' Macnair was referring to the latest advanced signal-intercept satellites that could pick up everything from cell phones to radios. Furthermore, no matter how much frequency scrambling or codes that were used, the computers quickly and easily tracked and de-coded the messages. As always the technology created its own problems. In this case it was sifting through the millions of calls to find relevant ones. Hundreds of words were "trigger-words" that made the satellites lock on and record the conversation. At GCHQ in Cheltenham it still meant a long, tedious process to find the nuggets amongst the dross.

'We need more information,' said Macnair, 'to give added or different trigger words. That way we could get more information more quickly.'

'If we concentrated our efforts in Israel for, say, forty-eight hours,' Isobel spoke pensively, 'we could vacuum up everything and listen to it all in about eight or nine hours, with what we've got right now. But that will mean everything else going by the board.'

Macnair nodded. 'I'll see what I can do. I need to talk to SACEUR as well as the Cabinet Secretary.' SACEUR or Supreme Allied Commander Europe was an American General in overall command of NATO who controlled the use of the assets in Europe. Macnair would need his permission to divert some of the satellites to look at the Middle East. The problem was, General Dwight Roberts had his hands full. What with a disintegrating Russia, Serbia at war with NATO and a deteriorating situation in Albania, Montenegro and Macedonia caused as a result of the war. Nearly two million refugees were on the march with nowhere to go and no one to support and protect them. Now this!

Macnair used the private satellite phone to get straight through to Roberts. 'Dwight? It's Malcolm Macnair.'

'Malcolm! Good to hear from you. Though I suspect you're calling to spoil my day.'

'Probably. Have you received the latest Intel reports on the Middle East?'

'Sure. It's going to hell in a basket and there doesn't seem to be too much that we can do about it. I've had the Pentagon on screaming for answers, as well as every government in Europe. Have you any ideas?'

'A few. Look, can you saturate Israel with everything you've got for the next two days? I'll get Cheltenham to concentrate on the area as well.'

'You think Israel is the key?'

'It has to be.'

'Come on, Malcolm. According to Washington, Israel can do no wrong. We turn a blind eye to every single abuse that Israel commits, whether it's against human rights or treaty violations. The governments of practically every single western country are terrified of the press and the Jews who are controlling it. If I suggested that Israel was to blame I'd be recalled on the next available plane.'

Macnair knew that there was more than a grain of truth in what Roberts was saying. A grain? More like a few tonnes. For years the West had turned a blind eye to whatever Israel did. Even when it was proven that the Israelis had nuclear weapons no action was taken. Unfortunately, Israel was changing from an undisciplined teenager to a grown-up bully. Fundamentalism was rife across the whole region, whether it was Moslem or Jewish and both were proving to be ugly, unforgiving and unrelenting. Neither side had learned anything from the minor and even major clashes of the last fifty years. Sectarian hatred was going to tear the whole area apart and if it did there was the danger that the rest of the world could be destroyed along with it. Nuclear weapons on one side, bacterial and germ warfare on the other – it didn't bear thinking about.

'There are too many indicators for my liking which show that Israel is up to its collective armpits in the trouble. I'm not saying it's their government, but I am saying somebody powerful and well connected is orchestrating what's been happening.'

'I see. Let me think about it. I may be able to do something without making too much noise. But you know we're stretched to breaking point here.'

'I know. What happened to the peace dividend?'

'We spent it,' was the laconic reply as SACEUR broke the connection. Roberts sat back in his chair and wiped the perspiration from his brow. It would not be for much longer now, he thought.

'He'll see what he can do,' said Macnair to the other two. 'Isobel, warn Sarah what's happening and tell her to expect help from NATO when it comes to tasking satellites over the area. Jim, recall the teams. I think we've got a busy time ahead of us. Also, increase the reward for information on Hunter by a further million. We'll use our own money, this time.'

'Sterling?' Carter asked.

'Of course sterling,' Macnair replied irritably. 'You don't think I meant zlotys, do you?'

When his two most important aides had left Macnair sat down at his desk, swung the chair round and put his feet up on the windowsill and looked at the beautiful day outside. A wave of sadness swept through him. Such a lovely world, he thought philosophically, and so many people trying to wreck it. The phone interrupted his thoughts and he sighed, swinging his feet down to the floor as he reached for the insistent instrument.

Incredibly no effort was made to close the door. Hunter stood poised to attack but the door was left hanging open. He stood behind it, hidden by the door and deep shadow. Three men walked nonchalantly across the deck and passed under a light. Hunter could see that two carried side-arms and one had what appeared to be an Uzi slung over his shoulder. They split up, one going towards the bow and the other two down each side of the ship, towards the stern. If further proof was needed that this was a well-run ship the deck patrol provided it.

He had only seconds to decide. Once the lifebuoy sentry was found to be missing all hell would break loose. Hunter decided that he needed more time and that left only one option.

Like a ghost he flitted along the port side, watching the back of the man he was trailing. The noise of the ship, the sound of the sea and the breeze over the deck all worked in Hunter's favour. He was half a pace behind the man when a sixth sense warned his prey, who suddenly looked over his shoulder. The man's jaw dropped in surprise and he reached for the gun at his waist as Hunter clamped a hand like iron over the man's fingers, crushing them around the weapon. Hunter smashed his fingers into the man's larynx, changing the yell that had formed into a faint, agonised gurgle and elbowed the man in the temple. He fell to the deck. Hunter quickly took the holster and gun and placed it around his own waist and ripped off the kaffiyeh. He placed it over his head and shoulders, dragged the inert body to the guard rails and slid the unconscious man overboard.

Hunter walked quickly towards the stern, pleased to note that he was as calm as though he were strolling in the park on a Sunday afternoon. Some park, he grinned!

The second guard was standing by the lifeboat holding one of the loosened strops. He looked towards Hunter and saw what he expected to see. A man wearing a gun and kaffiyeh walking towards him. He looked up at the lifeboat, turned his back on Hunter and gripped the ladder to climb up and look into the boat. It was the last thing he did on earth. With no finesse, Hunter smashed in the man's skull with the butt of the gun, took the Uzi and once more threw the body over the side.

He slung the Uzi over his shoulder and walked nonchalantly along the deck towards the bow. The third man was walking down the starboard side towards him. Hunter slowed his pace, wishing to meet in the shadow between two deck lights. He stopped in the darkest section and turned to the sea, leaning on the guard rail. The man said something which Hunter ignored. He stayed looking at the sea until a hand dropped on his shoulder. Hunter turned, drove his fist into the man's stomach and, as he doubled up, retching, Hunter tipped him overboard. The scream lasted only a second before it was cut off, lost forever.

So far, luck had been with him but now he needed to hurry. With four men gone any one of them could be missed at any time.

A few seconds later he was back at the superstructure and stepped through the door. Inside was a short corridor, with two doors on either side. The dim night lights illuminated the area well enough for him to see his way. The second door to starboard was what he was looking for. A watertight bulkhead door with Engine Room stencilled on it. He opened the door and stepped onto a catwalk, looking down into a cavernous space, well lit, the noise of machinery deafening. Instantly he saw that the ship had two Paxman diesels, well kept and gleaming bright. The other machinery he identified as two generators and a fresh water-making machine. On the aft bulkhead he saw the ready-fuel diesel tanks. The main tanks would be low down, probably aft, unseen from year to year. Diesel would be pumped up automatically, to keep the ready-fuel tanks full. This meant that in the event of an engine room fire, the minimum amount of diesel would help to feed the flames. It was a common precaution on any ship. Once fire or smoke was detected, the tanks could be isolated from a number of vantage points, including the engine room and the bridge.

All he had to do was to identify the isolation switch, turn it off, stop it from being opened too quickly, open the ready-fuel draining taps, go back topsides, launch the lifeboat and escape. He grinned; easy as pie. Except for one small detail – the two men sitting in the engineer's office on the starboard side of the engine room. So far neither had looked in his direction, seemingly engrossed in some sort of magazine.

He gripped the ladder each side with his hands and feet and slid the twenty feet down to the spotless deck-plates between the two diesel engines. There was no need for stealth or finesse. He walked boldly to the sound-proof door and opened it. The noise made both men look up. Hunter shot the first one through the forehead but the second one dived to one side and Hunter missed. The outcome was only delayed by an additional second or two as Hunter shot the other man, first in the shoulder and then through the head. At that moment the telephone on the bulkhead rang.

He ignored the sound and picked up a cigarette lighter from the desk as well as a heavy wrench and screwdriver. With the phone still ringing he rushed out of the office and into the noisy engine room. He quickly located the pipe and valve that fed the diesel from the stern tanks, turned off the valve and used the wrench to take the pipe apart. It moved easily, proving that the maintenance on the ship was as efficient as the running of the vessel. He dropped the U-bend of the pipe under the deck plates out of sight and turned on the valve. Diesel began to gush out, the pungent smell of the liquid making Hunter choke.

He picked up an oil can, used to check the water content of diesel samples – a problem requiring constant monitoring at sea – and filled it with diesel. He stuffed an oily rag in the top and darted for the ladder. He was aware of two changes in the noise level. The telephone had stopped ringing and one of the engines was already beginning to splutter.

By the door to the engine room he paused, lit the oily rag with the lighter, checked the diesel was well alight and threw it against the furthest bulkhead. Unlike petrol, diesel does not go up with a whoosh and a fire ball. The flames licked at the diesel on the deck, ignited the pool that was rapidly growing there and moved almost leisurely across the rest of the space. Suddenly the noise was raucous beyond belief as alarm bells rang throughout the ship and sprinklers came on automatically. Hunter stepped through the door, slammed it shut and hurried along the corridor to the fresh air outside. Strange, he thought, that they should make the mistake of using water sprinklers. The water would spread the flames, not smother them. What they should have used was carbon dioxide which would quickly smother the flames by starving them of oxygen. Maybe the ship was not quite as well organised as he thought.

Already there were loud voices being raised and feet running across the deck. He ducked into a shadow as half a dozen men suddenly appeared, some were armed but they were not looking to use their weapons. They went to the hoses and fire-fighting equipment liberally stowed around the deck. In the noise and confusion Hunter tried to slip away.

A yell from behind him was different to the others and he looked back. Somebody was shouting something and pointing at him. One of the men dropped a hose and reached for the gun slung over his shoulder. Hunter dived to one side, rolled behind a dwarf bulkhead, the low wall that helped to break up any heavy sea washing across the deck, and unslung the Uzi. Shots were fired in his direction but bounced off the steel wall. He put an arm around the edge and opened fire indiscriminately, spraying the area where the men had been standing. There were screams and curses but Hunter did not wait to see what damage he had inflicted. He crawled along the deck, rolled behind a large metal container which he saw contained life-jackets and ran aft to the whaler. At that moment the engines stopped and an artificial stillness fell across the ship. Looking forward, Hunter could see smoke billowing from the door in the superstructure and out of the main ventilators to the engine room. A harsh voice yelled an order and for the moment they forgot about him. The fire was their priority.

Hunter pushed the handle of the lowering gear and the davit smoothly trundled out. At the end of their run there was a slight jerk as the davits locked in position and the boat began to lower towards the sea, twenty feet below. As the boat went past deck level Hunter let go of the handle and prepared to clamber onboard. To his chagrin the hoist stopped and the whaler swung against the side. Without headway on, the ship was beginning to wallow in a short, choppy sea, the superstructure causing her to drift beam on to the wind. He pushed the handle again and the boat continued smoothly down. The boat was a few feet short of the water when the crew remembered him and three men suddenly ran into view. He dropped to one knee and emptied the Uzi at them. He saw one man sprawl back but he was sure he had missed the other two.

More shots were fired, this time from the port side and he realised that he was about to be caught in a pincer movement. He dropped the machine gun and dived over the side, his outstretched hands looking for the crew safety ropes which always hung from the davits of a lifeboat.

10

As he flew through the air Hunter was aware that he would smash himself on the whaler below. As the thought took hold his hands found the rope and his body jerked upright, his feet thudding heavily into the side of the boat. Another second and it would have been too late.

He dropped heavily into the whaler, scrambled forward and cast off the bow rope. The wind was pushing the ship away and a gap quickly opened up. Hunter crawled back into the stern, found the engine hatch cover and lifted it. He felt around for the stop lever and checked it was hanging open. Next he opened the diesel stop-cock at the bottom of the engine cover and pressed the self starter. As the engine burst into life, shots were fired from the ship and suddenly the air was alive with bullets hitting the boat and passing close to him. Ducking down, he drew the revolver, was about to fire when he realised that he would be wasting bullets.

Splinters of wood erupted off the edge of the boat and as he pushed the rudder over, turning the whaler's stern to the ship, the firing stopped. He was rapidly moving out of range and sight. Looking back he saw smoke billowing over the deck but no sign of any flames. Pushing the rudder hard over, he turned the boat to circle back towards the stern of the ship. He was a few metres away before he could read the name on the hull, *S.S. Salamander, Haifa*.

Thoughtfully he turned away once more and this time headed towards the distant land, a few lights still visible in spite of the fact that he was down at sea level. Keeping the North Star at about sixty degrees on his right and Arcturus almost dead ahead, he hoped he was heading for Italy.

During the night he munched hard-tack biscuits and drank copious amounts of water. His head jerked upright for what seemed the thousandth time and he decided to do something about it. He rigged a rope from one side of the boat around the tiller and to the other side. The whaler would now head in a reasonably straight line. Sitting on the duck-boards, he put his head back on the seat and fell into a fitful doze.

After about three hours the engine coughed and he sat up with a jerk. Finding a jerry can, he filled up the fuel tank with the spare diesel, careful not to spill a drop. He checked the rev counter making sure that the needle was firmly in the zone for the furthest range and hence the most economical use of the fuel. Looking ahead, he saw that the lights were becoming more numerous and brighter, proof that he was still heading in the right direction and settled down to sleep again.

About an hour later he sniffed the air. Faintly he detected the unmistakable scent of land. You needed to be a sailor to appreciate how, after the cleanliness of the air at sea, the smell of land was so, Hunter thought for a second, so real. It was the only description he could find. He stretched his aching body and stood up. He noticed that the North Star was no longer visible and even as he watched the sky, he saw Arcturus fading away and the bows of the whaler hardening in the strengthening dawn. Land was clearly discernible in the distance but, not knowing the height of the coastline, he had no idea how far away he was.

Hunter peered intently ahead. He could see very little detail but from time to time he thought he could make out a building or two. At that moment the engine gave a cough, spluttered and caught again. He was running low on fuel.

He began a thorough search of the boat. A further cough spurred Hunter on to lift open more seat covers and to rummage in the bow lockers. He threw away a kedge anchor to lighten the load unconvinced it would help much.

When the whaler was built as a man-overboard rescue boat

a great deal of thought had gone into its design. Lined with airtight compartments around the inside of the hull, the boat was incredibly buoyant. It had many stowages for such items as life jackets, bailers, spare rope and tackles, and most importantly, the rowlocks for use with the long, heavy oars it carried. The whaler was designed to be pulled by eight oarsmen, four each side.

Hunter sat in the middle of the boat, placed a rowlock to port and another to starboard and fitted two oars. He rested on them, listening to the engine splutter and cough. After a few seconds it cut out altogether and he took up the oars. When he had joined the Royal Navy, Hunter had spent two terms of the first year at Dartmouth Naval College before going to sea as a cadet. As part of their training the officers spent their third term living and working as ordinary seamen onboard frigates of the Dartmouth Training Squadron. When at sea, during the dog watches, the ships held races between them. At the signal, the ships reduced speed, launched their whalers and were pulled – the naval term for rowing – around the ship and hoisted inboard. The first whaler clear of the water won. Hunter was one of the oarsmen and his team never lost.

He leaned forward, put his head down, dipped the oars and pulled back in a long, steady movement. The boat moved ponderously through the water and Hunter settled down to the rhythm. In, pull, out. In, pull, out.

He watched the sun rise, blindingly, almost dead astern of the boat. He kept pulling. The whaler is a heavy boat and not designed to be rowed by one person. He tried not to think about it. Now that he had momentum he needed to keep it going, ignoring the ache in his arms and legs and the gut-searing pain across his stomach. He kept pulling. Sweat dripped from his face, stinging his eyes. He didn't dare pause to wipe it away as he doubted he would have the strength to get the boat moving again. His world contracted to the effort, he ignored the all encompassing pain and blocked out everything except the need to keep going. Noise penetrated his subconscious. Not the squeak of the rowlocks, or the rush of water under the hull or the wind that was beginning to whistle across the boat, causing white caps to appear in one of those quick, sharp blows the Mediterranean was renowned for. The noise was laughter and joyous squeals and the thunder of surf.

He stopped and looked over his shoulder to see a sandy beach thirty metres away. Wiping the sweat off his face using the sleeve of his overalls, his head drooped in exhaustion. He looked at the string of white hotels along the front and the mass of bathers leaping in and out of the waves as the wind turned the flat calm sea into a seething cauldron of fun. Hunter felt the boat beginning to surge towards the land and quickly back-pulled. The last thing he needed was to go crashing out of control through innocent holiday makers in a heavy boat causing accidents and distress. It took a few seconds but he turned the boat around and pulled away, energy coursing through him, the adrenaline of success buoying him up. The signs he saw along the beaches and the predominant words he heard shouted were Italian.

He paralleled the beach for nearly a mile and as he did so he dropped the gun and holster over the side. He had no intention of being arrested for carrying an illegal firearm. The flags and masts he saw in the distance indicated the presence of a marina and he decided it would be the safest place to land. Inconspicuous amongst all the other boats. Arriving at the entrance, he paused to reconnoitre the fingers of pontoons, saw an empty space near the fuelling jetty and manoeuvred the whaler alongside. Nobody approached him as he tied the boat up and clambered ashore. Wearily, he began to walk away. It was an effort to put one foot in front of the other at first, his muscles cramped and aching, but quickly his natural vitality and strength reasserted themselves. As he passed some of the luxury boats he greeted the people he saw sitting in the morning sunshine, enjoying their breakfast. The wind was picking up and he watched as a few of the boat owners began to move back inside to the safe, warm cocoons of their saloons. The sun was suddenly blotted out and the rain began in a deluge that soaked Hunter to the skin almost immediately.

He walked nonchalantly, as though he didn't have a care in the world. Penniless and without a passport or credit card, no proper clothes and looking like something the cat had dragged in, nonetheless he was smiling.

At the marina office he paused to look at the noticeboards which told him a great deal. He was at the marina at Polignano a Mare on the Adriatic coast of Italy. The largest towns were Brindisi, seventy kilometres south or Bari, thirty kilometres north.

However, before he did anything else he needed money. He walked into the nearest bank. In passable Italian he asked to speak to the manager. In perfect English the teller asked the nature of his business.

'I've had my clothes and papers stolen,' Hunter replied, smiling at the pretty girl. 'I need to contact my bank and make certain arrangements.'

'I can help,' she smiled. 'There's no need to speak to the manager. Robbery is not uncommon. Although,' she added hastily, not wanting to put off a tourist, 'it also is not that often an occurrence. Which bank is it?'

'Please contact Griffiths and Co in London. Tell the girl who answers the telephone that it is personal for David Griffiths and say the word saffron.'

'Saffron?' she repeated.

'Yes. You'll get straight through. Tell him Nick Hunter needs to speak to him.'

The teller dialled, used the word and was put through immediately. She looked at Hunter thoughtfully and said into the mouthpiece, 'Tall, black hair. I suppose you could say that he is good looking. Right. Thank you.' She hung up, blushing as Hunter grinned at her. 'He said that he will phone right back.'

Within two minutes the door marked *Manager* was flung open and a small, rotund gentleman rushed into the room. He paused for a second at the sight of Hunter but rushed over to him, his hand outstretched. 'My dear sir. Please come in.' He practically pulled Hunter through the door and as he did so said, 'Florianna, two coffees.' He was speaking to his secretary who scrambled to her feet and rushed to obey.

'Sir David is on the telephone.' He indicated the receiver lying on his desk.

Hunter picked it up. 'David? It's Nick.'

'My God, Nick, it's good to hear your voice. Do you know we

have the entire organisation looking for you?' The news startled Hunter. 'Both Macnair and ourselves have offered a million pounds for knowledge of your whereabouts. What happened?'

Hunter was even more surprised but managed to quip, 'I didn't think I was worth two million Turkish lira, never mind pounds. Look, a lot has happened. I need money, passport, the lot.'

'I told the manager to give you as much as you needed and that we would wire transfer the money to him along with a ten percent handling charge. I presume he's co-operating.'

'Yes, he's very helpful.' Hunter smiled at the little man who was standing anxiously near the door, pretending not to listen. Curiosity was eating him alive. To get a telephone call from a man as important as Sir David Griffiths was unprecedented at his small bank. Especially when it concerned somebody who looked like a pirate, and a poor one at that. 'I'll draw thirty million lira. That's about ten grand. Okay?'

'No problem. I have an idea. Pass the manager back to me.'

Hunter offered the little man the telephone and he eagerly took it. 'Yes, Sir David. No, Sir David. Certainly, Sir David.' Hunter tried not to grin. It was difficult to think of his cousin, only a year older than him and a life long friend, as Sir David. 'Yes, Sir David. A Platinum American Express. I shall see to it straight away.' He handed the telephone back to Hunter. At that moment that door opened and the secretary appeared carrying a tray of freshly made coffee and biscuits. The aroma made Hunter's mouth water.

'Nick, I've told our friend there to give you an American Express card and a PIN number. He can do that straight away. The quickest way back is to use the private jet and I'll despatch it to Bari where there's a small airport. It'll be there this afternoon. You can be back in Scotland by to-night.'

'What's the hurry?' Hunter's thoughts about the attractive teller and the possibilities for the evening faded. David did not issue orders like that. It had to be Macnair.

'The proverbial is hitting the fan all across the Middle East and you're needed. Macnair wants you, soonest. I'll make sure copies of today's newspapers are onboard so you can catch up with what's been happening. I'll tell your parents you're safe and sound, as well as the General, of course.'

'Thanks, David. I need to go shopping as I've no clothes, nix. I'll get to the airport for fourteen hundred.'

'Okay. The plane won't be much later than that. It's in Gatwick and ready to go to Switzerland with some of my staff, departing in half an hour for Bern. They can take a scheduled flight to Zurich instead.'

'Poor souls,' Hunter said with a grin.

Hunter caught the smile in his cousin's voice, 'Into every life a little rain must fall. Actually, as you well know, it's better to use our own plane than scheduled services most of the time. This time you're the priority. Hell, I might even make them fly tourist and not first class.'

'Just to show them how the other half lives?'

'Exactly that. Okay, Nick, that's it for now. I'll speak to you later.'

The receiver reverted to the dialling tone and Hunter hung up. 'Thank you for all your help Mister . . .'

'Paulo Parvatti. Please call me Paulo.'

'Thank you, Paulo. May I?' Hunter indicated the coffee. 'My name is Hunter. Nick Hunter. Call me Nick.'

The coffee was superb and the biscuits delicious. The secretary reappeared with a paper for Hunter to sign and the silver coloured platinum card of American Express. Hunter signed, pocketed three million lira and also put his signature on the back of the card. A few minutes later he was back on the streets after waving a reluctant farewell to the teller who was serving another customer.

It had stopped raining and the pavement was already drying as the sun came out. Hunter found a large store and bought shaving gear, a toothbrush and toothpaste and shampoo. Next he found a clothes shop and quickly selected a shirt, trousers, jacket, and underclothes. Within half an hour of leaving the bank he was back at the marina, making use of the extensive facilities for visiting sailors and their guests. By the time he left he looked and felt like a new man. At a small jewellers on the high street he used his American Express to buy a stainless steel Rolex Oyster Perpetual. The time was 10:58 hours precisely.

The railway station was small and filthy but had a friendly cafe that sold excellent coffee and fresh bread. The train, as usual, was late, grubby and littered with empty drink and food containers. Hunter sat alone in a first class compartment, prepared to enjoy the scenery. He fell asleep before the town was out of sight and woke up to the announcement that the train was now entering Bari.

He wandered along the platform, looking for signs of how to get to the airport. A brief enquiry at the ticket desk told him that his best bet was a taxi and he continued outside to find one. Seeing the signs for the harbour and ferry port he decided to take a detour. The taxi dropped him at the terminal where ships departed for Dubrovnik, Bar, Kérkira and Igoumenitsa. He walked past the ferry port and down to the docks. There were a number of tramp steamers and bulk carriers in port but not the one he was looking for. He walked along the harbour wall and stood at the entrance, gazing out to sea. Scanning the horizon, he did not expect to see anything, which was why he almost missed it. A dot in the distance gradually changed into two ships. He looked at his watch which showed 12:45 hours. He had plenty of time so he settled himself on a bench that had been thoughtfully provided for those who strolled so far along the harbour wall and waited. Half an hour later he was sure it was the ship he had escaped from under tow by a rescue tug. It was obviously making for Bari.

Hunter returned to the quay, stopped the first taxi he saw and headed for the airport, deep in thought. He needed to speak to Macnair urgently. When he got there he saw that the Lear jet had already arrived. Hunter passed through customs and by the exit to the runway he found the pilot. He was told that the jet was refuelled and ready to go. As a member of the European Union there was no need to show or even to possess a passport; it was only necessary to have one when leaving or returning to the United Kingdom.

The Lear jet was luxurious and although he had flown in it on a number of occasions Hunter was still impressed. He settled into the deep leather seats and closed his eyes, fighting waves of fatigue. As the plane lifted into the air he forced himself to sit up and reached for the first of a bundle of newspapers on the seat next to him. What he read chilled him to the bone. He scanned paper after paper, each telling the same story. Once they were airborne the pilot announced that he could walk around and use the phone if he wished. He immediately lifted the satellite telephone from the armrest and dialled.

'Macnair.'

'Sir, it's Hunter.'

'Nick, my boy, it's good to hear your voice. Your cousin told me what was happening. Where are you?'

'In the Lear. We've just reached cruising altitude. I would have phoned earlier but I didn't want to trust a land line.'

'Quite right. What happened? We've been trying our damnedest to find you but got nowhere. Sir David told me that he'd had upwards of two hundred agents searching, offering the reward.'

Hunter baldly filled in the facts and finished by adding, 'The ship is now under tow, approaching Bari – about three or four hours out, I would think. Her name is the *S.S. Salamander* and she's registered in Haifa. The masthead flag which I suspect is the shipping company's logo is yellow with an entwined S and D in black. I think the ship needs an official visit.'

'Maybe,' was Macnair's enigmatic reply. 'The ship belongs to Dayan.'

'Just as we thought. Why is he fomenting trouble for Israel?'

'We aren't positive,' he paused and then went on. 'But we think we may know. If we're right then the man is not only mad but he's one of the most dangerous men alive. We're just compiling a dossier on him, helped by Golightly and some of his people. So far what we've discovered is frightening beyond belief. Wait a moment, Isobel has something.' There was a pause and then Macnair continued. 'Dayan owns a dry-dock at Molfetta, twenty kilometres up the coast from Bari. That's probably where the ship's headed. We've received copies of signals sent out by the master of the *Salamander* claiming that an engine room fire killed two of the crew and asking for assistance. A tug was dispatched from Brindisi in the early hours and took the ship under tow. That's strange. To save time or so it's claimed, Italian Customs and Excise flew out by helicopter, cleared the ship for docking and left again.'

'Presumably it resulted in a cursory visit, a few bribes and they are clear to conduct repairs without further official hindrance. It still doesn't explain what they were doing on that mountain and why they took me alive instead of just killing me.'

'We think they wanted information. It's our belief that Dayan is working to a deadline and needs to know what we know or suspect about him.'

'We'd never heard of him until a few days ago,' Hunter protested.

'True, but he doesn't know that. After due reflection I think we should pay that ship a visit.'

Hunter replied immediately. 'I agree, sir. I didn't get much of an opportunity to see a lot as I was more concerned with escaping. I had the impression that it carried a lot of men. How else could they afford the manpower to have three of them carrying out intermittent deck patrols as well as a lifebuoy sentry? Are they there to guard something or were they just the men escaping from the Alps? Where was the ship bound and what is its cargo?'

'According to the Italian Coastguard it was heading for the Suez Canal and carried a cargo of grain.'

'That's a convenient way to hide a lot of contraband,' said Hunter. 'From people to arms or drugs.'

'Drugs aren't likely,' Macnair replied, 'but arms and people are. I think it's time to put some pressure on Dayan.'

'I may be able to help there, sir. There's a contingent of SBS at Naples,' Hunter was referring to the Special Boats Service, normally stationed at Poole in Dorset. 'A man called Lieutenant Douglas Napier is in command of a unit on an exercise. Get NATO to put him and a team onboard the *Salamander* and take the ship apart. Then let's see what happens.'

'Is that an order, Nick?' the General asked, dryly.

'No, sir. Merely a suggestion.'

'How do you know about the SBS being there?'

'I'm trying to recruit Napier, sir. I know him well having worked with him on a few jobs in the past. I think he'll be an excellent addition to the team and I know he's thinking about it. He said he'd give his decision once he returned from Naples.'

'I'll get onto it right away. If nothing else it will give us an opportunity to find out how much clout Dayan has.'

'Sir, with all due respect, I can probably find that out more easily than you. Let me ask the family.'

Macnair thought about it for a second. Hunter was right. "The family" had more contacts than TIFAT would ever have. Still, even they had not been able to find out where Nick was in spite of all their resources and wealth. 'All right, we'll both go at it. What?' Macnair's voice faded for a second. 'Sorry, my boy, I need to go. Something has just come in. Thanks, Jim. Nick, it's another explosion, this time in Mecca. I'll see you later.' The connection was broken and Hunter replaced the handset.

He undid his seat-belt, stood up, stretched and went aft to the well equipped galley. He helped himself to a cup of coffee and returned to his seat. His next call was to his cousin. Yet again, he needed the family's help.

In the meantime Macnair put a call into Langley. He wanted to talk to the Director of the Central Intelligence Agency.

11

Dayan was beside himself with rage. At only five feet six inches
tall he wore specially constructed shoes to add two inches to his
height. In his late fifties he was tanned, fit and had a shock of grey
hair that was carefully groomed at all times. Now he paced up and
down his office in Bethlehem unable to think coherently, flexing
his hands, wanting to kill somebody . . . anybody. He knew he
had to get the red mist away from his brain before he could begin
functioning again properly. Even his eyesight was affected as he
saw everything sharply defined but misshapen, the scenes like the
paintings of cubism. A cat walked past him and Dayan kicked
out. The cat saw the foot coming and darted, snarling, behind
the desk. There the cat turned and raised a claw, spitting anger
and hatred. Dayan turned away, the red mists clearing, his eyes
beginning to focus.

'One man! One man! He does all this damage? He rescues
the hostages, kills my men and now escapes after practically
destroying my ship!'

The two other men in the room with him knew to keep quiet.
In the mood he was in Dayan was capable of anything.

'Right! I'll teach them to mess with me. We will step up the
pressure. I want the following done.' As he spoke the cat slinked
out from under the desk, aware that his master's killing rage
had passed.

David Golightly, Deputy Prime Minister of Israel, was frightened.
It was not a feeling that he was used to, as personal safety had

never been a consideration with him. Frightened? No, terrified was a better word. Terrified for the future of his nation should the madman Dayan have his way. It beggared belief that anyone, particularly a Jew, could even contemplate what he was trying to do. Trying? Golightly shook his head helplessly, succeeding was a better description. He had managed to get some information to Macnair but would it be enough to persuade him to act? Golightly shook his head again, this time in frustration as he listened to the howling, harsh, acrimonious voices of the members of the Knesset. The voices of reason and moderation were being drowned by the bigoted, right-wing fundamentalists on the other side of the house. He looked around the debating hall of white hewn stone, his gaze resting on the menorah opposite the main entrance. The sculpture was by Benno Elkan and featured twenty nine reliefs with scenes from Jewish history. Golightly clenched his fists tightly as his eyes scanned the scenes. From left to right he looked at the prophet Isaiah surrounded by wild animals proclaiming the word of God; Rabbi Yohanan ben Zakkai leaving the burning city of Jerusalem to found a new religious centre in Yavne; The Golden Age of Jews in Spain; The Jews in Babylonian exile; Ezra reading the Torah to his people: Job with his friends; David's fight against the Philistines – David Golightly's mind skipped to the events that cemented the Jews in Israel – Abraham's sacrifice; Moses blessing Israel; The tablets of the law; The uprising in the Warsaw ghetto; Rabbi Hanina teaching the Torah in public despite the ban imposed by the Romans; Jacob struggling with the angel. Golightly read the words of the prophet Zechariah : "Not by might, nor by power, but by my spirit, saith the Lord of hosts".

The menorah had been donated by the British, as what? An apology? An act of contrition? If ever Israel needed the Lord, thought Golightly, it was now. A slip of paper was handed to him. He glanced at it and paled, his hand shaking. Quickly he walked out of the chamber, glad to get away from the noise and the accusations and counter-accusations.

He walked into his office, closed the door, sat at his desk and lifted the telephone.

'Golightly,' was all he said.

'You got the message?' There was no greeting.

'Yes. Are you certain?'

'We received the information from our sources in the Pentagon less than ten minutes ago. I checked to see that it was true. War has been declared against Israel by Iran, Iraq, Syria, Egypt and Jordan. The avowed intention is to invade and throw us into the sea. No Jew to be left alive in Jerusalem and those who surrender outside Jerusalem are to be shipped out or placed in concentration camps. It is to be a Holy Jihad conducted to the end, with the intention of making the whole of the Middle East free of all Jews.'

The receiver shook in his ear as Golightly asked in a voice strained beyond recognition, 'What,' it came out a croak and he cleared his throat to start again. 'What are the Americans proposing?'

'Right now Congress is in emergency session. The Senate will be meeting in about an hour. Frankly, according to my sources, it could go either way. There is too much evidence pointing at us as the perpetrators of many of the crimes that have been committed over the last few days. Furthermore, in spite of our influence with the media, more and more Americans are beginning to believe that we deserve all we get. That we are the cause of much of the suffering, that our Rabbis and extremists are as bad as the Imams and theirs. That we deserve each other.' There was a heavy sigh and the speaker added, 'I'm sorry, David. But I do not know what we can do. Fully mobilised we will never stand up to the whole of the Muslim and Arab nations. It's impossible.'

'Then Dayan will have his way. His vow has been to solve the problem once and for all.'

'I know. And you know that if I am ordered to fire, I will.' His brother, General Obadiah Golightly was the third highest ranking officer in the Israeli army. He was also in command of the small but deadly nuclear arsenal that the Israelis had stock-piled in open secret over the previous fifteen years. After all, the perceived wisdom was that nuclear weapons were not a deterrent if the other side neither knew about them nor believed that you would use them. His brother's assertion that he would use them was only to be expected. It was why he had the job.

'How long have we got?'

'Four days before they amass on our border.'

'How many?'

'Men? Ten million. Tanks? Three hundred thousand. Aircraft? Five thousand fighters and four thousand bombers. Need I go on? The nightmare we feared for the last fifty years is about to come true.' His brother's voice sounded odd as though he was being triumphant, that the word nightmare should have been replaced with dream, and the word feared, with hoped for, but that made no sense.

The Deputy PM shook his head and ignored his thoughts. 'It has been caused by our own people. We have allowed the right wing to become too strong. The Rabbis have preached as much hatred as the Muslim clerics. Even if we use the bombs and stop the attack we lose. No civilised country will ever speak to us again. We will lose no matter what happens. Can't the fools see that?' There was no reply. 'I must return to the chamber. They have to be told.' He replaced the receiver and bowed his head. He prayed for help and guidance. He begged God not to abandon them now. He begged Him to stop it before it was too late. Anger swept through him as he finished and he lifted his head to look upwards. God couldn't help. What was made by man could be destroyed by man. And he, David Golightly, would destroy the man who had brought them to this.

The door opened without knocking and three men stood there, armed, in flagrant abuse of the rules that said no weapons were to be carried inside the Knesset building. 'You will come with us.' Golightly recognised the epaulette pips of a captain.

'Get out,' the Deputy PM shook with anger. 'Get out before I have you arrested.' He reached for the telephone but the soldier fired a shot from his silenced revolver, missing Golightly's hand by millimetres, destroying the instrument.

'Now get up and come with us. You are a traitor to Israel and you will no longer spout your lying filth for all to hear.'

'What? What are you talking about?' Golightly was quickly

regaining his composure, his mind working overtime. He had been in many tight spots in his life and this was one that he had every intention of walking away from.

'You heard. Your party will sell us out to the Palestinians. Only the Likud could have saved us, not you socialist swine. The election was fixed from the start. You are coming with us,' said the young captain. 'If you resist we will shoot you. If you do not come willingly I will shoot you in each elbow and then you will come.'

'Why not kill me here?' Golightly asked bitterly.

'Someone wishes to speak to you. That is all I know. Now, up!' He jerked the revolver in his hand. His two silent companions looked ill at ease, their weapons, Uzi machine guns, still slung over their shoulders. Golightly wondered how on earth they had brought the guns into the building. Security was watertight, which could only mean that they must have had help. A lot of help from very senior men.

Golightly was a slight, balding man with a fiery temper and a quick wit. He had been with Brigadier Dan Shomrom who had led the Israelis on the successful raid on Entebbe Airport, Uganda on the 3 July, 1976. He had been a young lieutenant at the time and had had the satisfaction of shooting both Wilfried Boese and Gabriele Tiedemann, the first two German terrorists to die. One group of special forces paratroopers rescued the hostages, another blew up six Ugandan Air Force MiG-15, MiG-17 and MiG-21 aircraft and a third group secured the perimeter against a Ugandan Army counter-attack. Throughout the operation only three paratroopers were wounded until the time came to withdraw. Golightly was standing next to Lt. Col. Jonathan Netanyahu when the thirty year old, who was in command of the hostage rescue group, was fatally wounded. Golightly shot and killed the soldier responsible. The Israelis had spent 44 minutes on the ground and took away everybody, including the bodies of the three hostages killed. Since then Golightly had been involved in many such operations, prior to entering politics.

He had no intention of going quietly.He stood slowly, pushing back his chair, his hands placed flat on his desk. He hunched down, a beaten, defeated, middle aged man. His demeanour lulled the three soldiers into a false sense of security.

'Good,' said the Captain. 'Now walk slowly and carefully through the door and my men will walk either side of you and I will walk behind.' He holstered his gun and stepped aside as Golightly walked towards the door and paused.

One of the soldiers stood next to him, the Uzi still slung over his shoulder. Golightly kept his head bowed, his shoulders slumped, but a glance was enough for him to see that the gun's safety was off. He sighed, put his hand to his head and looked back as if it was his last look at his office.

The soldier nearest to him glanced away while the other two were looking ahead, trying to identify possible problems before they stepped into the corridor. Golightly hit the soldier in the throat with a devastating blow, his anger and fear giving him strength. The soldier's larynx and throat were crushed and he started to collapse. Golightly swung the Uzi under the soldier's arm and, holding it upside down, pulled the trigger. The gun sprayed across the room, simultaneously stitching a pattern of red buttons across the chests of the other two men. Both died instantly. The gun was dragged out of Golightly's hands as the soldier collapsed to his knees, looked up at Golightly and keeled over, dead. The Deputy PM was panting as though he had just run a marathon, the adrenaline rush which had carried him through the action was ebbing fast, leaving him shaking.

Armed guards came running from outside and the debating chamber emptied of its delegates as they poured out to see what was happening. Golightly knew that he had only one chance. If accusations of murder were thrown at him before he could act, he would be arrested and powerless to stop whatever madness was sweeping through his country.

He turned to the first two soldiers who arrived and pointed a finger at them. 'You two,' he barked, 'stand guard. You,' he pointed at a major who suddenly appeared holding a revolver in his hand, 'secure this area immediately. Nobody is to leave the building without my express instructions. Don't stand there gaping, man, get on with it.'

'What's going on?' A member of the Cabinet shouldered his way through the crowd of government representatives. His name was Saul Rabin, a distant relative of the former Prime Minister, Yitzhak Rabin. Unlike the other members of his family, Saul Rabin was an orthodox Jew who hated everyone and everything that was not Jewish. He was, Golightly knew, deeply involved with the troubles Israel was currently facing. He needed to stop the man before it was too late.

'Guard, arrest this man,' Golightly pointed at Rabin.

'What? How dare you! You cannot arrest me!' Saul Rabin seemed to swell with righteous indignation. A big man with a bushy beard and huge belly, he was a rabble-rouser and trouble maker in the Knesset. Golightly needed him out of the way for the next few hours at least. A pattern was emerging and Golightly was beginning to see a glimmer of light at the end of the tunnel. A tunnel that led to oblivion unless he could prevent it. He needed help. He needed Macnair.

The General listened attentively to Hunter's report. The only other occupant in the office was Jim Carter, who had asked searching and pertinent questions throughout the debriefing.

After landing at Edinburgh Airport Hunter had been met and taken through Immigration and Customs without any problems. A TIFAT car was waiting outside and from there it had been only a twenty minute drive across the Forth Road Bridge to Rosyth. It was early evening and the three men sat with a malt whisky at their elbows. Macnair and Carter had added a dash of water "to bring out the flavour", as any connoisseur would have recommended while Hunter had added a dash of soda as usual.

'I've had a message from David Golightly,' Macnair said. 'He has e-mailed a load of information. It proves that Samuel Dayan is orchestrating the trouble and, for some reason, wants Israel to go to war. Israel's only and I repeat, *only* response, if they are not to be over-run, is to use nuclear weapons.'

'Isn't the proof enough to stop him?' Carter asked.

Macnair shrugged. 'Maybe. But the real problem is time. He has to be stopped now.'

'Nuclear weapons won't solve anything,' said Hunter. 'Israel will be a pariah country as far as the West is concerned and the Arabs won't stop until the Israelis are wiped out. They cannot win.'

'Unless Dayan knows something that we don't. Or plans something we have no inkling of as yet,' Carter said, pensively.

'What do you mean?' Macnair asked.

'Let's assume that Dayan is, as far as his religion and fundamentalism are concerned, a madman. An obsessed maniac, if you will. He is also a very astute operator around the world. He's amassed a fortune in construction, shipping, electronics and the media. He has financed the – what's it called? – The Greater Israel Party, to the tune of ten million pounds or the equivalent. He has control of fifteen percent of the Knesset and is forcing matters his way. He must have something hidden up his sleeve. A Greater Israel cannot exist if the whole nation is wiped out. America can sabre rattle as much as it likes but the reality is they won't come to Israel's aid this time. That is even if they bother to sabre rattle, which I am beginning to doubt. The American press is, for the first time ever, blaming Israel for its problems. So what does Dayan know that the rest of us don't?'

The question was greeted by blank looks from the other two. At that moment there was a knock on the door and Isobel entered. At the sight of Hunter her face lit up with a smile, 'Nick! It's wonderful to see you.' She leant down and kissed his cheek. Suddenly noticing the looks on the faces of her two bosses, she stepped back, blushing. 'I'm so glad you're all right.'

Hunter smiled warmly at her. 'Thank you, Isobel. It's great to see you, too.' For the first time he looked at her, not as a colleague, but as an attractive woman. But then mentally shook his head. It wouldn't do, not with a colleague. Office or even service romances rarely, if ever, worked out.

'Have you got anything for me?' Macnair asked, quick to catch the interplay between the two of them.

'Oh, yes. Only it's not good, I'm afraid. Mobilisation by troops is now underway across the whole of the region and they are heading in one direction. Iran has been given permission by Iraq to cross its borders and to advance west. Oman, the United States Emirates and Saudi have also given permission for Iran to land troops by ship and to cross their territory. It appears that they intend to do as we did during Desert Storm.' Isobel was referring to the Gulf war against Iraq in the early nineties.

'You mean,' said Hunter, 'that they will amass their forces and then attack in one unceasing hit.'

'Precisely,' said Isobel. 'They'll go all the way to the Mediterranean.'

'Unless Israel's nuclear weapons stop them,' said Carter.

Isobel shook her head. 'It won't. I've played the scenario five times now and no matter what I do, the computer says that the Israelis will lose.'

'Every time?' Hunter asked.

'Yes. Well,' . . . Isobel hesitated.

'Come on, out with it,' said Macnair impatiently. 'What does "well", mean?

'Sir, there is one scenario when Israel can win, but quite frankly, it makes no sense, knowing what we know.'

Hunter suddenly grinned. 'Yes, it does.'

'What?' Isobel looked at him in surprise.

The other two men also stared at him. 'The computer game showed you that in order to win, Israel, or more particularly, Dayan, needed to have a major ally. A vast army, well equipped, who would help to carve up the whole Middle East between them. And,' he paused to sip his whisky, savouring the moment, 'we have one. Not only is it vast and well equipped but it is being invited into the territory by its so-called allies, who in reality hate them as much as they hate the Jews.'

'My God,' said Carter in awe. 'The Iranians.'

'Exactly,' said Hunter.

'Precisely,' said Isobel, robbed of her glory and looking hurt.

'Don't be upset, Isobel,' said Hunter. 'You put me onto it and when you think it through, it's the only explanation.'

'We don't know it's Iran,' said Macnair thoughtfully.

120

'True, sir, but I'm betting on it,' said Hunter, draining his glass. He stood up, walked over to the corner of the room and absent-mindedly refreshed his glass. He offered a drink to Isobel, who declined, and poured more whisky for the other two. 'It doesn't make sense for anybody else. The Saudis and Jordanians don't have the inclination. The Syrians aren't strong enough and the Iraqis would never go for it. But Iran? They have all their enemies in one place, being nuked from one side and annihilated from the other. It's priceless. They can take over the whole of the Middle East between them and by the time anybody recognises what's happening, it'll all be over. Greater Israel will become a reality with access to oil and land.'

'It will be contaminated by nuclear fallout,' said Carter. 'If the fallout gets into the substructure of the soil the oil will be useless for perhaps hundreds of years.'

'I'm not so sure,' said Hunter. 'There are two things as far as that goes. First of all,' he stood up and walked over to the map of the area that covered one wall, 'the troops and tanks will be amassed all along here. Not oil rich in any way. In fact, rough terrain that's no use to man or beast. All the oil wealth is stretched across this huge, sparsely populated area.' His hand swept across the map, covering Saudi Arabia, Oman, the Emirates and Kuwait. 'With their enemies' war machines wiped out Israel and Iran can take over huge areas and negotiate a peace that suits them. If . . .' Hunter paused, a thought taking hold and then blossoming, 'If the Israelis can guarantee peace across the whole of the territory. With huge tracts of land to offer, don't you think that it's possible that Jews from all over the world will want to emigrate there?' He began pacing the room, warming to his theme. 'Yes, that's it. A Greater Israel for the resettlement of Jews. Oil to finance the country and people to occupy it. My God,' he sat down heavily in his chair, 'it's so brilliant, so hairbrained, it could work. And once it's done, nobody will be able to reverse any of it. Greater Israel will exist and claim to be living inside secure borders and at the same time Iran will have what it wants most.'

'What's that?' asked Macnair.

'Iraq,' Hunter sipped his drink.

It made sense to the two senior officers and Isobel nodded. 'That's precisely what the computer comes up with,' she said.

'What are the casualty figures?' Macnair asked.

Isobel referred to the pad she was holding. 'The outcome depends on when the weapons are released,' she said. 'If Israel fires nuclear weapons as soon as they are threatened, then there will be millions of Moslems killed. The best estimate is two to three million within hours. At that point the Israelis will have lost so few soldiers the figures have no meaning. If Iran then turns on the Moslems then another few hundred thousand will die. The resulting carnage and mayhem would render command and control impossible.'

'The Israelis,' Macnair said, 'can sit behind their borders and let Iran take what it wants when it likes, while Israel can also help itself as the troops of Saudi, Jordan and Iraq do what? Run away? Disintegrate under the lack of command and organisation? Death at that level will wreak, what did you call it, Isobel? Mayhem? If all the forces were against Israel then they could attack and keep going, knowing that Israel could no longer fire nuclear weapons without damaging their own country. With Iran attacking from behind at the same time I think that they will cut and run. Don't let us forget that most of the troops are conscripts. Look what happened to the Iraqis once Desert Storm was unleashed.'

Hunter said, 'It was a turkey shoot according to the American flyers.'

'It'll be the same again,' said Carter, 'only I don't think the Iranians and Israelis will stop.'

'What can we do about it?' Isobel asked. 'We've only a few days to act. You know, it doesn't bear thinking about. All that death. And for what? Nothing ultimately.'

'It depends on your perspective,' said Hunter. 'As far as Dayan is concerned, he will go down in Jewish history as the greatest Jew of them all. Possibly greater than King David and Moses combined. A strong, wealthy Israel has been the Jewish Utopia for thousands of years. Their history is full of it. He could deliver.'

'The rest of the world won't sit idly by and watch it happen,' argued Carter.

'Maybe, but I could counter an argument that it will. A stable Middle East controlled by pro-western Israel is something we've all wished for. No, I think that Dayan could pull it off. How do we stop him? That's easy,' Hunter drained his glass. 'Kill him.'

12

'Our mandate, after all . . .'

'I don't need reminding of my mandate, thank you, Lieutenant Commander,' said Macnair coldly. Hunter wisely kept
silent, aware that he had possibly overstepped the bounds which
govern all military life, even the unique position they currently
occupied.

Nobody spoke as each of them turned over Hunter's words
and thought of the ramifications of such an action. Legally,
they could not do it. No organisation, not even TIFAT, had
the authority to kill someone who, in the eyes of the world, was
an innocent man; even if he was mad. If they carried out such
an attack and it became known, TIFAT would be finished and
the perpetrators brought to justice. That would, inevitably, make
Macnair an accessory and include any of the team who carried
out the operation.

Killing Dayan was a sobering thought which dissipated the
effects of the whisky they had been drinking. Isobel walked
across to the sideboard and poured herself a drink, handing the
bottle to the others. Pensively she took a sip, miscalculated and
took a gulp, coughing whisky into a handkerchief she grabbed
from a pocket.

'Is there,' asked Hunter, 'anyway that we can get permission?'

'From whom?' Macnair frowned.

Hunter looked surprised. 'The Government?' he suggested.

'Nick,' Macnair shook his head, sadly, 'forget what you see

124

in films and read about in books. It isn't like that in real life. If we declared war against Israel we might selectively try and do something though I cannot imagine what. Our intelligence agencies are just that – gatherers of intelligence. TIFAT is an anti-terrorist organisation that responds to situations – we don't create them.'

'What about Golightly, sir? Couldn't he ask for our help to avoid war?' Carter suggested.

Macnair shook his head. 'Israel is about to be invaded by ten million armed men who will push them back into the sea. According to the information I've received from Golightly, Dayan is, right now, mobilising every asset he has to protect Israel. He is publicly using his own money and resources to purchase sufficient hardware to arm the general population of Israel. Each day he is being seen as the saviour of Israel not its enemy. Only a few men know the real situation. Fewer have the courage to act.'

'Isn't it,' said Hunter, 'more likely that some so-called moderates in reality agree with him? That perhaps this could be the way to lasting peace?'

'At such a price?' asked Isobel, aghast. 'Peace at that price is not peace at all.'

'If you've lived and dreamt a Greater Israel for over two thousand years, what do a few more matter?' Carter said, lifting the cut-glass tumbler to the light through the window and watching the amber fluid sparkle against the sun.

'Years or thousands of years?' Hunter asked dryly.

Carter snorted in derision. 'Either. I suppose it doesn't matter. But for now, let's say ten or twenty years. They could achieve it, you know. Suddenly Dayan's madness makes chillingly good sense. Even his timing is almost perfect. NATO bogged down in Kosovo and the former Yugoslavia, the UN caught up in Africa, East Timor and Northern Iraq.' He sighed, 'And truth to tell, most of the West couldn't care less about Israel anymore. Their stiff-necked obstinacy and refusal to carry out United Nations instructions have left them isolated across much of the world.' He paused and then added, 'Yes, I think it all makes terrible, dreadful sense.'

'So what do we do?' Isobel asked.

'What we do,' said Macnair, 'is plan. Get on to GCHQ and ask Sarah to concentrate her resources on Iran as well as Israel. More particularly, see if she can pick up any communications between the two countries. We might get a few leads that way. Next, get Leo and Gareth working on everything they can find out about Dayan. We must locate him if we are going to do anything. Don't look so surprised,' Macnair smiled, reminding Hunter of a crocodile that has just spied his lunch, 'Dayan has to be stopped and hang the consequences. I'm not having millions of dead people on my conscience because I was afraid to act. I can defend my own corner and that of my men,' he looked up at Isobel, 'and women. In the meantime I want volunteers to go on leave.'

Macnair looked directly at Hunter, who raised a quizzical eyebrow in response.

David Golightly returned to the Knesset Chamber. Voices were already raised in heated argument and the Speaker was having a great deal of trouble trying to regain control and be heard. Golightly stood up and silently perused the room. He immediately identified at least seven of the men present as staunch supporters of Rabin. Two were talking animatedly together and one of them looked directly at Golightly. He indicated the Deputy Prime Minister to his colleague and both men stared at him. Hate poured down on Golightly and sent a shiver of fear up his spine. He mastered his feelings and glared back, saying nothing. After a few seconds one of the men, Isaac Dickstein, appeared to become unhinged for he suddenly lurched towards Golightly, screaming at the top of his voice.

Within seconds the rest of the room fell silent as the man advanced on Golightly. Dickstein was practically incoherent with rage but some words could be heard clearly. Predominant amongst them was the word traitor. When the man was still a few paces away it became apparent to others in the room that Golightly was about to be physically assaulted. Other members of the government surrounded the attacker and prevented him from advancing further.

Now, as Dickstein calmed down, the words became more coherent. 'This man is a traitor to Greater Israel and the Jewish people. Let me go.' He suddenly struggled to get loose but other hands quickly grabbed him. 'This is our opportunity to secure our borders once and for all. With our enemies massed at the border we can annihilate them with our nuclear weapons. Death to non-Jews,' he yelled.

There were gasps and astonished intakes of breath. Jews had and could live in peace with any religion. Never had it been part of their thinking or teaching to demand the death of non-Jews. Never. What was happening? What was going wrong with their world in the third millennium?

Dickstein realised that he had gone too far in his anger and passion and calmed down. 'I . . . I only mean should they attack us.' He looked about him, needing support.

'It's true,' said one of his supporters. 'Only if they attack us. Already there are over a million armed men at our borders. How much longer do we just sit here and watch their numbers grow?'

'We are still,' said Golightly coldly, 'trying to negotiate our way out of this mess. We cannot stop such a vast army if they decide to walk into Israel. It would be impossible. Our chiefs-of-staff say that the massed armies of Iraq, Jordan and Saudi alone are sufficient to walk all the way to the Mediterranean. With Syria from the north, Egypt from the west and Iran following behind we won't last two days. They'll come like a steam roller and flatten us and there's nothing we can do about it. We must get some answers and stop it now, before it's too late.'

'What answers do you think there are? There are none,' a voice said from the back. 'Our only hope is to threaten them with our nuclear weapons unless they leave us alone.'

'What do we do,' Golightly asked, 'if they ignore our threats and keep coming?'

'We do what we promise, and blow them all to kingdom come,' said a member of the opposition party.

'Can't you understand that it would not stop them? Once we use nuclear weapons, it is all over for Israel. It will be the end of two thousand years of dreams. No matter what the price, they will wipe us out. Can't you see that?' This time the impassioned speech was made by Levi Walanski, a second generation Polish Jew who was the Minister of Defence.

The argument broke out once more and pandemonium reigned. Golightly fought his corner as best he could, but he sensed a shift in the opinions of the men present in the chamber. Those who wanted to stop what was happening were beginning to lose the fight. Golightly shuddered, feeling as though the wings of death had brushed his face.

It made no sense, couldn't they see that? Unless . . . unless . . . the thought took hold. Unless there was something else. Dayan was behind the troubles, he knew that. His mind leapt off at a tangent as he tried to get to grips with the thoughts which were pushing at him. There had to be something else and he needed to find out what it was. Before it was too late. Looking around the chamber he made his decision. There was nothing more he could do. Israel needed help of a different kind and not just from Macnair.

He sidled from the room, ignoring the jeering and yelling members of the Israeli Parliament as fear and death stalked the room. Golightly shivered again. His imagination was working overtime.

There were now armed guards all over the building. Why they were there and to whom they owed their loyalty he could not tell. He only knew that time was running out fast.

As he reached to dial the number his hand was shaking. 'Obadiah?' he greeted his brother. 'Is there anything happening your end?'

His brother wondered what he should say. 'Some. None of it any good.'

'Alone?'

'No. But nothing I can't handle. But for how long I don't know. I've heard that there are ructions in the Knesset.'

'There are.'

'I've also heard that you were a prisoner.'

'Where did that information come from?' David Golightly asked, wondering how his brother had heard so quickly.

'I had a message an hour ago.'

The Deputy Prime Minister looked at his watch, surprised at the time. So much had happened in so short a time. 'From whom?'

'Someone claiming to be an ally and a friend.'

'He or she leave a name?'

'No, he didn't. But he did say that he would try and find out where you were being taken and let me know.'

'That was very kind of whoever it was,' said Golightly, glancing idly around his book-lined, shabby office. He frowned when he noticed three books of his set of Encyclopaedia Britannica were not sitting flush with the others. The volumes were his pride and joy and he frequently dipped into them, using them for information for his many speeches in the Knesset. The books were twenty years old and his daughter had frequently suggested that he get rid of them and use the new computer discs that not only contained far more information but were more up to date. However he liked the feel of the leather bound books, dipping into them for pleasure as well as useful references. He was always punctilious when he replaced them on the bookshelf. The hairs on the back of his neck stood up and he suddenly found that he was sweating. 'Obadiah, I suddenly think that I have a problem,' he spoke softly.

'What? What's wrong?' Urgency and concern were apparent in his brother's voice.

'Let me just look.' Golightly placed the receiver on the desk and walked softly across to the wall. He looked over the books but could see nothing. Very gingerly he felt behind the books and immediately felt something. Sweat oozed from every pore as he touched the detonator and felt the lump of plastic explosive. He withdrew his hand cautiously and walked back to the desk. 'It's . . .' he began but it came out a croak and he cleared his throat. 'It's an IED.' An impromptu explosive device was unsophisticated but lethal for all that.

'What?' his brother was outraged. 'How could anybody get into your office to place a bomb there? It's impossible!'

'It's not impossible, dear Obi, because somebody has done it. It seems that my enemies are determined to get rid of me one way or the other. Obi, you are in command of the detachment which controls our nuclear weapons. If ordered, will you use them?'

'Of course,' his brother replied, surprised by the question. 'But I won't like it,' he added after a pause.

David Golightly smiled grimly. He was not surprised by the answer. Just as every able-bodied man, woman and child would fight, so would his brother. Only his brother's arsenal was devastating and for a moment he wondered if Obadiah would be able to live with himself for unleashing so much death. Unless he, David Golightly, did something soon, millions were going to die, including him.

'David! What do you want to do about the bomb? I can get some men there who will have it rendered safe within seconds.'

'Thank you, Obadiah, but that won't be necessary. I'll take care of it. Now, the purpose of my call is to ask if you know what's happening. How many men are currently at our borders and who is still in transit?'

General Golightly looked at his computer screen, tapped a few buttons and waited for the down-loading of information from an American satellite. 'I'll tell you in one moment. I have been waiting for an update of the present situation which is expected any second. Ah, here it is. The Saudis, Jordanians and Syrians are almost all in place. The Iraqis are moving rapidly, having already deployed their fighter and bomber aircraft. The Iranians are behind schedule, according to this Pentagon report. They are a day or even a day and a half late.'

The Deputy Prime Minister's hand tightened around the receiver. Was that it? Was that what he had been missing? The Iranians in league with Dayan? A huge pincer movement that would wipe out many of Israel's and Iran's enemies in one hit? The possibilities teemed through his brain, overwhelming him, causing him to sit down in shock, the bomb in his office all but forgotten.

It also meant that Dayan could bring it off. He could create a secure Greater Israel and be remembered for eternity in the folklore that was Judaism. But the price! It was too high. An obscenity! Millions to die for the satisfaction of one man. No!

Two men! He was forgetting the Ayatollah in Iran. He too would go down in his own history as the man who secured and enriched Iran. Megalomaniacs playing the devil's own game. 'Obi, I need to go. I will e-mail some information you know where. Should I die then you must see that it is published as soon as possible. The world must know what has happened.' He replaced the receiver without waiting to say goodbye and sat at his computer.

Quickly he composed his thoughts and began to write. Clearly and concisely he wrote down his understanding of the information at hand. He named Dayan as the man behind the world-wide atrocities that had resulted in so many deaths already and which would cause millions more. He tried to phrase his words in such a way as to cast all the blame on Samuel Dayan and his cohorts, to reduce the opprobrium that would be heaped on the Israelis once the truth came out. And that was one of the problems. The truth would come out and Jews and Israelis would be hated world-wide. In his mind's eye he saw the pogroms starting all over again, as Judaism was blamed for the deaths of millions of men; blamed for setting off nuclear weapons not for legitimate defence but to create a Greater Israel. Why was it that every century turned up its quota of madmen? Now the ability to commit mass murder and destruction had become greater, the madmen were even more lunatic. As soon as he was finished he sent the e-mail to its secret destination for his brother to collect. Then he had a further thought and sent a copy to Macnair along with a request and suggestion. Once he was finished he decided it was time to escape. To save himself.

There was one door leading into the corridor which he normally used and a second which led to his secretary's office. His secretary was ill and for a cynical moment Golightly wondered if the man was really unwell or whether he had made himself scarce under orders. Remembering the unease he had displayed when he had asked Golightly if he could go early, the Deputy Prime Minister decided that he was not being cynical but painfully, truthfully honest. How far did the rot go?

He entered his secretary's office and carefully looked out through the door. Everything appeared normal apart from the armed patrols. He was about to step into the corridor and walk to the main entrance when he realised something. One of the two-man patrols hovering nearest to his private door seemed to be taking an unusual interest in both his office and the guard standing outside it. The other patrols were behaving more normally, walking the area, guarding the whole place, not interested in any one office or door. What would the two men do if he tried to leave? Could he rely upon the others patrols to save him? By the time they reacted it was more than possible that he would be dead. Should he call the patrols, point a finger and demand they be arrested? Cause a diversion and try to escape in the ensuing confusion? How appropriate, he thought, smiling grimly.

Back in his office he searched for something to implement his idea. He found nothing. Quickly he ransacked his secretary's desk drawers and in the bottom left hand drawer he found a roll of sellotape. In his own office he stuck the sellotape carefully to a copy of one of the encyclopaedias, and gave a tentative tug. The sellotape peeled off, leaving the book on the shelf. He thought for a moment or two and then espied his letter opener lying on his desk. Wrapping the sellotape around the top of the knife he carefully worked it down the spine of the book. He gave a tentative tug on the sellotape and was gratified to see the book move slightly. Returning to the door, he stepped through it and pulled hard. The sellotape stretched, took the weight and the book began to swing from the shelf. Even though he was braced for it and he was behind the wall the blast was terrific. The door slammed shut, breaking his arm like a matchstick, making him scream with the pain. Books, dust and debris flew everywhere, his desk over-turned and as he took a hold of his senses he heard yells from outside. Holding his arm he hurried to the other door, looked out and saw the guards rushing towards his office. When he was certain nobody was looking in his direction, he stepped out into the foyer and hurried towards the main entrance.

The Members of the Knesset were pouring out of the Chamber's doorway yet again, startled, fearful, curious. Some rushed towards the destroyed office while others were rushing towards the

132

exits. Disorder ensued. Nobody looked in the direction of their Deputy Prime Minister. Except for one man who nudged his companion. With an oath the companion ran to find a telephone.

13

The three men were alone when Macnair hung up the telephone. 'That was David Golightly.' He looked at his watch. 'It's now 18:30 hours, 21:30 hours over there. He's on the run.'

'What?' Carter sat bolt upright in his chair. 'On the run? From whom?'

Macnair shrugged. 'In effect, from Dayan. He has members of the Knesset after him and they in turn have army and police units loyal to Dayan helping to track him down. Originally they appeared to want to capture him, probably for interrogation. Now it seems they only want him dead.' Macnair briefly told the others what Golightly had said.

'What do we do?' Carter asked.

Hunter replied, stretching his long legs and leaning back in his chair. 'That's not a difficult decision to make. Go in and get him.' He spoke as if he was suggesting a stroll in the park.

'That won't be easy,' said Carter.

'It's a mess.' Macnair stood and began to pace his office. 'Who can help us? David is adamant that we can trust his Prime Minister. But right now he's paralysed with indecision and unable to establish control. What's the use of giving orders if they aren't obeyed? Having the police and army pursue David suggests that he's the enemy whereas we know it's Dayan. What's worse is that David knows as well as I do that I'll never get agreement to interfere in the internal politics of Israel. Not,' he added heavily, 'in a thousand years.'

'Sir,' said Hunter, 'that's self-evident. We need to get David out and safe so that he can tell his story, while we also stop Dayan. Otherwise a catastrophe is in the making which doesn't bear thinking about.'

Macnair nodded. 'I agree. It must be a clandestine operation using our own resources. Nick,' he looked piercingly at Hunter, 'you'll be on your own. If we rescue David, then there's a chance that we can argue a good case for our actions. If we fail to rescue him or fail to kill Dayan then the arguments will never cease and you know that the politicians will hang you out to dry, just to save their own necks.'

'Really, sir?' Hunter spoke with mock surprise. 'You astound me. You mean like the way we arm our troops to patrol Northern Ireland but when something goes wrong leave them to the courts and imprisonment? I signed the petition to get Clegg and the others out of jail. If the former Secretary of State for Northern Ireland hadn't been such a coward she would have backed them and pardoned them much earlier. So I have no illusions. But we can't sit and watch the Middle East go up in a nuclear holocaust. I'll get a team of volunteers together. We need to get out there fast. One or two ideas have occurred to me.'

'Where can we go? We'll need a ton of gear,' said Jim Carter, ever the Quartermaster and instantly identifying himself as a member of the team. 'And there are few if any friendly bases we can use.'

'Which means,' said Hunter, 'that we need a ship.'

'We need to be in the eastern Mediterranean within the next forty-eight hours if we're going to make any difference to what's going on there,' said the General. 'So where will we get a ship in time?'

Hunter's grin was pure delight. 'Easy. We buy the magazine *International Boats and Ships for Sale*, and find what we want.'

'We won't have time to get to the Med,' said Carter with some exasperation.

Hunter agreed. 'No, of course not. We buy the boat in Cyprus or Turkey. We pay cash. We fly the equipment out and drop it by parachute at sea. We'll need attack teams as well as a ship's crew. So we'll need a coaster sized ship that will house us all and at the same time have a turn of speed.'

'Just like that,' said Macnair, without a hint of scepticism in his voice. He stared at Hunter, looking at the idea from every angle. It had its merits but could it work? Somebody needed to be at TIFAT headquarters to work the computer systems, to liaise with GCHQ and to co-ordinate things from this end. That would obviously have to be Isobel. He needed Carter to take care of their logistical requirements and he could do that from Rosyth probably better than anywhere. Where should he, Macnair, be? Macnair grinned. He would take the long overdue leave to which he was entitled. Carter wouldn't like staying behind but there was no choice.

'Any better ideas, sir?' Hunter asked. The query was not insolent. Hunter had a huge respect for Macnair and his planning ability.

'None.' The General looked at his watch. 'Right, we need to get moving. Nick, can you arrange a banker's draft any-where in the world? We'll use our own money.' Only four people knew where the money came from, the three men in Macnair's office and Isobel. Although what they had done was completely illegal, Macnair was not in the mood to discuss it with greedy politicians and others who would start yelling human rights and unauthorised operations. The money was used to pay the families of anyone in TIFAT killed while in the line of duty or to supplement their pension in the event of injury and forced retirement. Macnair would ensure that his men would never want for anything in their lives. The money was also used to purchase specialised equipment available to civilians but not to the military, usually on the grounds of cost.

Hunter nodded. 'Easily, sir. I'll speak to my cousin. He can arrange to have any amount sent anywhere in the world at a moment's notice. It will be as good as cash so any transaction can be completed quickly. Let me go home and get the magazine and I'll see if there's anything we can use.'

As he was speaking, Isobel had knocked and walked into the

room. 'No need,' she said. 'If it's in a magazine it'll probably be on the net. What are you after?'

Hunter told her. 'Give me five minutes and I'll see what I can find out. In the meantime General, I've had word from Sarah at Cheltenham. There has been a great deal of contact between an area just to the west of Israel and Iran. It's mainly short bursts of microwave messages that have been scrambled. They'll be decoded by midnight at the latest.'

Hunter pointed out the obvious. 'There isn't anything to the west of Israel except the Mediterranean.'

Isobel shrugged. 'I'm only telling you what Sarah told me.'

'Unless it's a ship,' said Carter.

Isobel smiled. 'You men! You think that you're the only ones who can think for themselves. It cannot be a ship because the signal is coming from an absolutely fixed location about one thousand metres off the coast of Ashqelon.'

'Where's that?' Hunter asked.

'I looked it up,' replied Isobel. 'It's ten miles north of Gaza. Sarah is sending a satellite over there now to have a look.' She glanced at her watch. 'In about fifty minutes.'

Hunter stood up and walked across to one of the walls. The world was represented by twenty charts, each held on a sliding wooden panel. He found the one covering the eastern seaboard of the Mediterranean and slid it into view. He looked keenly at the chart but saw nothing. 'Depth of water two hundred feet and shelving fast. If it's not a boat then it could be a barge or an oil-rig. They have the necessary anchor arrangement to hold a structure as steady as Isobel says.' He turned to the room and said, 'You know, it makes a lot of sense. Dayan is not the type to sacrifice himself. He needs a secure bolt hole near enough to Israel to appear when he's needed and far enough away to be safe. What if the nuclear bombs and the Iranians don't stop the rest of them? What then? What if chemical warfare is used in retaliation? What's a better defence than a thousand metres of water to a structure, a platform, which can be secured? With his money it wouldn't have been difficult to make a comfortable bolt hole that's chemical and bacteriological proof. I suspect that's what we're going to find.'

'Even if you're right, there's no proof that Dayan will be there,' said Carter.

'No, of course not,' said Hunter. 'It's just the best bet we have. Isobel, see if you can find us a boat or a coastal ship on the internet. It'll have to be in the region of Turkey, Cyprus or even Egypt. It'll need to be able to go at a reasonable speed, say at least eighteen or twenty knots.'

'What sort of price range?' she asked.

Hunter and Carter looked at Macnair who frowned and said, 'Nick, I know nothing about ships and boats. You read the magazines. What do you think?'

'A million,' came the prompt reply.

Macnair didn't blink. 'A million it is. Pounds sterling,' he added.

'I was thinking dollars myself, sir,' said Hunter, 'but you're probably nearer the mark. Isobel, this is a list of criteria which may help you to narrow the search down.' He scribbled on a sheet of paper. 'I'll go and find the lads. We'll work on a list of equipment we think we'll need. I take it we use everything that's non-issue?'

Macnair nodded. 'Probably a good idea. You'll find most of the teams are on the base. I sent out a general recall two hours ago.' The recall worked automatically through a computer programme Isobel had developed. An automatic signal went simultaneously to all mobile phones. When it did the teams knew that only serious injury or death, their own, could excuse them from returning. 'I'll be on the ship with you,' he suddenly announced.

'Sir, there's no need for that,' began Hunter.

'He's right, sir,' said Carter. 'We need you here.'

'No, you don't,' said the General. 'And in any case, I'm fed up of being a desk-bound commander. This is my show and I'll run it my way. My force, my decision. Commander, I want you to make it clear to everyone that this is on a volunteer basis only. You do not tell them I'm coming along in case they think it'll give them some sort of protection should it all go pear-shaped.

Me being there won't make an ha'pence of difference to the powers-that-be.' He paused, 'Alternatively,' he paused again, 'tell them I'll be there. As far as they're concerned it is official. I can look after myself. As far as Isobel and Jim are concerned I'll be as contactable there as I am here. For the rest, I'm on leave,' he paused. 'Commander, sort out your teams. Jim, go with Nick and see what equipment we have that isn't British or Nato military. Isobel, you and I will . . . what do you call it? We'll surf the net looking for a suitable vessel. Nick, I'll phone your cousin.'

'Phone the bank at this number,' Hunter wrote it down on a piece of paper, 'and use the word saffron.'

'Saffron?' Macnair queried.

'We have a family code-word so that we can get through if it's an emergency. Otherwise you'll go for days without being able to contact him. He's a very busy man,' said Hunter dryly, 'and he spends a lot of time looking after the family fortune. If you use saffron you'll get him no matter where he is in the world. Usually within half an hour, even if he's busy. We never abuse it. Once a few years ago, when we had a family crisis, he cut short a meeting with the president.'

'Of Shell, ICI or some other conglomerate?' asked Macnair.

'Of the United States,' replied Hunter and left the room.

In some ways a password made sense to Macnair and the irritation he had felt at such tomfoolery quickly faded. He dialled the number and left a message along with his sat-phone number. He walked along the corridor to Isobel's office where he found her and her two assistants, Leo and Gareth, hard at work.

'I've found the web site,' said Isobel, 'and punched in our requirements. I'm just waiting for the search to conclude. Ah, here we go.' The computer screen changed and began listing boats and ships for sale all over the eastern Mediterranean. She began to add additional parameters, suggested by Hunter, honing in on one or two vessels. She wanted immediate purchase, easy access via an international airport, twin diesel engines, a lot of deck space, a large hold or a boat with plenty of storage space. By the time she was finished there were two vessels that fitted the bill, one in Cyprus, the other in Port Said, Egypt. She checked distances to Ashqelon and as it was nearly twice as far from the Cyprus boatyard, she decided to go for the Egyptian option. Two minutes later she had a full specification, internal drawings and photographs of the ship. More interestingly, she found out why it was for sale.

The Egyptian Customs Service was selling the boat after confiscating it from its owner, a drug smuggler who had been executed recently. The boat was named *Darnah*, was 140ft in length, had a 31ft beam and drew 15ft below the waterline. She – Isobel paused, why are all boats "she"? – had turbo-diesel engines with an impressive speed of thirty knots. The problem was the Egyptians wanted two and a half million dollars for her.

Macnair read the details of the ship and knew instinctively it was exactly what they needed. 'Buy it,' he ordered Isobel.

She shrugged and smiled. 'Two and a half million,' just like that, she thought. She did a mental calculation. That was one point six million pounds. She began to type information onto the screen but was only half way through when Macnair's phone sounded. It was Sir David. Briefly the General told him what his requirements were.

'Not a problem. The boat is in Port Said, you say. Wait a second.' Unknown to Macnair, Sir David was busy with his personal organiser. 'Right. Give me an hour and you'll have the boat signed, sealed and delivered. At least,' he added, 'delivered as far as the paper-work is concerned. I'll also have somebody give it the once over for you. After all, we don't want you buying a pig in a poke, do we?'

'You can do that?' Macnair asked, intrigued in spite of himself. He was used to wielding authority and, to some extent power, but he had never seen anything like the ability Sir David had to get things done.

'Of course. I have an agent in Port Said who looks after our shipping interests through the Suez Canal. We'd never get through there otherwise. Leave it to me. I'll be back to you within the hour.'

Macnair grunted his thanks and hung up. 'What is the likelihood of us flying out to Port Said tomorrow?' he asked Isobel.

'No problem, General,' answered Leo. Short and fat, he was the complete computer expert. He had already been into the internet looking for a flight. 'There's a plane to Rome leaving at eight o'clock tomorrow morning which connects to Port Said.'

'From Edinburgh?' Macnair asked.

'No sir, Heathrow,' was the reply.

'We can't have everything, I suppose. We'll use the helicopter to get us to Heathrow. What about booking tickets?' the General asked.

'I'll use our credit card and you'll be booked through,' replied Isobel. When the funds had been salted away for use by TIFAT, part of the arrangements had included a charge card with unlimited credit which was cleared automatically every month. The telephone at her elbow rang and she picked it up. After a few seconds she spoke, 'Well done, Sarah. That's exactly what Nick thought. Can you download the information straight away? You have? Pictures and all? Lovely, thanks. Any news on the deciphering of the messages yet? Okay, thanks.' As she hung up her fingers flew across the keyboard. 'We've got the pictures but the deciphering will take another hour.' A few minutes later the large wall-mounted screen came to life and a semi-submersible, oil drilling platform appeared. 'This is where the radio activity is taking place,' she announced. 'Just as Nick suspected. Sarah has already identified the rig as belonging to a company owned by Dayan. It was put there two weeks ago, ostensibly to drill for oil within Israel's territorial waters. Dayan has put out a story that information has come his way suggesting that oil is to be found there, contradicting the major oil companies' assertions that it's impossible.'

'Why impossible?' asked Macnair.

'There's a fault in the earth's structure, a real quirk of nature,' answered Gareth. Unlike his friend and colleague, Gareth was tall and skinny. His hair tied in a pony-tail that reached halfway down his back had been a source of extreme irritation to the General. When Macnair realised how brilliant Gareth was with a computer he stifled his irritation. Indeed, he rarely noticed the pony-tail nowadays. 'It's like a plug has been pulled and the oil drained from the whole area. Oil is all over the Middle East from Libya to Iraq, Syria and the rest of the Gulf but by-passes Israel and most of Egypt. The geologists reckon that the oil is there but at such depths as to be uneconomical. Dayan says that's not true and he's going to prove it. The only problem is he's making no attempt to drill yet.'

'It's a cover?' Macnair suggested.

Gareth shrugged. 'I can't say for sure, but it looks like it. He'll have to start drilling at some point or serious questions could be asked.'

'Unless more important issues are top of the agenda,' said Isobel.

'Like a war,' the General said heavily. 'I really need to speak to David Golightly. In the meantime get me General Ricardo Fellini. I want to see if I can put pressure on Dayan.'

A few moments later he was speaking to the Italian General, a senior officer at the NATO headquarters in Brussels. 'Ricardo, we need your help.'

'Malcolm! You only phone when you need my help. What is it this time?'

'Israel. I need to put a squad onto a ship in Italy, taking it apart – noisily.'

'I presume you have a good reason for wishing to do so?'

'Yes. I believe that Dayan is behind what's happening in the Middle East right now.'

'Dayan?' The one word contained shock, query, but something else as well, Macnair thought. Fear? Was there fear? No, it wasn't possible. Fellini didn't know the meaning of the word.

'We're pretty sure that's he's been orchestrating the unrest for his own ends. I want to start fighting back and fast. Time is of the essence.'

'But that makes no sense. We're working non-stop trying to solve the crisis but nothing is succeeding. You know that the Secretary General of the UN is making his way around the whole region talking to heads of governments in an attempt to stop them before it's too late.'

'It's already too late,' said Macnair. 'That's why I need to act. So can I put a team onto a ship and take it apart?'

'Which ship and where?'

'The *S.S. Salamander*, in dock at Bari in eastern . . .'

'I know where it is,' came the irritated interruption. 'But Dayan! Do you know what you're suggesting? It makes no sense. He's using everything he owns to protect Israel from invasion. I know that he has already spoken to the governments of at least five African countries and three former Soviet countries offering a fortune for help.'

'What sort of help?' Macnair asked.

'He has offered to hire their entire airforces. So far only the Ukraine has shown any interest. The remainder don't want to know. They're justifiably terrified of a back-lash by the Moslem states and of course, the reaction from the Moslems in their own countries. So what you're suggesting makes no sense.'

Macnair gripped the handset tightly, urgency in his voice. 'Ricardo, listen to me. I can't prove anything yet and even if I could I don't suppose anybody will believe me. But you're different. You've known me for nearly thirty years. You know I don't go off half-cocked and that I always make sure I'm as sure as I can be. Well this time I'm right. I know it's Dayan and I need to find more proof to let the world know the truth. That way we might be able to prevent a calamity and save hundreds of thousands, even millions of lives.'

'I'm sorry, Malcolm, but I cannot help you.'

'But . . .' The line went dead and Macnair slowly replaced the receiver.

In Brussels, General Ricardo Fellini wiped the sweat from his brow. He was certainly earning the money Dayan had placed in his off-shore bank account.

Hunter spoke to the assembled team. 'That's as much information as we have. We're going to Egypt to pick up a ship and from there to Israel. We'll be attacking an oil rig that we believe is

143

the headquarters for Dayan. If we're to stop the war before it even starts then we need Dayan dead. It's as simple as that. Full gear will be dropped at sea. We need to move fast so we're travelling light but Major Carter will arrange the air drop. This is a volunteers only job. Any questions?'

'Why volunteers only?' asked Don Masters.

'That's easy,' said Josh Clements, leaning against the wall of the gymnasium where they had assembled. 'It's because we don't have official backing for this one. Right, Nick?'

Hunter shrugged, a wry smile on his lips. 'If you don't know officially, you can't be held responsible. Let me just say that the General is coming along for the ride. He'll handle any flack if there is any. He's in charge on the scene and will take full responsibility. We don't need to know any more, should we ever be asked to explain ourselves.'

'That's answer enough,' said Clements. 'I know about Dayan. He moves in high places, the highest. It's no surprise that we can't get official sanction for this one. But,' he shrugged and smiled, 'you can count me in.'

The remainder of the team nodded.

'Everybody in?' Hunter asked. 'Good. Get your personal gear ready and take enough clothes to last four days. We're travelling by civilian airways so nothing obvious can go with us.'

'What about our hidden hardware?' Sam McReady asked.

'That's all okay,' replied Hunter. 'We know it can't be detected at the airports.'

The hardware they were referring to was part of their clothing. A belt that held a throwing knife, shoelaces that doubled as detonating cord and plastic explosives stuffed into the heels of their trainers. Each man carried a veritable arsenal of gear, all of which could be used in an emergency. Jim Carter had also perfected a gun made from a specially cast porcelain that was as strong as steel and undetectable by the machines found at airports. The bullets were made from the same material but so far he had only made a few dozen rounds. The bullets were hidden in the seam of a holdall while the gun was broken down into four parts and carried in different pockets. Hunter would

144

be carrying the holdall on this trip. Within Europe and the west there was never a problem as Macnair ensured the co-operation of the security services at any airport they used. However, other countries were not as co-operative which meant that no weapons could be carried overtly into Egypt.

'Burg will be flying us to Heathrow, leaving at zero four hundred. We'll catch a British Airways flight to Rome and then Egypt Air to Port Said. We take over the ship and get out of there.'

'Will the ship be victualled?' Peter Weir asked.

Hunter nodded. 'Fuelled and watered at least. As soon as we hit Port Said a couple of you can go to a local supermarket and get as much as we'll need. Remember that we'll need provisions for twenty for a week.'

Jim Carter had joined them and said, 'I've a better idea. I'll send detailed instructions to the shipping agent your cousin is using. The agent will be used to victualling ships so we can get what we want and depart as soon as we get there.'

'Has the ship been checked out?' Hunter asked, somewhat surprised at the speed of events.

'Yes. We've just heard. Sir David's phoned and said everything is A-okay. His agent knew all about the ship. Apparently at two million five it's cheap, so it must be some boat. The General wants you. He's having difficulty getting permission to examine the *Salamander* and he wants to talk to you about Napier.'

Hunter nodded and walked back to the General's office.

'Did Jim tell you I'm having trouble getting permission to put Napier and a team on to Dayan's ship?'

'Yes, sir. Somehow I'm not surprised.'

'Well, I am. Has Dayan so much influence and power that he can penetrate the highest command echelon of NATO? If he has, how many others has he contaminated? It's occurred to me that if I try harder there will be a danger that Dayan will get to hear of our plans. And although I want to shake him up it's no use to us if he thinks we can be stopped before we even begin. So, if I asked Napier to take a unit of men to Bari will he go? Knowing it's unofficial?'

Hunter had half expected the question and had been mulling over what he knew about Lieutenant Douglas Napier, Royal Marines, Special Boats Service. They had worked together twice, once on a clandestine operation into the Sudan and once on an exercise in Scotland. Napier had proven to be tough, ruthless and a good planner. Which was why Hunter wanted to recruit him to TIFAT.

'I would say that he's the type to plan carefully and then go at it as hard as he can. He would have an exit strategy as well as an attack plan. He'd do it whether or not it was an official operation providing he knows that we'd do everything we can to back him up. We often spoke about the way the politicians hung the lads out to dry in Northern Ireland. It made him as angry as me. So,' Hunter shrugged, 'he has as little faith in our political leaders as,' he grinned, 'you do, sir.'

Macnair kept a straight face but Hunter's smile was so infectious the General suddenly smiled back. 'So cynical and still so young. I need him to get on board that ship and take it apart. If he finds anything useful he's to get the information back to us as soon as possible. He's not to pussy-foot around. These are deadly and, using an old-fashioned term, evil men who are planning to kill millions for their own perverted idea of a safe country. I don't want Napier to be gentle.'

Hunter nodded. 'In that case we need to make sure he can get out.'

'I've considered that. I'm sending Schwarzkopf to Bari. Isobel has been busy on the internet again, this time looking for a helicopter. Schwarzkopf can pick up Napier and fly out to us. I've checked distances and fuel and he can probably make it if we can find an Agusta A.109A.'

'Why not get Burg to fly onwards from Heathrow after he drops us?' Hunter asked.

Macnair shook his head. 'I thought of that but it won't work. The refuelling and flight times are useless. It will be better for Schwarzkopf to arrive reasonably rested, check out the helicopter and take it from there. He says he knows the helicopter as he flew one three years ago in Switzerland. Isobel is working on purchasing one right now. She's found a dealer in Rome who can supply what we want. It'll cost about £156,000. If needs be, when they reach us, we can ditch the helicopter or, if it's possible, land it on the *Darnah*. I've sent for Schwarzkopf to have him look over the airworthiness certificates and log book which are being faxed to us.'

At that moment Isobel entered the room. 'I've agreed a price for the helicopter at £134,000 and Burg is waiting for the faxes now. Sarah phoned to say that they're beginning to decipher the information they collected between the rig and Iran and will be down-loading it as it comes off the computer. If we just log on,' she moved to the General's computer, 'we may find out something useful.'

14

David Golightly had reached the busy street and was hurrying through the bustling crowd when he looked back. Three, no, four men were following him. Chasing him. He bumped into a pedestrian, agony shooting up his broken arm as he mumbled an apology.

The hot, dusty street was beginning to take on an odd coloured hue around the edges of his vision. He needed help and he needed it fast. He looked back but saw nobody who posed a threat. Had he imagined the men? Stumbling, he recovered and walked faster. Sweat was beading on his brow and he could feel his body alternating hot and cold flushes. Damnation! He was reacting to his broken arm when he needed all his wits about him.

Droves of school children were heading for the Israel Museum. The sham of normality jarred his nerves. Oblivion was days away and these children were looking at the past when there was little hope for a future. The thought brought his jumbled mind back to reality. If he didn't do something quickly his future was going to be only minutes long. He ducked down a side street and turned left, then right, losing himself in the myriad of small alleys which made up the sprawling city of Jerusalem.

His arm was throbbing and his mouth and throat were parched. He wanted help badly but first he needed to find some place to hide up so that he might, just *might*, survive the next few hours. He looked about him, unsure of his bearings for a few seconds and then he smiled. Instinct and instinct alone had brought him to this place. He was in the area known as Nahalat Ahim, amongst the thousands of small apartments to be found in the area and near one that he knew only too well. A widower, for some years he had been visiting a lady friend, a discreet lady friend, who looked after a number of clients on a regular basis. He knew that he ought never to appear without phoning first. That was the arrangement. But this was an emergency.

He turned another corner and looked back. His heart began thudding as he saw two soldiers running towards him, although there was no indication that they had seen him. Mustering his strength he ran down the alley, the thought of a bolt-hole giving him strength. Looking back, he saw that the soldiers were not in sight. Another corner and he had reached the door. He pressed the entry button. No answer. He pressed again, and again.

Just as he was giving way to despair an irritated voice came tinnily out of the microphone at his elbow. 'Yes? What is it?'

'Miriam, thank God. It's David, let me in.'

'David! You know my rules. You must . . .'

'Miriam! Shut up and for God's sake open the door. Now!'

The buzzer sounded and Golightly fell through the doorway, slamming it closed behind him. He leant against the door, his heart pounding, gulping in air as though he had run a marathon. He heard feet running past, voices raised in query. The cool of the unlit corridor washed over him and the sweat on his face began to dry. He heard a door at the top of the stairs open and a tentative voice, 'David?'

He pushed himself from the door and staggered up the rough hewn steps to the third floor. Miriam was standing in the doorway of her apartment, a towel around her head and wearing a dressing-gown. At the sight of him her irritation quickly turned to consternation and she helped him into the small living room.

'David! What is it? What's happened?' Her dressing-gown fell open, revealing a beautiful sight which, for the first time, failed to inflame the Deputy Prime Minister's ardour.

Golightly sank onto a leather sofa and let his head fall back. Waves of giddiness washed over him as he tried to control an urge to vomit. In spite of the cool interior sweat broke out on his forehead and he croaked. 'Water, please.'

A glass of water was placed in his hand and he greedily gulped it down. Refreshed, he had control once again and he said, 'Help me with my jacket. My arm's broken.'

'But what happened?' Miriam repeated, helping to take off his jacket and roll up his shirt sleeve. She bit back a gasp when she saw the lump on his arm and tentatively touched it. Golightly gasped in pain and she said, 'It's your radius. It's broken. You need a hospital. It needs an x-ray and setting. Thank goodness the skin isn't broken. That's something, at any rate.'

Golightly shook his head. 'Can't. I need you to strap it up for me and give me some pain killers. I've too much to do.'

'David, don't be stupid! If you don't get this treated properly anything could happen. You could even lose your arm.'

'Never mind. I've got to stop the war. This can be seen to later.'

Fear sparkled in her eyes as she raised a hand to her throat. 'You mean it's happening? They are really going to attack? All those men? What will happen? Oh, God! Why can't you stop it?'

'Miriam! Be quiet! I'm trying to stop it but I need help. I'm being chased by men who want a war. Our own men. Soldiers! Now, please get me some painkillers. Then pull my arm and push the bone back into place. You were a nurse. You can do it.'

'That . . . that was a long time ago,' Miriam whispered. 'All right! All right! I'll do it. Just give me a second to compose myself.' She pulled the dressing-gown tightly around her and stood up. She went into the bathroom and returned with a plastic container of tablets. She fumbled with the top, dropped the container and cursed.

'Take it easy, Miriam,' said Golightly. 'I need your help but not for long. I'll be out of here soon. Now, give me the pills and go and find something to use as a bandage.' He stood up and went across the small room to the tiny kitchenette and helped himself to a bottle of still water from the fridge. He didn't bother with the glass but upended the contents of the bottle into his mouth. Next, he levered open the lid of the pills and shook four into his hand. He put all four into his mouth and washed them down with another mouthful of water.

Miriam returned with a dishtowel and used a pair of scissors to cut it into strips. Golightly closed the fingers of his injured arm around a cupboard handle and used his other hand to hold the door closed. 'I'll pull and you push the bone back,' he gasped. Sweat shone on his brow and he bit back a gasp of pain as Miriam tentatively touched his arm. 'Push it. Fast. I can't hold on much longer.' With a sudden thrust Miriam pushed the bone back into place causing Golightly to gasp and sink to his knees with pain and shock. Deftly, her training coming to the fore, Miriam wound a strip of the towel around his arm. The pain was slowly receding and Golightly was able to clamber to his feet.

'Thanks, Miriam. Nice and tight but leave the blood flowing.'

'I know,' she said huskily. 'I still remember what to do.' Miriam had been a nurse with the Israeli army for five years until she had found an easier way to make a living. Looking after the needs of rich and famous men – discreetly – was the way she had chosen. She was tall with a figure built, as she often said, for comfort and not for speed. Despite receiving many proposals of marriage she had never been tempted. Miriam liked her freedom and independence and when the question of children was brought up she always argued that the world was not a fit place for children.

With his arm strapped and the pills taking effect Golightly was regaining his strength and stamina. He reached into his jacket, which was lying on the sofa, and found his mobile phone. Switching it on, he pressed in a four number access code and waited for the acceptance signal. Next, he pressed a speed dial button and placed the receiver to his ear.

'Ruth? I need your help. Where are you? Good. Can you pick me up at Jason's Tomb in half an hour? Good girl. No questions but come armed and ready for trouble.' He switched off the phone. By this time his arm was a dull ache and he was in control once again. 'Do you have a gun?' he asked Miriam.

She nodded. 'Yes. I was given a revolver two years ago for personal protection after I was threatened by that Sephardi.'

Golightly nodded, remembering. A rabbi of the Sephardi had denounced her as a prostitute and had threatened to kill her. A gun with a permit was issued to Miriam for self-protection. It was never needed as a senior police officer had made it clear to the rabbi what would happen should anything befall Miriam. Golightly guessed it had been another one of her clients who had intervened on her behalf.

Miriam scrabbled around in the bottom of a cupboard and eventually found an old shoe box. She handed it to Golightly who lifted the lid to find a German Weihrauch HW-9 nestled there. He knew the weapon, as it was popular throughout Europe and the Middle East. Inexpensive, it fired .22 cartridges from a .38 frame and was deadly accurate. He ignored the spots of rust on the handle but quickly checked to see that the gun was loaded and that the barrel was clear. He tucked the weapon into his waist band and put on his jacket.

'Miriam, I can't thank you enough. If anybody comes looking for me, you haven't seen me and you don't know here I am. All right?'

Miriam nodded. 'Yes. Can you tell me what's happening? Who's after you? What men?'

'Samuel Dayan is trying to have me killed. He's behind everything. Now, don't look so shocked and stay quietly here. I'm hoping to solve the problem in the next few days.'

'How? How can you solve it?'

'It's better that you don't know. Just leave it to me. Look, I need to go. Remember, not a word.'

Golightly gave her a peck on the cheek and left the apartment. Miriam stood at the window and watched the hunched figure shamble along the street before picking up the telephone. She dialled a number from memory. 'Samuel? It's Miriam. David Golightly has just left. He's making for Jason's Tomb, in the Rehavya Quarter. Yes. He's armed.'

Out in the alley the heat hit Golightly like a blow. He paused for a few seconds to get his breath, one hand holding his aching arm, and then moved cautiously back the way he had come. At each corner he stopped, knelt and looked around the edge of the building, hoping that the slight movement he made would be missed as anyone searching for him would be looking at normal height.

He was on Ussishkin, the street that ran north to south through Nahalat Ahim before he saw anyone who could be a possible enemy. Two armed soldiers were standing on a corner a hundred metres away taking an inordinate interest in the passers-by. They had their work cut out for them as the street was teeming with pedestrians, many men in western casual clothes but as many incongruously wearing suits with kaffiyehs. Many women wore burkas or kangas and some Muslim women wore yashmaks. Golightly paused, wondering what to do. Then, across the street, he saw a clothing shop, advertising in its window western and traditional Arab dress.

The pavements on both sides were teeming with people, some being forced onto the road. This in turn made the heavy volume of traffic slow. Keeping his head down Golightly briskly walked across the road, inconspicuous amongst the throng. He went straight into a shop, looking neither left nor right.

There were few customers but the shop was well stocked. One side was given over to western clothes, suits and jeans, while the other side displayed African and Arabic garb. It took only minutes to find a dark blue haik, a large Arab garment made of cloth that draped over the head and about the body. He put it on over his suit under the watchful eye of an Arab shop assistant.

He said nothing, afraid of being recognised by his voice as well as from his many television and newspaper appearances.

He handed over a wad of shekels and said, 'Keep the change.' Walking quickly out of the shop door he turned left. With his head bent, his face and body were hidden under the cloth. By hooking his thumb into his belt he supported his injured arm. In his other hand he gripped the gun tightly, ready for use.

Some perversity, a challenge within him, caused him to walk close to the two soldiers who had not moved from the corner. They barely glanced in his direction. Emboldened, David Golightly lengthened his stride and walked more quickly, jostling past pedestrians, murmuring an apology in Ivrit whenever he accidentally bumped into anyone. He crossed the main arterial road of Ramban with its bumper to bumper lorries, cars and buses and was nearing Jason's Tomb on Alfasi Street, a leafy suburban thoroughfare. The tomb was not much to look at. It dated back two thousand years to the Maccabean period. A cave with a rusting iron gate. Facts about the cave flooded Golightly's mind, especially the idea that during the era of Jason the people had believed in an afterlife, burying cooking utensils and food along with the corpses. Would he enjoy an afterlife, he wondered? As he slowed down, his eyes darting everywhere, Golightly was overwhelmed by the sense of history that surrounded him and the terror that was imminent. With a sigh he sat down on one of the numerous benches in the area, surreptitiously looking about him, careful not to draw any attention his way. He noticed two soldiers hanging about a street corner, then another couple, then another. All were alert, watching carefully, their weapons cradled and ready for immediate use.

He was aware that Israel was in a state of hypertension. People had a manic, panicked look about them, rushing around, unsure of their future. Those who could were trying to leave the country, while those who were of military age had already received their papers calling them up. As he watched, the phrase "headless chickens" came to mind. God alone knew what it would be like once the war started. He looked past the Tomb and saw more soldiers, then yet more approaching. They knew! They were there for him! They were going to stop him at all costs. But how? It was unthinkable! Who? He gasped. Miriam! It couldn't be! It had to be! There was no other explanation. Despair washed over him for a few seconds but he quickly rallied. If it was war they wanted he would start his own small one right here. He wouldn't go quietly, that was for sure. He had six shots. He would make every one count.

Ruth! He had to warn her. He took his phone from his pocket and pressed the numbers. 'Ruth? Don't come. I'm surrounded. You'll never get me away.'

'Too late, Papa, I'm on Alfasi Street and one minute away. Where are you?'

'Ruth! Don't stop,' panic was in her father's voice. 'We won't survive. They'll cut us down. There are at least ten maybe twenty armed soldiers all looking for me. They knew I was coming here. They are ready. Now keep going.'

'Where are you?'

'I won't tell you. Just keep going.' Golightly looked up and down the road at the traffic trying to find her. First he saw the car and then her. She was driving a battered Datsun, a car he had never seen before. But with her head tilted to one side in concentration, to him she was unmistakable. Somebody was with her.

'Who's in the car with you?' His voice sounded harsh even to him.

'Jacob Mordecai. He's one of us.'

By "one of us" Golightly assumed he was also a Mossad agent but on whose side?

'Okay, Papa, I see you. On the bench hidden beneath the haik.'

'What? How can you . . . ?' Golightly began.

'I'd recognise you anywhere Papa, and besides, if you can see Jacob there aren't many other people it could be. Now, walk slowly towards the road and I'll stop next to you. Take it nice and easy and don't draw any attention to yourself. Got that?'

Golightly knew when to argue and when to hold his peace with his headstrong, self-willed daughter. Resignedly he got to his feet and shambled towards the edge of the pavement. Perversely the crowds were thinning and Golightly felt exposed, the skin crawling between his shoulder blades as any second he expected to hear a shout and feel the thud of bullets extinguishing his life once and for all. He stopped, and looked right and left. The car was only metres away and sliding to a halt next to him. He grabbed the handle, wrenched open the door and climbed awkwardly into the back, the haik now a hindrance when he wanted to move freely and quickly.

'Duck down, Papa, while we get away from here.' Deftly Ruth manoeuvred the car into the traffic and drove away. 'Papa, meet Jacob. Jacob meet Papa.'

'Hullo, sir,' the voice was American, educated.

Golightly stayed slunk down in the seat, his gun ready, his eyes scanning left and right. Not to be outdone in courtesy he said, 'Pleased to meet you. Thanks for coming, Ruth.'

'My pleasure, Papa. This place is crawling with soldiers. My God, are they all looking for you?'

'Yes, I think so.'

'Oh hell!' said Ruth. 'They're stopping the traffic. Two cars ahead. Damnation, they're putting up road-blocks. What do we do now?'

The young American answered, 'Drive up to the barrier and I'll flash my passport. Sir, you get down between the seats and make like a bundle of clothes. Quick, we're being called forward.'

Golightly did as he was told. He felt the car jerk forward and come to a stop. He heard a voice say, 'Who are you and where are you going?'

'Hey, bud, here's my passport,' Jacob said.

There was a second or two's silence. 'And you? Who are you?'

'Just the driver,' said Ruth.

The car moved forward slowly and then there was a yell. David Golightly heard the sinister snicker of a rifle bolt and the same voice called out, 'Stop! Stop, I say!'

Ruth accelerated away in a screech of tyres as gunfire thudded dully into the back of the car. The rear window blew out and pellets of glass showered Golightly's back. The car lurched to the right and then flew round a left hand bend, out of sight of the gunmen.

'Papa, are you all right?'

Golightly sat up, his legs cramped, back aching and his arm throbbing. 'That was close. We need to change cars and get out of sight. They'll have helicopters up looking for us soon.'

'Who's doing this? Who has the power to call in the army, sir?' asked Jacob.

David Golightly eased back in the seat, a whiff of exhaust fumes from the car being sucked in through the gaping hole behind his head. 'Samuel Dayan. The country's gone mad and he's leading it into becoming the world's pariah state at best or to possible annihilation at worse.'

'Dayan? The industrialist?' came the shocked reply from the American.

'The very same.'

15

The helicopter landed at Heathrow. Macnair stayed in his seat while he finished down-loading the information he needed from Isobel into his lap-top computer. Sarah at GCHQ had come up trumps. The signal traffic from the oil rig to Iran was enough to hang Dayan, should he ever get to a court of law. Or, better still, be sufficient to justify any action Macnair took should the proverbial hit the fan. It was all there, dates, times, intentions. The carve-up afterwards. Suddenly he realised that there was a new dimension to what needed to be done. His mind worked overtime as possibility and opportunity played out in his thoughts.

'Sir, we've got a problem,' Hunter broke into the General's thoughts. 'They've just closed Heathrow.'

'What? What do you mean?' Macnair looked at Hunter sharply.

'We're the last aircraft in. All planes and other aircraft are being diverted all over the UK.'

'Not again?' Macnair asked, as the implication of what Hunter was saying sank in.

'I'm afraid so, sir. I've just received a message to say that eight incidents have taken place across Europe. There are no details, but Paul Meadows called. As you were busy, Isobel patched him through to me. A plane has been hijacked and is landing in ten minutes. The hijackers have identified themselves as the League for the Elimination of Israel. If it's the same lot and not a copy-cat operation then we know what to expect.'

Macnair nodded. 'Delay, obfuscation and a bomb.'

Hunter nodded. 'And nobody's getting in or out in the meantime. Meadows knows we're here as I've asked him to let us take off again for Gatwick or even Schipol. He said he's thinking about it.'

'There's no point,' said Schwarzkopf, entering from the cockpit. 'Unfortunately we don't have enough fuel even to get to Gatwick. So we need to re-fuel before we go anywhere. And there's no guarantee we'll get a connecting flight from there,' he added, pointing out the obvious.

'How long to take on enough fuel for Paris? There's bound to be numerous flights to Rome from there throughout the day,' said Macnair.

'By the time we submit a flight plan and refuel I guess we'll be delayed at least two, maybe three hours. Flight time to Paris followed by a possible connection?' Schwarzkopf shrugged. 'To stick with the original time scale we need to fly from here as scheduled.'

'That can't happen,' said Macnair.

'Sir, knowing what we know, why don't we go straight in? The hijackers will blow up the plane and kill many people anyway, so why not hit it hard and fast as soon as it lands?' Hunter suggested.

'Because we can't be sure it is the same lot. What if it isn't and there is a real possibility of the hostages being released? What then? We're putting lives at risk for no reason.'

Just then Hunter's phone warbled and he answered it. He spoke briefly and flicked it shut. 'Well, there's your answer. That was Isobel. So far the Israeli embassy at Buitenhoff, the Hague, has been destroyed and three planes blown up. One in Paris, one in Egypt and one in India. The pressure is being applied because two of the planes were blown up by the Army for the Protection of Israel.'

'Damnation. Dayan is forcing matters faster than I thought,' said Macnair. 'We need to get to that rig p.d.q.' He paused, his fingers tapping a furious tattoo on the cover of his lap top. 'What do you suggest?'

'It's a 757,' said Hunter. 'As soon as it stops I'll go under the tail and open the baggage doors. We'll go in through the bottom, up the ladder into the forward section galley area. We'll take it from there.'

'What if you don't move fast enough and they blow the plane?' Macnair asked.

Hunter shrugged. 'If we move fast they won't be expecting trouble. They know as well as we do that we only make a move once negotiating has failed. That's why they're getting away with all this carnage. The hijackers have an agenda we've never seen or contemplated before.'

Macnair nodded, weighing up all the possibilities, the chance of success. Finally he nodded. 'All right. Three of you only. If it goes wrong and the plane blows we'll have the airport opened again sooner rather than later in any case.' He looked into Hunter's calm eyes. 'The only difference will be that you won't be coming with us.'

Hunter nodded. 'There is something else we can try. We drop the baggage out of the hold as fast as we can and get it away from the plane. I don't think the explosives are carried into the cabin but are amongst the baggage. Otherwise there's the danger of it being found when passing through the security checks at the airports. So there is always the chance that if we get the baggage away it can't be detonated.'

'Alternatively you could search the luggage for the explosives,' said Schwarzkopf.

Hunter shook his head. 'It'll take too long. Dropping the baggage out of the hold could make the difference between survival and devastation,' said Hunter, 'and if we shifted it further away then even better. It's worth a try, at any rate.'

'Okay, let's go. Three of you only into the plane,' the General ordered. 'The rest are to go into the terminal and book onto the flight.'

A short while later Macnair, Hunter, Badonovitch and McReady stood with Paul Meadows, the Head of Security at Heathrow.

'I can't allow this,' said Meadows. 'What if we can negotiate a peaceful settlement? There's too much at risk.'

Macnair explained why he thought that the outcome was more

likely to be a bomb blast and many deaths but Meadows merely shook his head.

After a pause Macnair nodded his head. 'All right, if that's the way you want it. In that case I shall write a note to you now, stating that in my opinion the hijackers intend to blow up the plane and you prevented us from stopping it. You can then take full responsibility.'

Meadows blanched. 'That's not fair,' he protested. 'You know as well as I do that the policy is to negotiate in the hope that some lives, if not all lives, can be saved.'

Macnair shrugged. 'That's not how the papers will play it. I think they're more likely to have a go at you for not listening to the experts – us – rather than hoping nothing would happen.'

Meadows glowered at Macnair. The man found himself in that most disquieting of places colloquially known as between a rock and a hard place. If they did nothing and the plane blew up he would be damned. If he allowed Macnair's men to attempt to retake the plane and it went up, he'd still be damned. On the other hand, if they succeeded, then he'd be praised to high heaven. It looked like there was only one choice.

'All right, Macnair. The plane only landed two minutes ago and is taxiing to hangar three. Let's go! We can be there within seconds of it stopping.' He turned and walked from the room, indignation and anger seeping from every pore and displayed in the tautness of his bearing.

The plane was on the hard-standing near hangar three. The engines were winding down and the brakes had been applied. All windows had their shutters down, keeping prying eyes out and fearful ones in. Hunter, Badonovitch and McReady checked their weapons and in file darted towards the tail of the plane, out of sight of any passengers or anybody in the cockpit. At the baggage hatch Hunter quickly undid the handles and opened the door. In the meantime Macnair was patched via the control tower to the plane's pilot.

'Air France 3542, this is the control tower, over,' said Macnair.

'This is Air France 3542,' was the reply followed by two clicks. Good, it meant that a hijacker was in the cockpit but not listening to the radio, only to the pilot. The new international codes for secret communications in the event of a hijack appeared to be working. Macnair had the book of codes spread out before him; he hoped the pilot could remember them.

'How many passengers and crew and is everybody all right?'

'One hundred and twenty six passengers, two flight deck and four cabin crew,' the pilot replied. It was followed by three clicks, caused by the pilot pressing the transmit button three times. Three hi-jackers, one in the cockpit, two in the cabin.

'Are there any injured passengers?'

'No. No passengers are injured,' followed by two clicks. It meant that the pilot did not know precisely where the other two hi-jackers were.

'Any crew hurt?'

'No. No crew injured,' followed by one click.

Macnair checked the code. If the pilot remembered the correct codes, by answering the way he did, he was telling Macnair that there were two men and one woman hijacker. If the pilot had repeated the word hurt followed by one click it would have meant one man and two women and a repeat of the word hurt followed by two clicks would have meant all men. Using the word injured followed by two clicks would have meant all women.

Now came the big one. 'Do you want anything sent to the plane? Like additional food?'

'No. No additional food. Nothing. I am being told to stop transmitting. Out.' The connection was broken and Macnair sighed. He had told the pilot that a rescue attempt was in progress and the pilot had agreed to it.

Macnair made one more attempt to raise the pilot, asking to speak to one of the hijackers. Silence greeted his attempt. The General transmitted what he had learnt to the three men in the hold of the plane.

Hunter handed down bag after bag to Badonovitch who handed it to McReady. He in turn was busy laying the bags flat on the concrete, a good six to eight feet separating the bags from the underbelly of the plane. They worked fast and silently. Even so it still took nearly ten minutes to empty the hold but finally all the luggage was removed.

The two men joined Hunter who had climbed the short ladder to the hatchway into the cabin. The three had their silenced guns ready, tense and poised to move.

'Hunter,' Macnair transmitted into their ear pieces, 'I've just had one of the hijackers on. He says that no harm will come to any of the passengers, provided we do nothing. We are to leave them alone for the next two hours.'

'A similar pattern as before, sir,' Hunter replied.

'I agree. It's a go, Nick. Now.'

'Roger that, sir.'

Hunter pressed a shoulder against the hatch and slowly straightened his legs. The hatch moved a millimetre at a time as he carefully pushed it upwards. When it was barely more than cracked open, Badonovitch reached around Hunter and fed a thin optic fibre thread into the cabin. Hunter let the hatch drop back. The fibre was hardly thicker than a strand of hair but had minute sensors all along the first five centimetres, pointing in different directions. Badonovitch held the palm sized monitor in his hand and flicked through each sensor like changing channels on a television. Each picture showed a bit of the forward galley, two just dark blobs of the cabin floor. The galley was empty.

'Okay, boss. In you go,' said Badonovitch.

Hunter heaved up the hatch and silently clambered up the ladder. The other two men quickly joined him, hidden from the passengers by the forward bulkhead. The door to the cockpit was on their right, the aisle into the main cabin to their left. Hunter held the optic fibre at waist height and pointed it into the cabin.

The faces of the passengers were strained, fearful, anxious. They all knew that of the numerous hijackings which had taken place recently most of the hostages had been killed. What assurances had been given to get the men, women and children sitting in the plane to acquiesce to the hijackers demands?

A stewardess was walking towards the front of the plane. One man holding a gun was standing halfway along the cabin. There was no sign of the third hijacker, the woman.

The stewardess stopped to speak to a passenger, giving reassurance, smiling; offering hope when she had so little to give. Hunter saw that she was a mature woman, a professional, who had seen it all. Well, perhaps not, thought Hunter as she stepped into the galley and stopped in shock.

'Shshsh,' Hunter put his finger to his lips. 'Where's the other one? The woman?'

If the stewardess was surprised that Hunter knew that the third hijacker was a woman she hid it well.

'At the very back. Sitting down.'

'Damnation,' Hunter said. 'We need her out in the open. Up here even. We need a clean shot at her before she realises what's going on.'

The stewardess's reply startled Hunter. 'Give me the gun and I'll shoot her.'

Hunter frowned and looked at the other two. Both men shrugged. It was probably their best bet. 'You can't get close enough without the gun being seen. You've nowhere to hide it,' Hunter said.

'I'll take the drinks trolley. I'll give juice to the children but pass quickly through the cabin. I can hide the gun under a cloth.'

'Have you ever fired a gun before?' McReady asked.

'I belong to a shooting club. I'm good with a rifle and adequate with a handgun. At the distance I'll be from her I won't miss.'

A voice shouted from the cabin and the stewardess stepped into the aisle. 'I'm getting drinks for the children,' she said in a loud voice.

The hijacker yelled, 'Come here! Now! Or I shoot someone. Now!' He screamed the last word. The man was a teenager, his complexion and accent suggested he was Arabic.

Hunter reached into his holster and placed a spare, unsilenced gun on the top of the drinks trolley that the stewardess was busily pulling out. She dropped a towel over the gun and walked up the aisle. Hunter spared a thought to her bravery and then looked at the monitor showing her progress along the aisle via the optic fibre camera. She stopped halfway to the first hijacker and handed out a drink. The team could not hear what the hi-jacker said but the stewardess replied in a loud voice. 'We must give the children something. Why can't you let them go? Show some goodwill.'

The reply was inaudible but the angry gesture with the gun was unmistakable. The stewardess walked more quickly along the aisle as though she wanted to get it over with as soon as possible. Before her courage failed her.

'Ready?' asked Hunter. His eyes glued to the monitor, watching the hijacker. 'He's standing looking her way. His head is swivelling, looking at the passengers. He's stopped, looking at one in particular. His head is moving on, looking this way. Any moment now. She's almost at the rear of the plane. A clean head shot, Jan, then, we'll go into the cockpit.'

The bang was a shocking noise that stunned the passengers and hi-jacker alike. Badonovitch stepped into the aisle and using a silenced weapon blew the hijacker's head away even as McReady lay on the deck and smashed his feet into the cockpit door. Hunter, bent low, stepped over McReady and into the cockpit and came face to face with the startled hijacker. Hunter also shot the man in the head, killing him instantly. Pandemonium was breaking out in the cabin as the passengers began yelling, screaming, climbing out of their seats just as the explosion went off and the tail of the plane lifted a few feet before smashing back down onto the concrete, shattering the rear wheels.

Those people who had risen to their feet were thrown down, some were injured, the majority merely shaken as they fell back into their seats. Hunter staggered before running up the aisle.

'Sit down. Sit down, all of you. We'll get you out!' Frantically he searched for the one who had set off the bomb. The one whose face didn't fit. There, that one. The one reaching into a bag. Pulling out a round black object. The man looked up, a snarl of contempt, hate etched in his face. He reached for the pin as Hunter's shot created a third eye in the middle of his forehead and the grenade fell onto the cabin deck. It rolled, unprimed, into the aisle and Hunter scooped it up, dropping it into a pocket. The stewardess was lying in the aisle, the explosion and movement of the plane having thrown her heavily to the floor. When Hunter reached her, he knelt beside her and turned her over gently, relieved to discover that she was breathing normally although she had a large lump on her forehead.

Already others were getting the plane evacuated. Emergency doors had been thrown open and slides had appeared. Passengers were sliding down to safety, away from the terror. Hunter stayed where he was. The explosives must have been in one of the suitcases they had placed at the rear of the plane. When it had gone off the force would have dissipated in all direction, including upwards. If the suitcase had been near the main wings the highly inflammable aviation gas could have gone up as well, turning the plane into a firebomb. They had been incredible lucky.

He tenderly picked up the stewardess and carried her to the centre escape slide. He placed her on the slide and let her go. By now the plane was empty apart from Hunter, Badonovitch, McReady and the senior pilot.

'Thank you,' said the pilot, holding out his hand to Hunter. 'You saved our lives.'

Hunter shook his hand and indicated to the others to go down the slide. A few seconds later he followed.

The airport was opened again within minutes, as the business of shuttling people all over the world resumed. Planes began to land and those that had been held on the runway began to taxi and take off.

Hunter and the others joined the remainder of the team in the departure lounge waiting for the flight to Rome. Meadows ensured that their flight was given priority and on that day it was the only aircraft to take off on schedule.

Once onboard the plane, reaction set in. Hunter leant his head back against the seat rest and fell asleep. Next to him Macnair was busy with his computer, reading the information he had received from Isobel, collating it into some semblance of order. Preparing his ammunition.

16

Ruth pulled into a car park and stopped in a corner under the shade of an old tree. At that moment nobody was chasing them, nobody shooting at them. They needed a different vehicle, something robust and fast. It took her only a moment to recognise a Land Rover Discovery and she said to Jacob, 'Over there. The Discovery. Can you get it?'

'Sure, nothing could be easier. Let's just all of us stroll across and I'll have it open in a jiffy.'

'Right,' said Ruth. 'I'll get the bags from the boot.' The three of them climbed out of the Datsun and Jacob went ahead to open the Land Rover. Ruth unlocked the boot and lifted out two holdalls. She handed one to her father, hefted the second in her left hand and held a gun ready in her right. In Israel many people carried weapons as it was normal to join the Israeli Defence Force at the age of 18. Because each person was responsible for the safe keeping of their weapons, whether in or out of uniform, it was not unusual to see many men and some women carrying guns when wearing jeans and tee shirts and not just in combat fatigues. The loss of a weapon could result in a punishment of up to seven years in prison. After their initial national service of three years for men and two for women they were required to serve thirty days every year until the age of thirty-five for men and thirty-four for women. Now, with the threat of war hanging over them, more guns than ever were in evidence on the streets.

Jacob was an expert at breaking into cars and he already had the doors open and the engine running. Golightly did not bother

167

to ask him how he had done it, aware that some of the skills taught at Mossad were highly illegal but eminently practical.

'Papa, can you use a gun?' His daughter looked over her shoulder at her father, seeing the exhaustion etched in his face.

'Naturally I can use a gun,' he replied, 'I have one here.' He reached into his pocket and withdrew the revolver he had acquired from Miriam. As he did so pain lodged itself behind his eyes as he contemplated her betrayal. Then he shook the feeling away, concerned with the present and the future, not the past.

Jacob drove and backed the vehicle out of the parking slot. He stopped at the road, turned left and accelerated away. None of them heard the yell of outrage as the car owner watched his Discovery vanish into the distance.

'I must speak to General Macnair,' said Golightly, reaching into his coat pocket for his sat-phone. Within moments he was through to Isobel who switched him through to a high security line. 'Where is General Macnair?' Golightly asked, his politeness masking his impatience and desperation.

'He's airborne,' said Isobel. 'He's caught the connection from Rome to Egypt where he intends boarding a ship. He's on his way to the rig.' Briefly she updated the Deputy Prime Minister on their status and immediate plans. 'Right now it appears that Dayan isn't there but is expected within twenty-four hours, according to the information we've intercepted. He'll want to be where he thinks he's safe.'

'I need to reach the General,' said Golightly. 'I could be of use.'

'General Macnair agrees, sir. He phoned me before he caught his plane. He's hoping that you'll find a way to get to him somewhere off Ashqelon. You have his sat-phone number so you ought to be able to speak to him when he gets to Egypt. He has an idea that you can be useful in stopping the war. I don't know what he has in mind but he did say that he needed you.'

'All right, thank you, Isobel. I'll try and make contact later. Now I must flee my country like a criminal.' On that bitter note he broke the connection.

'Well?' his daughter looked back at him, concern reflected in her eyes and the set of her mouth.

David Golightly conjured up a smile and said, 'General Macnair has a plan. I just hope its a good one.'

'Who's General Macnair?' Ruth asked.

Golightly laid his head wearily on the back head-rest and answered. 'He's in charge of the new organisation known as TIFAT.' He told them some of his conversation with Isobel.

'I've heard of those guys,' said Jacob. 'Supposed to be tougher than the SEALS and Delta Force combined – but also with brains.'

'Something like that. Well, he's working on a way to stop this war. He has, so I am told, a plan. What it entails and whether it will succeed or not I have no idea. I only know that I've got nothing else to run with. If I'm stopped I'll be killed.' The thought made Golightly sit up and shake off his lethargy. 'Ruth, you have to get out. Leave me to go on alone. If you're picked up tell them that you helped me to escape from terrorists. That you know nothing else.'

'Papa, be quiet,' Ruth spoke sweetly. It was a tone of voice that Golightly knew only too well. 'You cannot make it alone and you know it. Which is why we're going to help you. I have given ten years of my life to Mossad and now I believe that I am facing the biggest fight of all. And shockingly it is not a fight against our external enemies but against the enemy within.' She sighed heavily, fear and doubt intermingling in the sound.

'Who are you, Jacob?' Golightly asked suddenly.

'Me?' was the startled reply. 'Just the hired help.'

'No, I don't think so. The way you opened the door to this car, the way you handle yourself all speak of Mossad. Your accent speaks of something else.' Golightly paused and then added, 'How stupid. CIA?'

'Well, sir, I guess there's no reason why you shouldn't know. Although in the strictest sense I was told to tell only your daughter who I really am.'

'What are you doing with Ruth?'

Jacob paused, thinking about his reply; then shrugged as

though coming to a decision. 'Two days ago we got a request at Langley from General Macnair. He was concerned about your safety. The General didn't know and still doesn't that Ruth here is a Mossad agent and, I may add, reputed to be a very good one.' Ruth blushed at the unexpected compliment. 'So my boss figured it would be easier to get to Ruth than to you and that we could work together.'

'I didn't believe him, Papa,' she said apologetically. 'I'm sorry. It was too far fetched. We're on the brink of war and your life is in danger? From annihilation if we're invaded but then all our lives are at risk. So who else? The Palestinians? Hamas? None of it made sense. And the trouble was, Jacob couldn't tell me why or who was trying to kill you. When you phoned I had decided that we needed to see you and find out what was going on. It seems we came along just in time.'

'What's your story, should we be stopped?' Golightly asked.

'I'm a distant cousin and journalist who is using his family contacts to speak to you to get your perspective on the future. If anybody cares to check they'll find me accredited to *Time Magazine* as a respected but free-lance journalist.'

'And have you been published, should anybody enquire?' asked Golightly.

'Yes, sir. We have real writers submitting work on my behalf to *Time*, *Newsweek* and *Global International*.'

'Now I know we're in trouble,' said Golightly with an attempt at humour, 'when the journalists arrive by the same plane as the rich depart. As regards to the future, I don't think Israel will have one unless we stop this madness. And right now it seems that Macnair is our only hope. What's the view from Langley?'

'Heck, sir, I don't know. All I can tell you is that you aren't very popular. The Jewish lobby has been . . . I can't say silenced, but certainly put on the defensive by what's been happening. You're being called terrorists and worse in the media and being compared to fanatical fundamentalists from all religions. The consensus appears to be that whatever happens you've got it coming.'

The harsh words were like hammer blows to Golightly. There

were no surprises in Jacob's words, but still they had the power to shock. 'It . . . it's not like that. The manipulation has been brilliant. Most Israelis think that we're the victims. They think that the so-called Army for the Protection of Israel is a Moslem organisation designed to create the atmosphere we now find ourselves in. Instead it is an Israeli force and our enemies know that to be the case. The League for the Elimination of Israel is Moslem but financed by a Jew and our enemies *don't* know that. My God, but its clever. The deception and lies that have been woven have brought us to this and only a handful of people know the truth.' Even as he spoke an idea was forming and the Deputy Prime Minister lapsed into silence for a few seconds. 'That could work,' he said, as though speaking to himself.

'What could?' Ruth asked.

'An idea I've just had. I must get to Macnair. He's our only hope.'

'So you keep saying, Papa. And we'll do our best.'

'Where are we?' Golightly suddenly became aware of the dusk and rapidly falling night, the few lights of isolated farmsteads and the deteriorating road surface.

'We've just passed the Kennedy Memorial.' Ruth was referring to the fine memorial to John F. Kennedy atop Mt Orah, a landmark in the area. 'We'll be back on the main road to Ashqelon in about fifteen minutes.'

'Then what?' asked Golightly.

'Then we keep going,' replied his daughter, 'and try and get you to the General.'

David Golightly closed his eyes for a few minutes, the cool of the air conditioning causing him to shiver as the heat of the day dissipated rapidly with the onslaught of nightfall. The bouncing eased and was replaced with the steady hum of tyres on a tar-surfaced road and he fell into an uneasy sleep.

'Papa, wake up. There's a road block ahead. I can see cars stopped.'

The Land Rover crawled to a halt as Ruth reached over her head and pushed the switch on the internal light. 'Right, we get out, Papa, and let Jacob carry on through. He's travelling on his

American passport so he should be all right. We'll meet you one mile the other side,' she said to Jacob.

Ruth opened her door, the inside light stayed off, and she dropped lightly to the ground. She whipped open her father's door and helped him out. 'Come on, Papa, time to take a walk.'

She led the way onto the dark hillside, sand and gravel beneath their feet. The large shoulder bag which she hoisted onto her left shoulder was never far from her. Reaching under her jacket, she withdrew a revolver, and thumbed the safety off. The ground was firm beneath their feet and they made rapid progress. Within seconds they had walked around a hillock and were out of sight. Golightly stumbled a few times, the pain in his arm beginning to make itself felt, but he ignored it.

Ruth stopped and said, 'Shshsh. There's something up ahead.' She stooped down and walked slowly around the side of the hillock. After a few seconds she knelt on one knee and reached into her bag. The nightscope she placed to her eye showed the world in a green hue. She took her time, quartering the landscape, ensuring she examined every stone or possible hiding place. She passed over a lump, paused and turned back. Then she smiled as she saw the goat raise its head and look directly at her.

'False alarm,' she whispered. 'Let's go.'

Three more times they stopped as they slowly made their way past the roadblock. A hundred metres away, in the still night, they could hear doors opening and closing, voices raised and arguing. Engines growled and whined as they stopped and started. The clattering roar of an exhaust with a hole in it suddenly rent the air and slowly drew away down the valley. Father and daughter kept going until Ruth stopped and said, 'This should be far enough. Let's get back to the road.'

They walked down a shallow ravine and up the other side. Behind them were high hills, and as they cautiously peered over the top of the ravine down onto the road, the moon rose in the sky behind them and bathed the view in a white light. They were out of sight of the roadblock and watched as a few cars passed left and right. One stopped a few hundred metres down the road. It was the Discovery. They stayed off the road, paralleling it, until they

172

were opposite the car, and then walked towards it. They heard the sound of metal on metal, a curse, the ring of a spanner being dropped. When they reached the car they found Jacob had raised it on its jack and was kneeling by the rear nearside wheel.

'Puncture?' Ruth asked.

'Nope. But I was ready to let the air out should a patrol come along. I wanted an excuse to be parked. Come on, climb aboard while I drop the jack.' He threw the jack and wheel-brace into the back of the vehicle and climbed into the driver's seat. The engine started with a quiet purr and he drove sedately away, keeping the noise to a minimum.

'Any problems?' Golightly asked.

'Not really. I was asked what I was doing here and so I showed them my journalist's ID and a letter of appointment from *Time* commissioning me to do an in-depth analysis of the situation in Israel. I made a few supportive noises and they let me through. I did ask if I could expect any more delays as I wanted to get to Gaza as soon as possible. But they said they didn't know. They claim to be looking for fifth columnists who could cause problems when the war begins.'

'So they think there'll be a war?' Golightly asked.

'I would say that, from the way they were talking, that yes, they're expecting a war. One of them said that it will be the war to end all wars.'

'That's what they said about World War One,' said Ruth, 'and look what happened afterwards.'

'Ruth,' her father said, 'do you have any pain-killers in that bag of yours?'

'Sure, Papa. Here.' She handed over a bottle of pills. Golightly swallowed three of them, his parched throat constricting, protesting at the passage of the pills.

'Thanks. Now, let me try the phone again.' He took out his sat-phone and pressed the buttons. He was greeted with the recorded message that the number called was unavailable. 'Damn!' he said. 'Come on Macnair, where are you?'

The plane from Rome had been late taking off. The Airitalia

173

Airbus had been late arriving from Moscow and so Macnair and his men had been forced to kick their heels at Leonardo Da Vinci Airport, Fiumicino. Finally they boarded.

In the cabin Hunter had his eyes closed with his seat as far back as it would go. In his mind he was playing what they needed to do. Macnair was alongside him, still working on his computer while the remainder of the team were scattered throughout the aircraft. He was in the aisle seat at the rear of the plane when the voice of the stewardess broke into his thoughts.

'. . . telling you there's something strange about them.' She spoke in Italian.

'About who?' asked a second stewardess.

'Look at rows three, eight, nineteen, twenty four and,' she dropped her voice to a loud whisper, 'the last one here. Tell me what you see.'

'Passengers. Mainly men and two women.'

'The men. Can't you see anything special about them?'

There was a pause before she replied, 'No, I can't. What are you driving at?'

'They . . . they are so . . . so aware. Look again. Have you ever seen passengers as fit looking? So . . . I don't know what. So tough?'

'Now that you come to mention it I don't suppose I have. You don't think . . .'

'I don't think anything. After all those hijacks, the bombs . . . all those passengers killed. I'm going to warn the Captain.'

'What are you going to tell him?'

'That I'm uneasy.'

'He'll tell you not to be so silly. That you're letting your imagination run away with you.'

'Maybe. But he could warn ahead, just in case.'

The last thing Hunter wanted was to be met by Egyptian officials at Port Said so he undid his seat belt and stood up. He smiled when he stepped into the galley and said, 'It's okay, ladies.' He spoke in Italian, ignoring the little gasps of concern and the sudden fear in their eyes. 'You're right. Here's my NATO identity card. Those men are travelling with me. You have nothing to fear and no need to alarm the Captain.'

Both stewardesses looked at the card. The NATO emblem showed clearly over the plastic card, along with Hunter's photograph and rank. The stewardess who had wanted to speak to the Captain said, 'That means nothing to me. I've never seen one before. You could have made it up.' There was defiance in her demeanour replacing her original concern.

Hunter's smile widened. He appraised her pretty face, her dark hair and slim figure before he said, 'Look, I can appreciate what you've just said but think about it. We're landing in twenty minutes. If we were going to cause any trouble there wouldn't be anything that you could do about it. In fact, I could stop you here and now from talking to the Captain, or to anybody else, ever. So just let us land and disembark quietly. Okay, Nina?' Hunter read her name-badge. He switched to English. 'Here is my British passport as well. You have nothing to fear. We are on a sort of working vacation, all of us.'

The two stewardesses nodded and said something to each other in an Italian dialect that Hunter could not follow. They giggled and nodded and Nina said in English, 'Thank you. Please take a seat as we will be landing shortly and I have to make certain announcements.'

Hunter nodded and sat down, relieved. There had been enough delays without any problems at Egyptian customs.

'Well done,' said Macnair. 'I couldn't have handled it better myself.'

Which, Hunter thought, was praise indeed.

The airport was dingy, dirty and smelled of Africa. The team carried only hand luggage and customs was perfunctory so they quickly moved through and out of the airport.

Three taxis took them the thirty kilometres to the port where they found the *S.S. Darnah*. The men stood looking at the ship, drinking in the sight of her sleek lines, rakish funnel and spotless paint work. They hefted their bags and walked up the gangway. At the top they were met by two men, one armed and dressed in some sort of uniform, the other in a business suit.

'My name is Achmed al-Megrahi. I represent Sir David Griffiths.'

Hunter stepped forward and extended his hand. 'Nick Hunter. How do you do? I gather you have received the payment and have papers for us to sign?'

'Yes, thank you.' He turned to the man standing next to him and spoke in Arabic. The man gave a sloppy salute and walked down the gangway. 'Let us go up to the bridge. You can check the ship over at your convenience and I can come back in the morning when we can complete the necessary paperwork.'

'That won't be necessary,' said Macnair, 'we are quite satisfied with the information we received. As long as the ship is fuelled and watered we'll be on our way. Masters, Weir, check the engine room.'

'Yes, sir,' said Masters and walked along the deck. They had all spent time studying the plans of the ship that had been faxed to Isobel and so had a good idea of where to go. Details of the engines and their operation had been included so it would not take them long to familiarise themselves with the machinery.

On the bridge al-Megrahi said, 'You will find everything in order, gentlemen, but you will not be leaving tonight. The port is closed until zero, six-thirty hundred hours tomorrow morning. And then you will need a pilot and that will take many hours more as the pilot's office is closed for the night.' He shrugged his shoulders expressively, lighting an evil-smelling cheroot as he did so. 'You may as well join me at a nearby hotel and relax.'

'Thank you,' said Macnair, 'but we'll spend the time getting to know the ship and making sure that we can leave as soon after six thirty as possible. Let us deal with the paperwork now and we can say goodnight. Are all the keys that we need on board?'

'All keys are in the cabinet behind you,' al-Megrahi pointed with his cheroot, a coldness in his voice. 'Here is the key to the cabinet.' He undid his case and extracted a bundle of papers. 'You sign here,' he pointed with his pen. 'Thank you. Now here,' he turned to another page. Macnair signed another seven times before al-Megrahi was satisfied. 'Thank you,' he swept the papers together and put them into his briefcase. 'I bid you goodnight.' He stalked away, leaving a smell of harsh tobacco behind him.

'Our time is being cut away hour by hour,' said Hunter.

'No it isn't,' replied Macnair. 'Get the engines flashed up and acquaint yourself with the layout of the bridge. I'll find the charts for Port Said. We're getting out to-night.'

At that moment Macnair's sat-phone warbled and he answered. 'Ah, David, just the person I wanted to speak to.'

Simultaneously, Hunter's phone also rang.

17

Burghard Schwarzkopf had, a few hours earlier, landed at Bari airport. He had been met by the agent for the company selling the helicopter and together they had walked across the airport to a grassed corner away from the main runway. The Agusta helicopter was waiting for him and he spent time checking it out thoroughly. The most important job he had to do was to ensure the paperwork was correct and that all maintenance had been done by reputable companies. As near as he could tell that was the case and he was relieved to find a new international airworthiness certificate. He switched on the ignition and looked at the dials as the batteries warmed up the engine and electronics. He checked the fuel gauges and scowled. There was enough for a test flight and no more. He had flown an Agusta a few years earlier and as he sat in the pilot's seat memory flooded back.

'All right to do a circuit?' he asked the agent. The man nodded in reply and as he did so the helicopter lifted half a metre off the ground and Schwarzkopf spun the machine around. He did that a few more times, indulged in a series of hops back and forth and then called up the control tower for a test flight. It was granted and he flew a circuit of the airport. He landed, took off immediately in an almost vertical climb, hovered and landed again, finally satisfied.

'Excellent,' he said to the agent. He handed over a banker's draft for £134,000 and signed the papers. He was now the owner of an Agusta A.109A. He shut down the engines, climbed out of the cockpit, shook hands farewell and wandered over to the

178

hangar looking for somebody who could sell him some fuel. The evening was warm, not a cloud in the sky nor a breath of wind to stir the leaves and grass. The smell of aviation gas hung heavily in the air. Like all aviators, it was a smell that he relished.

In the hangar was a small partitioned office and he knocked before entering. The elderly man sitting at the battered desk looked up and said, '*Si?*'

'Sorry. No speak Italian. English?'

The old man shook his head.

'French?'

Another shake. Schwarzkopf was about to try and explain what he wanted when the man said, '*Aber, ich spreche gut Deutsch.*'

Schwarzkopf grinned. 'How did you know I was German?' he replied in the same language.

The old man looked at the pilot's name tag and nodded. '*Der Name ist Deutsch und dein Akzent ist nicht amerikanisch. Was willst du?*'

Schwarzkopf explained what he wanted and the old man nodded. '*Kein Problem. Folg mir.*'

The old man led the way to the back of the hangar. There, a small tractor with a bowser attached stood ready for use. He climbed on to the tractor, settled in the seat and started the engine. It exploded into life with a roar and belch of diesel smoke. Schwarzkopf walked back outside, the old man following.

They refuelled the helicopter and returned to the hangar. '*Das macht eine Million, fünf hundert und sechzig tausend, sechs hundert und sechs und zwanzig lire.*'

Knowing the price of avgas Schwarzkopf was about to protest at the day-light robbery but sighed and took out a wad of notes and paid. '*Gib mir eine Quittung,*' he said. The old man handed over a receipt for the money.

Outside once more he watched as a number of small light aircraft landed and then he strolled across to the helicopter. Having spent a few minutes sitting in the cockpit again getting a feel for the controls, he started the engines. He looked up as the pair of Allison 250-C20B turboshaft engines thundered into life and the four blades of the main rotor began to turn. The engines shoved out 420 shp – shaft horse power – each and could easily carry seven passengers and their gear at a speed of 170 knots. Range was the potential difficulty and Schwarzkopf needed an answer to a tricky problem. He doubted they could fly as far as the ship without refuelling. When they had worked out the original speed and range problem they had forgotten one simple fact. A helicopter used more fuel in warmer climes simply because the air was thinner. Pushing south across the Mediterranean was going to be a problem. His. So he would have to solve it. He sat for ten minutes looking at the gauges. One of the engine temperature gauges was reading slightly warm and he tapped the glass. The needle fell back into the correct range. Re-setting the barometric pressure, he called the control tower and received permission to take off. He hauled back on the cyclic control with his left hand and the helicopter lifted smoothly into the air. Retracting the tricycle under-carriage he flew at three thousand feet, circumnavigating the airport again before heading out to sea. A mile off-shore he really put the helicopter through its paces. After twenty minutes he was satisfied. He returned to Bari and landed near the hangar. He went inside to see the old man. An hour later and considerably poorer, Schwarzkopf left.

The helicopter was filled to over-flowing with avgas but more importantly he had built a jury-rig to hand pump fuel from two 50 gallon drums that he had installed in the port side of the cabin after throwing out two seats. The hose was taped to the fuelling point and kept in place using a rubber sealant. The set-up was completely illegal but for a bribe of six hundred thousand lire the old man had been a great help. The drums and materials he had used had been thrown in for nothing. The avgas was about the most expensive in the world.

By 21:00 hours Schwarzkopf was sitting in the dark, looking at the night sky, waiting. On time he saw the flashing lights of a twin engined plane and watched as it came in to land. A few minutes later four men appeared dressed in the uniform of Italian customs officers.

The man in the lead was about five-five, maybe five-six,

stocky, tough and fit. 'Captain Schwarzkopf?' he held out his hand.

'Lieutenant Napier?' They shook hands, the pilot aware of the immense strength of the man, the latent energy he radiated. 'Call me Burg.'

'Douglas. This is Tam, Eddie and Joe.'

They shook hands. 'Where did you get the uniforms?' Schwarzkopf asked.

Napier smiled. 'It was simplicity itself. We got them from the Italian equivalent of *Gieves of London*.' The reference to the famous haberdashers and military uniform store was lost on Schwarzkopf who merely shrugged. 'What's the plan? What do we do after we take the ship apart?' Napier asked.

Schwarzkopf said, 'I've flown over the ship and had a look. I can land about forty metres away.' He opened up an aviation map of the area, 'Just here. There appears to be lights in the area so there shouldn't be any problem. I suggest that I take off in one and a half hours' time and hover out at sea. You call and I'll come running.'

Napier said, 'Give us two hours. In fact be ready for midnight. That'll give us time to get to the docks and have a good look round before we make our move. I gather we're to create a good deal of trouble.'

'That's the instructions we've had from the General. He wants to start putting pressure on Dayan. We'll join him off Israel when you've finished. I understand you're thinking of joining us permanently.'

'It's an idea I'm toying with. Luckily, we'd just finished the NATO exercise when I got the call from Nick. We're on leave for four days before we're due back in Poole.'

'What about weapons?' Schwarzkopf asked.

Napier hefted a canvas holdall and Schwarzkopf suddenly noticed that each of them carried one. 'All here. We only travelled from Rome so no Customs and Excise. We brought our own gear.'

'Right,' said Schwarzkopf. 'Take this.' He handed over a round disc like a fob watch on a chain. 'Hang it around your neck. If you get into trouble thump it against your chest and it activates a signal.' He squeezed the disc and a beeping noise sounded. He reached into his pocket and took out a small, square, metal box, like a match-box and showed it to them. 'This will bring me running. He pressed a button on the side and the noise stopped. 'It's for emergencies. If things get too hot I can be with you in ten minutes from here. From the sea I can be there in two minutes. Okay?'

'Okay. Thanks. If things get too hot we'll try and head out to sea.'

'How will you do that?'

'I received satellite pictures of the area from some woman in Scotland.'

'That's Isobel,' said Schwarzkopf.

'Isobel, that's right. It shows pedallos and other small boats dragged up on the beach at night just a few hundred metres from the dry dock. If we get into trouble that's where we'll head.'

'Good. Once I'm close we can be in contact on the personal radios so I'll be able to find you. Nothing else? Okay. There are taxis out the front.'

Lieutenant Douglas Napier of the Special Boats Service was in his element. Or as he liked to think of it, as happy as a pig in the proverbial. From the information he had been given by Isobel he had worked out a plan of action and how he was going to get onto the ship and then away again. In fact the former was easy. He was going to walk on board. He had three different plans for the latter. Hopefully his preferred exit route would work – he and his team would walk off the same way they had walked on.

The two taxis dropped them at the dock gates. They paid the fares and marched straight towards the dry dock gates. The area they were in was in one corner of the port, away from the rest of the shipping and ordinary traffic. At the gate was a sign warning them to keep out. The gate was padlocked. Tam took a small hydraulic cutter from his bag, placed the pincers around the clasp of the lock and turned the knob at the bottom of the handle. The irresistible pressure built up and the pincers closed, cutting through the mild steel like a hot knife through butter. They opened the gate just far enough to slip through and walked slowly towards the dockside where the gangway was situated.

The ship loomed above them. Standing on the edge of the dock they could see that it fell away in a series of steps all the way to the bottom. A fall into the dock could mean injury or even death. The boat was propped up by lengths of wood like telegraph poles stretching from the ship's sides to the dock walls. It was pitch dark where they stood although there were lights shining around the deck high above their heads.

Napier pointed and the men went to work. Barely half an ounce of plastic explosives was needed for each length of wood. The detonating device was electronic and could be set off by any of the four men.

'Okay, let's go.' Napier whispered into his throat mike. As they approached the bottom of the gangway they slipped their ear-phones out of sight and walked onboard the ship. As Napier set foot on the deck two men appeared silently from behind a door. One had a gun and he pointed it at the lieutenant.

'What do you want?' he asked in English.

'Customs,' Napier replied, with what he hoped was an Italian accent. 'We have come to search this ship.'

'I don't know nothing about no customs so get off.' He gestured with the gun.

'Sorry,' said Napier, 'but I have my orders.'

'Now listen, I said off. I know nothing about it and you aren't coming on here. Not to-night, not ever. We were inspected at sea earlier. Do I make myself clear?'

'Please do not wave that gun, it might go off. Me, I am very nervous around guns.' Napier raised his hands in the air.

'Good. Well let me make it clear that you get off, pronto.'

'You will be in trouble threatening Customs like this,' said Napier, nervously.

'No. You will be in trouble. Now go before I have you thrown off.'

'I am sorry but that is not possible,' Napier moved a few paces along the deck and the others stepped down off the gangway.

There was something about the four men that made the holder of the gun nervous. He gestured again, the barrel moving away from Napier's stomach. Napier's blow was to the throat, poleaxing the man even as he clamped his hand over the gun and kept it pointed away from him.

Eddie used a rubber covered lead cosh on the temple of the other guard who was unconscious before he hit the deck. They secured both men with thick tie-wraps, stuffed gags in their mouths and dragged them out of sight.

'Let's go,' Napier led the way up to the bridge. It was deserted. Quickly they looked through the cupboards and drawers but found nothing. 'Okay,' Napier spoke softly into his throat mike, 'let's get below. Joe, stay here and keep a look out. If anybody approaches let us know.'

'Roger, boss.' He opened his holdall and removed a Colt Commando Model 733, the favourite weapon of the American Special Forces and Federal Agencies as well as other armed services world-wide. Its length was seventy-six centimetres but with the stock retracted it was reduced to only sixty-eight centimetres. It carried a magazine of either twenty or thirty rounds of 5.56mm by 45mm NATO standard bullets and, most importantly, could be fitted with a highly effective silencer. Tam and Eddie had the same gun as Joe and fitted silencers while Napier screwed a silencer to his Austrian Glock 18 revolver. The extended 33 round magazine in the handle made it look like a small machine gun. 40% of the gun was plastic; it was a light, self-cocking automatic of great accuracy and a favourite with the Austrian Army and American Police.

The three men moved silently from the bridge down into the main living quarters. They looked in the cabins but found nobody until they went down another deck and heard voices. The sign on the door read "crew's mess" and they paused outside, listening to laughter and indistinct speech.

'Tam, you and I'll take care of this place. Eddie, you finish checking the ship for any uglies. Ready?' Napier stood to one side of the door, Tam on the other. He turned the handle and pushed the door open. It was a typical sailor's mess-deck and galley; formica tables bolted to the deck with hard-back chairs to sit on, a sitting area of comfortable chairs with low tables and a serving hatch off the galley. The room was thick with smoke from the eight men who were seated at the tables in two groups, playing cards and drinking beer. The door swung open and the silent figures standing with guns in their hands caught the attention of one man. He gaped, his mouth dropping open, a lighted cigarette falling unheeded onto the deck. Another man looked in the same direction and gave an oath, which startled the remainder into looking as well.

Chairs were pushed back and men began to stand up when Napier yelled, 'Sit! Now!' He waved his gun and the men subsided back into their seats.

They were a motley bunch, dressed in clean tee shirts or string vests, jeans or shorts. They had long hair and stubble on their faces but there was one obvious characteristic that struck Napier immediately; they were all fit looking and had the aura of awareness that only came with a great deal of training. Napier realised that he needed to take action fast if he was to retain control of the situation. He also realised, just as Hunter had said, that this was no ordinary ship. Most crews on a ship like the *S.S. Salamander* would be fat, slovenly and dirty. These men may have needed a haircut and a shave but there was no doubting their military backgrounds.

'You are making a mistake,' said one of the men. He went to stand up but Napier pointed his gun at him.

'Don't move. Or I will shoot, believe me.'

The man sat still and glowered at Napier. He was in his early thirties with brown hair and a bushy moustache. He rested his hands on the table and looked at Napier with scorn.

'I suggest, Mr Customs Man, that you leave this ship immediately. If you do you may live. If you do not . . .' he shrugged expressively.

Napier grinned. 'If I do not?'

'You won't leave the ship alive.'

'You,' Napier pointed at one of the men, 'stand up slowly and walk over to that chair. Sit down.' Napier followed and

185

stood behind the man, Tam keeping them covered. 'Now put your arms on the rests and don't move. The man did as he was told and Napier quickly slid a tie-wrap around each arm pinning it to the armrest. 'Now you. Move there.' He indicated another man to move to another chair and quickly did the same again.

'You won't get away with this,' said the man who had spoken, hatred in his eyes.

'Oh, I think we will,' Napier replied.

They continued the process of securing the crew until the last one, the speaker, remained. Napier was expecting trouble and he got it. As the man stood up Napier appeared to become careless and stood too close to the man, his gun pointing at the deck. The man moved like lightning, striking a stunning blow at Napier's arm, a blow that would have broken the arm of most men. Instead, the shock of the blow jarred the man as though he had hit solid rubber. Napier's short punch to the kidneys sent the man into agonising spasms, retching for breath, agony searing his body. As he collapsed to his knees Napier picked him up by the scruff of his neck and single handedly dragged him to a chair and dropped him in it.

Napier bent his face to the man's and looked him in the eyes. Contemptuously he said, 'You're scum. You and this rabble. Tell Dayan,' Napier was gratified to see the flicker of shock cross the man's face at the mention of the name, 'that we're coming for him. Wherever he is, we'll get him. Before, during or after the war. It'll make no difference.' Napier had been told to pass on the message and to make it forcefully. He was satisfied that he had carried out his orders.

They spent the next few minutes securing each of the crew's legs to the chairs using the same tie-wraps as before. When they were finished Napier led the way out of the room.

As soon as they were gone the crew struggled to escape. After a few seconds it became evident that they were securely trussed up and one by one they lapsed into inertia. Frustration and anger washed over each of them in turn but from time to time one or other would strain at the tie-wraps until their muscles creaked and their eyes popped. To no avail.

Napier and Tam systematically searched the living quarters. Half way through Eddie rejoined them to report that there was nobody else on board. It was in the Master's cabin that they finally found the safe. Even as Tam squeezed plastic explosive around the hinges Napier was looking at his watch. Forty minutes to go. It was taking longer than planned. The explosion took the hinges off and the door fell onto the deck. Inside the safe were wads of money, papers, floppy disks and a gun. It all went into Tam's holdall.

'Boss,' said Eddie, 'the hold is still filled with grain of some sort. Wheat I think but I'm not sure.'

'So? What's your point?' Napier frowned.

Eddie shrugged. 'I'm not sure. But shouldn't the grain have been taken off? Won't it go rotten or something?'

The three men exchanged puzzled frowns and shrugs. Napier said, 'No idea. But I still don't see what you're getting at.'

'Is there something hidden in the grain? It looks pretty deep to me and it struck me that a hell of a lot could be under there.'

'Let's take a look,' said Napier. The three men clambered down into the hold. A vast cavern with mountains of wheat grain in large open hoppers spread out before them. 'It can't go off,' said Napier, 'but what doesn't make sense is why the docking authorities allowed the ship into the dry dock without first removing the cargo. That would have been the normal procedure.'

'Do you think something could be hidden in there?' asked Tam.

'It's possible. But we can't look. We need huge suction pumps to suck that lot out,' replied Napier. 'Unless,' he paused and then grinned.

'Unless what, boss?' asked Eddie.

'Unless we drain the wheat out,' said Napier. 'Come on. We need to hurry.'

He led them back up to the main deck. Napier checked in with Joe before leading the way down into the dry dock. The bottom of the dock was thick with oily mud and sand that reached up to their ankles, each step caused a faint smell like rotten eggs to be released. It was typical of ancient dry docks the world over.

'Right, put plastic in circles all along the bottom. Say twelve inches in diameter. I'll follow and place dets with ten second intervals so that the noise won't be too loud.'

Quickly and quietly the men worked their way along the hull, placing plastic explosives shaped like a bar of *Toblerone* chocolate in a circle on the rust stained metal. Napier followed, sticking a single detonator into the soft plasticine like explosive. They were around the hull and on the other side when the first explosion occurred. There was a dull bang followed by the noise of the piece of the hull falling into the mud. Fifteen seconds later came the second explosion. Eight others followed in succession. They were now nearly back where they had started from when the explosions commenced on their side of the hull. The three men stepped back around the hull and out of harm's way as the last explosion went off. Tam and Eddie were already reaching inside the hull to the second skin to repeat the process. Napier followed behind, setting the detonators. This time, as they were protected from the explosions by the ten inches of space between the inner and outer hulls, Napier set the detonators to go off after only three seconds. The bang reverberated inside the hull and as the first explosion faded and the metal disc dropped between the hulls with a loud clang, the wheat started to pour out of the hold.

They kept going, fingers aching from kneading the plastic into shape, heads reverberating from the noise of the explosions and nerves stretched taut as they realised that time was running out. Even as the third hole was blown the grain from the first one was beginning to dry up. Napier frowned, there should have been a great deal more wheat than that. Finally they had finished and even as the last circle of plastic explosive was set off they were climbing out of the dock and back onto the ship.

'Tam, check the crew again. Joe,' Napier contacted the bridge, 'is everything quiet?'

'Yes, boss. I don't think those bangs could have been heard very far because they were muffled by the dock wall and the ship's hull.'

'Good. We'll take a quick look in the hull and be on our way. We've twelve minutes until the chopper gets here.'

Inside the hull the wheat had drained out of most but not all of the containers. The ones that had emptied still had layers of grain in odd shapes laying in them. Napier climbed down into one of the hoppers and wiped his hand across a surface scattering the thin layer of grain away. The stencilled legend on the box read ATROPINE. Quickly he brushed grain from other surfaces. Every box contained atropine. He knew it was used as an antidote in the event of a bacteriological bomb going off in the vicinity of troops should their special suits and masks not be fully effective. Troops were issued with instructions. At the first sign of nausea or dizziness they were to ram the atropine holder against the muscle of their thigh. The needle would plunge deeply into the tissue and release the atropine. They had about two minutes to do it if they wanted to live but with the knowledge that they were releasing one deadly toxin to kill another. The joke had always been if the enemy didn't kill you the cure would.

'What have you found?' Napier asked into his throat-mike.

'Shells, boss,' said Eddie.

'Same here,' said Tam. 'But not HE. They're all chemical or bacteriological shells.'

'Damnation,' said Napier. 'What do we do now? We can't destroy them yet we can't let them leave here.' His question was greeted with silence. 'Okay, let's go up top and get out of here. The helicopter'll be here any minute.'

They climbed out of the hull and onto the deck. Napier used his sat-phone to call Macnair. It was engaged. He broke the connection and phoned Hunter.

'Nick? Douglas Napier. We've got a problem.' Briefly he told Hunter what they had done and found.

'Good work. Let me speak to the General and I'll be right back with you. In the meantime, remove the detonators from one side of the log-braces. I have an idea. Be ready to get the hell out of there as soon as Burg arrives.'

Napier called Joe off the bridge and the four men stepped ashore and began to walk to where the helicopter would land.

They had passed the end of the dry dock when the shooting started and Eddie had his head blown open. A bullet ricocheted off a metal stanchion and hit Napier in the middle of the back, knocking him to his knees.

18

Thanks to the Kevlar jacket he was wearing Napier was only winded. His phone rang and he was on his feet even as he answered it. The three men were crouched behind a metal rubbish skip, returning fire, Eddie's body lying between them.

'What the hell's happening?' Hunter asked.

'We're under attack from the ship. We're on the quayside,' – as he spoke Napier pressed the signal disc hanging around his neck, – 'and I've just sent out an SOS for the 'chopper.'

'Right,' said Hunter. 'In that case, blow the charges. An Italian para-military squad is on its way to look at the cargo. We've warned them that the crew are armed and dangerous and to proceed with extreme caution. Their ETA is seventeen minutes.' The crew on the ship were still firing, bullets flying all over the place, keeping the three men pinned down. Tam and Joe had worked themselves into positions on either side of the skip and were firing whenever there was a lull from the other side. It was clear that the crew's intention was to send men ashore to outflank the three of them.

'Burg's just come in sight and moving like a bat out hell. Got to go.' He broke the connection and at the same time set off the electronic signalling device to the explosives. There were four men on the gangway as the loud bang went off. The ship seemed to hover upright for a second and then it pitched over on its starboard side, breaking the gangway like a reed, pitching the four men to their deaths in the bottom of the dry dock.

The firing stopped as bodies were flung off the ship, some

falling to the bottom of the dock and others hitting the quay. Those who weren't killed were seriously injured. Above the racket of the helicopter the wailing of sirens could be heard in the distance. Napier slung Eddie's body across his shoulders and the three men ran to the helicopter which had landed on the edge of the light, near the outer perimeter wall.

The door was opened as they approached and Schwarzkopf stood in the entrance, a gun at the ready. He made no comment as the body was unceremoniously thrown in and the three men climbed aboard. He had already left them to shut the door while he climbed back into the pilot's seat. Having rapidly scanned the instrument panel, he hauled up on the collective and at the same time fed fuel to the engines. The helicopter lifted into the air like an express elevator, leaving the death and destruction they had caused far below them. He pushed the cyclic forward and turned south-east, heading rapidly over the dark water, leaving the lights of Bari behind.

Napier was already on the phone to Macnair. 'Sir, Lance Corporal Edward Woodstock is dead. We have his body. What should we do with it?'

Macnair replied, 'Bring him here. We'll have a burial at sea later today. Tell Captain Schwarzkopf that we're listening out on two zero three megahertz. We still haven't left harbour yet so also tell him to head for Port Said and I'll get further information to him as soon as I can.'

'Roger that, sir. We'll be in touch.' He relayed Macnair's instructions to the other two. Now that the fighting was over and the adrenaline rush had subsided they were tired. They put Eddie into a body bag and zipped it up, hiding the gruesome reminder of their former colleague. Typical of fighting men the world over, Tam and Joe settled back in their seats and promptly fell asleep. Napier went forward and clambered into the co-pilot's seat. Schwarzkopf nodded and lifted a set of earphones which he handed over. When Napier was settled in his seat and the earphones were switched on the background clatter of the engines and rotors faded to a low murmur.

'I just spoke to Macnair,' said Napier. 'They are still in Port

Said and he says to head straight there. He'll get back to us once they're at sea.'

'I hope there's no change in the weather, in that case,' said Schwarzkopf.

'Why's that?' Napier was looking out of the cockpit window, enjoying watching the moon rise in a cloudless, star-filled sky. The white light was like a giant searchlight, a finger beckoning across a flat calm sea. He saw a number of ships' navigation lights, the green starboard and red port lights as well as the white masthead lights of merchant ships. To starboard of the helicopter he could see land and a huge cluster of lights, indicating a large town or city. 'Brindisi?' he queried.

'Yes. Hang on a moment I just want to re-check my calculations.' He fiddled with the inboard computer system and then said, 'I thought so. It's eight and a half hours flying time to Port Said at 150 knots provided we don't get a head wind or we don't need to detour due to bad weather.'

'That's all right, isn't it? I see you've got on extra fuel.'

'Yes, and I reckon we have enough for seven and a half hours of flying so we can expect to go feet-wet around about breakfast time.'

Hunter stood at the console and studied the instruments. He had read the faxed instructions that Isobel had sent him but it was not the same as looking at the array of dials, buttons and handles. Hunter was aware of Macnair at the back of the bridge, impatient, raring to go. He turned the ignition key halfway and held it there for thirty seconds. Down below in the engine room the heaters warmed the diesel in the starboard engine's injectors. He turned the key fully and the engine burst into life, the only indication being the flickering needles on the dials. He looked at them as they settled in the green zones. Oil pressure, water temperature, idling revs, all appeared normal. He did the same again with the port engine. Now he could feel a slight throbbing through the soles of his feet as both engines smoothly ticked over.

Don Masters opened the port bridge door and put his head in. 'Ready to go, boss. We have stern and bow ropes on only.

We took in the springs,' he confirmed, referring to the ropes that went from the stern forward to the jetty and from the bow astern to the jetty.

'Okay, Don, thanks.' Hunter pressed two more buttons to start the bow and stern thrusters. The flickering dials showed that they were working. Next he moved the helm fully to port, then to starboard and back amidships. 'Right, sir,' he turned to Macnair, 'I'm ready whenever you are.'

'Can you handle her?' the General asked.

'We'll soon find out,' was the laconic reply. Hunter went out onto the starboard bridge wing to study his surroundings and to get a feel for the weather. There was a hot breeze coming off the desert and pushing the ship off the wall. From the chart he knew that he had a tight turn to starboard about two cables ahead of the ship, the same again to port and then a gentle turn into the main shipping lane out of the harbour. The advantage with the port being closed was that there should be no other shipping to get in his way. The disadvantage was that the Egyptians could take serious umbrage at their departure and try and stop them.

He stepped back onto the bridge after first clipping the door open.

Peter Weir appeared in the doorway. 'Three soldiers have appeared. One of them yelled something I didn't understand. Now they're pointing a gun at us.'

Hunter and the General went out on the bridge wing to look down on the quayside. Three slovenly looking soldiers stood on the quayside, two pointing guns at three members of the crew who had their hands in the air.

'We haven't time to negotiate and explain,' said Macnair. 'We need to get away as soon as possible.'

'Sir, can you go and talk to them? Distract them?'

Macnair nodded. 'Remember, no killing.'

'Roger that, sir. Let's go,' Hunter added to Weir.

Hunter and Weir crossed the bridge and went down to the deck on the side away from the quay. They both stripped to their shorts. Hunter lowered the jumping ladder over the side and quickly climbed down followed by Weir. In spite of the

194

heat of the night the water was cold and felt oily. They swam the short distance to a set of steps and, like ghosts, stepped up and onto the quay. They walked noiselessly in the shadow of a tall building until they were directly behind the three soldiers. Macnair seemed to go mad. He suddenly ranted at the three men, jumped up and down and generally gave the performance of an irate idiot. The soldiers looked at him with their mouths agape and heard nothing from behind them. A swift blow to the neck felled two of the men and as the third was turning to see what was wrong Hunter hit him in the solar plexus, caught hold of his shoulders and smashed him to the ground. The soldier's head hit the concrete and he went out like a light. Hunter checked for a pulse and was relieved to find it beating steadily.

Both men climbed back on board and Hunter went immediately to the bridge. Even standing in his shorts he exuded a natural authority when he said, 'Let go fore and aft.' He addressed Joshua Clements, standing on the bridge wing.

'Let go fore and aft,' Clements repeated the order, softly, to the men on the deck. As the ropes snaked free the ship began to drift away from the wall. Hunter moved the wheel in his hands, getting a "feel" for the ship, trying to guess how she would respond to his wheel and engine orders. For the moment he was satisfied as the distance from the wall slowly increased and they were lining up to take the first ninety degree turn to starboard.

Hunter kept the revs low and pushed the gear levers on both engines into ahead. There was a slight change in pitch and tempo from the engines and then the screws were biting and the ship moved slowly forward. He kept to the port side of the dock to give them room to swing round the corner. The moon had risen and cast a white glow across the docks which were also well lit by street lighting and beacon lights telling the mariner where the main navigation channels were. He turned the wheel a few degrees to starboard and the ship instantly responded, bringing the bow round a few degrees. Hunter looked aft to ensure his stern was clear and then turned the wheel firmly to starboard. The ship came round and began to swing towards the exit channel. Almost as soon as the swing was on he began to ease the wheel, knowing that if he went too far they could easily overshoot and the ship would end up jammed across the entrance. It was easier to increase a turn than to go back the other way and still retain control. Hunter grimaced. From the feel of the wheel he surmised that the ship's shafts were turning the same way and that created a paddle wheel effect he had to compensate for. Not difficult, just awkward.

They were sailing with no lights, a white, ghostly hull with nobody in sight on the decks. A ghost ship, to all intents and purposes. The men were scattered around the deck, hidden, armed, ready for anything. After five cables – one thousand yards or half a sea mile – Hunter turned the wheel to port and she moved to the left. Now there was more sea-room and Hunter pushed the throttles up a few notches. The powerful diesels responded immediately and the ship picked up speed. He eased the wheel a few more degrees to port, checking astern of him as he did so. There was plenty of room. They were now in the main shipping channel, passing between huge merchant vessels berthed on either side of the port.

'Those ships are helping to keep us masked,' said Macnair. 'With luck we can be away before anybody knows that we've gone.'

The words were prophetic. At that moment the radio, guarding channels 16 and 12 simultaneously, burst into speech. '*Securité, securité*. Unknown vessel moving in harbour, stop immediately. Unknown vessel moving in harbour, stop immediately. Harbour launch will be with you in a few minutes.'

'It looks like,' Macnair breathed, 'I spoke too soon.'

'The Harbour Authorities have us on radar, sir,' said Hunter, 'which I expected. The launch will probably take ages to get here as it's kept about two miles upstream.'

'How do you know?' Macnair asked.

'I read it in the *Admiralty Sailing Directions*,' said Hunter. 'We call them "Pilots" and they contain just about all the information we need to get out of Port Said. I knew there was radar coverage but hoped that as the port is technically shut it wouldn't be manned. Proves how wrong I was.' He eased the throttles forward another notch and watched the speedometer creep up to seven knots. This was their speed through the water. With an ebb tide behind them their speed over the ground was closer to eight knots. The radio burst into more chatter, angrier, more insistent.

Hunter said over his shoulder. 'Sir, can you switch the radio off, please? We aren't stopping. It won't tell us anything we need to know and is just an intrusion. Josh, tell the lads to expect trouble from the stern.' Clements went to leave the bridge when Hunter called him back. 'Collect all the marker flares from around the deck. There should be six of them. They're man overboard markers and throw up a lot of dense red smoke. If the launch does come after us throw the lot in the water. That ought to slow them down.'

Clements grinned and left.

Hunter eased the ship into a gentle right hand turn and aimed her bows for the port exit. The open sea was less than six cables away. From astern came the sudden sound of machine gun fire and the silence of the night was suddenly shattered.

Macnair darted out onto the bridge wing while Hunter pushed the throttles all the way forward. 'It's the harbour launch. Hell, that's like no launch I've ever seen. It's a small gunboat. That's a GPMG they've got there.' The general purpose machine gun fires 7.62mm rounds of heavy ammunition at a rate of 750 rounds a minute. Belt fed, it could cause huge damage to a ship like the *Darnah*. Hunter grabbed the microphone to the ship's tannoy system even as he felt the ship leap forward as the revs built up rapidly. 'Throw the marker buoys over. All of them,' he ordered.

Six markers went over the stern and immediately the sea behind them was thick with dense red smoke that billowed across the shipping lane. The firing continued but none of the shots came near the ship. They were already passing fifteen knots and the bow of the ship was beginning to pitch slightly as they approached the swell of the open sea. The firing stopped and as the ship went between the flashing lights of the harbour entrance, Hunter looked back. The whole of the area was filled with dense smoke, the enclosed space hampering the light breeze from dissipating it. The firing stopped and there was no sign of the pursuing boat.

'I don't suppose they'll come after us. We're already doing,' Hunter checked his instruments, 'over twenty knots. This is some beauty of a ship,' he added appreciatively. Once past the entrance he turned further to port and steered a course of 350 degrees. He lined up the automatic pilot, switched it on, and let go of the wheel. As if an invisible man was steering, the wheel tracked left and right the few degrees necessary to keep the ship on an exact heading. 'The auto-pilot will steer far more accurately than I can,' he announced. He went out onto the bridge wing to look astern. There was still no sign of their pursuers and he returned to the bridge to check the radar. In the middle of the harbour he could see a bright, stationary, yellow dot making no effort to follow. Hunter guessed that either their radar wasn't working or it had not been switched on in their haste to chase the *Darnah*. Whatever the explanation, it meant that they were safe. 'Sir, if you don't mind, I'll take a quick shower and get dressed. If you need to change course or speed hit that switch and you take back control. There's nothing on the radar except those five anchored vessels,' he pointed to them, 'waiting in the roads.' He used the term to indicate the area where ships, waiting to enter port, anchor until they have a clear passage or until the local harbour pilot can join them to steer them in. 'Those white lights are the anchor lights and correspond to those five radar dots. Josh, you keep a look out while I get the men fed and into their pits. We've a long day ahead of us.'

'Aye aye sir,' Clements gave a half salute and a wide grin.

Hunter went below, showered and dressed in tee shirt and shorts. The night was warm and muggy, typical of the Eastern Mediterranean in early summer. The remainder of the team were already in the main saloon, two of them making sandwiches and one opening tins of soup and pouring them into a single pot. Hunter briefly wondered what a mixture of tomato, mushroom and chicken soup would be like.

'You lot settling in?'

'Sure, boss,' said Don Masters. 'This is some cruise liner. It's got everything we need.'

'Except girls,' said Badonovitch, biting into a thick cheese and pickle sandwich. There was laughter.

'Is there a lifebuoy sentry?' Hunter asked.

'Yes, boss. I've made a roster, half hour each,' replied Masters.

'Good,' Hunter paused and then added. 'Okay, listen up. Get some sleep. We've a busy day ahead of us and it'll be starting in about,' he looked at his watch, 'four hours. We need to get ready to take on the helicopter if we can. If we can't then we'll ditch it and get Burg and the others on board.' He then added, 'Incidentally, I know you don't know any of them but one of the marines was killed tonight. Shot. We'll be burying him later in the day.' The announcement cast a pall over the room as they each contemplated the death in their own way. It was no consolation not to have known the dead man. He was one of them; one of the good guys.

Back on the bridge Hunter studied the chart; the radar and the weather picture for the area he received when he tuned into the right satellite. Macnair was sitting in the captain's chair, his feet on the console in front of him, watching the sea. Whenever a cloud passed across the moon the night was plunged into pitch blackness with not even a light on a passing vessel to suggest there was any life outwith the cocoon of the ship.

Hunter said, 'I think we'd better switch on the navigation lights now, sir.'

'Agreed,' said Macnair.

Hunter found the switchboard and turned on the port and star-board navigation lights, the masthead light and the over-taking light on the stern. Next he checked the LORAN (LOng RAnge Navigation aid), a highly accurate American system for fixing a ship's position, with the sat-nav picture. Both agreed to within ten feet of each other. Satisfied he stifled a yawn and said to the General, 'Sir, why not go below and get some sleep? I'll call you if I need anything. Hiram has already got his head down and will take over from me in a couple of hours.' Hunter read all the dials on the console, satisfied himself that all was running smoothly and checked their speed. Twenty-one knots with a potential six to nine still available. Few ships ever achieved their claimed maximum and even if they did it was usually at the expense of far too much fuel being burnt to justify the extra knot or three.

At that point Macnair's telephone sounded. 'Macnair,' he growled, fatigue making him irritable.

'Sir, it's Schwarzkopf. I have double checked my figures and I can tell you that we'll run out of fuel about forty to fifty minutes before we get to you.'

'Right,' all trace of irritation was gone. 'Give us your exact position and we will head directly for you and not go to the rendezvous. In the meantime throw out anything that's a dead-weight.'

'What about the body?' the pilot asked.

Macnair sighed, aware of his unintended pun. 'He's dead and won't know any better. Weight it down so that it sinks. Tell Napier that in accordance with our policy for all members of TIFAT, a substantial sum will be paid to the dead man's next of kin.' Should anybody ask where the money came from it would be stated that it was paid out of a trust fund set up by Sir David Griffiths, as a token of appreciation. It was the kind of idea and gesture that appealed to Hunter's cousin and he happily went along with the deception.

'Right, sir, I'll do that,' said Schwarzkopf. 'This is my lat and long from the sat-nav. I checked it at Bari and it should be accurate to within a few metres.' He read off the co-ordinates.

'Got it,' said Macnair. 'We'll see if we can get any more speed up ourselves. Our position is,' he read their latitude and longitude to the pilot, 'and our course is?' he looked at Hunter who had been busy with the chart.

'Three three five true.'

'Three three five true,' Macnair repeated. 'Keep us in the picture but if we don't hear from you I'll assume everything is all right.'

'Okay, sir.'

The connection was broken. 'You got that?' he asked Hunter.

'Yes, sir. I'll fiddle with the engines and see if I can reach a compromise of speed and range. From the information Burg passed, I reckon we should meet in about six and a half hours from now. The weather forecast is fine with a westerly breeze backing north-north-west. Which is in our favour.'

'Agreed. Right,' Macnair stood up, 'I'm going below for some sleep. I'll leave you my phone. Call me if you think it's necessary. All navigation and ship handling decisions are yours. Goodnight.'

'Goodnight, sir.'

The dawn found them steaming at a maximum speed of twenty-seven knots towards the helicopter. Hiram Walsh was on the bridge with Don Masters and both men savoured the glorious sunrise as the stars faded and the dark sky slowly turned from indigo to blue.

Below decks the men slept soundly enjoying the calm before what was going to be one hell of a storm.

19

The body had been wrapped in a blanket, weighted with loose equipment and dropped into the sea. The seats had been unscrewed and ditched along with their weapons and ammunition. The first of the 50 gallon drums had been drained dry, the aviation fuel pumped into the main tanks. The drum had then been thrown out.

'How's it looking?' Napier asked Schwarzkopf.

'Like it's a beautiful day. The dawn is only a few minutes away and the wind, what there is of it, favours us.'

'That's not quite what I meant.'

'I know,' Schwarzkopf shrugged. 'Truth is, I don't know. We're certainly a lot lighter and that will help. The wind has given us an extra five knots over the ground and that's also to our advantage. The ship is steaming full speed towards us and . . .'

'I know, that will help. But is it enough?'

'That I don't know. Worried?' he looked at Napier.

The unperturbed gaze that was returned to him looked as though it belonged to someone without a care in the world. The smile confirmed it. 'Nope. I just wondered whether we'd be getting our feet wet, that's all. We still have the liferaft on board. It's an eight man inflatable. If we ditch it we could make all the difference.'

Schwarzkopf thought about it for a few seconds before he nodded. 'We've got lifejackets under the remaining seats. Gas operated. They'll do. Ditch the liferaft. You'll need this.' He reached down the side of his thigh and removed a sharp aviator's knife, handing it to Napier. 'Slash the raft before you shove it overboard. Otherwise it'll inflate and a beacon will set off an air-and-sea search that'll have half of NATO scurrying about the area.'

'Wilco,' said Napier, undoing his seat belt and climbing into the back of the helicopter. Quickly he cut into the strong rubberised felt container and pushed the knife as deeply into the packed liferaft as he could. A few seconds later the starboard door slid open and the liferaft was thrown out. Napier stood watching it tumble through the air until it vanished with a faint splash into the deep blue sea. It rapidly sunk from sight. He stepped back from the wind, slid the door shut and went forward. Tam and Joe were both asleep or at least sat slumped with their eyes shut.

Napier returned to the co-pilot's seat and strapped himself in. 'How much longer have we got to go?'

Schwarzkopf pressed a button on his console computer and replied, 'About two hours give or take a swim.'

'What's this about Eddie's wife getting a million?'

The pilot glanced at Napier but saw only mild interest. 'Nick's family have a huge trust fund. One of us dies our next of kin gets a million. That's all I know.'

'Seems pretty generous to me. Why do they do it?'

'I asked Nick the same question. He was embarrassed by it but he said it was a charitable trust and the trustees had agreed to make the payments whenever it became necessary.'

'Could you finish pumping the avgas over? We can get rid of that last drum then.' Schwarzkopf wiped a weary hand across his face. 'Christ but I'm tired. Even using auto-pilot it's knackering. Is there any more coffee left in the Thermos?'

'Sorry, no. It's bone dry.'

'Sling that overboard as well,' he said with feeling, as though the inanimate object was to blame for being empty.

Napier pumped the av-gas out of the drum and into the fuel tanks. He worked the hose into the corner of the drum after he tilted it, to get the last possible drop out. Once he was satisfied that there was no more, he opened the door and dropped the drum into the water. Back in the cockpit he surveyed the wide expanse of sea. Ships were passing left and right, one or two large enough to land a helicopter on.

'I'll call Nick and get an update on their position,' Napier said.

'I've just done it,' the pilot replied. 'I was waiting to check the fuel to do another calculation.' He looked at the needles showing the fuel remaining in the two tanks and then checked them against the digital readouts which told him in pounds weight precisely how much they had left. 'In theory, we should make it.'

'I hate theories,' said Napier. 'How about in practice?'

'In practice I doubt it. That's why I'm going lower.'

'Why? So that we can land more easily?'

'No, because there's a typical Med pressure inversion taking place and there could just be a better tail wind down there.' He pushed down on the collective and eased the helicopter lower. They dropped past 5,000ft, 4,000ft, 3,000ft, and then Schwarzkopf said, 'I thought so. The tail wind is now at fifteen knots. We're getting the Eastern Mediterranean equivalent of the mistral. The wind is from the north-west and cold but it could make the difference.' He put the numbers into the computer again and updated the fuel remaining. 'We now have a greater margin for error and mishap. But it's still touch and go. It's straight on or straight in.'

'What do you mean?' asked Napier.

'Straight on board or straight into the drink,' was the sobering reply.

The sun was now warm and heating up the cockpit so Schwarzkopf opened an air vent that let in cool fresh air but kept out the noise. He directed the airstream at his face, fighting his fatigue.

'Zulu One this is Mother, over.' The call came over their radio. The callsigns were not internationally recognisable as neither the ship nor the helicopter wished to call attention to themselves.

'This is Zulu One.'

'We have you on radar. You are forty-six miles away and closing fast. ETA fourteen minutes.'

'Roger that,' said Schwarzkopf. He checked the display in front of him. There was no margin for error left. 'I'll only get one try. A second and we'll ditch. Alternatively, we ditch alongside and take a swim.'

'It's a possibility. The General and I discussed that very thing,' said Hunter, 'but we would like to have the helicopter if it's at all possible.'

'That's what I thought,' said Schwarzkopf, his hands busily taking the helicopter out of auto-pilot and once more under his control. 'Where's the wind over the deck?'

'Red two zero.' That meant the wind was coming from twenty degrees to port and was about right for a landing.

'Look ahead,' said Napier.

Schwarzkopf looked out of the canopy at the white ship belching smoke and steaming straight at them. He then looked at the ship's stern. At that point he broke into a stream of profanities in German. In the same breath an engine gave a cough hinting at fuel starvation.

Schwarzkopf's hands flew across the console. He shut down the fuel feed to one engine and opened the transfer valve to suck the last of the av-gas from one tank to the other. Throttling back, he brought the helicopter down to maximum fuel save with the blades moving just fast enough to keep them flying. He had bought them about two minutes' extra flying time. The ship passed beneath the helicopter and a cable to port. He turned after the ship and followed her. At the last moment he lowered the undercarriage, preserving the last teaspoon of fuel that he could.

Normally when making an approach to land on a ship the helicopter travels alongside, hovering just off the deck and to one side. This gives the pilot an opportunity to gauge the effect of the wind across the deck and the relative forward motion of the ship to the helicopter. The landing pad is usually six or eight times bigger than the one in front of Schwarzkopf at that moment and a fully trained flight deck crew should be in attendance should anything go wrong. In normal conditions, the flight deck officer uses two batons, like Ping-Pong bats, red and green to signal the helicopter in. As soon as the helicopter hovers over the right spot he brings both batons down fast and the helicopter lands. After the approach is made and the helicopter is ready to land the pilot watches the flight deck attendant and obeys his instructions. He does not make any movement decisions for himself except to break away should he consider that he is flying into danger or difficulty.

Schwarzkopf had no flight deck attendant for the simple reason that there was nowhere for one to stand even if they had a trained man in the team. It was one skill missing. The task ahead of Schwarzkopf could only be performed by two kinds of pilot – the suicidal kamikaze hell-bent on flames of glory, or the natural born flyer, verging on genius. Macnair had persuaded Schwarzkopf to join TIFAT because he had proven to be the latter. According to his records he was considered one of the top three helicopter pilots in NATO, which meant the world. The thought passed through Schwarzkopf's mind that the one man he knew to have been a better flyer had been Fred "Sweeney" Todd, who had been killed by Habib off the coast of Scotland.

Schwarzkopf drove the helicopter straight in. Like an arrow heading for a target, he compensated for the movement of the ship which was now down to about five knots giving the *Darnah* just enough way-on to keep a steady and true course. Nothing was transmitted to him from the ship for which he was grateful as unnecessary chatter in his earphones right then was the last thing he needed.

The stern grew larger as he moved steadily towards the deck. The engine coughed and the helicopter jerked under his hands. Less than a cable to go and he was heading straight into the after superstructure, the only consoling thought being that when they smashed into it there would be no fuel to burn them alive. Or cremate them if they were already dead.

The helicopter flew within a metre of the superstructure and was half a metre off the deck when Schwarzkopf dragged the cyclic back as hard as he could. As the helicopter came into the hover he pushed the collective down. The helicopter reacted

206

like a galloping stallion when its reins are pulled up hard. It came to a dead stop in the air and dropped down onto its haunches. The three wheeled undercarriage compressed with the force of the landing, and the helicopter bounced precariously. This was a very dangerous moment as the helicopter could literally bounce back into the air and over the side. Schwarzkopf pushed the collective down, pressing the helicopter onto the deck even as the motor began to cough and splutter and fade. Two men suddenly appeared from each side of the superstructure, ducked beneath the still turning rotor-blades and clipped a hooked tackle to each of the two rear wheels. The tackle was roved to advantage, the hauling part of the rope connected to the block attached to the helicopter. Both men sat on the deck and threw their weight backwards. The slack was taken up in the tackle and the helicopter was securely pinned to the deck.

Napier wiped his brow, the only indication of his nervousness, and said in a not quite normal voice, 'Nice landing, Burg.'

Schwarzkopf nodded his head. He was exhausted. He wearily removed his headphones, undid his seat belt and stood up on legs that were not quite steady. He shoved open the cockpit door and lowered himself to the deck.

At that moment the General appeared around the corner and marched towards the pilot, his hand outstretched. 'Magnificent, magnificent.' He shook Schwarzkopf's hand. 'Go below, get some hot food and a drink. We'll re-fuel and get you ready. Flying ops will be at about twenty hundred hours.' He turned to the squat, tough looking man standing to attention. 'At ease, Lt Napier. We don't stand on ceremony here. But you still call me sir.' Macnair smiled to take any sting out of his words. 'I'm sorry about what happened to Lance Corporal Woodstock. However, we've a much greater problem than one death, regrettable though it is. All of you get some food and sleep and come up to the bridge at fourteen hundred hours. I'll brief you then as to what's going on.'

'Thank you, sir. You'd better have these,' Napier handed over

207

the disks, papers and money he had taken from the *Salamander's* safe.

'Thank you. They could prove useful.' With that he about turned and walked forward. TIFAT, he thought, has found three excellent new recruits.

The ship was already heeling to starboard and the speed increasing. The helicopter weighed the stern down but not so much as to make the ship unstable. The added weight had, to a certain extent, been compensated for by ditching the bulky, leather covered chairs and sofas from the ship.

Napier and his men went below decks to find something to eat and to get some sleep. Schwarzkopf saw to the securing of the helicopter to the deck before doing the same. As he walked forward he paused to look at the horizon. It was a clear, beautiful day and the phrase "God's in his heaven and all's right with the world" sprang to mind, before he remembered that millions of people would die unless they could stop a war. He sighed before continuing below.

On the bridge Hunter was sitting in the Captain's chair, a cup of strong, white, sugarless coffee in his hand. He loved being at sea and all that the command of a ship entailed. He missed it and suddenly began to doubt whether his move to TIFAT had been a good one or not. He enjoyed the excitement – the danger – but for how long? What did he really want to do with his life? He sipped the coffee, doubts assailing him. The General stepped onto the bridge from down below and looked at Hunter, somehow aware of Hunter's introspection. 'We all get them, Commander.'

'Sir?' Hunter looked over his shoulder, sliding to his feet, relinquishing the chair to his superior officer.

'You were just pondering your future. How much you enjoy sitting on the bridge of a ship, being in command.'

Hunter smiled and nodded, placing his mug in the holder fixed to the armrest of the chair. He walked to the LORAN console and compared it to the sat-nav read-out before marking the ship's position on the chart. Next, he checked their course and speed and moved the autopilot direction dial two degrees clockwise – to starboard.

'We all have doubts especially if we consider the long term prospects of our careers. I'm at the top of mine and TIFAT will be my last job. Although how long I'll keep it is in the lap of the gods. If this operation turns to rats then I won't be here for long. Indeed, I don't suppose TIFAT will last if that's the case. If we succeed then it may be a different kettle of fish but we have a lot to do to *make* it succeed. And anyway, how far do you want to go with the Navy?'

'It's a fair question, sir, and I've often asked myself that. I suppose the truth is I was already getting a little bored when you came along. I don't want to go through seven or eight years in the hope of promotion to commander, perhaps get passed over and then quit. And let's face it, commander is the first rank of self respect. Also, we all hanker for command of a ship, which is what it's all about. And there are less than forty sea going units which have any command attraction and the competition for those is fierce. My family want me in the Firm and I can get a pretty high-powered job anytime I leave.' He shrugged. 'But I have enough money not to have to work again. I like adventure,' he paused, embarrassed that he had confessed so much. 'I guess I want TIFAT with times like this thrown in.' He gestured around the ship.

Macnair nodded. 'You're one of my most valuable assets on the operational side, along with Hiram. You're focused and you get on with things. All in all you're what TIFAT needs. There are more like you and if you want out you can go anytime you like, I won't try and stop you. But,' he smiled, 'you'll miss us more than we'll miss you.'

Hunter smiled back. 'That's probably true so I'll just get on and enjoy it.'

At that moment the radio broke into life. 'Mother this is Beta 6.'

'Beta 6 this is Mother. How do you read?'

'Loud and clear. ETA overhead thirty minutes.'

'Roger that. Thirty minutes. We'll be ready.'

'Sir, can I leave you to keep watch? I'll get the boats turned out and the men made ready. When this lot arrives we'll have our work cut out storing and prepping the gear.'

209

'Carry on. I've plenty to do as I need to speak to Isobel and David Golightly – if I can contact him. I'm also going to call Ibn ben Saud. As Minister Without Portfolio for Saudi Arabia he has a lot of influence with the ruling family. I may be able to talk enough sense to him that he'll listen and get the attack delayed. Even one day could make all the difference. PACER SKY has just updated information to GCHQ and Isobel has forwarded it to us.' PACER SKY was a satellite-based reconnaissance system that transmits real-time radar, visual and infra-red data. The up-to-the-minute information on enemy troop positions and movements was invaluable to commanders of western forces. 'GCHQ assesses the attack as being only thirty-six hours away. The only force not quite ready is Iran and they're only procrastinating so that they can attack from behind, as we know.' He looked at his watch. 'We're making good progress. It's only just after ten hundred hours. I need to dump this lot,' he waved the pack of information he had been given by Napier, 'on to Isobel. She can sort out the wheat from the chaff and tell us if there's anything important here.' He began getting his laptop and sat-nav phone in tandem to down-load the information on the disks to Isobel.

Hunter went to find Don Masters and to wake up Hiram Walsh. All hands were needed for the next few hours.

Sticking with their decision not to use recognisable callsigns twenty-five minutes later the call come over the radio. 'Mother this is Charlie 4, over.'

'Charlie 4, loud and clear,' replied Hunter once more on the bridge.

'We have you in sight and are descending through fifteen thousand feet. We will hit two five at three cables to starboard and start unloading.'

'Roger that. We're ready.' The Lockheed C-130 Hercules would straighten out at two thousand five hundred feet and start dropping gear six hundred yards to starboard. Hunter reduced speed to less than two knots, giving the ship just sufficient headway to maintain her course.

The "Herky Bird" droned into view and the rear door dropped

open. Almost immediately pellets of equipment fell out and dropped for two thousand feet before the parachutes opened. They snapped open high enough to take the weight so that each pallet hit the sea with scarcely a splash and the automatic inflation gear burst open. They counted them out.

'That's seven, eight, nine. That's the lot,' said Hunter. 'No, hang-on. Another one's just . . .' he paused. 'It's a jumper.'

'What?' Macnair grabbed a pair of binoculars and focused them on the person dangling from the end of the 'chute. 'I might have guessed,' he said, pleased in spite of himself.

'Jim?' Hunter queried.

'Major Carter it is,' said Macnair. 'I told him to stay out of it, but it looks like he's disobeying me.' He looked at Hunter. 'I'm pleased to say.'

'We'll certainly be able to use him,' said Hunter 'we've a lot to get done once we get this lot onboard.'

Already the two lifeboats, port and starboard, were launched and in the water. They chugged across the sea to the nearest pallet and hooked it onto a line already made ready for the purpose. The lifeboat moved over to the next and repeated the hook-up. Each rope was three metres longer than the previous one so that the pallets strung out in a line astern without getting in each other's way.

One of the lifeboats made straight for the parachutist first. When a jump into water has been made it was all too easy to get entangled in parachute shrouds and drown. Carter's feet hit the water and as they did so he hit the release button on his chest. The parachute fell away from him cleanly and as the water rushed over his head the hydrostatic release valve on his inflation vest opened. The vest inflated and he bobbed to the surface. It had been a text-book jump. He grabbed hold of the side of the boat and was immediately lifted in by Badonovitch, the Russian Spetsnaz. 'Thanks, Jan. I'm okay. Let's get those other pallets.'

They headed across the water and hooked onto four pallets, the other five already being dragged back to the *Salamander*. Twenty minutes later all the gear was on board and the ship was back on

course at twenty-five knots and heading for Israel. When Carter
reported to Macnair on the bridge the General was speaking to
the Israeli deputy prime minister.

'David? Where are you?'

'Holed up just north of Gaza. We had a few problems getting
here but nothing we couldn't handle. I'm not sure but I think we
were recognised about half an hour ago, so somebody might be
out looking for us by now. The car's hidden in a cave, as are
we. We can't be seen from the air but ground troops could get
to us easily enough. What is your ETA?'

'Four maybe five hours, David. Sorry, but we can't make
it any sooner than that. Do your best to stay alive. We need
you.'

'I'll do my best. I'll start transponder transmitting in four hours.
I'll use two-two-two giga hertz. Okay?'

'Understood. Two-two-two giga. I'm phoning Ibn ben Saud,
to see if he can get the attack delayed. I've an idea I want to
share with him.'

'Okay,' said Golightly. 'See you soon.' He broke the connection and added, 'I hope,' under his breath.

Macnair's next call was to Ibn ben Saud. Macnair had met
the man briefly when TIFAT had rescued him from Habib on
the west coast of Scotland, saving ben Saud's life. Macnair was
owed and it was time to call in the debt.

'Hullo? Is that Ibn ben Saud? Ah, sir, this is General Malcolm
Macnair from TIFAT.'

'Malcolm, what a pleasant surprise. Though hardly an auspicious
occasion with a war about to start.'

'That's precisely why I'm calling you.'

'I thought it might be. What can I do for you?' The cultured
English was Eton and Oxford.

'I want you to try and postpone the attack for at least twenty-
four hours.'

'What? But . . . but that's impossible,' ben Saud was practically spluttering. 'The attack will take place in less than forty-
eight hours and Israel will be no more.'

'It's a trap. It's you who'll be no more.'

212

'What? What did you say?'

Macnair explained for the next fifteen minutes. When he was finished ben Saud said, 'That's impossible. It can't be.'

'It is and I can prove it. I'm collecting all the information right now. I will also supply all the proof you'll need. I intend e-mailing it to all front line heads of state and as much of the media as possible. The spotlight of publicity could help stop the attack just as easily as any decision taken by the rulers.'

'Yes. Yes, that is so, my friend. I understand. You want me to phone the king and tell him what you have told me. You then wish me to persuade him to contact Assad and the rest of them and try and convince them to postpone the attack until you can produce David Golightly.' He sighed. 'It is a tall order.'

'I know it is. But what if I'm right? Will waiting matter that much?'

'If you put it like that, no. But is there some motive you are not imparting? Are you up to something I don't see?'

'Sir, I assure you I am not. If I am wrong you will have delayed twenty-four hours. Considering the length of time Israel has been a thorn in your collective sides one day won't matter.'

'Perhaps, perhaps not,' Ibn ben Saud paused, thinking. 'At the same time you will send your evidence of this, what shall we call it . . . Conspiracy?'

'As quickly as possible. Sir, millions of lives are not worth gambling with at this stage.'

There was further silence and just as Macnair was thinking the connection had been broken Ibn ben Saud said, 'You are correct. I will make the call right now. What are you doing? You say you are going after Samuel Dayan but when? When can I tell my king that Dayan is either dead or under arrest?'

There was something in the man's tone that sent a warning bell through Macnair. There was nothing he could put his finger on but suddenly the General didn't trust the man on the other end of the phone. 'We will be attacking the rig the day after tomorrow at zero three hundred hours.'

'Good. I will pass that on.' Ibn ben Saud broke the connection.

213

As he put down the phone he smiled and made his call. 'Samuel? It is I, ben Saud. I have some important information for you.' He repeated what he had just learnt.

'Excellent. In that case I will go to the rig today and tomorrow we will prepare for the attack. You have done well, my friend. Soon your family will be ruling in Saudi.' Ibn ben Saud hung up, leant back in his chair and contentedly contemplated the future. He would create a dynasty that would last a thousand years.

20

Macnair frowned at Hunter. 'You heard?'

'Your end, sir. I thought we were attacking to-night.'

'We are. I just didn't trust ben Saud and the way he asked the questions. Perhaps I'm becoming paranoid in my old age. However, there's no harm done, one way or the other. Send somebody down to wake up Schwarzkopf, will you? It's time we had a strategy meeting.'

His phone rang and he picked it up. Before he could say anything he heard Golightly's voice. 'Malcolm? It's David.'

'David? Is everything all right?'

'We're still alive, if that's what you mean. I'll set the transponder whenever you say. All's quiet at present. Helicopters have been criss-crossing for the last few hours obviously searching the area and I guess it's us they are looking for.'

'How's the arm?'

'Bearable. What happened in Italy?'

'They found chemical and bacteriological shells. The Italians are creating a stink right now. Some men were killed and seriously injured but a few are able to talk yet won't. They are all claiming that they knew nothing about the shells or the atropine. But considering how they started the shooting match that doesn't hold much water. It's really irrelevant anyway as the war will start long before the Italians achieve anything. Dayan hasn't even bothered issuing a denial. I suspect he will wait a couple of days and then say yes, they are his, needed for the defence of Israel. The action of a true patriot.'

'Traitor, you mean. When do you plan to extract us?'

'At zero one hundred hours. We're steaming as fast as we can to the area but my pilot wants at least a few minutes' flying time in hand when he gets there – for emergencies. Try and hold out until then.'

'Okay. Ruth is gesturing, I need to go.' Golightly said goodbye and went to the mouth of the cave. He looked at his watch, 23:10 hours. Nearly two hours to go. His daughter touched his arm and pointed. It took a few seconds but then he saw what she was pointing at. Soldiers, spread out, searching. 'What do we do?'

'Run. Can you make it?'

'There's still plenty of life in the old dog yet, daughter dear. Don't fret.'

'Sure there is, papa.' She leaned over and kissed his cheek. 'We stay ahead of them until the 'chopper comes. They'll find this cave soon and the car. I think we had better set a small trap.'

'Ruth. Some of them are kids. Conscripts who don't know why they are here or what they are doing. Innocents.'

Ruth paused as she opened her rucksack. 'I know. That's why we'll bring down the cave entrance before anybody gets in. It may delay them a while.' Quickly she made her preparations while Jacob Mordecai kept a watch at the entrance. It was a cloudless, star-filled night. The moon cast its white glow across a bleak landscape of hard hills, scrubby pasture and small bushes. Irrigation work had started two years earlier and was only beginning to bear fruit as behind them grass of sufficient quantity to support a few sheep was beginning to take hold.

'Ready,' said Ruth. 'Let's go.'

The three of them crept out of the cave and down into a shallow gully that went uphill and further into the wilds. They kept low, aware that it was all too easy to be seen against the backdrop of the night sky. They could hear the soldiers blundering around, the occasional expletive clearly carrying in the still air.

Then a voice said, 'The cave is just ahead. We have it covered. Get ready.'

At that point Ruth pressed the transmitter and a thunderous

roar went up, earth and rocks blown sky high, the entrance to the cave buried under tons of rock.

'I didn't mean to use so much,' she said. 'Explosives have never been my strong point. Come on, while their ears are ringing and they're getting their wits back, we can make some tracks. With luck it'll delay them for a while.' She hoisted her shoulder bag into a more comfortable position and strode out, her long legs eating up the ground. The two men followed behind her, trying to match the cracking pace she was setting. By following a narrow path the terrain was not too difficult or harsh on their feet. But even so, David Golightly was soon trying to get his breath as the toll of the last few days caught up with him. He gritted his teeth and bore it. Even though Ruth was his daughter he wasn't going to admit that he needed her to slow down. He moved his arm, cradling it, the ache beginning to turn to pain. He glanced at his watch. It was only fifteen minutes since the last time he had looked.

'That's all the gear checked and ready, sir,' Hunter reported. Hunter helped himself to a cup of coffee from the machine they had taken from the galley and installed at the back of the bridge. 'I gather we'll be launching in fifteen minutes?'

'Correct. Schwarzkopf has put a fifty gallon drum inside the helicopter. He'll take off half an hour earlier. Which is just as well as David's just off the phone. They're running for it with the army on their heels. He reckons they're maybe ten or fifteen minutes ahead but no more. If they maintain that lead all well and good but it's doubtful they'll be able to do so. David's hurt, relatively unfit for what he's doing and getting on in years. So we need to move fast. I've told the pilot that he's to take the BLU-96 and drop it behind the troops to encourage them to keep their heads down. He's then to go straight in. I don't want any more Israeli casualties if we can help it but the safety of David Golightly is paramount. It is above all other considerations. I need him alive for what we have to do.' The BLU-96 is a fuel-air explosive bomb that disperses oil into the air. It is many times more powerful than a conventional bomb of a similar size due to the fact that it does

217

not carry its own chemical oxidisers. Hunter was surprised that they had one but thought it better not to ask how Carter had acquired it. The BLU-96 would certainly be a great inducement for any ground troops to stay low.

Hunter checked the ship's position. 'We're on time for our part of the operation,' he said.

'Agreed. You'll launch ten miles off shore. We'll keep going.' The plan was to slow down for a few minutes, launch the chariots and then continue along the coast. If a radar watch was being kept from the rig the ship's blip would be seen moving serenely at ten knots. Slowing down for two or three minutes would not be noticeable – they hoped.

'I've received the information from Isobel that Napier collected. It was encrypted but not difficult to crack,' said Macnair, pacing the deck, looking out of each window, watching the white, green and red lights of various ships passing a few miles away, going in all directions. 'They contained further proof, if further proof was needed, of Dayan's machinations. However there was other information which may turn out to be valuable. The whereabouts of a second base at a place called Quneitra.'

'Where's that?' Hunter asked, picking up a pair of binoculars and scanning the dark night.

'The Golan. On the border with Syria and a short hop from Lebanon. Isobel is collating as much information about the place as she can. She's also got Sarah Fleeting sending a satellite to take pictures. I need to know everything I can about Dayan. We mustn't lose him.' Macnair hit his fist into his hand for emphasis. 'Are the teams ready?'

'Yes sir. We've rigged jury-rigs either side for all six chariots. We'll have them in the water within a minute of stopping and you can be on your way. We've checked the communications and sat-nav gear and all six sets are working perfectly. The magnets have been stowed as well as the weapons. So, yes sir, we're ready.'

Macnair nodded. 'Good luck, Nick. We want that installation destroyed and Dayan killed. By the time you do that David and I should have been in contact with the front line states and, I hope, convinced them that Israel is not to blame. More to the point,

I want to convince them that there is only one megalomaniac working with the regime in Iran. With Dayan dead we should be able to stop the war and get things back to normal.'

'Maybe the Israelis don't want normal,' said Hunter.

Macnair nodded. 'I've had the same thought. However, whatever the solution to Israel's problems, it isn't this. Get ready. Launch is ten minutes away. Remember, we also want information. It's clear that this whole affair has not been planned and implemented by one man although I may be able to persuade Israel's enemies that it has. No, it's taken an international conspiracy to allow things to get this far. I want the names of the other co-conspirators.'

'Understood, sir,' said Hunter, leaving the bridge.

Jim Carter was standing on the starboard side of the bow, a chariot hanging from a jury-rigged crane, ready for launch. 'I've re-checked the gear,' he greeted Hunter, 'and everything works as it should. The new batteries should last three times as long so there's plenty of power. I've checked the sat-nav displays and aerials but there's no substitute for trailing through the water to see if they work properly. They're all fully armed and the electro-magnets all work. That's about it.'

'Thanks, Jim. We'll be going in five minutes. Okay, Jan?' Hunter asked Badonovitch.

The Russian smiled. 'Sure, boss. Ready when you are.'

'Standby for launch,' Macnair announced over the tannoy system. 'Slowing down now.' The ship's engines were put into reverse and the way was coming off rapidly. At two knots Macnair put the engines into forward and the ship drifted along at launch speed. The teams worked quickly, lowering the chariots, donning diving masks and slipping into the water. On each of the chariots the same procedures were being followed. The carrying straps were being unhooked, engines buzzing into life and electronic consoles were switched on.

Hunter spoke into his throat mike. 'Alpha clear.' He was teamed with Badonovitch.

'Beta clear.' That was Napier and Tam Wilkinson, a Special Boats Service Sergeant.

'Charlie clear,' said Colonel Hiram B. Walsh, teamed with David Hughes.

'Delta clear.' That was Don Masters and Peter Weir.

'Echo clear,' said Joshua Clements, teamed with Sam McReady.

'Foxtrot clear,' said Alexander Dupois, a French lieutenant from the Foreign Legion Parachutists, teamed with Doug Tanner, an American SEAL.

'Mother, you can go now,' said Hunter. The twelve men watched as the ship increased speed and carried on its way, leaving them to bob about in the swell, uncomfortable until they were submerged.

The divers sat on the chariots as though on motorbikes. The diver in front controlled the depth, speed and course. The man behind looked after the communications, their position and monitored the engine's dials. Steering a chariot at a set depth and on a fixed course, heading for a particular target, mile after mile is a demanding task requiring dedicated effort and months of training. The six lead divers were experts.

'All set? Over,' said Hunter.

The reports came in, one by one. Hunter opened up the throttle and pushed the steering wheel forward. The chariot glided beneath the surface of the water with barely a ripple. The electric motor changed pitch as the depth increased and the two contra-rotating screws bit into the water and pushed the speed up to five knots. A screen pushed the water to either side making the whole more streamlined than if the diver sat without protection. At eight metres Hunter levelled off and set course for the rig. It was a two hour journey. The remainder of the chariots formed a diamond, twenty metres apart, the dark keeping them hidden from each other.

Out of the back of each chariot a thin, tough, nylon coated thread of copper floated to the surface, held up by a cleverly designed colourless piece of plastic. This was an aerial that received and transmitted different types of data depending on what the second diver asked for on his console display. It enabled contact between the other chariots and back to the ship. It received sat-nav signals that told them precisely where they were and the course and distance to go to their target. On the display in front of them, each diver could see the formation of the chariots and watch that each one stayed on station. As they were breathing pure oxygen through re-breather sets which scrubbed the carbon dioxide out of the exhaled gas, no tell-tale bubbles escaped to give away their whereabouts. The only problem when using pure oxygen is that at depths below ten metres or two bars of pressure, the oxygen becomes toxic and can be fatal. Hence the requirement to travel at a specific depth. Although the second diver controlled the console for the ancillary equipment, the console and switches were duplicated for the lead diver in case the other man was no longer able to carry out his duties.

Hunter felt a surge of well-being course through him, at odds with the challenge ahead, as he glanced at the console and checked the other five chariots. Speed through the water was deceptive as trillions of minuscule phosphorescent plankton swept past suggesting they were travelling far faster than reality. He checked his communications with Macnair, received a "loud and clear", and settled down to enjoy the ride. The distance to go on the digital readout was eight miles and closing.

Burghard Schwarzkopf started the engines, raised a thumb to the man sitting next to him and threw the helicopter off the ship backwards. The engines screamed as he twisted the throttle and manoeuvred away from the ship. With only inches to spare between the tips of the rotors and the ship's superstructure it had been the only way to get airborne. He would not be landing back on board when they returned.

'I'm glad you're with me, Joe,' Schwarzkopf said into his microphone. 'I gather you aren't one of us?'

'If you mean TIFAT, sir, that's correct. However,' lance-corporal Joe Spalding of the Special Boats Service grinned, 'from what I've seen I think I'll put in for a transfer.'

The pilot glanced out the corner of his eye and returned the grin. 'Once you're in you won't want to leave. The General looks after his men and we've access to the best equipment in the world – private or military. It's some operation, I can tell you and if things go on the way they are, special services

221

forces from all over the world will be queuing up to join. So get in while you can.'

Spalding looked slightly despondent. 'I may not be good enough,' he said doubtfully.

'The General must think so otherwise you wouldn't be here. We've an hour and forty minutes to go before we start searching for the transponder. In the meantime can you give all the weapons one last check and do a test firing out of each door?'

'Sure, no problem.' Spalding undid his seat belt and clambered into the main cabin. On each side of the helicopter was mounted a GPMG. Spalding checked the ammunition belts, drew back the bolt on one of the guns, let it go, pushed the safety off and test fired out the door. He did the same with the second gun. Next he checked the submachine guns and pistols including an RPG, rocket propelled grenade launcher, used against tanks by the infantry. It did not take long before he was re-seated next to the pilot.

'All okay.'

'Good. I've checked the Sea Rays as best I can. All systems are go up to but short of firing so we've done all we can. Now all that's needed is for us to enjoy the ride.' The Sea Ray is a small, inexpensive air-launched antiship missile carried by helicopters. Carter had supervised their installation giving Schwarzkopf six missiles. At a push they could be used air-to-air. They had eighty kilometres left to go. The moon was bathing the water in a clear light in a cloudless sky and barely a ripple of wind ruffled the surface. Flying at fifteen thousand feet over open sea nobody took any notice of them and wouldn't until they were within ten kilometres of Israel. Being one of the most closely guarded borders in the world Schwarzkopf knew that speed and stealth were of the essence; either that or a big bluff.

The helicopter flew smoothly over the water, passing through the night like a great bat, its lights extinguished, the noise of the engines and rotors lost long before anybody on the surface could hear them. If anyone chose to look up and happened to glance in the right direction they would have seen the flickering of stars as the helicopter passed overhead.

Luck was with them that night. At ten kilometres from the coast Schwarzkopf took the helicopter down to twenty feet and zoomed in at wave-top height. Only an hour earlier the radar which covered that section of the border went on the blink. It transmitted only intermittently and the picture was badly deteriorated. In view of the high tension and level of alertness gripping the Israelis at that time, the two men in the helicopter did not know how lucky they were. The Israelis were in the mood to shoot first and ask questions later if anything unauthorised approached their country. Even if the attack was coming from the west the Israelis never allowed their judgement to influence their paranoia.

Twenty minutes later Schwarzkopf switched on the transceiver. The signal he was receiving was automatically fed into a sat-nav display that showed him where David Golightly was hiding. He knew his distance to go, heading and time of arrival. It also told him that Golightly was on the move.

David Golightly, his daughter and Jacob Mordecai were running for their lives. Although to term their tired plodding across rough terrain as running was a misnomer. Golightly's arm was aching, his body craved rest and if it hadn't been for the support of Ruth he would have collapsed. His face was ashen, his breath a rasping gasp as he forced one foot in front of the other. Ruth had her father's arm across her slim body and was supporting half his weight as she urged him along. She kept going but in her heart she knew it was hopeless. Rescue would not – could not – come in time. She was going through the motions, determined not to give up. She had her father's grit and determination, but while part of her mind kept them going another part grappled with a problem that was nagging her. How on earth had the troops come after them so quickly and so unerringly?

Mordecai was covering their backs, three or four paces behind, easily keeping up with father and daughter. They were climbing steadily now, a gentle strength-sapping incline that would force them to stop sooner rather than later. At that point a triple bleep sounded and Golightly seemed to gain strength.

'That's the signal from the helicopter. They're closing fast. Must be less than ten minutes away, otherwise I wouldn't have received the signal. Thank God for Macnair. The helicopter is half an hour early.'

'There's a hillock just ahead,' said Ruth. 'It looks steep this side but there may be a way up on the other side. Papa, we must get you out. That's the priority. Go around and try and climb to the top. The helicopter can pick you up from there. We'll see you get away, cover you, if need be, and then escape ourselves.'

'I don't think that's such a good idea,' said Mordecai. 'If we stick together we can all get out.'

They had reached the bottom of the steep incline and stumbled over rocks and dirt around to the other side to find an incline of forty-five degrees and less. It was just possible they could scramble up.

Ruth put her hand in her pocket as she turned to look at Mordecai. 'No, let my father go up. The helicopter can pick him up from there and get him away. We can then move fast out of the area and fall back on our covers.'

Mordecai pulled the catch back on the revolver he drew from his waist and said, 'Sorry, but I can't let you do that.'

'That's what's been bothering me,' Ruth said, as Golightly straightened in shock. 'They came too fast. You've been telling them where we are. Transmitting a signal of some sort. Why didn't you stop us before?'

'You weren't with me at the roadblocks so I had to go along with you. Besides, I've no intention of dying, just yet. I needed you exhausted and off guard so that I could have you taken alive, if possible. If not, you were to be killed. I've got you alive. The others will be here any minute and all is well.'

'Nice one,' said Ruth. 'So who are you really working for?'

'I told you. The CIA. We support Dayan and what he's doing. That's one of the reasons he's come so far so quickly.'

Both Ruth and David Golightly stood rooted to the spot, shocked to their cores at what they had heard. They heard a voice shouting in the distance and Mordecai turned his head a fraction to reply. As he did so Ruth shot him between the eyes.

'Papa, you heard. It is imperative you get away.' She was already kneeling by the body, searching the pockets. She found what she was looking for, stood up and kissed her father's cheek. 'They'll come after me. Now go. Climb the hill and wait for the helicopter. I can get away without you.'

Before Golightly could protest Ruth turned on her heels and began to run. She moved with the grace and fluidity of a gazelle. Her father stood and watched her go, his heart heavy, knowing she was right. He felt ashamed that she was taking such a risk to save him. It wasn't right. It wasn't the order of things. He was the protector. It was his sacred task and honourable duty to look after his daughter. He started up the hillock, a shrunken figure, shame and helplessness grinding him down. He heard more shouts and scrambled faster, on his knees and using his good arm. He prayed that nobody would stumble on to the body of Mordecai. The implications of what had been told to them began to take hold of him and now, along with his other feelings, came despair. Was it a rogue CIA action or was it sanctioned? He needed answers, desperately.

Shots suddenly sounded, loud in the still air and he paused, almost at the summit, his breath rasping into his lungs, his heart pounding from exertion and fear, not for him but for his daughter. He knew that she was a superb athlete, capable of running a marathon if need be. She was tough, resourceful and fearless and, before joining Mossad, had been selected to represent Israel in handgun and rifle shooting at the Olympic games. Even so, he thought, she was a woman with trained troops after her.

He reached the summit and as he did so he heard the noise of the helicopter. He fumbled in his pocket for the transponder and pressed the transmit button twice followed by a further three times. It told the pilot that he was alone for now but that the enemy was in the vicinity. Suddenly the helicopter was coming straight at him. Golightly took out a torch and flashed it at the incoming helicopter. The hillock he was standing on was not big enough to allow the helicopter to land and it hovered next to Golightly. The door was open and a figure was yelling at him to hurry. He darted across to the machine and tried to climb on

225

board. A strong hand grabbed his shoulders and heaved him in unceremoniously. The helicopter took off like an express lift, dodging the pinpricks of light that came from the barrels of guns shooting in their direction.

The deputy prime minister lurched to his feet and staggered to the cockpit. 'My daughter,' he shouted. 'She's down there. They're after her. Can we give her some help?'

Schwarzkopf was already wheeling the helicopter to starboard and picking up speed to get out of the area and back to safely, as he had been instructed. 'We've got to get you back,' he shouted. 'The General said at all costs we must get you to the ship if we're to stop the war.'

'I know, I understand. But she's my daughter. She's risked everything to get me out. Please, can you do something to delay the troops who are chasing her?'

Schwarzkopf thought for a second and then switched his radar to heat imaging. Clearly on the screen tiny dots could be seen, strung out, heading in one direction. Three hundred metres ahead of them was a single running figure.

'Do you think that's her?' Schwarzkopf shouted, pointing.

'It must be,' was the reply.

'Okay. Let's see what we can do.' Schwarzkopf turned the helicopter, checked his height and the trajectory setting and released the BLU-96. He then swung the helicopter to port and thrust the cyclic fully forward, the throttle open wide. As the helicopter accelerated past 100 knots there was an almighty explosion behind and the fuel oil incinerated the area. The white hot flare blocked out the radar screen for a few seconds and then the picture returned. Schwarzkopf adjusted the set and said, 'Only one person moving. That do you?'

Golightly sagged in shock and relief. 'My God. I didn't mean . . . I mean. Oh God.'

'Look, Mr Golightly, I have to get you back. I was told at all costs. The lives of a few do not and General Macnair repeated, do *not*, count for a jot against what may happen in a few days. I don't have enough fuel to hang around and get us back to the ship. If that's your daughter, she's safe,'

Schwarzkopf paused and added. 'We can go back for her. We've enough . . .'

The words were barely out of his mouth when a jet thundered across the nose of the helicopter. It was a Hawker Hunter, a ground-attack aircraft obsolete in Europe but still in active service across the third world.

On the Guard frequency came the heavily accented English order, 'Identify yourself this instant or be shot down.'

'Shit! Where did that come from?' Schwarzkopf asked rhetorically. He recognised the aircraft and knew it carried missiles as well as machine guns mounted in the wings. The helicopter was no match for it unless it could go where a jet couldn't.

Another order was passed, this time in Ivrit. 'Mr Golightly, can you talk to him? Bluff him? Get him to leave us alone?'

'I can try.'

'Hurry up,' Schwarzkopf ripped off his headphones and handed them over. 'Press that button to transmit.'

'Aircraft this is helicopter, what do you want?' Golightly asked nervously, speaking English.

The aircraft had moved away, turned and was lining up to come back at them. The intention to attack was obvious. At that moment the warning system on the console started to bleep and Schwarzkopf made ready to fire his own missiles, aware that Sea Rays were not a very clever option to use against a jet aircraft. He gave instructions to Joe Spalding.

The pilot of the aircraft spoke Ivrit. 'Who are you and what are you doing here?'

Speaking Ivrit, Golightly bluffed, 'We . . . we are from Gaza. We are returning there now. We had the idea to come and fly here in the moonlight.' Then he had some inspiration. 'My girlfriend wanted to fly here. We are doing no wrong.'

The aircraft was flying steadily towards them, the attack radar still locked on them. If the bleeping grew any faster then a missile would be on its way and there would be nothing Schwarzkopf could do about it except head straight down for the ground and pray.

227

The bleeping wasn't changing. It looked as though they might be getting away with it.

'We detected an explosion in the area. Did you see anything? Over.'

'No, no, nothing,' Golightly said. 'We wish to return to Gaza, you can follow if you desire.'

'I have better things to do,' the aircraft pilot's voice was suddenly young and excited. 'There will be a war soon.'

'Yes, I know. Now please, can we go?'

The aircraft had closed to a hundred metres and was circling the helicopter like a huge bird of prey.

'He's unsure what to do,' Golightly said to Schwarzkopf who had put on a second pair of headphones.

Both men heard the pilot on open voice net say, 'Control, it is a helicopter from Gaza. I believe there was an explosion in the area but can't see anything. What should I do about the helicopter?'

'Shoot it down and RTB.'

Schwarzkopf acted first. The pilot was still absorbing his orders to shoot and return to base when Schwarzkopf yelled over his shoulder, 'Fire, Joe!'

Spalding slid open the doorway, aimed and began firing the GPMG. Schwarzkopf turned the helicopter keeping the aircraft on his port beam, giving Spalding as stable a platform as possible. Luck played as great a part as skill. The GPMG fired at a rate of 750 rounds a minute and was belt fed. It is normally fired in short bursts to prevent over-heating, wasting ammunition, and more to the point, there was danger of using up all the ammunition too quickly. In this case Spalding had his instructions. He held the trigger down while the rounds of ammunition spat out the end of the barrel in a non-stop stream of lethal metal.

He moved the gun up and down a few degrees not attempting to aim it steadily at the aircraft but keeping the gun pointed in the middle of the target. The rate of fire was such that the bullets smashed into the side of the aircraft, tattooing a pattern along the fuselage from top to bottom. Spalding kept firing even as the aircraft appeared to stand still for a second. Amazingly, the plane broke in half and dropped from the sky. It was too low for the pilot to even think about bailing out and he had only said MAYDAY once when the plane hit the ground and blew up.

Schwarzkopf was already heading east, back to the ship, when Spalding climbed into the seat next to him. David Golightly stood like a statue, gripping the back of the pilot's seat, his mind in a daze. So much death already, he said to himself and it hasn't even started yet.

Ruth had been thrown to the ground by the force of the explosion. The blast of hot air had past over her like a dragon's breath and left her winded. She sat up, stretched her arms and legs, felt herself for any damage and looked back. Nobody appeared to be coming after her. She staggered to her feet and looked up at the sky in time to see the jet arrive. She watched the interchange and the explosion before turning her back and walking rapidly south. She urgently needed transport. If Samuel Dayan was not on the oil rig he would be at The Golan. She had made up her mind that she would have to stop him at whatever the cost. It was time to re-establish herself as Ruth Mazen, executive aide to Dayan.

The helicopter escaped to sea without further mishap. Schwarzkopf reported to Macnair and they exchanged positions. They were still five miles apart when the helicopter coughed and Schwarzkopf switched off one engine. They slowly dropped from the sky and landed on the sea. The automatic inflation gear failed to work and the helicopter began to sink.

21

'Foxtrot this is Alpha, any problems?'

'Affirmative, boss,' Tanner replied. 'We're losing power.'

Hunter looked at the screens in front of him and did a quick mental calculation. Twenty minutes to go, power for fifty-five or sixty minutes left. 'Close on Echo and tow for ten minutes.'

'Roger, boss.'

Hunter watched as Foxtrot and Echo merged into one blob. He knew that they would be passing a tow-line to hook onto the nose eye. The blobs separated slightly and returned to the formation, easily keeping up with the remainder. The only problem was that the batteries of Echo would be draining more quickly. 'Delta, take over in five.'

'Roger, boss.'

They piggy-backed three times, keeping to the planned estimated time of arrival. 'All hold,' Hunter ordered. The formation came to a hover and Hunter moved slowly upwards until he was only a metre and a half below the surface. 'Jan, take control.'

'I have control,' Badonovitch replied.

Hunter pressed a button on his console and the latest modification to the chariots appeared – a periscope as thick as a car aerial with night-intensifier optics that turned the world bright blue. Other colours weren't masked as they were with the old fashioned green night-goggles shown on spy films. With the new optics it took only a little practice to learn to distinguish other shades and colours.

He adjusted the controls and the top section of the periscope turned freely. This enabled the user to get an all round view without turning the chariot. There were two contacts as he expected. The rig and its stand-by vessel, the latter a legal requirement the world over – a safety boat in case of emergencies, to help fight fires or evacuate the rig crew if necessary. In this case it was assumed that the boat was also being used for protection.

He spent a few seconds examining the rig. It was as they had been shown on the plans Isobel had acquired. An old American construction from the Sedneth Corporation, it had four main legs, a helicopter pad and a drilling platform and stack. Hunter increased the magnification and minutely examined the rig. Apart from the preponderance of armed guards it was quiet enough. He was finally satisfied, and pressed the button to slide the periscope home. 'Heads up,' he said into his microphone. 'I counted twelve guards on watch which probably means a heavy contingent inside. The rescue vessel is about half a mile away so we need to go up the inside of the legs. You know what to do. Good luck and move in.'

There were no acknowledgements, it would be a waste of breath. Each pilot opened up his throttle and the chariots moved slowly forward. Within a few minutes they were under the rig, in deep shadow, invisible to any eyes prying in their direction. They surfaced in the middle, twelve dark figures astride floating bombs with enough explosive power to blast half a dozen rigs into oblivion. Their diving masks were the latest in high-tech equipment. A flick of a switch on the side of the goggles and they immediately became light intensifiers. Again, unlike the green goggles these reacted immediately should light flare up. Whereas the older type left you blinded for a second or two, these new goggles had a micro-chip which worked at the first hint of light and compensated for the change even before the user's eyes realised anything was happening. Carter had bought them at an arms bazaar in the Far East only weeks earlier.

The swell of the sea approaching the land was magnified within the confines of the structure and was uncomfortable to ride on. The chariots moved across the water to each of the legs, two chariots to two legs and one to each of the others. They sank to relative calm four metres beneath the surface. Each man slipped out of his seat and began to work.

Hunter swam up to the rig leg and felt its surface. As expected, it was encrusted with tiny molluscs and other sea organisms that meant a poor surface for the magnets to grip. He removed a knife from the sheath strapped to his right leg and quickly scraped the surface clean.

While he was doing that, Badonovitch had used a spring loaded hook to fix a rope to the eye on the bow of the chariot and to swim around the rig leg and back. He tied off the end of the rope ensuring that the chariot could not drift away. Next he dropped a weight connected to strong thin nylon from the stern of the chariot onto the sea bed. It was self tensioning and held the chariot horizontal.

Hunter undid the catches on the aft containers and opened the cover. He lifted out a specially moulded plastic coated electro-magnet and strapped it to his left knee. Later he would strap another magnet to his hand. When he pressed a button on the side of the hand-held magnet, powerful micro-batteries operated the magnet. His right knee and left hand magnets were connected by a tough, thin wire and operated simultaneously. He strapped a further magnet to his right knee. The two hand magnets he clipped to his waist. It only took a few minutes to unload the remainder of the equipment which he hung from a further magnet he fitted to the rig. To this he clipped a wire reel and attached it to his belt. As he moved, the wire on the reel paid out behind him.

'Alpha One ready,' he said into his throat-mike.

Within a few seconds he had acknowledgement from the whole team and swam upwards. Heads bobbed to the surface. Four of the men remained submerged, busily setting explosives and detonators around the legs. The remaining eight men shucked their diving gear and pressed an electro-magnet onto the rig, clipping the gear to the magnet, leaving it ready for immediate use. It was their emergency route off the rig.

The swell was bobbing them up and down, a dangerous place to be, and so they moved with a sense of urgency. Hunter unclipped the magnets from his waist and slipped the Velcroed straps over his hands. Reaching as far as he could above his head with both hands, he tucked his knees up to his chin and pressed the buttons on either side of the electro-magnets. He stuck to the rig like a limpet, the swell no longer moving him up and down. Straightening his legs he lifted his body out of the water. He let go the button on his left hand and immediately the magnet stopped operating and he was able to move his left hand and right leg up the rig. He repeated the process with the right electro-magnet and he began to crawl upwards. Some of the men preferred to move their left hand and leg and then their right while others preferred Hunter's method. The team had practised this on many occasions and they went up the near vertical sides as easily as though they were taking a walk across a Scottish glen. Sixty feet above the sea Hunter reached the first platform. His breathing was normal, his senses heightened, exhilaration coursing through him.

'Alpha One in place,' he whispered. Acknowledgement followed quickly, each man having reached a platform. Hunter removed the electro-magnets from his knees and hands, felt behind him, unclipped the reel from his belt and unfolded the winding handle. The reel was four inches in diameter and was driven by a powerful battery operated motor. He pressed a button and sent a signal down the line. The magnet holding the packages to the rig switched off and the equipment fell free. Pressing another switch, he gripped the reel tightly and let it haul the packages up to him. Should the battery fail, the handle could be used instead. Within moments the packages were in his hands and he began to open and assemble his equipment. When he was finished he undid the zip on his dry suit that stretched across his chest and pulled the rubber neck-seal over his head. He quickly removed the suit and left it rolled up and ready to be used again should the need arise. He hoped that it wouldn't.

Hunter, like the remainder of the team, was dressed in a dark grey, lightweight cotton combat suit that was comfortable to wear and allowed easy movement. It was similar to the outfit worn by Japanese *Ninja*, the martial arts experts whose history of clandestine operations stretched back a thousand years. Hunter slipped on a pair of thin cotton gloves and a balaclava. From one of the packages he took grey soft soled canvas shoes that laced up over his ankles. As the moon set and the night turned dark, two hours before the dawn, he was like a ghost as he finished his preparations.

A faint slithering sound made him look down as Badonovitch appeared and Hunter helped him onto the platform. 'Okay?'

'Yes, boss. The charges are set and the chariot's ready to go. I've checked the batteries and guess it'll take us a mile or so.'

'That's what we expected. Let's hope it won't come to that.'

While they spoke Hunter was helping Badonovitch to get his equipment ready. Within minutes they were finished.

Hunter whispered into his throat mike. 'Alpha ready,' speaking for himself, Alpha One and Badonovitch as Alpha Two. The other charioteers used the same system.

Acknowledgement came over the radios and the team moved cautiously up the ladders that would take them to the main deck. The weapons they carried were coated in a thin rubberoid material that prevented any loose clinking and any untoward noise. Each man carried a silenced revolver of his own choice along with a silenced Heckler and Kock G11, undoubtedly one of the most peculiar looking guns ever made. In production in Germany for one year from 1989–1990, it fired a special caseless cartridge, a block of explosive with a bullet buried in it. The firing mechanism lay inside a plastic casing and the recoil varied with the type of fire selected. The magazine held 50 rounds and was ideal for their purpose. The safety catch, on the left side above the trigger had four positions. Rear ('S') position was safe; forward one notch ('1') single shots; forward two notches ('3') three-round bursts; fully forward ('50') full automatic. There was no barrel as the whole gun was a piece of plastic 750mm long by 112mm deep by 50mm wide. In the middle, sticking out, was the grip and trigger and sitting on the top was a superb sighting mechanism. Although odd looking, it was comfortable to use and shot well. It delivered its three round bursts at a rate of 2,000 rounds per minute and for close work, like the team expected that night, it always hit the target. The built in silencer was reckoned to be the most efficient in the world.

Both McReady and Weir also had specially manufactured sniper rifles, each gun made to fit the build and desires of the shooter. Either man would have been a contender for a gold medal at Bisley, the toughest shooting competition in the world.

Like spectres the team rose from the depths. The first shot was fired by McReady who killed a guard standing by the edge of the helicopter pad, urinating. The head shot threw the body into the water, the splash not even reaching back to anybody on the rig. Weir killed a man who was standing on the other side of the pad next to the helicopter, an old Wessex Mk1. He fell with a clatter against the side of the helicopter but again the noise drew nobody's attention.

Walsh and Hughes climbed to the next deck, where the derrick was to be found and they each shot a guard at close quarters.

Napier and Wilkinson hid behind an oil drum. The two men approaching them were carefree, nonchalant, not expecting trouble. At less than a metre, Napier and Wilkinson stood up and fired three rounds into each of their targets. The bullets smashed both men backwards onto the deck, their guns clanging loudly, metal on metal.

The team froze and waited, listening; nothing. Like the others, their bodies were dropped unceremoniously into the sea.

Joshua Clements stood still, his grey clad body invisible amongst the drilling paraphernalia littering the deck. A guard sauntered past him, less than half a metre away. The specially blackened, two edged knife favoured by the SAS was as invisible as the man holding it. Clements took a pace forward, clamped a hand over the man's mouth and thrust the knife into his heart. He held the body up by tucking his arm under the chin, shuffled the two further paces to the deck edge and dropped the body into the water.

Hunter and Badonovitch killed their targets just as easily and quietly.

Dupois and Tanner had the most trouble. The two men they had targeted had unexpectedly gone inside the rig. After a few minutes they re-appeared, each carrying a cup and in the still of the night the smell of coffee wafted across the deck. The two guards sat straddling a pipe, facing each other, talking softly. They showed only their heads and as each man bent forward to take a sip of coffee there was always the likelihood of missing the target. Dupois touched Tanner on the sleeve and indicated his intention. Tanner nodded and started carefully across the deck while Dupois walked towards the two men, knowing he was hidden in the gloom of the drill stack behind him. Tanner would have to cross a lit section of the deck to get a clear shot and although the two guards were drinking, each man had a rifle lying across his knees. Something was noticed by one of the men and he strained his eyes, looking directly at Dupois. He frowned and said something to the man opposite him who looked over his shoulder. Each man thought he was seeing a ghost as Dupois shimmied into sight. They sprang to their feet, terrified for a second or two by the grey apparition walking towards them. Tanner stepped across the light and fired two bursts, one into each. Dupois followed with a single head shot into both although the shots were superfluous. They threw both bodies into the sea and reported to Hunter. The upper-deck was theirs.

At that instant the searchlight on the rescue vessel came on and bathed the rig with half a million candles of white light. Simultaneously a klaxon sounded. All hell broke loose.

22

The helicopter settled quickly in the water and the three men barely had time to get out before it vanished beneath the sea. Schwarzkopf and Spalding were wearing aviator's life-jackets, thin tubes of cloth around their necks. Each man pulled a rip-cord and their jackets inflated automatically, tearing apart the Velcro fastenings. Schwarzkopf took David Golightly's good arm while Spalding held his belt, supporting him while they waited for the ship to appear. In spite of the fact that they were in the Mediterranean the water soon began to feel cold although it was neither numbing nor debilitating like the waters of the North Sea at that time of year. The sea splashed their faces, salty and disagreeable, a nuisance rather than a danger. Schwarzkopf's automatic alarm was set to a special frequency monitored only by the ship. It also acted as a homing beacon and twenty minutes after hitting the water the ship came in sight.

A boat was launched and the three men watched it approach. They were hauled into the dry, thankful to be rescued. As the boat went alongside the ship Macnair appeared, leant down and called, 'Are you all right, David?'

'Yes,' Golightly said weakly and then repeated himself more strongly. 'Yes, I'm fine. Thanks to you and your men. Is everything ready?' As the boat reached deck level Macnair offered his hand and helped the Deputy Prime Minister off the boat.

'Just about. I've spoken to London and Washington and they've agreed it's worth a try. My logistics officer is setting up the CNN link even now. I'll take you below for a shower and change. We've a lot to discuss and little time to do it in.' Macnair appeared to have forgotten Schwarzkopf and Spalding but suddenly paused and looked over his shoulder. 'Well done, you two. Get changed and get something to eat. We're going in, full charge, in about an hour.'

'Aye, aye, sir,' said Schwarzkopf, wearily. What was that English saying? No rest for the wicked.

Macnair led Golightly below to the stateroom. It was plushly decorated, a deep-pile carpet covered the deck, the bulkheads were lined with rosewood and the green leather furniture looked invitingly comfortable. In one corner was a well-stocked bar and in another a door led to an en-suite bedroom. The stateroom covered the width of the ship and would have done royalty proud.

'Go in there,' Macnair indicated the door to the bedroom, 'and put on the robe. Throw out your clothes and I'll get them dried.'

Golightly did as he was bid and reappeared a few minutes later.

'Can I get you anything? A drink? Coffee?' Macnair indicated the freshly made coffee percolating.

'Coffee please. I'll take a shower and have a shave and try and make myself look respectable,' said Golightly.

Macnair, in the act of pouring the coffee, looked at the other man and frowned. 'That had been my idea but looking at you I think it would be better not to do that. We'll broadcast you as you are. Chased across Israel, barely escaping with your life, desperate to stop a war that will kill millions. Your clothes will be back in twenty minutes or so, dry but rumpled.'

David Golightly took the proffered cup of black coffee and added three spoons of sugar, stirring thoughtfully. 'You know, Malcolm, that might not be such a bad idea. Make it appear more dramatic, more, what? Urgent?'

Macnair nodded. 'Yes. We must impress the urgency of the situation on them in every way we can. We've only just picked you up from a downed helicopter and whisked you in to do

238

the broadcast before it's too late. To save the lives of women and children, mothers and fathers, brothers and sisters, family and friends. David, you must emphasise the sheer waste, the futility. We have to appeal to their egos while at the same time making it clear that if they attack they will have lost the moral high ground because they and the world will know the truth. And what's more, if they attack, then Israel will be left with no choice but to fight back as hard as it can. The waste will be phenomenal. It is in reality a no-win situation. That plus the other information we can send them should be enough to convince them.' Then he spoilt it by adding, 'I hope.'

'What information?' Golightly gulped at his coffee, the enormity of the next hour or so suddenly leaving him feeling overwhelmed.

'We have the transcripts of the broadcasts from Dayan to Iran which we will supply along with the codes. We will show them where they originated and we will then show them a satellite picture of what's happening on the rig, right now.'

'What is happening?'

'We don't know for the moment. GCHQ will be sending pictures in,' he looked at his watch, 'about three-quarters of an hour from now. The last message I got was that the team was safely on board and taking out the sentries. Since then we've heard nothing.'

Golightly drained his cup, stepped across the cabin and placed it down on an easy table. As he did he caught a glimpse of himself in the mirror behind the bar and paused to look critically at himself. What he saw was a lined, tired face, close to exhaustion. Pain was etched there along with determination and something more. Anger, yes and a thirst for revenge against the madman or madmen who had brought his country so close to possible annihilation. Even with Iran behind them it was impossible to achieve. Unless . . . unless there were others involved as well. He suddenly sat down, shock showing in the way his mouth dropped open.

'What is it?' Macnair asked, concerned.

'There are others, Malcolm. There has to be. Even with Iran,

239

Israel cannot succeed. Or maybe they could but at such a huge loss it would be a Pyrrhic victory. Others are conspiring as well. Perhaps the Arabs and Jordanians. Oh, not the rulers. But underlings who have day-to-day control and can give the orders. That would make sense. Iraq and Syria wiped out but surrounding states left intact to share the spoils. The price, control passing to those who support Israel and Iran. God, what an unholy alliance.' He went on to tell Macnair about the CIA agent, Mordecai.

Macnair nodded. 'I don't think this goes to the White House. However, I came to the same conclusion thirty-six hours ago. That is why I've instructed my men to retrieve all the information they can from the rig. It's not just the death of Dayan we need. We got some useful stuff when we attacked the ship in Bari but nothing that will lead us to any of the leaders. All we did find was that Dayan has two bases, the rig and one in the Golan.'

Golightly nodded. 'I know. My daughter is on her way there now. In case Dayan has gone there or will escape there from the rig.'

Macnair was about to make a caustic comment about what a solitary woman could achieve but thought better of it. They had enough work to get through without any acrimony. At that moment there was a knock on the door.

'Come,' Macnair said.

'Sir,' Jim Carter opened the door, 'we're ready and here are Mr. Golightly's clothes. Reasonably dry,' he held up the crumpled clothes that would not have looked out of place on a scarecrow. The deputy prime minister took them and with no embarrassment slipped off the robe and quickly dressed. 'I've tuned in to CNN,' continued Carter, 'and set up the camera. I've set up the data link with Syria, Lebanon, Iraq, Turkey, Jordan, Egypt, Saudi Arabia, Kuwait, UAE, Oman, Qatar, and the Yemen. We have tapped into government computers in all the countries and established video links with them all.'

'Any leaders?' Macnair asked.

'I'm afraid not, sir. Some are pretty low level employees but I have told them all that this is of vital importance and that they will either be heroes or be damned by the world when CNN

240

broadcast what's been going on. I think I can safely say that they are all intrigued enough to listen, even if they are losing their beauty sleep.'

Macnair nodded. It was as much as he could hope for right then. He just prayed that it would all change in twenty minutes. 'Are you all right?' Macnair queried Golightly.

Golightly grimaced in reply. 'These are uncomfortable, that's all. The salt is making my clothes stiff, leaving them unpleasant to the touch. But I can survive it,' he smiled wanly. 'Okay, let's get started.'

Carter led the way down to the crew's salon. It was a large, comfortable room filled with a vast array of equipment. Two cameras of broadcast quality stood on tripods facing a table, behind which were two chairs. A bank of computers, data-link gear, televisions and specialised radio equipment were all in evidence. On one screen was the face of Isobel and on another, Sarah Fleeting at GCHQ.

Golightly and Macnair sat behind the table and faced the cameras. Jim Carter and two TIFAT specialists manned the cameras and the transmitting equipment. Carter pressed a switch and pointed a camera at the two seated men. A red light came on. 'Broadcasting now.'

'Good evening, gentlemen,' said Macnair. As he spoke, TV screens came to life, each showing the face of the vital contact in each state they had contacted. 'My name is General Malcolm Macnair. Let me tell you that we are talking to the following countries.' He reeled off the list of countries around Israel and the eastern Mediterranean. 'You will all recognise David Golightly, the deputy prime minister of Israel. He will tell you what has been happening in his country and I will send the proof. I suggest you then relay the information to either your superior officers or your rulers. You can hand over the proof to them and let them decide. David.'

'Gentlemen,' said Golightly, his haggard features filling the screen, 'in one hour we will broadcast live on CNN the information we are giving you now. I beg you to listen to what I have to say with an open mind. I am speaking to you in the hope that I can prevent the deaths of millions of men, women and children.'

'They will all be Israelis,' spat out the Syrian delegate, 'and will be no loss.'

Golightly shook his head. 'You are wrong, my friend, so listen carefully. What has happened has been a plot by one man.' He held up his finger. 'One man who has made a pact with the Devil to bring us close to a war which nobody will win. He has the help of others as yet unknown to us. There may be a victory but at what cost? Israel will retaliate with everything in her arsenal, and that includes nuclear weapons.' There were gasps from the men looking at Golightly. He had finally admitted publicly what the world had known for years, that Israel was a nuclear state.

'So you admit it. You have nuclear weapons,' the outraged face and voice of the Jordanian interrupted.

Golightly nodded. 'Yes, I admit it. And they will be used.' There was a cacophony of protests at which Golightly raised his hand, 'Please, gentlemen, please. Hear me out. This is not an Israeli government plot. One man, Samuel Dayan, in league with Iran has caused this to happen. He has orchestrated *the whole affair* from beginning to end. He financed both the so-called Army for the Protection of Israel *and* the League for the Elimination of Israel.'

'It's true,' interrupted Macnair. 'We have managed to trace payments of large sums of money to organisations all across the world who we know are involved with terrorism. Dayan has made promises for much more money to be paid should his plan work. Remarkably, he even persuaded these groups to commit the hijackings and killings he needed to cause the backlash we see now. Somehow, he even got the perpetrators to commit suicide. Whether that was through bribery or coercion we don't know. But he managed it. You are now poised to walk across Israel but . . .' Macnair broke off. 'I'll let the Deputy Prime Minister finish the tale.'

'Dayan has Iran and others to help him. We don't know yet to what extent some of your leaders are involved.' There were protests from the screens. 'I don't mean the King or the President of your countries, but I do mean senior people, officers and ministers. All in it for their own ends. That is the only scenario that makes sense.'

'How do we know that you are telling the truth?' asked the delegate from Oman.

'Gentlemen, you will receive information via your sat-data links in one minute. It will contain transcripts of conversations between Iran and Dayan. It will tell you exactly what has been going on. You will notice that the signals are encrypted and so we will also send you the codes you need to decipher the messages. You can feed them into your own computers and listen yourselves.'

'That proves nothing,' sneered the representative from Qatar. 'It could be some sort of elaborate hoax.'

'To serve what purpose?' Golightly asked. 'Please believe me when I tell you that we are all being duped. Iran is now moving into place behind you. We believe that some of your forces will not fight as they will be ordered to one side. Iran and some regiments more loyal to their generals than to their presidents will side with Israel. I can only guess at what has been offered in the way of bribes but I believe that it isn't money but power.' David Golightly sighed, aware that he was not making any headway with the impassive faces that glared at him with hatred. 'Look, please, why am I doing this? What have I got to gain? Can any of you tell me?'

'We know neither what you have to gain nor why you are doing this,' said the man from Syria, 'but we do know that we do not – cannot – trust you.'

Golightly nodded his head wearily. 'I understand. All right, GCHQ in England is sending the information to you all now.' He looked at the screen showing Sarah Fleeting who nodded. 'You should look at what is there and pass it up the chain of command. In one hour we will contact you again. If you possibly can, try and get a senior government official to contact us. We will be attacking Dayan's bolt hole in about twenty minutes and you will be able to watch what happens on the sat-link that we have set up for you. You should also tune in to CNN in forty-five minutes when we will be broadcasting the events to the world. The broadcast will contain a plea to stop, to turn back before it's too late. Gentlemen, we've all been duped and unless we apply commonsense now, Armageddon will ensue.'

With that Carter stopped the camera. 'Will it work, do you think?'

Macnair shrugged. 'Possibly. If we can convince only one or two of them it may be enough to halt the war – even temporarily. The real solution is to stop Dayan and let the world know that we've succeeded.'

Just then the internal phone rang and Macnair answered it. He listened and then replied, 'Right. I'm coming up immediately. Tell the team to stand by.'

Carter looked at the general quizzically.

'The rig is five miles away. There's a fierce gun battle going on. We're in range for personal radio contact. We can't raise Hunter but we do have Walsh and a few of the others answering. They're trapped between the superstructure and the safety boat and taking a pounding.'

Carter nodded and strode for the door. 'That,' he said, 'is something we can take care of right now.'

In the bow of the ship, Carter and two of the team ripped open the wooden casing which stood five feet high by four feet square. The weapon was so new NATO had yet to give it a designation but Carter had obtained it for a vast sum of money only two weeks earlier from its American manufacturer. As Carter pressed a button immediately the self contained power plant flashed into life. A flick of a switch and a thin aerial rose twenty feet into the air. Next he turned on the display and within two seconds they were looking at the rig and the safety boat. The combination of radar, video and heat detection sensors all fed through a computer system to give a perfect picture. No matter how bad the weather, they would receive a clear picture at the console.

One of the men had broken open another box and removed a metre long, thin cylinder with a trigger sticking out half way along the tube. He held the tube at waist height, supporting the end on the guard-rail. It was not necessary to aim the tube but it was pointing ahead of the ship. Carter manipulated a joy-stick on the console and moved it until cross hairs on the display were centred on the safety boat. He pressed a red switch on the joy-stick, watched as a green light came on and said, 'Shoot.'

The man pulled the trigger on the tube and the missile launched. Once the green light had come on it indicated that the target had been acquired, identified precisely and the information passed to the missile. No matter where the safety boat moved the missile would track it. As the missile left the tube, stabilising fins sprung out and after an initial wobble the missile headed as straight as an arrow into the air, reached its zenith and angled down at the target. Although it was less than ten centimetres in diameter the missile had a range of twenty miles and carried a lethal warhead the equivalent of a missile three times larger. The explosive in the warhead was a honeycomb, precisely designed so that the force of the hundreds of tiny explosions all merged at one point, a metre ahead of the missile. It could blow a hole in steel six inches thick, pass through it and then, a nano-second later, explode a second time. This time the explosion was lateral, blowing out with the same devastating force. Carter had seen one of them hit a tank. The tank had blown apart like an egg being smashed with a sledge hammer.

A second missile was already in the air when the first reached the top of its trajectory and dropped onto the boat.

Hiram B. Walsh and his men were, not to put too fine a point on it, up the proverbial creek without a paddle. Up until the point when the searchlight had caught them and the shooting had started everything had gone well – too well, maybe, he thought. Now they were in trouble.

Walsh checked in with his men. Everybody apart from Hunter and Badonovitch were accounted for. He had last seen them climbing on top of the living quarters superstructure, where they had passed out of sight. If he didn't do something quickly he knew that they would be overwhelmed within minutes. Their ammunition was running low and they had no more grenades left to throw. He had no alternative but to blow the legs and they could all take their chances. Even as he made the decision the first missile landed in the bow of the boat. It exploded a metre above the boat and punched a hole two metres wide through the wooden deck, the metal deck one down, the bilge deck and out through the hull. It then exploded in the first hull space and blew holes through the port and starboard hulls and the forward and after bulkheads. When the second missile exploded fifteen seconds later in the stern of the boat, there was virtually nothing left to do. Seventeen men died instantly, the shooting stopped and the boat simply vanished.

The shock of the event silenced the defenders on the rig as they watched the safety boat disintegrate. Walsh and his team recovered quickly and poured fire into the crew's quarters. Now no longer caught in a trap they could move against the enemy. Suddenly it went quiet.

A voice called out, 'Boss, it's Alpha Two. Stop shooting. They're all dead.' Badonovitch came out slowly. Over his shoulder he carried a leather satchel, blood seeped from a bandage wrapped around his forehead and he was limping.

'Where's Alpha One?' asked Walsh.

'I don't know. The last I saw of him he was chasing some of them down below. I . . .' at that point Badonovitch keeled over.

A short while earlier, Hunter and Badonovitch had seen the problem. Walsh and the team were pinned down on the wrong side of the helicopter pad, caught in the beam of the searchlight from the safety boat. Whenever they tried to move a hail of bullets filled the air. Hunter knew that already at least three of the team had been hit.

'Jan, fire at the searchlight. See if you can knock it out. I'm going over the top and onto the roof. If I can find a vent I may be able to drop a grenade or two inside that might even things up a bit.'

'Roger, boss,' Badonovitch replied. He knelt in the shadow of

246

an orange painted lifeboat, took aim and emptied his magazine. The light went out and the firing stopped for a few seconds. He moved just in time before the area he was hiding in was shredded with heavy machine gun fire. The lifeboat was ripped apart and hung in tatters from its davits. Bits and pieces of the boat tumbled down to the deck and bullets ricocheted in all directions. One bullet bounced off the metal deck and scraped across Badonovitch's brow, digging down to the bone. Blood poured from the wound as he stumbled. He was blinded for a few seconds before his eyes cleared and he could focus once again. He pulled the balaclava off his head, reached into the hip pocket of his coveralls and pulled out a field dressing. He ripped it open with his teeth and wrapped it around his head, reducing the blood flow to a trickle. Even the army-issue bandage was a mottled grey.

The respite Badonovitch had won for the team enabled them to move to more secure positions, although they were still pinned down. A second searchlight suddenly illuminated the area and more bullets poured down around the team. This time they were better protected but even so, the ricocheting bullets were dangerous and still lethal. A few found exposed limbs to smash into, others were expended on the Keflar body protectors. One was fatal.

'Jan,' Hunter spoke into his throat mike, 'can you get up here? I'm setting plastic around a vent cover. I hope we can get in but I need help.'

'Roger that, boss,' Badonovitch replied and groggily shuffled across the deck. He reached the relative safety of the superstructure and searched for a way up. His hands reached for an eye-bolt and he curved his fingers round it. He heaved, lifting himself up with one hand and, as his strength was failing, slammed his other hand onto the edge of the roof. He let go the eye-bolt, grabbed the roof and pulled himself up and over. He lay halfway across the roof for a second, gathering his strength. A bullet hit the side of the superstructure and ricocheted into his thigh, lodging in the top of his leg. He grunted with pain and rolled across the roof.

247

Hunter saw that Badonovitch was in trouble and snaked on his stomach to his side. 'Are you all right?'

Badonovitch nodded. 'I think so,' he gasped. 'Head's okay but just got hit in the leg.'

Hunter ripped the trousers open and had a look. Blood was pouring from a deep wound but a glance showed that the bullet was still lodged inside. 'Jan, you're lucky. The bullet's still in there but no artery seems to have been hit. There's a lot of blood but nothing a dressing won't stop.' Even as he was speaking Hunter was ripping open a field dressing and wrapping it around the leg. 'The charge is set. I'll blow it and see what happens.'

Badonovitch nodded, sitting up, his natural strength reasserting itself after the double shock of two bullet wounds. Hunter set off the charge that blew open the lid of the ventilation shaft. Next he picked up a piece of timber and pushed it over the opening. It was blown out of his hands by a fusillade of bullets. Hunter took two hand grenades, pulled the pins, counted three seconds off the five second fuze and lobbed them both into the opening. They exploded as they hit the deck and, even as the blast was ringing in his ears, Hunter was dropping down the shaft. Badonovitch hung his torso over the opening, ready to fire at anything that moved. Nothing did. He grabbed the edge of the shaft and swung down, landing awkwardly on his good leg.

'Okay?' Hunter asked.

'Okay, boss.' The Spetsnaz was unaffected by the blood, gore and dismembered bits of body parts that were scattered around the corridor in which they found themselves.

'We need to find the rig superintendent's office. That's the most likely place to find what we're looking for,' said Hunter, swallowing the bile in his throat. He had seen and caused enough death in his time, but it could still affect him when he least expected it.

The muffled sound of battle came to them. They knew the team were having a hard time but killing Dayan and getting the information Macnair wanted was the priority. Hunter tried to raise Walsh on his radio, but the steel walls of the rig blocked out the transmission. All lights on the rig had been extinguished but, thanks to their night vision goggles, both men could see as clearly as in daylight. As they slunk along the corridor the sound of firing receded. A turn of the corridor led them to a set of stairs which they carefully went down. Offices were found left and right. The end door on the left was marked *Superintendent* and they paused outside.

'Ready?' Hunter asked.

'Affirmative, boss.' Badonovitch knelt to the side of the door while Hunter gripped the handle. He twisted it and slammed the door open all in one movement. As it smashed back against the metal wall they were surprised at what they saw – no ordinary office but a luxurious room. Even as they recovered from their surprise, shots rang out and sprayed the doorway. As they ducked they saw a man's back vanishing through an opening in the other side of the room. The man turned and put his hand out to the side of the doorway. As an electric door slid shut Hunter recognised him. It was Dayan.

Badonovitch had already thrown a flash/bang grenade into the room and as the huge noise and brilliant light deafened and blinded the room's occupants, Hunter and Badonovitch stepped through the door and shot the two men they found there. Hunter darted across to the other side and looked for the doorway Dayan had vanished through. At first he could see nothing. It was only after he made a careful examination of the walls that he saw the vertical hairline cracks. He searched for a handle or a button, anything, but could find no way of opening the door. Badonovitch in the meantime was pointing a small box with a short antennae around the room.

'Boss, two definites.' He looked at the flickering dial.

'Where?' Hunter asked.

'There and there.' Badonovitch pointed and then added, 'The rest is clear.' He had pin-pointed two booby-traps. When first manufactured in Czechoslovakia in the late fifties, plastic explosive was undetectable. International pressure had persuaded the Czechs that in order to detect the explosives and stop it being smuggled into aeroplanes and other high risk terrorist targets, it needed to give out a recognisable odour. Special oils had been added and now, with the right equipment, it was possible to find the explosives, even when hidden in a sealed container. The equipment was now found in all major airports in the civilised world. It was the uncivilised part that still gave the problems.

Hunter quickly looked at the first device and found it to be a simple time switch. He cut the wire and easily disarmed it. The second was not so simple. It was hidden behind some panelling and he realised that it had been placed there to protect a safe.

The safe was two feet square with a double tumbler, two-handled lock that was out of place on an oil rig. If he had tried to open it, even using explosives, the second load of explosives would have detonated and not only blown the safe and its contents to smithereens, but also injured or killed anybody in the room.

'Trembler arm and sensor,' Hunter said, looking closely. 'No timer. At least two kilos of Semtex, maybe more. Serious stuff, Jan.'

'Sure, boss. Serious stuff. What are we going to do?'

'You're going outside while I dismantle it.' He looked over his shoulder at Badonovitch. 'Go on.'

'Sure, boss,' Badonovitch shrugged but made no attempt to leave.

'Stupid Russki,' Hunter said with good humour.

'Better get a move on, boss. We need to move it,' Badonovitch said, as though he didn't have a care in the world.

Hunter recognised the set up and knew that first of all he needed to stop the trembler arm from working. He took a sheet of paper from the desk and carefully inserted it between the two terminals at the end of the trembler. Their width determined the degree of sensitivity of the arm. These were a millimetre apart and about as sensitive as it got. Hunter let out his breath as the paper slid between the terminals. He then detached the trembler from the plastic explosives and threw it away. The sensor was heat and noise operated and could not be too delicate as it would be too easy to set off. Hunter placed his thumb and forefinger around it, drew it steadily from its plastic bed, cut the wire and threw that away. A careful examination showed no other firing device and he removed the PE as an added precaution.

'Jan, you blow the door while I blow the safe,' he ordered.

Badonovitch used the last of his plastic explosive to run a seam down one side of the door through which Dayan had vanished. He helped himself to the explosives that Hunter had just rendered safe to finish the job.

Hunter always used the minimum plastic required to get a job done and could slice through steel as though he were using a hot knife on butter. He took the PE and broke it into thin strips. Carefully he kneaded the plastic along the hinges and down the edge of the door around the lock. Having made sure there were no breaks in the explosive strip, he pushed in a detonator. At that moment Badonovitch blew the door. It ripped cleanly away down one side and along the top. A kick with his good leg shoved the door in.

He carefully looked through the opening and reported, 'A set of steps going down, boss.'

'Okay, keep watch while I open this,' said Hunter. He set the timer and flattened himself against the wall. The explosion came in less then three seconds and Hunter took hold of the door by its two handles and ripped it open. Inside were floppy disks, bundles of paper and a number of loose leafed ledgers. 'Jan, shove this lot in your grip while I go after Dayan.'

'I'd better come as well, boss,' said Badonovitch.

Hunter shook his head. 'No. Get this lot up top to Colonel Walsh and give him a hand. You can attack from behind. I need to go after Dayan. Look, we've two objectives, information and Dayan. This looks like the information the General is after and Dayan went that way. If you secure the rig come after me then.'

'Okay, boss,' Badonovitch slung the bag over his shoulder, checked his weapons were loaded and ready to fire and limped out of the room. He went along the corridor and up the steps, following the sound of gunfire. Seconds later came an explosion and a lull in the firing. Shooting started up almost immediately and Badonovitch stepped round the corner and shot three men in the back. He shouted to Walsh to stop firing.

The team moved quickly to search the rig and help Hunter. It took only a short while to realise that there was nobody left alive on board apart from themselves. There was no sign of Hunter or Dayan. They had vanished into thin air.

23

Hunter slid like a ghost down the iron steps, one hand resting lightly on a safety rail, the other holding his cocked gun. He was outside the living quarters descending to the sea. The safety boat was sending a withering fire onto the rig and he paused. Should he go on or return and help the others? He dismissed the thought. Dayan was his target. The remainder of the team had to take care of themselves. As he looked at the boat again he saw it disintegrate before his eyes and he grinned. Macnair was charging in.

He dashed lightly down the steps, throwing caution to the wind. Suddenly he stopped in surprise. A hydraulic platform was slowly descending to the sea. On it was a rigid-raider, the sort used by marine forces the world over. Made of dark green plastic, it was capable of speeds up to sixty or seventy knots with a payload of ten men and all their equipment. There were four men sitting in the boat. At that moment it reached the water. Hunter leant over and was raising his gun when he was shot. He had been bending over and the bullet scraped across his back and threw him off his feet. He tumbled three metres into the boat, startling its occupants. The man who had shot him stepped from behind a control console and jumped down beside Hunter.

'Is he dead?' he asked.

One of the others bent over Hunter and checked him. 'No, he's breathing all right. No sign of blood anywhere.'

A rough hand ripped open Hunter's clothes and exposed the Kevlar vest. Unceremoniously he turned him over and looked at Hunter's back. 'He'll live,' he said, ripping off Hunter's headset and goggles and throwing them overboard. 'Feed him to the fish.'

'Wait,' said Dayan. 'We'll take him with us. We need to know what they know – who he is and what's happening. How did he come to be here now, a day earlier than expected? I need answers if we're to continue or,' he paused ominously, 'if we are to survive. We need to know what we're dealing with. Let's go.'

The platform had sunk beneath the sea and the boat was drifting in the swell. One of the men pushed an electric start button and a 120hp Evinrude outboard burst into life. He pressed a second button and started a second engine, pushed the gear lever into ahead and carefully manoeuvred the boat away from the rig. As soon as they were out from under the rig he rammed open the throttles and the rigid-raider took off like a missile for the shore, less than a mile away. The boat skimmed the sea, bouncing from wavelet to wavelet, phosphorus in the water sparkling either side of the boat but disappearing in the wake. The engines roared defiantly but no shots were fired in their direction.

They barely slowed down as they hit the gently shelving beach, their momentum taking them well onto the land. The four men clambered out of the boat, two grabbed Hunter and dragged his inert body onto the sand before picking him up, one man taking his legs, the other his arms. Hunter's head lolled back, occasionally glancing off a rock, the pain bringing him back to consciousness. He lifted his head aware that he was being carried. He was about to say something, thinking it was his own team who had him, when he heard a voice speak Ivrit. Feigning unconsciousness, he wondered why they were bothering to carry him and didn't just shoot him and get it over with.

They hid behind a sand dune, watching the sea. It soon became apparent that nobody was following them. After a while the sound of a helicopter came clearly from the east and landed in a storm of sand. The men picked up Hunter and carried him to the open door where he was thrown into the back of the helicopter. The engines started and within minutes they were airborne, keeping low, skimming the land, a poor target for anybody who might be looking for them. Dawn was not far away.

A few minutes later the pilot decided that they were safe and the helicopter rose to its normal cruising altitude. Speaking to air traffic control at Ben-Gurion airport, situated midway between Tel Aviv and Jerusalem, he received permission to fly to Haifa. They skirted the coast, flying half a mile off-shore under radar control, until they reached the city. Haifa, Israel's third largest city, had a population of a quarter of a million people. With war looming it was like a ghost town, with hardly a light showing. It was eerie to know that so many souls were gathered together, united in fear at what was to come. But for some, those few who were in the know, a wild elation gripped them. At last Israel would become the dominant country in the Middle East, powerful, rich, with safe borders. Soon Greater Israel would become a reality!

At Haifa the helicopter dropped to wave height, falling out of radar control and skirted the city, flying illegally low. North of Haifa it turned east and headed for Tiberias, the only town on the Sea of Galilee, with a population of 40,000. As the fresh water lake, fed by the River Jordan, came into sight, the helicopter veered to port and now headed north, skirting the shore. The Sea of Galilee has been known by different names over the millennia. In the Old Testament it was known as the Sea of Kinnereth, derived from the Hebrew word *kinnor* meaning harp, purposedly because the lake is shaped like a harp. In the New Testament it is first referred to as the Sea of Galilee although to the Israelis it remained "the Kinneret". Capernaum became the most important site on the lake when Jesus made it the centre of his ministry in the Galilee. With the destruction of Jerusalem, Galilee became the new centre of Jewish life and the lakeside saw the establishment of synagogues and religious study schools all over the area. It was where Dayan's power base was to be found, amongst the zealots and fundamentalists of the Jewish faith. Many lived in Tiberias, a wholly Jewish town since the war of 1948, when the defeated Arabs were forced to leave.

A short while later the helicopter passed over Ha Yarden Park

Reserve and followed route 888 north. Upper Galilee was to port, the Golan to starboard. The disengagement zone between Israel and Syria was twenty-four kilometres away. Much of the area they were now flying over was made up of different nature reserves, interspersed with small villages and towns. The helicopter was now flying along a steep, narrow valley, hidden from the prying eyes of ground-air radar and other border sensors. However, now they were in maximum danger of either being shot down or merely seen. As they approached the border and the disengagement zone, the sensors on the helicopter began to pick up, albeit fleetingly, search radars and other overt and covert sensors. The valley they were in twisted and turned and was so narrow in places that the slightest slip by the pilot would have sent them crashing to their doom. He had flown the route many times before and boasted that he could fly it with his eyes shut. It was not a boast he wished to prove.

They flew over the highest point of land, directly above the observation station found there and into the UN-patrolled border with Syria. Ahead was the abandoned town of Quneitra. It had been the major town belonging to the Syrians in the Golan and was mostly inhabited by Circassians, Muslim immigrants from the Caucasus. It had been captured and destroyed by the Israelis in 1967 but was returned to Syria under the terms of a cease-fire. Even so, it remained a ghost town until Dayan made the Syrian President an offer he couldn't refuse. Damascus lay only 30 kilometres to the north-east.

Sand blew up in the down-wash of the helicopter blades as it landed in a deserted square, surrounded by decaying buildings. The rotors were still turning slowly when the men climbed down from the helicopter. Two of them grabbed Hunter and unceremoniously dragged him from the helicopter then dropped him on to the sand. Hunter, deciding it was time to regain consciousness, sat up and looked around him. He was not restrained in any way and his captors seemed indifferent to him. As he stood up he was ignored, as he stretched and worked the kinks out of his muscles. He watched as a cat jumped down from the helicopter and wandered across to an open doorway. Feeling behind him, he pressed his hands into his back, trying to assess any damage from the bullet. Relief flooded through him as he realised there was very little injury. With interest he scanned the deserted, ramshackle buildings. In the strengthening light he could see from the state of the place that nature had begun to reclaim the land. He wondered where they were. While he wandered around four of the men took up positions around the helicopter and pushed it towards a dilapidated building with double doors hanging crazily as though about to fall off. Dayan stood to one side and watched as the helicopter was trundled away.

To Hunter's surprise, though he didn't show it by so much as a twitch of a muscle, the doors swept silently open to present a large open space. The sun reached over the wall and in the bright light he couldn't see far into the dark interior but what he could see was swept clean and kept tidy. The helicopter vanished inside along with the four men and the pilot. Hunter was contemplating attacking Dayan and then taking his chances when Dayan interrupted his thoughts.

'Don't even think about it. You'll be shot before you get two paces and this time it won't be a body shot.'

Hunter stopped, poised like an athlete, every sinew ready to explode into action.

'You were contemplating trying to kill me,' Dayan looked across at Hunter fifteen metres away. 'We have ignored you because there is nowhere for you to go and you have been under close surveillance since we landed. You cannot see them but right now three guns are pointed at your head. If you think I am bluffing take a pace towards me.' Dayan stood with his head on one side, contemplating Hunter like a specimen under a microscope.

Hunter reasoned that if they had been going to kill him they would have done so by now, so he took a pace towards Dayan. Three shots rang out almost as one and dust and sand erupted half a metre in front of him. He stopped.

Dayan smiled and said, 'You see. We are not as lax as you might have been thinking. Go towards that door.' He nodded in the direction opposite to where the helicopter had vanished. 'You will be met and escorted below.'

Hunter sauntered in the direction indicated, taking a better look about him than the cursory glance he had so far paid to the place. As he did so he realised that his first impressions had been wrong. The town was not dilapidated. It was made to look that way. Now that he examined the area closely he realised that what he had thought were the dark holes of doorways and windows were actually covered over and painted. Someone had gone to a lot of trouble and expense to make the area appear deserted.

He paused in the darkness of the doorway and blinked, unable to see in the gloom. The brutal blow into the small of his back was totally unexpected and sent him to his knees. The second blow fell across his upper arm and for a second he thought it was broken. It took all his will power but, after flexing his fingers, he ignored the two blows and looked slowly behind him. His eyes were now accustomed to the lack of light and he could make out two figures standing either side of the doorway. One carried what appeared to be a pick-axe handle. He was hefting it in his hand, metronomically lifting and dropping it into his palm. From the look of him Hunter had no doubt he intended to use it further. The man stepped forward and swung the pick-axe handle at Hunter's other arm.

Hunter was ready and even as the handle whistled through the air, he was rolling to one side. He came to his feet like a cat, crouched, ready to defend himself. The man he was facing was built like an orang-utan. Long arms, a squat body and a completely bald head. He also moved like a simian and quickly faced up to Hunter, an evil grin on his face.

'Stay back,' he said in a cultured English accent, at odds with his appearance. 'He's mine.'

The other man shrugged and moved to the doorway, silhouetted against the bright sunlight. The gun he was carrying hung down by his side.

Hunter shuffled warily to his right, concentrating on the man with the pick-axe handle, who was again lifting and dropping it into his hand with a loud, smacking noise. As Hunter moved around in a circle he tried to find something to defend himself with, but the room was completely bare. Not even dust or sand on the floor, just four bare walls in a room at least ten metres by ten. As he watched his adversary, Hunter had the impression he knew the man from somewhere. Suddenly he remembered.

'Sheffield,' he spoke the name aloud.

'You know me?' was the surprised response.

'I know you,' Hunter said with contempt. 'Or at least I know of you. You were thrown out of the Paras for mistreating new recruits.'

'How do you know? It was all kept quiet at the time. Didn't want to sully the name of a great regiment,' Sheffield said with a sneer.

'I was at One Para finishing a jumping course. The enquiry had just finished and you were being escorted back to your quarters. A friend of mine pointed you out. I saw you again an hour later walking out with your gear. So this is where you ended up. With this carrion.'

'They don't mind my, what shall we say . . . History? No! *Curriculum vitae*,' said Sheffield. 'But you're right. The little Nancy boys couldn't take it. They ganged up on me and put in a complaint.' The pick-axe handle was no longer moving but gripped tightly in both hands. He held the shaft so hard he appeared to be trying to crush it, anger and hate distorting his features.

At that point Hunter made his move. Stepping forward, he pirouetted on his left foot and, toes curled up, with his right leg sent a shattering blow into Sheffield's thigh. Hunter's foot bounced off it, as though he had kicked solid rubber. It was a blow that would normally have broken the leg. Sheffield didn't even flinch. Instead he grinned. Warily Hunter backed off, circling, watching his adversary's eyes. The slight narrowing of the eyes warned Hunter just in time. As Sheffield sprang forward with the club gripped in one hand, Hunter dived to one side and the bone-breaking blow sailed harmlessly through the air. The momentum of the swing left Sheffield off balance for a nano-second and Hunter sprang in like a coiled cobra. Two gut pounding punches with his fists did little more than cause Sheffield to gasp and although Hunter tried to duck and weave his way out of harm's way, a blow to the head from Sheffield's open right hand sent Hunter reeling into a corner of the room. Dazedly he used the wall to climb to his feet, fear beginning to gnaw at his belly. Sheffield made no attempt to follow up the blow, content to let Hunter regain his feet and fighting stance.

'I'm enjoying this,' said Sheffield. 'It's been a long time since I had a really good work out. You'll die, of course, but it'll be a slow and painful death. We want some answers from you but we won't start asking them until I'm ready.'

Hunter said nothing but continued to circle Sheffield. When the eyes changed, instead of moving out of harm's way Hunter did the opposite. He ducked under the swinging pick-axe handle and jabbed with his right hand, knuckles bent, into Sheffield's throat. A second blow with the side of his left hand into the carotid artery in the side of the neck should have killed Sheffield. Instead it felt to Hunter as though he had smashed a side of dead beef. Sheffield staggered back, more injured than he cared to show, shaking his head, a killing rage surging through him, his little eyes glints of hatred. Now he was more careful, less cocky, aware that he was up against a formidable opponent. Sheffield swung the shaft and even as Hunter moved he realised too late that it was a dummy and the swing became a jab that smashed numbingly into his shoulder and threw him against the far wall. His head thumped back into the bricks and a grey mist descended over him for a few seconds.

Wearily he clambered to his feet, holding onto the wall with one hand, expecting a further onslaught. None came. Sheffield stood, feet apart, waiting for Hunter to recover, enjoying his game of cat and mouse. Hunter knew that it was only a matter of time, but he would go down fighting as long as he had breath in his body. He needed to summon *ka-shi*. It was the only chance he had. Literally it meant spirit strength. A combination of meditation and martial arts together helped to drag strength from his inner being. Groggily Hunter shook his head, only partly feigning the soul weary tiredness that was coursing through his veins. He turned his mind inwards on himself, summoning the strength that he knew existed in the core of his being. It was an act of desperation. There was nothing only . . . only a flicker. It was there, coming now, like a volcano about to erupt. Slowly his strength flowed from deep within, coursing along his arms, legs and into his fingers and feet. He took a hesitant step forward, disorientated, looking wildly about for a way out. Sheffield grinned and hefted the shaft rhythmically in his hand. At that moment Hunter exploded into action.

The marshalling of his strength and stamina erupted in a continuous movement of action. He kicked, elbowed, smashed hands, fists and fingers into Sheffield. He moved in a blur, totally focused, each point of contact carrying every ounce of energy and strength that he had. Hunter knew he could not last. This was a suicidal attack which, if he lost, would leave him utterly exhausted and vulnerable to a counter-attack. It was a once only attempt to survive or die trying. In spite of the ferociousness of the attack Hunter knew he was losing. Sheffield landed a few blows but *ka-shi* kept Hunter immune. Sheffield was taking the kind of blows which could maim or kill any other man and yet he was still standing. True, he was being hurt but not seriously damaged. Hunter put everything he had into his right foot as he desperately tried to kick Sheffield between the legs. He connected. Sheffield dropped the pick-axe handle, shock and pain etched in his face, his hands gripped across his front, swaying and roaring in agony.

Hunter heard the snick of a gun being cocked and felt a blow to the side of his head. He heard the same dulcet tones he had heard in the Alps. 'We need him alive for interrogation.'

Hunter lay on the ground, exhausted, as a beautiful face leaned down and looked him squarely in the eyes. 'He's unconscious and will be for some time.' She closed her eyes and opened them again. Hunter understood and closed his own, beginning his mantra, urgently seeking a deep meditation to regain his strength. He knew that he would need time to recover. Even as his mind sought the comfort and safety of deep meditation he heard her.

'That is the second time I have seen *ka-shi*.' There was awe in her voice. 'You are an amazingly strong man to have withstood such an attack,' she said to Sheffield.

261

'The second time?' Sheffield questioned, his voice a rasping croak.

'Yes. I saw it some years ago. The person who performed *ka-shi* killed six tough men and badly injured a seventh. Two of them he killed after he was already dead.'

Macnair sat with David Golightly. Each had a cold cup of coffee at his elbow, waiting, thinking, hoping. They had made their broadcast to CNN which even now was relaying it across the world.

The internal phone rang. 'Macnair,' said the General picking up the receiver. After listening for a few moments, he hung up.

'That was Hiram Walsh. They've made the rig safe.' Seeing Golightly's perplexed look he added, 'They've removed the explosives and recovered all the gear. It's a crying shame about Dayan. However, we're certain now that Dayan has another location at Quneitra, in the Golan.'

Golightly nodded. 'It makes sense. There are any number of supporters for his way of thinking to be found near there,' he could not keep the bitterness from his voice. 'The fools. I wish they'd hurry up. Unadulterated fools.'

Macnair didn't need to be told who "they" were. Israel's survival, indeed, the survival of the whole Middle East rested on the shoulders of men who, in essence, were Golightly's and Israel's enemies. They had to recognise the truth when it was shown to them! Doubt coursed through him. Didn't they?

The door was flung open unceremoniously and Carter looked in. 'Sir, they are beginning to get back to us.'

'Who's there?' Macnair asked.

Carter grimaced. 'The same as before.'

With a heavy heart Macnair said, 'Doesn't look good, in that case. We needed at least Prime Ministers or Presidents for this call. Damnation! Don't they know what will happen if they don't call off this useless, stupid war?'

'Stupid? Yes, I suppose that sums it up,' Golightly said. 'Stupid and pointless.'

Macnair nodded. 'This war will be particularly brutal and

nasty. The death toll will be horrendous and at the end of it nothing will be achieved. There won't be a Greater Israel, David, you know that. The world cannot, will not, sit back and let it happen. Israel has already been allowed to get away with too much. With proof that Dayan has orchestrated the situation, the U.N. will be forced to act. And what's more, many in the U.N. will enjoy watching Israel being whipped and humiliated.'

Golightly nodded sadly. It was true. Israel had ignored or broken many U.N. edicts, much to the chagrin and anger of the Arab world. If the attack wasn't stopped, Israel would cease to exist.

Both men sat facing the cameras. The same serious faces appeared before them on each of the screens. It was with dread in his heart and fear in his soul that Golightly looked at the men.

'I have the President for you,' said the Syrian representative.

All the others made similar announcements until Macnair and Golightly faced either the Presidents or senior government officials from all the states concerned. Both men allowed a glimmer of hope to shine through. Perhaps their prayers had been answered after all.

'Gentlemen,' Macnair spoke, 'we trust that you have looked at the evidence?'

'We have,' replied the President of Syria in his deep, gravelly voice. There was a long pause and the two men waited expectantly. 'We have considered the evidence and we have spoken at great length together,' he paused again, enjoying turning the screw into Golightly. 'We have very little doubt that what you have told us is the truth. We have halted the attack on Israel.' Golightly felt a surge of joy on hearing the words. 'But,' and his heart sunk again. 'But,' the President repeated, 'we will not withdraw until Dayan is either arrested or dead. We have been in contact with the Iranians and they deny it absolutely.' He paused again. 'We do not believe them.' Now the President allowed himself a small smile. 'We have never believed them . . . about anything. They are withdrawing to Iran. Their contention is, if we do not believe them, then they cannot be our allies. It is all nonsense, of course. However, we are also worried that if

263

Dayan isn't stopped, he will be able to persuade the hotheads in the Israeli military to carry out their attack without Iran. That they will rely solely on weapons of mass destruction. It is not beyond the wit of man to so delude himself. Do you agree?'

It was a tense moment for Golightly. If he denied the possibility then he would destroy his credibility. If he agreed, there was still a chance that his country would be attacked in a pre-emptive strike to annihilate the warmongers in Israel before nuclear weapons could be used. He took a deep sigh, and replied, 'Sir, I agree with you. We are working now to stop Dayan. We are trying to identify all those who are on his side both within Israel and in other countries. We have already issued arrest warrants for a number of his followers and our forces are working to execute those arrests even as we speak.'

The President of Syria nodded in satisfaction. 'Mr Golightly, you have twenty-four hours. That is all the compromise we can come to. We must have proof that Israel has ceased to be a threat and to do that you must stop Dayan. Far be it for me to advise you, but,' he paused for a moment before continuing, looking deeply into Golightly's eyes, 'I suggest that Dayan is not arrested. It will cause too many problems, too much unrest.'

Golightly was about to protest that Dayan should at least have a fair trial before being imprisoned as there was no death penalty in Israel. However he realised that was not acceptable. He nodded, wearily. 'We, that is,' he inclined his head towards Macnair, 'the General and I, are in full accord with you, sir. It will be for the best if Dayan were to die. We are working on the problem even now. His supporters will have the pleasure of a lifetime in prison, but not Dayan.'

'Good. We will announce to the world that we are stopping our attack. We will not announce our intention to renew the offensive if we don't have a satisfactory result within twenty-four hours. I recommend that you keep that piece of information to yourselves. To release it may yet cause your fellow countrymen to launch all-out war.'

'I agree. I will be back in touch as soon as I have any information to give you.'

264

There was a plethora of goodbyes in various tongues before the screens faded. Golightly let out a sigh of relief before sinking back in his chair. He was soaked in sweat and was disconcerted to find that his hands were trembling. He looked at Macnair, who had sat silently throughout the exchange. 'Well?'

Macnair shrugged. 'It's all we could have hoped for. I wasn't aware that arrest warrants had been issued for Dayan's supporters.'

'They haven't. I need to speak to the Prime Minister. He is currently with the Chief Justice waiting to issue warrants. He needs names and for that we need the information we hope your assistant is uncovering. In the meantime I'll call my brother. I need to make sure he knows what's happening. I think there are about half a dozen officers who are capable of ordering the use of our nuclear weapons and they are scattered across the country. That way they cannot be wiped out in one action. However, they only give the orders. You need, I believe, two officers in every location to fire the weapons.'

Macnair nodded. 'We have the same system in the UK. Two keys and a special card are needed.' Even as he spoke a thought occurred to him. 'Is it possible to fire a missile without a senior officer giving the order? We have dissolved the act of firing . . .' Macnair was aware that he was sounding pompous but couldn't help himself, 'to the officer on the ground. Hence a nuclear submarine captain can fire off a missile but he needs the missile control officer's key as well. He has access to the necessary codes and in fact all three of our services practise preparing the missiles and bombs for firing right up to the point of release. In theory a rogue officer could fire off a missile or release a bomb in spite of the fact that all personnel are carefully screened and selected.'

'We do the same. However, what if a senior officer promotes men who will do as they're told and gives them control of nuclear weapons?' Golightly shuddered and sweat burst out on his forehead. 'We have to move very fast. We need those names urgently.'

Macnair nodded, aware of the urgency of the situation. 'I need to report to my political masters,' he said. 'It will help if you speak to them as well.'

Golightly nodded in agreement. 'That will be no problem. Not to put too fine a point on it, you've helped save the world from a catastrophe.'

As they sat in contemplative silence Macnair's phone warbled. Lifting the receiver, he listened for a moment and then said, 'I'm waiting. I see. Thanks.' He hung up. 'That was Isobel. The names are coming in now. She thinks she has a lead as to where Dayan could be and hopes to get back to us in the next ten minutes or so.'

'I'll phone my brother,' said Golightly, 'and warn him that we must do all in our power to prevent the missiles being fired. We must not allow defeat to be snatched from the jaws of victory. We are so near to preventing mayhem across the country. No, not just across the country but the world.'

Carter came in and handed a sheet of paper to Macnair. Golightly had dialled the number and the phone was ringing when Macnair reached across and disconnected the call.

24

Ruth Golightly sat at the table, her hands clasped around a cup of tea, a frown reflecting her thoughts. She still hadn't been allowed in to see Dayan and time was running out. She knew that she had to kill him and in so doing would inevitably be killed herself. Well, she told herself, what was death other than a continuation of the same journey? Her being existed and could never be extinguished and so she would return. As somebody else, but she would return. She sighed. It was no good. She liked being Ruth Golightly and did not want to depart this world just yet. She wanted marriage, children. A different . . . a better life. She smiled wryly, there was no hope of that now. She had to kill Dayan. But how if she wasn't even allowed near him?

What about Hunter? Mentally she shrugged. She had done all that she could for him. A quick death was the best that she could offer. Better than to be tortured by that brute Sheffield. He would punish Hunter dreadfully for what had been done to him. There were no depths to his depravity and Hunter had done something no other person had ever achieved. He had hurt Sheffield, badly. How on earth had Sheffield stayed on his feet? It was an uncanny testament to his brute strength because she knew that any other man would have been dead. Awe and dread filled her at the thought of Sheffield. If she managed to kill Dayan, she did not dare to be taken alive.

The door opened and a bearded face looked in. 'Mr. Dayan wishes to see you,' it said and immediately withdrew. She stood up, wiping her suddenly sweating hands on her shirt, her heart pounding, her lips dry. Maybe she would get her opportunity in the next few minutes. She swallowed, her senses heightened to such a degree that she saw everything in sharp focus and hard lines. For a moment she appeared to lose connection with reality and then normality returned. Her breathing steadied, her nerves stopped screaming and she was able to moisten her lips. She walked out of the room.

Along the corridor she followed the back of the man who had summoned her. Her feet silent on the bare concrete floor. The empty corridor had doors left and right, but they were shut. She knew that they were the sleeping quarters of the small army of men that supported and protected Dayan. They were three levels below the ground. On the level above was Dayan's quarters and above that the offices, dining halls and kitchens. The armoury was below them, along with the communications centre and the cells.

The man was waiting at the lift, the door held open. He said nothing as she stepped in and he pressed the button to go up one level. When the door opened they stepped straight into another world. They entered a huge, luxuriously furnished room. One wall was covered with books, many of them of a religious nature, of all faiths. Ruth knew that Dayan had read many of them and that his knowledge on the religions of the world was encyclopaedic. It had led him to the conviction that there was only one true faith – Judaism.

A huge television set sat in one corner, and to her startled surprise, the screen had been smashed. Dayan was pacing up and down, every gesture, every move bristling with anger. Between Ruth and Dayan was a large oak desk and in front of the desk stood Sheffield with four other men. Each was armed, each had a shocked look on his face. Ruth stopped in bewilderment, aware that something momentous had happened. Her gun was in its holster at her side, the flap undone, ready to be drawn and fired in an instant. She knew that she would only get one shot before she would be cut to pieces and that one shot would have to be fatal. It would need to be a clear head shot but she needed to get into a better position.

'What has happened?' she asked nervously.

'A CNN report has just been broadcast across the world,' replied Lionel Goldstein, an American Jew who had moved to Israel ten years earlier and who had immediately joined Dayan's movement. Now he was number two in the organisation. An imposing man in his late forties he had a shock of grey hair, a small pot belly and a hooked nose. His piercing blue eyes looked permanently angry. Lightning seemed to be flashing from them as he smashed his fist into his left hand with a loud clapping noise. Dayan by comparison contented himself with his pacing, muttering to himself as though in a private argument.

'What did the report say?' Ruth asked.

'That we had been responsible for all the terrorist attacks throughout the world and that we have been fomenting the war,' replied Goldstein. 'It has also just been announced that there will be no attack on Israel and that the Iranian forces are returning to Iran. It is all over,' he said tiredly, dropping his hands to his sides.

Dayan stopped pacing and suddenly pointed at Goldstein, his finger quivering, anger thickening his voice. 'I will have you taken out and shot if you talk of defeat,' he snarled. Goldstein paled, fear flooding his face, aware that Dayan would do precisely that. 'We can still succeed. Send the signal ordering the release of the nuclear weapons against the forces currently massed along our border. We will wipe them out in a pre-emptive strike and claim that we had no choice. That it was the only way for Israel to survive. To strike first and not respond to a cowardly Arab attack. Well, don't just stand there, get on with it.'

It's now or never, thought Ruth. I have to kill him before the signal is sent. Nervously she edged to one side, aware that she would be dead within the next ten seconds. At that moment the door swung open and smashed against the wall and an aide rushed in.

'Sir! Have you seen what's going on?'

'You fool!' replied Dayan. 'Of course I have. Iran has retreated and there is no attack.'

'No, sir,' the man nervously licked his lips, suddenly fearful for his life now that he had more bad news to impart. Suddenly he wished that he had not so impetuously rushed into the room.

'Well? What is it?' Dayan barked.

The man hesitated and then blurted out the news. 'Arrests, sir. They're arresting everyone.'

'David,' said Macnair, not unkindly, 'you must act and act now. Phone the PM and give him the information he needs.'

The anguish in Golightly's voice was reflected in his face when he raised his head from his hands after nearly two minutes as he came to terms with what he had been shown. 'Why, Malcolm? What did he hope to achieve?'

Macnair shrugged, sad for his friend, words superfluous.

Golightly pulled himself together, sat up straight and became angry. 'He may be my brother but he's a traitor to all of mankind. He will pay for what he's done.' He reached for the phone, dialled and was immediately connected.

'PM.'

'Saul? It's David. I have the list of main supporters of Dayan. You aren't going to like what you hear but we need to move fast.'

'I know. I have been discussing it with Peter.'

Golightly knew that he was referring to Peter Mendelson, the Minister of Defence, the only man the PM could trust until the list was in his hands. Golightly read off the names. When he had finished there was a stunned silence.

'Are you still there?' Golightly asked.

'Yes,' was the croaked reply. 'My God, David, this is,' he paused, 'this is devastating.'

'Not as devastating as it will be if we don't stop them,' Golightly replied.

There was a moment's silence before the Israeli Prime Minister cleared his throat and replied. 'I agree. These are madmen and have to be stopped. There are what? Fifty-seven names on this list. I see the Minister of Health is named which somehow I'm not surprised at.' He hesitated before he said, 'And your brother. I am so sorry but there can be no exceptions.'

'I know and I agree. He is the key to releasing the weapons. We must find all those named before it's too late.' Golightly added, 'I ask only one thing. Please let me know the time my brother is to be arrested. He's a proud man.'

He said no more. After a pause the Prime Minister said, 'I understand. I shall see what I can do. Now, I must go. There is a lot to be covered. Oh, and David, well done and thank General Macnair for us. We owe more than we can possibly repay and we won't forget.' He hung up.

'*Shalom*,' Golightly spoke to a dead line.

Captain Isaac Isaacs was not a happy man. He was, in fact, terrified. Nervously he licked his lips but they still felt dry. His hand shook and he steeled himself for what he had been ordered to do. For five years he had prayed for this day. When the news came that the invasion was not going to take place he had felt relieved but somehow, cheated. Then angry. His anger sustained him when he received the telephone call from the General, enabling him to follow his orders. But now doubts were invading him, frightening him into an almost catatonic state. When he had immigrated to Israel from America seven years earlier, he had known that he wanted to create a safe, secure Greater Israel, the predominant power in the Middle East. He had been quickly recognised by Dayan's organisation and although only a corporal in the catering corps in America he was promoted to lieutenant and transferred into an active company. Promotion followed quickly and now he was second-in-command of a small missile site capable of firing nuclear weapons. In accordance with the general mobilisation order issued earlier, the missiles had been prepared for launch. Then had come the news that the attack was off. The Arabs and their allies were going home. Relief had flooded through Isaacs leaving him giddy and light-headed with joy. That had turned to the all-consuming anger he now felt and he was steeling himself to act. First of all he needed the firing key from Major Barak, his commanding officer. To get it Isaacs knew he would have to kill him. He was dressed, sitting on the edge of his bed, pulling on a shoe when there was a knock at the door.

Surprised he called out, 'Who's there? What do you want?'

'Police. Open up. Now.'

Shock left him paralysed for a few seconds. Police? Here? Why? What did they want? What could they know? But he knew that he was fooling himself. There was only one reason why they would be knocking on his door at that time of night. Before he could reply there was a thunderous crash, the door flew open and half a dozen men rushed in. Isaacs was hurt and bloodied by the time the handcuffs had him secure. The police were aware how close Israel was to *Armageddon*, the biblical prophecy of a great battle between good and evil at the end of the world. They were too frightened for themselves and their families to bother with any niceties.

'Take him away,' said Major Barak, striding into the room, 'before I shoot the bastard.' As Isaacs was led away Barak turned to the police officer standing next to him. 'Are you sure that there is nobody else here connected to this . . . this obscenity?'

The policeman shrugged. 'His was the only name we had here. There are dozens of arrests taking place all over the country. We can only get to the ring leaders. There are probably hundreds of sympathisers and low-grade helpers, but we don't know who they are and probably never will. If we cut off the head the body should die.'

'We hope,' said Barak.

'Amen to that,' said the policeman.

Colonel Alexander Tradesman knew his duty. He had sworn an allegiance to Dayan and when the order came he did not hesitate. A tall, slim man in his early fifties, he was a career soldier, having served with the Israeli army all his adult life. He knew that Dayan's vision was right. Within days Israel would be a new, greater country, led by men of vision and courage. Men like himself. He stroked his pencil-line moustache with his left fore-finger, a nervous habit he had when fear stalked him. Although he would rather have died than to admit that he ever felt afraid. He was in command of two missile batteries and over the last three weeks he had acquired copies of the second missile release keys he needed to fire the nuclear weapons. Now he was in the control centre, preparing the missiles for firing.

The missiles were smaller versions of the American Minutemen, the huge transportable missiles that had been the backbone of the American defence system throughout most of the Cold War. The Minutemen and Polaris missiles fired from nuclear submarines would have wiped The Soviet Union from the face of the earth. Of course America would have been wiped out as well but that was the price worth paying for freedom. Better dead than red had been the slogan throughout the fifties and sixties. The Israeli missiles were a miniaturised version of the Minutemen, improved by Israeli scientists and engineers, using information stolen from America by Israeli supporters. A fifth of the size of the Minutemen, they packed a punch almost as great. Well, better dead than over-run by the Arabs, he thought. The order he had been waiting and praying for had come through five minutes earlier.

It was not too late, the General had told him. Israel would provoke an attack and wipe out her enemies once and for all. Tradesman did not hesitate as he placed his key into the firing console and turned it clockwise. He referred to the books, ensuring that he followed the procedure precisely.

In spite of the highly effective air-conditioning in the control van he was sweating heavily.

The heavy knocking on the door startled him. 'Open the door. Now!'

Tradesman paused and then resolutely continued what he was doing. The control room was secure and could not be forced in the usual way. There was no further knocking and Tradesman ignored what might have been happening outside. The firing sequence was complete on both sites and all it would take would be to press both buttons simultaneously. Four missiles would be launched, each carrying a warhead equivalent to the combined force of the bombs dropped on Hiroshima and Nagasaki at the end of the Second World War. For a nano-second he was aware of the control room vibrating and in that nano-second he knew he had failed.

The explosives stacked hurriedly around the control room were massive and represented an overkill factor of five. The mobile control room vaporised. Dazed and bruised policeman and soldiers picked themselves up off the ground and looked at the huge crater they had made. They looked towards the missile sites, terrified that they would see the four rockets lift into the air. Nothing happened and, as the ringing faded in their ears and breathing became easier, a ragged cheer went up.

Israel operated five sites, each with two missiles. At the remaining two sites nothing happened simply because the men trusted by Dayan to carry out his orders had vanished. When the news had broken that the attack was not forthcoming they had simply left their posts and returned to their homes. The four men, all officers, were arrested before they could flee the country.

General Obadiah Golightly had no qualms about what he had done. His orders had gone out and he was confident that at least six missiles would be fired and the war over before it began. He poured himself a large brandy and rolled the liquid around his tongue, savouring the taste. He had been a widower for nearly ten years, ever since his wife had been killed by a Palestinian attack intended for him. Since then, with no children, he had dedicated his life to this moment. His support of Dayan was unfailing and unquestioning. A great man, thought the General, raising his glass to him, confident that the outcome would be a safer, prosperous, *greater* Israel. He frowned at the faint noises coming from outside and tried to identify what he was hearing. Rattling? Scratching? What was it?

He was sitting in the living-room of his barracks quarters having left the command centre only moments earlier. The men under his command were rejoicing that the war appeared to be over before it began and he had left them to their joy. Only he knew differently.

From the safety and seclusion of his quarters Obadiah Golightly had sent the orders to fire the missiles. He was waiting for confirmation that they had been fired before rushing back to the command centre to take charge. His private, mobile phone rang and with a smile he flipped open the receiver.

'General Golightly,' he said, savouring the moment. The words he listened to filtered into his brain from a great distance, the shock causing the glass to slip from his fingers.

'You bastard,' his brother's voice said. 'We know what you've tried to do. What you've been doing. It's over. Finished.' The strength of his anger and fear caused David Golightly to talk in short, abrupt sentences. 'We know. We know what you've done. We stopped it. The reports have come in. No missiles will be fired. You will be tried, sentenced and never leave prison. The police are coming for you even as we speak. There is no escape.'

'Wait. David. I . . .' Obadiah Golightly rallied and spoke in a voice dripping with venom. 'What have you done? What have you done?' he repeated himself. 'This was our chance to make Israel secure once and for all. No more deaths, no more fear. You fool. Think of Mary.'

'Mary was killed by the Hizballah by mistake. I mourned her loss almost as much as you did but that does not justify what you've done,' David Golightly tried to keep the contempt from his voice but failed. 'Oh, Obi, Obi, it's over. It was wrong. The end does not justify the means. You will spend the rest of your life in prison doing hard labour. Or,' his voice cracked with emotion, 'or you can go with God.'

His brother disconnected and General Obadiah Golightly sat still, shock paralysing him. Now he heard it again. The noises from outside. Men coming for him. He heaved himself to his feet and walked across the room into his bedroom. The door to his quarters smashed open as he put the gun in his mouth and pulled the trigger.

*   *   *

275

Macnair and Golightly received the reports one by one. Finally Macnair said, 'That seems to be all of them. I'm sorry about your brother.'

David Golightly shook his head. 'It doesn't matter. It was for the best. Since Mary died . . . was killed, he has been a changed man. I knew it but never thought for a moment he would carry out such a mad scheme. His bitterness and hatred were there if you looked closely enough although usually he kept it masked. We don't, as a rule, promote unbalanced men to become generals. With my brother we made a mistake, for which I am responsible.'

'You?'

'Yes. Thanks to my political influence I was able to smooth the way for Obi's promotion when perhaps other, more deserving men should have received it.' He sighed and added, 'I shall resign as soon as this is all over.'

'You'll do no such thing,' said Macnair sharply. 'If it hadn't been for you Israel would have been at war. Your country needs you now more than ever. I suggest . . .' before he could continue Carter burst into the room.

'Sir, Isobel is on the computer satellite line. She needs to talk to you both.'

'Right. Thanks Jim. We'll be right with you.'

The two men hurried after Carter. In the computer link room the face of Isobel Sweeney filled one of the screens, a frown on her face.

'Isobel? What do you have for us?' Macnair asked.

'I'm sorry it took so long, General but I was confused. Sir,' she addressed herself to Golightly, 'you did say Dayan is the richest man in Israel?'

Golightly nodded. 'By far. It has been estimated that he is worth at least five billion dollars. Maybe more.' He shrugged.

'Yes, that's what I thought. It was why it took so long to get to the bottom of his affairs. I tried to add to his assets when I should have been subtracting. He isn't the richest man in Israel but the poorest.'

'What?' Golightly goggled at her.

'I think the term is "negative assets". His debts are over five billion dollars. According to the information I have, a small loan with the Bank of Japan will be called in sometime in the next forty-eight hours. If it is, then the whole of Dayan's empire will collapse. The knock-on effect will be devastating to Dayan.'

'Are you sure?' Macnair asked.

'As sure as I can be,' Isobel replied. 'There's no doubt that he's in heavy debt to practically every major bank in the world. Some of his assets have been used three, even four times. I wish I knew how he managed it,' she tried some bleak humour, 'I'd do the same.'

Golightly shook his head as the enormity penetrated his mind. 'Do you mean that this whole . . . whole affair was because Dayan is broke and his loans are about to be called in?'

Isobel shook her head. 'I can't say that, sir. I'm only telling you what I know. It appears that when he built the Assis Dam he lost something like half a billion dollars and it has been downhill from there ever since.'

Golightly's eyes opened wider in surprise and then understanding dawned on him. 'I remember now. At the time it was reported – rumoured is a better description – that he had lost a fortune on the project. Dayan insisted that he had made a fortune and sued various media groups when he showed that he had made a profit of half a billion and not a loss.'

Isobel nodded. 'Well, he lied. He also had a great deal of backing from your government. I checked some of the names involved. Senior members of the Likud Party worked to cover up the mess. Since then Dayan has been pulling one stroke after another. Like I said, it seems the whole edifice was about to come crashing down. He must have known what was going to happen years ago and perhaps he did plan the whole confrontation just to save his business empire. Perhaps the timing is coincidental, I just don't know.' She paused and then added, 'But I doubt it somehow.'

'Dayan was going to allow millions to die for money?' Golightly said, the shock still in his voice. 'It's monstrous. Unbelievable. We must get him.'

277

'I think I can help there,' Isobel said. 'I've found the proof I needed that Dayan has property in The Golan, near Syria. According to the inventory I've found, the property has been turned into an underground fortress. Which makes sense if you want to avoid a nuclear bomb dropping on your head. For what it is worth, I think that's where he'll be.'

25

Hunter knew that he had not achieved full *ka-shi*. It was beyond him. He had dragged strength up from within himself but not the all-encompassing, devastating force of *ka-shi*. The ferocity of his attack against Sheffield had been the combined application of his superb training and stamina and his absolute determination to kill Sheffield. The fact that he had failed left Hunter stunned. The strength of the man was awesome. If the woman hadn't appeared when she did Hunter had no doubt that he would be dead now. Who is she, he wondered?

One advantage of not achieving *ka-shi* was that his strength was quickly returning. He felt bruised and battered, the blows he had received from Sheffield now making themselves felt. He stifled a groan and sat up, flexing his aching muscles, checking that nothing was broken. Gratefully he realised that his injuries were superficial. He did a dozen squats followed by stretching and limbering exercises and already his aches and pains were beginning to recede. Now, he thought, I have to get out of here.

He examined the room. It was white-washed stone, four metres by four metres and if he stood on his toes Hunter could reach the ceiling. It was lit by a single light, recessed into the ceiling. There were no windows and the door had no handle. Tentatively he pushed against it and then tried harder. It did not yield as much as a millimetre. Along the wall opposite the door was a bare concrete bench. He wore only shorts and tee-shirt, the remainder of his clothes having been taken from him. His watch was missing. He sat down on the cold concrete slab and closed his eyes, husbanding his strength.

He had no way of telling how long he sat there. He was sure he had dozed but when he heard the door creaking he was immediately wide awake and stood, ready for action. He was surprised when the girl walked in. Seeing Hunter wide awake she quickly put a finger to her lips.

'I expected to find you semi-conscious,' she said quietly.

'You did? Why?'

'After that *ka-shi* attack.'

Hunter shook his head. 'I didn't achieve *ka-shi* although I tried. I'm not good enough and doubt I ever will be. I just flung everything I had at the brute but it was like attacking a brick wall.'

Ruth nodded in understanding. 'It was an impressive performance. You hurt Sheffield badly. He's asked Dayan if he can have you.'

'And what did Dayan say to that?'

'That you're all his but before he has his fun he has to check the defences around the whole area. I told them that you will probably be unconscious until the morning and Sheffield said he'd wait until then.'

'Thanks. And thanks for what you did up there. I took the hint and closed my eyes. How long do I have?'

'What? Oh, it's eleven o'clock. I came to wake you up to see if you could hide somewhere until you'd recovered fully and then you could try and escape. But to be honest I can't think of anywhere you can hide. But as you appear to have recovered you could try and get out. By the way, who are you?'

'My name is Hunter, Nick Hunter. I work for TIFAT.'

She nodded, 'I thought so. General Macnair's outfit.'

Hunter grinned. 'That's one way to describe it. Who are you?'

'My name is Ruth Golightly.'

'David Golightly's daughter?'

'You know my father?'

'I met him in Scotland,' was the laconic reply.

'You? You were with the team that rescued them off that ship?'

'I wouldn't put it as strongly as that. They were doing a pretty good job for themselves as far as I remember. What are you doing here?'

'It's a long story. I work for Mossad. Dayan doesn't know who I really am. I was infiltrated into his organisation nearly a year ago but it took me most of my time to get into a position to find out what was happening. In the last few weeks I've been trusted enough to be given a free rein. Switzerland was the first operation I'd been on for Dayan.'

'What's happened?'

'The war is off. Key personnel from Dayan's organisation have been arrested so effectively he is finished. I don't know what he intends doing, where he can hide. He might try and brazen it out but I doubt it. He's irrational. When I slipped away he was issuing orders as though he had command of an army, which is not the case. He and the others are behaving like trapped rats wanting to wreak revenge against those responsible for what's happened.'

'Like your father?'

Ruth shrugged. 'He's top of the list, along with the Prime Minister. It's been announced on the television that a warrant for Dayan's arrest has been issued. Dayan thinks he's safe here for now which may be the case. Somehow I have to let the authorities know he's here but the communications room is locked and I don't have access to it.'

'Where is it?'

'Along the corridor. Seven, no eight doors along on the right.'

'Won't that depend on which way I'm going?' Hunter asked.

'What? Oh, sorry. You're at the end. You can only go one way. Look, I'll leave the door unlocked. Wait until the dead of night and then try and escape.'

'Why don't you come with me?'

'I can't. There's something I have to do first.'

Hunter realised immediately what she meant and said, 'Don't

281

bother. You've done enough. We'll get out of here together and before we go we'll do as much damage as we can. The others will be able to deal with Dayan.'

Ruth hesitated. She knew there was little chance of her surviving even if she did manage to kill Dayan. Perhaps Hunter was right. She could try and get away with him and leave someone else to arrest Dayan, or kill him. After all, he was a spent force. No longer a threat to the country. It was time to escape. She liked life and suddenly she had an overwhelming desire to continue with hers. She nodded. 'Yes, all right. If we can get away then we can tell my father where to find Dayan and they can send in a heavy force to get him. He won't be able to escape.'

Hunter wasn't so sure but said nothing. 'Why a heavy force? How many men does he have?'

'I guess somewhere between seventy and eighty. Maybe more.'

'All combatants or are there cooks and bottle-washers?'

'Even cooks and bottle-washers can fight if they have to,' she replied, dryly.

Hunter nodded. 'True enough. You said the communications room is eight doors along. What's behind the others?'

'I don't know. Just empty cells like this one, I think. Why?'

'No reason. Okay, why don't you go now. Come back at three o'clock and we'll get out of here. In the meantime I'll see what damage I can do. Okay?'

Ruth nodded. She found his overwhelming belief in his own abilities comforting, reassuring. Yet her commonsense said it was totally misplaced. She smiled tentatively. To escape with him was a better alternative than being killed if she attacked Dayan.

Hunter smiled at the black haired, brown eyed beauty standing before him. She was about five feet six inches tall, slim and looked fit. He had an urge to get to know her better.

'Where are the weapons kept?'

'There's an armoury on this floor. The other end of the corridor. But that's locked as well.'

'All right. You'd better go now.'

Ruth checked the corridor and quickly left the cell. As soon as she was out of sight Hunter followed, sliding the two heavy bolts across, relocking the door. He shivered. The air was cold and after a few seconds he realised there was a draft coming from somewhere. The corridor was well lit with naked bulbs dangling from the ceiling. As he crept along he reached up to remove a bulb but snatched his hand away at the heat. He slipped off his tee-shirt to protect his hands, unscrewed the bulb and placed it gently on the floor. As he passed each bulb he repeated the performance. There were open doors on either side of the corridor and when he looked in Hunter saw that they were replicas of the cell he had left. The first locked door had the legend *Communications Centre* neatly painted on it. There were no bolts but a heavy lock, operated by punching in a series of numbers. Hunter did not waste his time fiddling with it but kept moving. There was a short side corridor to the right where he found a lift and a stairwell. The draft of fresh air was now on the back of his neck and looking up he saw a metre square grill. It made sense as fresh air would have to be brought down into the building either by using fans or a natural air duct. It was easier to operate an air duct.

Back in the main corridor he found doors left and right that were bolted. He opened the first one, not knowing what to expect. Other prisoners? Zilch? His luck was in. He felt along the wall, found a light switch and flicked it on. The single bulb illuminated a room that was lined with racks of cardboard boxes. He pulled one down and looked inside. It contained soap, another held shampoo. He tore open more boxes, finding scrubbing brushes, mop heads, rags. In a corner he came across a set of step ladders. Another box contained dark blue overalls of various sizes. He found a pair to fit him and slipped them on. Hunter thought that if he needed proof that the place was run on military lines, this was it. The military penchant for cleanliness and orderliness was well known to any serving or ex-service personnel and the room reeked of both. The last box contained various eating and cooking utensils. He up-ended the box and riffled through the contents until he found a sharp kitchen knife. He put it into the leg pocket of the overall, feeling better. It wasn't much if he came up against a man with a gun but it was better than nothing.

The next room yielded racks of dried and tinned food. He

located a tin of peaches, rammed a hole in the top with the knife and gratefully drank the sweet juice. Immediately he felt better, hunger and dehydration having left their mark on him. He used the knife to make the jagged hole big enough to let him hook out half a peach, which he stuffed into his mouth. Ambrosia, the food which gave the Gods their immortality, could not have tasted better. Other rooms yielded more useful gear. In one he found camouflaged jackets and trousers and a pair of combat boots. The green, rubber soled boots laced above the ankles and were both rugged and comfortable. He stripped off the overalls and put on the trousers, jacket and boots. He found a room of tools, everything from picks and shovels to electric drills and screwdrivers. The last door facing him at the end of the corridor had *Armoury* painted on it. It was locked with the same coded arrangement as the Communications Room. Hunter carefully examined the door. Whereas the other doors had been made of wood, this one was steel. He tapped it with his knuckles. It sounded solid. The door was opened by twisting a large round wheel in the middle, very much like the watertight doors found on ships. Two heavy dead-bolts locked the door in position, each one three inches by half an inch.

'*Scheisse, warum ist hier kein Lichte?*'

'*Ich weiss nicht,*' said a different German voice.

'You've been told before – speak English,' said a third with an American accent.

'I asked what was wrong with the lights.'

'Dayan forgot to pay the electricity bill,' was the facetious answer. 'Now forget it and get to the radio room. We've a hell of a lot of signals to send and Dayan is mad enough as it is.'

Hunter heard their feet clattering along the corridor, moving away from him. He had stepped into a doorway as soon as he had heard the voices, the knife in his hand. He let out a sigh of relief. Time was running out. He had a lot a to do and right now the three men in the communications centre were preventing him from doing it. However, they had solved one problem for him. They had opened the door.

As silently as a cat he retraced his steps. He paused outside and he heard the men moving around, chairs scraping on the floor. Then, the pungent smell of tobacco smoke as someone lit up. There was an immediate outcry of protest in German and the American said, 'For Christ's sake put that damn thing out. Don't you know that smoking is bad for your health?'

'Many things are bad for your health, my friend,' came the cold, accented reply. 'I will finish this cigarette.'

Neither of the other two argued further. Hunter knelt down and carefully looked inside. The smoker was the biggest, burliest man in the room. Although he was sitting sideways to Hunter, Hunter could see that he was as tall as himself, broad-shouldered but running to fat. The nose was misshapen, the eyes narrow slits beneath a sloping forehead. The cigarette burned, clenched in his right hand as his fingers operated a keyboard. In spite of the sausage-like fingers his hands flew across the keys. The other two men sat with their backs to the door, one was writing and the other was flicking switches, bringing the console in front of him to life. Hunter recognised the communications system, a *Sperry-vec SW137*, which he had last used as a sub-lieutenant onboard the minehunter, *H.M.S. Maxton.*

Hunter retreated back along the corridor to the tool room. He found the rack of chisels he had noticed earlier and thoughtfully weighed a few of them in his hand. He selected two of them and looked around to see if there was anything else he could use. On another rack was a row of hammers of all shapes and sizes. He selected two, a blacksmith's set-hammer and a machinist's straight-peen. The straight-peen had a stout handle and was ideal for throwing, while the set-hammer was a solid lump of iron which fitted into the hand, the thumb and forefinger comfortably wrapping around the slots at the square end of the head. One to throw, one to smash, Hunter decided. The chisels he discarded. Pausing in the doorway, he looked along the corridor, ensuring it was empty. He walked back towards the communications centre. A change in the light pattern through the door warned him in time. He stepped back and into the short corridor leading to the stairs.

'*Ich gehe auf die Toilette.*' A man stepped into the dark corridor and walked around the bend straight into Hunter. The startled oath died on the man's lips as Hunter brought the set-hammer smashing down onto his head. He collapsed without a sound. Hunter felt for a pulse but found nothing. He grabbed hold of the dead man's collar and dragged the body into the nearest cell. The odds were now considerably altered in his favour.

At the door to the communications room Hunter paused and looked inside. The big man was still at the keyboard while the other, wearing a pair of headphones, was bent over the console, his back to the door. Hunter stepped into the room and took a pace towards the nearest man. He must have caught some movement from the corner of his eye because he looked up, saw Hunter, gave an oath and started to stand, reaching for the gun carried in the holster at his side. Hunter swung the straight-peen into the man's hand even as he was drawing the weapon from its holster. Bones broke and the man yelled, the noise warning the other man who looked over his shoulder. Hunter threw the set-hammer at his adversary's head which was only inches away from his outstretched arm. There was a sickening crunch and the man collapsed. The other man was on his feet and had drawn his gun. Hunter threw himself to one side as the gun went off and the bullet sailed past his ear, burying itself in the wooden door opposite. Hunter was on his knees six feet away and in desperation threw the remaining hammer at the man's head. The man had lightning reflexes and ducked. Hunter missed but the sudden movement caused the man to jerk the gun and the shot that was intended for Hunter's torso instead grazed his upper arm. Before the man could aim and fire again Hunter leapt at him, knocked his gun hand to one side and hit him in the throat with the extended fingers of his right hand. His left hand, held like a chopping axe, he brought crashing into the side of the man's neck and the carotid artery. It had been the same combination of strikes that he had used on Sheffield only this time the outcome was different. The man gurgled, his eyes bulged and he dropped dead. Hunter breathed heavily with relief. If the third man had been there Hunter knew he would not have survived.

He dragged the two bodies into the same room as the other

corpse and removed the belt and holster from one of them. He strapped it to his waist and proceeded to help himself to the dead man's watch. He retrieved one of the guns and found it to be a French MAB PA-15. The gun held fifteen 9mm Parabellum rounds of ammunition and was one of the most commonly found revolvers in the world, having been sold commercially from 1960. A second gun, the same model, he slipped into a pocket before turning his attention to his wounded arm. The bullet had grazed his upper arm and left it seeping blood. He knew he should not leave it to fester. Heroes in films ignored wounds without any ill-effect. The reality was that even a minor wound could quickly turn ugly if it wasn't treated. He checked the corridor and went back along to the room containing the cleaning utensils. He found a rag and a bottle of disinfectant. He dabbed the wound, the pungent smell of household detergent lingering on his arm. He tied a rag around his arm and put his jacket back on. He flexed his fingers, satisfied he had done all he could to prevent infection.

The corridor remained dark and empty, the only light coming from the communications centre. He returned quickly and sat at the console. Although the equipment was at least twenty years old it was still in use around the world. Powerful yet sturdy, it could take the wear and tear of constant use on a small ship which operated in the foulest of weather. The only drawback was that world-wide communication was achieved using Morse. He twisted the large frequency tuning dial in the centre until he reached 102.45 megahertz. He did not make the mistake of putting the earphones on, blocking out any other noises around him, but held them to one ear.

Morse was no longer the usual means of communicating world-wide having long been overtaken by satellite and e-mail. The *SW137* – short-wave model 137 – could transmit in clear language up to a hundred and fifty miles and on a good day perhaps as far as two-hundred and fifty, depending upon the atmospherics. However, using Morse, Hunter knew he could transmit to Australia without any difficulty.

Hunter's Morse "fist" enabled him to send and receive at

an approximate speed of eight words per minute, the standard required of all Royal Naval seamen officers of his generation. He had practised the Morse Code by encrypting in his head signposts and car number plates as he drove his car. It was a habit he had developed when he first began to learn the Morse Code and one he found difficult to break even now, although he no longer practised it as obsessively as he had in the past.

Hunter flexed his fingers and started tapping the key. Dash, dash, dot, dash, pause, dot, pause, dash, dot, pause, dash, dot, dot. Quebec, Echo, November, Delta, over, was what he transmitted three times. He waited a few seconds and was about to repeat the signal when he heard the reply. He frowned, pencil poised and listened to the series of long and short beeps that sounded in his ear. It seemed to take forever as he established his identity, each word spelt out slowly.

'Chess this is Rook, over,' he transmitted. Over was dash, dot, dash, the letter kilo.

'Rook this is Chess, loud and clear, over.' They were receiving him without difficulty.

'Chess this is Rook, please connect me to King or Queen, over.' The callsigns had been designed in the early days of TIFAT for use in an emergency. Easy to remember, they immediately triggered an automatic trace when used. Chess was the headquarters in Rosyth, King was Macnair, Queen was Hiram Walsh.

'Roger that. Voice on 98.5 megahertz, over.'

Hunter breathed a sigh of relief. With an automatic fix on his position and knowing Macnair's location the operator had decided that voice contact was possible.

'Roger, out.' Hunter quickly turned the dial and broadcast in clear voice. 'This is Rook, come in King, over.' He let go the transmit button and the earphones crackled and hissed.

'Rook, stand by please, over,' the communications operator for the watch onboard the *S.S. Darnah* replied.

After a few minutes, which seemed like an eternity to Hunter, Macnair's voice sounded in his ear. 'Nick, is that you, my boy?' The voice was faint but clear.

'Affirmative, sir.' Briefly Hunter told the General what had happened since the attack on the oil-rig. 'I now intend getting the hell out of here,' he finished.

'I concur with that. Isobel had already confirmed Dayan's bolt-hole and we are currently working on a plan of attack. We are having political problems with the Israelis because your position confirms what we already suspected – you are in the disputed border territory between Syria and Israel. The Syrians are not happy for the Israelis to enter the area with a large force of men and the Israelis are not prepared for the Syrians to do likewise. Also there is a question of national pride. The Israelis want to take care of Dayan themselves, while the Syrians are arguing that in view of what's happened, Israel has forfeited any rights in the matter. It's the usual political clap-trap, over.'

'Since when has that ever bothered you, sir? Over.'

'It doesn't, usually. But now there are some seriously heavy and loud noises being made across the world from America to China and throughout Europe. I've been practically ordered to do nothing. Over.'

'Sir, we can't let Dayan off the hook at this stage and from what I've seen of him he probably has contingency plans ready, just in case everything did go pear-shaped. Also, you did say practically ordered, over.'

Macnair chuckled. 'I knew I could rely on you to understand. I've had no direct orders but I have had serious suggestions made to me that we've done all we need to. I don't agree but I'm waiting for the green light. If we're allowed in we'll be there at zero three hundred tomorrow which is,' there was a pause, 'twenty-five hours from now and the earliest we can manage. Over.'

'Sir, I think that will be too late. Over.'

'It's the best we can do. If needs be, Dayan can escape and the international community can hunt him down. Over.'

'General, at the last count there were over a hundred and eighty-five arrest warrants outstanding for men and a few women who are wanted for crimes against humanity. You know as well as I do that the chances of serving those warrants are practically nil. Over.'

'Damn it, Nick, I know but it's the best I can do. I won't go off half-cocked and risk the lives of my men. I also daren't risk another incident between Israel and Syria, in case it flares up into something a lot more serious. We are on a knife edge as it is. There's an emergency meeting taking place even now at the United Nations and demands for reparations from the Israelis are already being made. It's a huge international mess which will take months if not years to settle. Over.'

'Understood. I have an idea,' Hunter said, thinking furiously.

26

Hunter needed to prevent Dayan escaping before friendly forces could arrive. To do so he had to work fast. He left the communications room with the light on. Should anybody arrive they would be attracted to the lit room like a moth to a flame in the dark. He would keep an ear cocked and, hopefully, he would hear anybody arriving and be able to deal with them.

In the tool room, tucked away in the furthest corner, he found what he was looking for – an oxy-acetylene cutting torch. What he couldn't find was a means of lighting the gas and returned to search the pockets of the smoker he had killed. He found a cheap throw-away plastic lighter.

He wheeled the heavy bottles into the corridor, turned on the gases and lit them, adjusting the flame until it burnt blue with a pale yellow tip. The flame was a loud roar in the quiet confines of the corridor. He had found leather gloves but no safety goggles so he averted his face when he applied the torch to the top metal bar holding the door to the armoury locked. Sparks flew in all directions as he drew the flame along the metal and pungent smoke was released as he made a ragged cut. After a few minutes he removed the torch and looked at his handiwork. The bolt was still held in place by a thin thread of metal and Hunter aimed the flame on the thread and held it there. It melted away. He used the torch on the lower bolt and quickly made the cut. He turned off the gases, grateful for the sudden quiet. In spite of turning his head away and slitting his eyes Hunter was seeing spots and he closed his eyes for a few moments until they returned to normal.

He listened intently but the corridor remained silent. He put his foot out and pushed at the heavy door. It swung open and he stepped into the armoury, careful not to touch the still hot metal. He groped along the wall, found the light switch and flicked it on. He sucked in his breath at what he saw. The last time he had seen such an array of weapons had been on board the aircraft carrier *U.S.S. Eisenhower*. There were racks of Uzis, GPMGs, Brens, Kalashnikovs with their famous banana shaped magazine, Dragunovs and yet more racks of American weapons from Thompsons to Barrett light machine guns. There was a complete rack of Smith and Wesson revolvers while another rack was neatly lined with revolvers and pistols from all over the world. Yet a further rack contained hand-held Stinger launchers and Chinese Dragon Hawks. There were enough weapons and ammunition to fight a small war. Even, Hunter thought laconically, a medium sized one.

The room stretched twenty metres away from him and was at least fifteen metres wide. The armourer, whoever he was, was a methodical man. Taped to the wall next to a desk Hunter found lists of what was in the room. The contents of the safe surprised him. The detonators and timers which he read off the list were, he knew, obsolete. However, he had trained on them years earlier. He quickly ran his eyes down the list, looking for what he wanted. He grinned. Everything he needed and more was to be found there. He dragged the oxy-acetylene bottles into the room and positioned them near a heavy metal safe as tall as himself and equally wide. He shoved the door to the armoury shut and placed a chair behind it. If the door was opened he would hear the chair scraping on the concrete floor and be forewarned. He hoped.

On the lists of contents he had noticed safety goggles and quickly located them. He needed finesse for the next cut. The safe had a central dial to set the combination and a brass handle on the right to open the door, next to a keyhole. The hinges on the left were recessed but still evident. It was an old-fashioned monster built to be fire and damage resistant, because of its contents. According to the lists detonators, detonating cord, electric cable and timing devices were to be found inside.

He lit the torch, adjusted the goggles and began to cut carefully and cleanly down the right hand side of the door. The steel surface of the door was only a thin skin covering thick pig iron. By the time he had worked the burning flame down the length of the door Hunter was sweating profusely. He switched off the torch and filled a bucket of water from a sink in the corner. He threw the contents over the door and repeated the action three more times. The immediate vaporisation into hissing steam had abated sufficiently by the time he threw the last bucketful to let him stick his knife into the cut. He drew it down the safe, frequently hitting iron he had not cut through. He re-lit the torch and drew the flame along the cut a second time, continuing to throw buckets of water then tried again with the knife. Twice it stuck. He used the torch a third time, cutting only in the area where the knife had jammed. More water and he was able to take hold of the door and pull. It swung open, revealing a solid steel container five feet deep.

Before going through the contents of the safe, Hunter opened a cupboard where he found complete webbing sets. The webbing was designed to carry enough gear to make a fighting soldier self-sufficient for as long as forty-eight hours. He filled the water bottle, checked the contents of the medical bag and placed hand-grenades in a pouch. Another pouch he filled with k-rations, the high protein food concentrate designed to give energy but no waste product. Slinging a heavy General Purpose Machine Gun and two ammunition belts across his shoulders, he staggered under the weight along the corridor. He hid the gun and webbing in a room next to the small corridor and returned to the armoury.

Hunter was spoilt for choice when it came to choosing another weapon. He discarded the idea of a machine gun as it was easy to squander ammunition, deciding instead on a rifle for long range work. It was then he discovered the VAL Silent Sniper, left off the inventory. The Russian-built rifle was only made known to the West in 1994. A silent semi-automatic rifle firing a heavy 9mm bullet at subsonic velocity, it boasted a special cartridge capable of defeating all levels of body armour up to 400 metres. The magazine carried 20 rounds and fully loaded weighed only

2.5kg. Hunter knew that Badonovitch had suggested to Macnair they get hold of one for TIFAT.

He filled pouches with boxes of ammunition and empty magazines. Into other bags he stuffed plastic explosives, safety fuse and detonating cord or cordtex. From the safe he took a specially manufactured tin into which he fitted five No. 82 Mk 2N electric detonators and five No. 80 Mk 1N safety fuse detonators. Each one sat snugly and separately in a padded sheath. Wrapping the tin in a rag, he placed it in a separate satchel. Hunter had a healthy respect for the instability of detonators.

He checked the time. He had been in the armoury nearly fifty minutes and knew that he was running out of luck. Slinging a length of rope over his shoulder, he picked up the bags he had packed and walked along the corridor. The Russian rifle was cocked and ready for use, held casually across his chest, the quickest position from which to aim and fire, other than being held at the shoulder. He dropped the bags under the ventilation grill, collected the step ladder and a battery operated screwdriver. Climbing the steps, he scraped the paint off the four screws holding the grill in place and undid them. He pushed the grill up out of the way and climbed after it. The only item he had looked for but not found was a torch and so he resorted to the cigarette lighter. In the flickering light he could see that the shaft was at least a metre square and went straight up. To his relief he saw there were metal handles fading into the darkness above him, presumably, he thought, to aid maintenance. He put his foot on the lowest and pushed down. It easily held his weight. Climbing down into the corridor, he laboriously carried the bags and weapons into the shaft, item by item. He tied the rope to one of the handles and dropped the end through the hatch. Finally, he climbed back down and replaced the set of steps in the storeroom. All that was left now was for him to set a booby trap or two.

In the armoury he started work from the back. He placed half kilogram blocks of plastic explosives amongst the weapons and ammunition throughout the room. Each block had a hole through it into which he threaded lines of cordtex. The detonating cord is an instantaneous detonating fuze consisting of a textile tube with a plastic finish with an explosive core in the form of a white powder whose detonating velocity is 20,000ft/sec. Being almost immune from detonation by friction, ordinary shock or flame, it was very safe, only burning slowly and not detonating under ordinary conditions of fire. Were it subjected to intense heat, or tamped or confined in any way while burning, it would work like high explosive. At each block Hunter tied a simple knot in the cordtex, thus ensuring an explosion.

The blocks and cordtex he secreted carefully throughout the armoury, using black masking tape where necessary to hide the white cordtex. He then set an electric timing device which he hid very carefully.

At the safe he set the first trap. He used two Mk 1 safety fuse ignitors. If the ring spindle at the end of the fuze was pulled away and released, a ball moving between the striker and the spindle would hit a cap and make a flash, igniting the safety fuse, burning and igniting the cordtex. In this case, as he wanted an instantaneous explosion, Hunter by-passed the safety fuse and fitted the detonators to the cordtex. He fixed the detonators inside the safe by taping them to a shelf and ran a thread from the ring of the spindle to the handle of the door.

The next trap, using a similar set-up, he set in the drawer of the desk. A third trap he placed in the racks of the machine guns and the fourth at the door to the armoury. Each trap had its own quantity of plastic explosives, as though it was a stand-alone explosion. However, near each trap Hunter took time to place three Mk 1N No. 80 safety fuse detonators. The two inch tubes, half filled with a mixture of lead azide and mercury fulminate, were primary explosives. They needed to be treated with caution as they could explode if dropped onto a hard surface. Hunter taped three of the detonators together and placed them so that their open end faced the explosives but were hidden less than half a metre away. From the detonators he led cordtex to the main explosive charges he had laid in the armoury. Anybody finding the traps would locate the first quantity of plastic explosives. If they didn't find one of the traps and set it off, the resulting sympathetic detonation would explode the three detonators. They in turn would ignite the cordtex which would set off the main charges. Hunter hoped that either Dayan's men would be so careless as to set off one of the traps which in turn would set off the main explosives or that they would find each of the traps. Just as long as they didn't find the main explosives and the timer.

In the communications room he placed plastic explosives with an electronic timer set to explode in two hours. He hid the device buried beneath paper files inside a wall cabinet. He switched off the light. The die was cast. If the bodies weren't discovered or the damage he had done to the armoury door found, the explosion in the communications room would set the cat amongst the pigeons. He only needed Ruth to appear to make good their escape.

Hunter climbed the rope into the ventilation shaft and replaced the grill. He sat down wearily, his head resting on the wall, his eyes drooping. A scuffling noise jerked him wide awake. He lifted one edge of the grill and looked down. He was aware of a figure cautiously creeping along the corridor from the stairs and assumed reasonably that it was Ruth. Just in case, he got his revolver ready.

'What are you doing?' A harsh voice asked behind her and she jumped in surprise, spinning round, crouched, ready to attack.

A gun was pointed at her head, the click of the revolver's hammer being pulled back, an ominous sound in the quiet of the corridor.

'Nothing. I . . . I was coming to check on the prisoner.' She had an inspiration. 'Sheffield ordered it.'

'That's strange. I have just left him and he said nothing to me. In fact we have spent half the night examining our defences and there has been no opportunity for him to speak to anyone without my knowledge. You're lying. Put your hands up, bitch. We're going to see Sheffield.'

'Wait!' Ruth was thinking furiously. 'I am telling the truth. Can't you see that something is wrong? The lights are out. There's no sound from the radio operators and they were sent down earlier. Something is wrong. Come on! We need to investigate.'

She turned around and, heart pounding, expecting a bullet in her back at any second, she moved further along the corridor.

The man hesitated and then came after her. 'Stop, I say. Or I will shoot. I mean it.' He had stepped further along the corridor and was standing beneath Hunter's hiding place. Hunter did not jump onto the man's back as he was more than likely to fall and hurt himself. Instead he dropped behind him and smashed the butt of his gun into the man's head. The momentum of the drop and the movement with his hand smashed the man's head to pulp and he fell dead.

'Oh! You scared me to death!' Ruth gasped, relieved to see him.

'Here,' he held his hands together in front of him, creating a stirrup, 'jump up and throw down the rope you'll find there.' She stepped onto his hands and he flung her upwards. Simultaneously, Ruth leapt and flew easily through the trapdoor.

'Here,' she dropped the rope and he tied it around the dead man. He grabbed it and climbed up alongside her. He pulled on the rope and dragged the body into the ventilation shaft.

'Are you okay?' he asked.

'Sure. What about you?'

'I've been having fun.' He told her briefly what he had done and the conversation he'd had with Macnair. 'We have an hour and forty-five minutes or thereabouts to get away. I'll climb the shaft while you tie the gear to the end of the rope. When I get to the top I'll haul it up while you follow behind and prevent it snagging. All right?'

'All right,' she whispered.

Hunter climbed steadily, easily. The air became cooler the higher he went. Just as he was thinking he had to be near the top his head smashed into another grill, surprising him. He reached up tentatively to find it was a flimsy metal mesh. He bent his head and put his shoulders up against it. He strained upwards and after a second or two the mesh tore open and he clambered over the edge into a large room. He reached down, gave three sharp tugs on the rope and began pulling the equipment up. It was heavier than he expected and he was soon straining on the rope. After a few minutes the first of the bags reached him. At the end of the rope was the heavy GPMG and the belts of ammunition. Ruth followed right behind, unsnagging the load whenever it caught on one of the handles.

'We're on the roof,' she whispered. 'This is a stand-alone room perched on the top containing filter equipment for fresh air.'

'I figured as much. I've brought you a spare webbing set. Let's get you kitted up and we'll get out of here.'

Macnair was frowning. He had a serious problem. Since David Golightly had flown off the ship to return to the Knesset to attend an emergency meeting of the Israeli parliament the *SS Darnah* had been steaming north. Since the beginning of the affair Macnair had been moving men and equipment to areas accessible by helicopter in the Lebanon and the Turkish held part of Cyprus. For the last twelve hours they had been ferried to the ship. There were now forty-eight fighting men plus equipment on board. The men were everywhere, in corridors, on the open deck and in fact would have to hot-bunk it before long. The last time a vessel was voluntarily so crowded, thought Macnair, was on board a WW2 submarine.

His problem was that he had no means of ferrying his force into the Gaza to attack Dayan's stronghold. The helicopters he had been using were civilian and inadequate. He needed proper military helicopters but as things stood Israel was paralysed with fear and indecision. The rest of the Middle East was not prepared to get further involved unless it was under terms totally unacceptable to Israel. The reparations debate in the UN was not helping and Israel's politicians were already arguing that there was no justification in blaming Israel. The Israeli mind, thought Macnair, was amazingly selective. Capable of self-deception on a scale no other nation had ever achieved. They had ignored every UN mandate that did not suit them, demanded aid from the Americans as though it was owed to them, violated as many human rights as the Chinese and justified too many decisions and actions on the grounds of religion and national security.

Macnair looked pensively at the sheet of paper he was holding.

No one apart from Isobel knew of its existence. To have achieved what he had, Dayan had needed help outside Israel. Important help. Macnair had no idea how it had been achieved, whether coercion, bribery or honest support had been the motivating factors but the list contained the names of men and women around the world, of all nationalities, who had been helping Dayan. Perhaps they still were, thought Macnair. The problem was that in some cases they had also been supporting Macnair. A classic CYA (Cover Your Ass) scenario or had they been two-timing TIFAT? There was no way of telling without further investigation and, reading the list, Macnair knew there was very little likelihood of that happening. Macnair, like all good generals, knew when to attack and when to fold up his tent and quietly sneak away until another day. This was a day for the latter. But he would use TIFAT's considerable financial base to dig deep and get proof. It may not be court-of-law proof but it could be enough to be of use in the future, should favours be needed. He frowned. Was blackmail that easy? When was it justified? Was it ever? Was he creating a monster because he thought it was for the better good? Where were the checks and balances needed in any democracy to stop incompetent, even evil, men from achieving power? He sat in pensive silence terrified at the thoughts that were bubbling up, reluctantly coming to a conclusion that he knew was inevitable.

He looked down the list again. A few names caused him immense sadness. One could be of help. But before he called on that person, Macnair had important work to do.

He picked up the sat-nav phone and called Isobel in Scotland. He could hear the weariness in her voice when she answered.

'Isobel? Sorry to disturb you. Were you sleeping?'

'What? Oh no, General. I was thinking about Nick. Wondering what was happening since he contacted us.'

'He's all right for now but I need your help to get him out.'

Isobel immediately perked up. 'Right. Just tell me what you want me to do.'

When Macnair had finished she was somewhat disappointed. 'Is that all? Is there nothing more?'

'No. I need the information as quickly as possible. I need to know why he did it. He's the one man on the list right now who can help. How long will it take?'

'It depends. If he was coerced then I'll need to dig into the information until I find it. If he was bribed with money it may be easy enough. If he was persuaded to help because of his beliefs then I may never get what you're looking for. Let me call you back as soon as I think I have anything.'

'Right. Also have Sarah monitor the area around Quneitra as closely as she can. We may be able to learn something as events unfold.'

'I already have done,' Isobel replied.

Macnair smiled. He should have known. 'Good. That's all for now.' He broke the connection stood up and stretched the weariness out of his bones. He busied himself making a fresh pot of coffee aware that he didn't need any more caffeine, only something to do while he waited. With a mug in his hand he stood at the window looking out into the black night, seeing only his reflection, wondering if the man looking back at him had what it took to do the job he had fought for. He shook his head, turned away, banishing his doubts. There was no one else right now. He put the mug down, sank into a comfortable chair, leaned back and closed his eyes. Within minutes he was asleep. The phone woke him forty-five minutes later.

At the end of his conversation with Isobel he said, 'Good work. Send me what you've got. All the details including the account numbers. It should be enough.' He broke the connection, paused, took a deep breath and dialled a number. The phone rang for a long time. Finally it was answered.

'Roberts,' said the annoyed voice of the Supreme Allied Commander Europe.

'It's Macnair.'

'Malcolm? What do you want at this ungodly hour?' Irritation tinged with anger came clearly over the telephone.

'I want you to listen. Don't interrupt and then you can do what I tell you.'

'How dare you!' The irritation was gone, venom filled the

300

voice. 'Do you know who you're talking to? I'll break you for this. You're finished. You don't come on the phone in the middle of the night and make demands.'

'Yes, I do,' Macnair cut in. 'Especially when the man I'm talking to is a traitor to humanity and has betrayed his office.'

'What? What are you talking about? What nonsense are you spouting? Are you drunk?'

'Shut up, Dwight,' Macnair said harshly, angrily, his hand gripping the phone so tightly it was in danger of being crushed. 'I know about your support for Dayan. I know exactly what you did for him and what he paid you. Though to abuse your position as you have is beyond me. Now I want your help and you're going to give it to me.'

His words were greeted with silence as the man on the other end of the line, the most powerful military officer in Europe, weighed up what he had just heard. He was about to bluster, demand an apology, get angry, when commonsense prevailed. Macnair was not the type to go off half-cocked. It was one of the reasons he had been chosen to head TIFAT. For the first time in his life, after a career of facing and beating all the odds, Roberts was suddenly unsure of himself. It was a feeling that blew up in the pit of his stomach and mushroomed through his body, paralysing him. Sweat broke out on his forehead, the receiver suddenly became slippery in his hand. What did the swine know? He sat up, swinging his feet to the floor, control reasserting itself. He cleared his throat. He needed to know more. 'What?' To Macnair's satisfaction Robert's voice sounded strangled, tinged with fear, although the anger was just below the surface, barely under control. Macnair knew that he needed to keep the other man off balance, not give him time to think – to keep the momentum going – to get what he needed. Roberts was rallying quickly. 'I don't know what you're talking about. I may have agreed with Dayan's original aims but I have never agreed with his methods. Never. A secure Greater Israel is one thing, war is something else.'

'Nice try, Dwight, but it won't wash. I'm telling you I know precisely what you've done and what you've been paid. I can

301

even tell you the numbers of your bank accounts in Switzerland and the Caymans.'

That shut General Roberts up for a few seconds as he thought frantically, wishing now that he had not drunk himself into oblivion earlier, needing his wits about him like never before. His worse nightmare had come true, even though he had tried to convince himself that Dayan would not have been so stupid as to keep a record of their dealings. That he would have honoured their arrangement and expunged all information connecting them. He should have know better, he thought bitterly.

'Malcolm, I . . .'

'I don't want any of your excuses,' said Macnair. 'What you did was inexcusable. Despicable. You betrayed your office for five million dollars.' There was a sharp intake of breath. 'Oh yes, I know the exact details. Dayan kept impeccable records.'

'Malcolm, please, you have to understand. I needed to. I retire in three years and I'm broke. I'm in debt up to my ears. My pension won't even pay the interest on what I owe. I survive now because of my office. Free accommodation, food, drink. Allowances that make life bearable. I needed the money. I'm broke,' he repeated.

Macnair's skin crawled at the thought that the weak and greedy man on the other end of the phone wielded so much power in Europe. 'You can't be,' Macnair said, drawn into the discussion in spite of himself.

'I'm telling you, I am. Three divorces leaves you gutted,' said Roberts. 'Along with poor investment advice and speculating on a property venture that failed. When I retire I go down, all the way. It's not an option.'

'Too bad. You've betrayed your office and your country.'

Roberts took a deep breath. 'I knew when you got involved that Dayan's days were numbered,' he said bitterly. 'I just hoped and prayed that he would move fast enough so that you didn't stop him. May you rot in hell.'

'Dwight, you're a disgrace to your uniform. However, you can still survive this,' Macnair paused, letting the bait dangle.

After a few seconds Roberts said tentatively, 'How?' It came out as a croak and he cleared his throat, repeating himself, 'How?'

'By giving me the help I need. The Sixth Fleet is currently operating in the Eastern Mediterranean.'

'Correct. Between what's happening in Bosnia, Serbia and Israel, it's the only place for it to be.'

'Right. I want eight helicopters to carry a team of fully armed and equipped men into combat and I want them tomorrow at zero one hundred hours.'

'What? I can't do that! I don't have operational control. That's with the Pentagon as you well know.'

'The Pentagon doesn't approve of or order sorties, it gives strategic orders and leaves the tactics to the local officer commanding. In this case Admiral Charles M. Myer. I believe he's a friend of yours.'

Roberts did not ask how Macnair got his information. Nothing Macnair did or knew surprised him any longer. 'That still doesn't mean I can get Chuck to supply you with eight helicopters. What for, for God's sake?'

'To get Dayan.'

'What? What do you mean? You haven't got him?' Hope sprung up in Roberts.

'We know where he is but the fact that we haven't got our hands on him doesn't help you one little bit. We lifted detailed information from Dayan's files telling us all we needed to know. The detail is such that any court in the world will believe it is true. I know that you supplied Dayan with important information and helped him to build a secret arsenal of weapons. I know that you did all in your considerable power to keep any investigation away from Dayan and in one case you actually altered a report to protect him. It's all there along with the money. What you don't know but what we've found out is that Dayan has the ability to recall the payments he's made to you and the others. Your control over the money is, to say the least, tenuous.'

'Others?' Roberts clutched at the thought. Maybe there was help available after all.

Macnair guessed what he was thinking and said, 'Others. But

you'll never know who they are and in any case they cannot and will not help you. It's too late for that. It's over, finished. We need to tie up the loose ends once and for all and draw a line under the whole sad and sorry affair. Dwight,' Macnair had wielded the stick, it was time for the carrot, 'nobody will ever know. Not from me anyway. Now, you can tell Myer that this is a directive from the President. It is needed in the interests of world peace. Tell him anything you like. I want eight helicopters here tonight.'

'Where's here?' Roberts asked, resignation in his voice, an idea beginning to form, hope rising again. There was possibly another way to deal with Macnair, he thought.

'You don't need to know. I can talk to Myer directly, you just need to give the order. And don't try anything. I don't trust you. Be aware that copies of the information I have been sent to safe places. If you try anything you will be ruined, I promise you that.'

The idea of telling Admiral Myer that Macnair's ship held Dayan and his men and therefore was to be destroyed without hesitation faded.

'Is that all?' Roberts asked.

'That's all. I can take care of the rest.'

'And afterwards? What will you do then? Release the information anyway?'

Macnair was surprised at the question, especially in view of what he had just been saying. 'Of course not. I told you, you keep your end of the bargain and I'll keep mine. Nobody will ever learn from me of your involvement. However, you will resign. You cannot be trusted to hold such an important job. You've sold your soul to one devil and are capable of doing it again. After all, why stop at five million dollars?'

'No! No, I can't! I won't! I'll do as you say but I keep my job. It's not for long. I leave in two months. To the Pentagon. My last years before retirement. You can't deprive me of those.'

'I can and I will,' Macnair paused. He did not want to pressurise Roberts so much that he would do something stupid. A cornered rat will fight no matter what the odds and Macnair

304

needed Roberts' co-operation. 'All right. I'll make a compromise. You can stay until you finish this tour. You will then resign on the grounds of ill-health. You don't go to the Pentagon but slip into obscurity to enjoy your money, if you can. If you do that then it will be the end of the matter as far as I'm concerned,' he paused. 'Well man, what do you say?'

'I say you're a bastard,' snarled Roberts, 'and one day you'll go too far and somebody will get you.'

'In that case you had better hope and pray it won't be in your life time. If it is you'll be disgraced and will end your time in a state penitentiary somewhere.'

'All right, damn you. I agree. Give me an hour. You can contact Myer after that.'

'Get an aide to signal me with call signs and authentication tables,' Macnair ordered and broke the connection. Only then, as he flexed his fingers, did he realise how worried he had been about the outcome. If Roberts hadn't agreed to help, Macnair would have ruined the man but that was no consolation. His priority was to get Dayan and, if possible, save Hunter.

Jim Carter entered the room. 'I heard your voice. May I join you?'

'Please. I was about to send for you. We've work to do. Where are we?'

'Just past Haifa. I've told the officer of the watch to slow down,' even as he spoke the engine noise changed and the ship began to reduce speed. 'We'll enter a box pattern in an hour's time for the rest of the night. At daylight we'll head west and turn round when we need to. That way we won't draw any attention to ourselves. What about transport?'

'The Sixth Fleet will co-operate. I'm waiting for authentication and call sign details.'

Carter nodded, not surprised that Macnair had somehow managed it. 'We'll be ready to go. Hiram has everything organised. However, he estimates that loading time will be two hours and that's if everything runs smoothly.'

Macnair nodded. 'That's what I figured. Even at that there's no room for error. Even if we lift two men at a time, with all the gear, it'll still take too long. What's more, in the dark there is every likelihood of an accident. It's sod's law.'

'At sea they call it dos's law. Sod's law backwards. If anything does go wrong it goes wrong twice as bad as anywhere else. But I can't see an alternative.'

Macnair picked up an internal telephone and called the bridge. 'Officer of the Watch? Send me down a copy of the chart we have for Northern Israel and Southern Lebanon.' He listened for a moment. 'Yes, that's the one. Thank you.' He hung up. 'There is an alternative which, according to an old fashioned cliché, will kill two birds with one stone.'

Carter raised a quizzical eyebrow and poured two coffees, curious to hear what Macnair was now planning. There was a knock on the door and Peter Weir opened it. 'You want this, sir?'

'Thank you, corporal. Is everything quiet?'

'Yes, sir. The OOW said to tell you that we will be starting our box pattern in half an hour.'

'Good. Thank you,' Macnair dismissed him. The box pattern meant the ship would alter course ninety degrees every five miles, sailing in a clockwise direction. Macnair spread the chart on the table and pointed. 'Twelve miles north of the town of Nahariya is the Lebanese border. The nearest town in Lebanon is Sour, fifteen miles north. Along this stretch is desolate coast, much of it is sandy beaches. I propose that we ferry all the men and equipment ashore using the boats and the helicopter. By the time the Americans arrive we should have everybody and everything ashore. The helicopters land, we embark in minutes and away we go. The likelihood of an accident will be minimised and we won't waste any time.'

Carter nodded. 'That's a good idea but I've just thought of something else. Look at this shore. If this chart is accurate there's deep water just here all the way into here.' He pointed with a pair of dividers. 'Why don't we drive the ship right into the beach? Drop stern anchors and then rig jackstays from the deck to the shore. We can rig two, maybe four jackstays and have the gear ashore in no time. And it will be a lot safer.'

Macnair nodded. 'Good idea. Do we have enough wire and rope?'

'Probably not, but we can get the Americans to supply us with what we need. They'll have standing equipment we can rig in no time. One sling load will do it.'

Macnair nodded. 'All right. Use half the men to establish a safe beachhead while the rest hump the gear. I'll talk to David Golightly and tell him to keep the Israeli army away if he can. The last thing we need is a fight with the Israelis or an unprovoked attack by their air force. Let's plan to hit the beach at sunset tonight.'

A teleprinter in the corner began to rattle. Macnair walked across to read what was spewing forth. 'The green light from Roberts, including authentication codes for the next forty-eight hours. That should reduce the risk of error. I'll call Myer now . . .'

'I shouldn't just yet, sir. Let him have his sleep. He'll be more receptive in the morning and in any case, there's no advantage in waking him. We can't do anything before daylight and we have all day to achieve our objectives.'

Macnair nodded. 'You're right. I'll get some sleep as well, so should you. We've a long day ahead.'

27

Hunter had checked the equipment and was now eating a complete k-ration meal washed down by distilled water with added glucose and salts. He checked his watch. 'An hour to go. Ready?'

Ruth nodded. 'Whenever you are.'

'Have you told me everything you can think of?'

She shrugged. 'Like I said, I haven't been here often and I haven't seen everything. As far as I know there is only the one helicopter and the two garages containing the Jeeps and lorries. Apart from the armoury down below the men have their own weapons. There could be a ready-use store somewhere but I haven't come across it.'

Hunter nodded. 'There's bound to be. It doesn't make sense to keep all your weaponry buried so far under ground it would take too long to get at it. There must be an arms store within easy reach. Let's just keep our eyes open and hope we find it. Remember, stealth and silence at all times. When the crap hits the fan make for the archway and wait there. If I don't make it get the hell out of here and keep going. If you don't make it I'll do the same. Right?'

'Right.'

'Let's go.'

The rope was threaded around the top of the ventilation shaft which stuck three feet proud of the roof. Hunter threw both ends over the side of the building and Ruth clambered the seven metres to the ground. She gave two tugs and Hunter retrieved the rope.

The equipment was in three bundles and he lowered each of them down to her. He followed and once on the ground pulled one end of the rope to retrieve it. From the vantage point of the roof they had spent many minutes examining the layout, looking for sentries, trying to detect any activity. At first the buildings had seemed quiet and deserted but as the minutes had past they began to detect a movement here, a cough there. Somebody had lit a cigarette and across the courtyard two guards had come together and had exchanged a few words. Slowly it dawned on Hunter that the place was alive with guards. If the roof they'd been on hadn't overlooked a narrow alley at the back they would never have been able to climb down undetected.

They left the GPMG and its ammunition at the corner of the building. For what Hunter planned all they needed was contained in the bags they carried and on the webbing they wore. Hunter put his mouth close to Ruth's ear and whispered, 'Good luck.'

She nodded and they went in different directions.

Hunter moved stealthily, keeping to the shadows, pausing frequently to listen and to smell. In the clear night air his other senses, not sight, would warn him of any danger. There was no moon and no cloud and the shadows cast by the walls were more imagined than real. However, there was one thing working in their favour – no one was expecting trouble from within. Dayan's men were concentrating outwards, the enemy their fellow Israelis. In spite of their demeanour, their bravado, fear pervaded the compound as each of the men wondered what the future would hold. For years it had been dreams of fame and fortune that had sustained many of them. The adoration of their fellow Jews, the establishment of a stronger, *Greater* Israel. Of the men under Dayan's command only half a dozen were mercenaries, there for the money. The remainder were fanatics, prepared to die but determined to escape and fight again. As Dayan had told them, the battle wasn't lost until the last man was dead and they were far from that. Their movement would live to fight another day. Stronger and better supported than ever. It would only take time and they had plenty of that. After all, they had been fighting for two thousand years already. They only needed to escape, to recoup and continue the battle. Dayan knew that fanatics were the easiest people to lead, the greatest self-deluders, martyrs to the cause, whatever that might be.

Hunter found the side door Ruth had described to him. It was unlocked and he swung it open slowly, carefully. It moved silently and he stepped into the deeper gloom, a ghost in the shadows. He paused. The all-pervading odour was a mixture of oil, petrol and diesel. Cars and lorries in an enclosed space. The floor was even underfoot and Ruth had told him that the garages were kept spotlessly tidy. Hunter moved silently around the perimeter of the room. He estimated it was thirty perhaps thirty five metres square. There were doors leading to storerooms every few paces. Hunter looked into each of them and found them well stocked with tools, oil, diesel tanks and the paraphernalia of spares needed to maintain a fleet of vehicles. One door led to a corridor and into the main building. It was fireproof, made of metal and opened inwards. Hunter brought a stack of five litre cans, full of oil, from a storeroom and stacked them alongside the door. He hid a handful of plastic explosive amongst the cans and set the detonator. He tied a piece of string from the door handle to the ring spindle of the detonator and the trap was set.

He placed a lump of plastic explosive on the side of the main diesel storage tank and set a timer. Next he worked his way amongst the cars and lorries. Checking inside the nearest cab, he saw that the key was in the ignition. It made sense to leave the keys there. He did not have sufficient detonators to set each one individually and so ran cordtex between each vehicle. Running a junction spur of the white cord to each vehicle, he tied a double figure of eight knot in the end and wrapped plastic explosives tightly around the knot. Unlike a detonator there was no guarantee it would explode, however nine times out of ten it worked. Anyway, he had used enough explosives amongst highly inflammable material to ensure that nothing survived. What he had laid he had no doubt was over-kill. Satisfied, he made his way to the door he had entered by and took a cautious look outside. All was still quiet.

Easing himself through the opening, he took a deep breath

of fresh air, clearing his lungs after the pervading smell of the garage. The quiet of the night was torn apart by the shockingly loud noise of machine gun fire that had him diving for cover.

It took a second to realise that he was not the target and that the firing was coming from the other side of the compound. He saw a fleeing figure and heard yells and then one voice could be heard above the rest ordering them to stop shooting. Silence fell over the compound and Hunter could hear the faint murmuring of men talking to each other over their radios. He looked at his watch. Twenty minutes to the explosion in the communications room.

He unslung the Russian VAL Silent Sniper rifle and flicked off the safety. Silhouetted against the skyline Hunter could see a sentry who looked deformed in the light. It took a moment to realise he was wearing old-fashioned night intensifier goggles and was in the act of raising a gun to his shoulder. Hunter's shot, as silent as a sheep's cough on a mountainside, took the man squarely in the torso and threw his body over the edge of the wall. There was a distant clatter but no scream and nobody fired at Hunter. Night vision goggles compounded Hunter's problems. It was time to get the hell out of there.

Another man appeared on the other side of the square followed closely by a second and third. They were crouched down, the man in front pointing. They too had the disfigured appearance of men wearing goggles. Hunter set the gun to automatic, aimed and fired, sweeping the gun right to left. It was eerie to hear the stutter of coughs instead of the loud clatter of bullets but it was just as satisfying to see the three men either being hit or throwing themselves under cover. Ruth was two thirds of the way back to where Hunter was hidden when a machine gun opened fire and bullets sprayed around her. Hunter realised that it came from above his head, less than five metres from where he crouched. Assuming they wore goggles Hunter broke out into a cold sweat at the thought of how lucky he had been not to have been spotted and shot.

He looked up but could see nothing, the sentries hidden by the angle of the roof. Taking three hand grenades, he pulled the pins and lobbed them one after the other on to the roof.

He heard the clatter, the yells of consternation and then the explosions swiftly followed one another. The gun stopped and Ruth took the opportunity to run as fast as she could.

When she reached Hunter she gasped a few lungfuls of air and said, 'Sorry. I was spotted by one of the guards. He didn't challenge me but just started shooting. They're as nervous as newborn colts. I thought I'd get away with it when I identified myself but he didn't give me a chance.'

'Did you set the explosives?'

'Yes. In the helicopter and in the other garage. Just like you told me.'

'Well done. We've been lucky so far. They've got night vision goggles so if we move they'll see us easily.'

'I know, I noticed. What can we do?'

Hunter grinned wolfishly. 'They're the old fashioned type. They take time to respond and a bright light will leave them blinded for a minute or more.' He was reaching into a bag as he spoke. He withdrew a Very-pistol and a handful of cartridges. 'Fire this and keep firing until you run out of shells.'

'Why? What will you be doing?'

'I'm going to the garage you were in.' He reached into another bag, took out a timer and turned the dial. He connected it to a detonator and shoved the detonator into a lump of plastic explosive. Next he added half a dozen packs of more plastic and said, 'As soon as you've fired the pistol throw this against the gates and keep down. Okay?' He checked his watch.

Ruth nodded, her fear and nervousness masked by her training and professionalism.

'Right, fire now.'

Ruth pointed the pistol into the air and pulled the trigger. There was a bang followed by a loud whoosh and the brilliant white star-burst of light brightened up the sky and the compound. Before she could open the chamber and put in another shell Hunter was running. He sprinted, head down, shoulder blades hunched involuntarily as any second he expected a bullet in the back. There were yells and wild shots fired. Another four star-shells burst into the night. There were further yells and the shooting stopped. Hunter reached the door to the garage, paused to see it was all clear and ran inside. There were half a dozen lorries and three Land Rovers parked there. He checked the nearest Land Rover to make sure it was not one that Ruth had booby-trapped, climbed into the cab and started the engine. He was not surprised yet gratified to see that the tank was full.

The layout of the garage was similar to the one he had been in and he quickly located the diesel tanks. Ruth had set explosives to go off in twenty-five minutes; he set them on the side of the tank to go off in three and a half. Next he placed the last of the plastic on top of the bonnet of one of the lorries, checked his watch and set the timer for one and a half minutes. The plans he and Ruth had made were now being changed on the hoof. He darted back to the Land Rover, jumped in and drove straight at the door, smashing through it.

His abrupt eruption into the square took the sentries by surprise but one of them quickly recovered and opened fire. Bullets thudded into the back of the vehicle while Hunter swerved left and right trying to dodge the hail of death. Grenades exploded behind him and the shooting stopped. Then the bomb sitting on the lorry exploded blowing out the windows and rattling the walls. Almost immediately the one on the diesel tanks went up and flames shot into the air. Firing was indiscriminate, in all directions, as panicked men shot at shadows, convinced a major force was attacking. Hunter stopped next to Ruth and she piled into the Land Rover. He sat composedly, waiting.

'Get out of here,' Ruth screamed. 'What . . .'

There was an almighty explosion and the gate disintegrated. Hunter slammed his foot on the accelerator and the Land Rover shot forward and through the gate. Nobody fired at them. The turmoil and mayhem that was going on behind them masked their escape. The sentries thought they were under attack from an outside force that had somehow penetrated the compound. The last thing they thought was that anybody was trying to get away.

Hunter held tightly to the wheel of the bucking, swinging vehicle as they bounced over rough terrain. Ruth looked back.

Already the flames were dying down, the shooting fading behind them. 'The GPMG!' she exclaimed. 'We left it behind.'

'There wasn't much choice,' said Hunter. 'Check what we do have. I think they'll be too busy to come after us but you never know.'

Ruth quickly ran through the gear she had on and in her webbing. 'First aid kit, three hand grenades and my pistol and fifty rounds of ammunition. Sorry, but I lost my rifle.'

'No matter,' Hunter said, feeling around his own webbing. 'Two grenades, pistol and rifle. Here, check the ammunition.' He handed over the contents of a pouch and Ruth quickly counted it up. 'Eighty rounds for the VAL and a spare clip for the pistol.'

Hunter hit a large stone and the Land Rover bounced heavily. He slowed down, fearful of landing on a large rock with the sump and causing serious damage to the vehicle.

'What do we do now?' Ruth asked. 'Keep going?'

'No. We circle back.'

'What! Are you mad?' Ruth was aghast. 'We've only just got out. We were lucky beyond words and now you want to go back?'

'I want to make certain that Dayan doesn't escape.'

'How can he? We've destroyed all of his transport. He's holed up there until he can find another way out.' Ruth gripped tightly to the safety bar in front of her as they bounced uncomfortably along.

Hunter was aware that what Ruth had said made sense. They had stopped the war and now it was time to escape. They wouldn't stand a chance against a concerted attack by Dayan's men and their deaths wouldn't achieve anything. Reluctantly he nodded. 'Okay. Let's get the hell out of here. We've set enough explosives back there to raze the place to the ground. It's time we looked after ourselves.'

The explosion was underneath the rear passenger's wheel. The Land Rover lifted, stalled and flipped onto its side, sliding down the rough scree of a steep gradient, sparks flying, tortured metal screeching.

Ruth hit her head on the windscreen, stars dazzling her.

Hunter's head painfully hit the roof. His grip on the steering wheel kept him from falling against the door as the window shattered and the vehicle bounced over the rocks. If his shoulder hit the side he could do untold damage to himself as rocks and stones flew past, some being scooped up and into the cab. They slid for a hundred, maybe two hundred metres before coming to a halt, slewing round as the ground levelled off. Incredibly the engine was still running.

'Are you all right?' Hunter asked as he tried to manoeuvre himself around to stand on the door. He held on to Ruth, helping her.

'I . . . I think so,' she touched her forehead. 'I've a lump coming, but nothing much. It hurts a bit.'

'Come on, we need to get out.'

'What happened?'

'Either we hit a land mine or somebody fired a rocket or heavy shell at us,' Hunter replied. 'I think it was a land mine.'

Ruth groaned. 'So much for a quick and easy getaway. It's a long walk.'

'Not so far,' said Hunter. 'I reckon we can be over the border and safe in two maybe three hours at the most.' He looked up. An oyster grey was lightening the sky to the east and the stars were fading rapidly. 'Dawn is fast approaching.' He had turned off the engine and pushed open the passenger door. He easily climbed out, reached down and pulled Ruth up beside him. 'We'll leave the weapons and ammunition. Take one first aid kit, two k-rations and all the water we can carry. We'll travel light and fast. Sit still for now while I scout ahead.'

'Why?'

'If that was a mine then we could be in the middle of a field. I don't relish the idea of stepping on one.'

'All the mines were cleared from here years ago. I think we were just unlucky enough to hit one that's been forgotten.'

'Maybe. On the other hand ten minutes' more light and we can be sure. It's not worth the risk.'

'How can we be sure? Mines are buried not to be seen.'

'They used to be. The UN charter on mines says that they

should be banned but if they are used then they must be marked so civilians won't walk over them and at the end of the conflict they can be easily cleared.'

'So what's the point of using them?'

'They slow down or stop vehicles from troop carriers to tanks from crossing a piece of terrain. Listen to me. I sound like I'm giving a lecture! If the Syrians played by the rules they could have laid a fresh mine-field around here in the last few weeks to box Israel in. It would make sense. And if they want world opinion on their side they will want to be able to say – Look! We did it by the book. The mines can now be removed with no danger.'

'Or it could be an old mine.'

'Do you want to risk it? For the sake of a few minutes?'

Ruth shuddered, 'I guess not. How will you be able to see them?'

'They're marked,' said Hunter, 'like that one over there.'

It took a second for his reply to sink in and then she exclaimed, 'What?' She whipped her head around looking in the direction he had pointed as though a snake was about to strike. She sighed with relief when she saw nothing. 'That's not even funny.'

'What?' It took Hunter a moment to understand that she could not see what was obvious to him. 'Look. There, that white stone. And that one. And that one.'

Ruth looked again. 'I can see white stones scattered across the ground, so what?'

'Ruth, a standard method of pin-pointing the whereabouts of the mines has to be established for each new field. As well as detailed maps showing precisely where each mine is buried. Most armies don't bother. The Serbs in Kosovo are an obvious example. There was no reason to think that the Syrians would do what they were supposed to but they have. They wanted to be seen as whiter than white once Israel was wiped off the map.'

'How do I know you aren't kidding? For some perverse joke.'

Hunter was about to retort angrily but shrugged and walked away. He knelt by the nearest stone, prodded the earth gently with his knife and then used it to scrape the loose dirt and small rocks away. Within seconds he had exposed the round deadly object and lifted it out. Ruth stood where she was, her eyes wide. She was brave in the normal sense of the word, but it took a special kind of courage to deal with unexploded mines and bombs. When asked, Hunter jokingly put his choice of profession down to the frontal lobotomy he'd had as a child. He unscrewed the plunger, lifted it out, unscrewed the base of the plunger and dropped the detonator into the palm of his hand. He threw the plate sized disc to Ruth and said, 'Here, catch.'

She had recovered her poise and did so deftly. She looked around her in the strengthening light and said, 'We're right in the middle, surrounded by white stones.' She shuddered, 'We were lucky not to have hit more than one.'

'I know. Come on, let's get walking. If Dayan's men are chasing us they'll have to follow on foot as well. The advantage is on our side. We just need to be careful where we put our feet.' He was examining the plunger from the mine. 'Look,' he pressed down and there was an audible click. 'That sets it. You lift the weight and bang. It can be set from ten pounds to fifty pounds. Ten pounds is anti-personnel, fifty pounds is anti-tank.'

'What's that one?'

Hunter grimaced. 'Ten pounds.'

'That proves it. How can we trust the Syrians? The mines might not be by the rocks.'

'There wasn't any point in putting the markers there in the first place if that was the case. Just because you're surrounded by enemies all out to get you there's no need to be paranoid,' Hunter joked feebly.

Quickly they sorted the gear. Hunter hefted the VAL in his hand, reluctant to leave it. But, he rationalised, Dayan's men wouldn't be coming after them. Escape lay in speed. Over the border and into Syria. Damascus was within walking distance and if they weren't picked up by a border patrol they could find help at the British Embassy. If they were picked up by the Syrians, Hunter was sure that Macnair would get them out.

'Let's go.' Hunter took the lion's share of the gear and helped

317

Ruth to discard everything that was not essential. They walked side by side away from the wreckage, towards the rising sun. At the last moment Hunter decided to keep his pistol and an additional ten rounds of ammunition.

Hunter took the precaution of checking another three rocks to make sure they did mark the position of a mine. They did and he set off at a cracking pace, Ruth easily keeping up with him. Twenty minutes later they were standing on a gentle incline and looking towards the hills of Syria when they heard the sound of a vehicle followed by gun shots. The ground around them erupted as bullets flew into the hard packed sand and gravel, ricocheting in all directions.

28

When the shooting started Dayan had been asleep in his quarters. He was exhausted as he battled to save his life and his movement. He had been in communication with all his contacts world-wide, demanding, cajoling and blackmailing them into helping. Finally he was satisfied that he had done all that he could and that there was a possibility of saving something from the mess. The Knesset was in uproar, some members were calling for Dayan's arrest and others insisted that he was not to blame but was a hero. Political chaos was being fermented by his organisation which was expert at obfuscation. He felt sure that if he muddied the waters enough he could survive. He was beginning to believe that if he blamed David Golightly and Macnair's outfit for going off half-cocked then he could get away with it. His mind raced with ideas and possibilities. Finally he fell asleep, plotting and dreaming.

The sound of gunfire was somehow a part of a dream which became more real. It penetrated his conscious until he snapped awake. At that moment the door to his quarters burst open and an aide appeared.

'Sir, we're under attack,' he announced breathlessly.

Dayan threw back the bedclothes and said, 'I know that, you fool. What's happened?'

'I don't know. I heard the shooting and rushed to wake you.'

'Well find out. Call Goldstein or Sheffield and tell me what's going on.' He dressed quickly and strapped a pistol to his waist. Nervously he waited. He was not prepared to expose himself to danger, rationalising that he was too important, that without him the movement would collapse. Dayan had spent a lifetime hiding the fact that he was a physical coward. He had hidden it well behind his bombast and bluster, his bullying and superior intellect.

The aide seemed to take forever as Dayan paced nervously back and forth. He heard an explosion followed by another. More shooting followed. He was considering climbing into the specially constructed bolt-hole to hide when the aide finally returned.

'Sir, it appears that the prisoner has escaped. We are not under attack. They are trying to find and kill him now.'

'What?' Dayan stopped pacing, the subsiding fear and over-whelming anger causing his face to suffuse red. 'Get Goldstein here! Now! I want to know exactly what's happened. Go on, get on with it,' he thundered as the man hesitated.

A few moments later Goldstein came rushing in. 'Samuel, I . . .'

'Do you have him?' Dayan interrupted him.

'No. He had help. The girl. Ruth.'

'What! Kill her! Kill them both!'

'We're trying,' replied Goldstein. 'Only they've caused havoc. The helicopter has been blown to smithereens and so have most of the lorries and cars. It was only a fluke we had a lorry and two Jeeps in another garage otherwise there'd be nothing left.'

Dayan went berserk. He smashed over a table, threw a vase against the wall, drew his pistol and emptied it into a sofa. He was beside himself with rage and looked ready to kill Goldstein, who suddenly feared for his life. Finally Dayan's rage abated, he took deep, gulping breaths and said, as calmly as he could, 'Find them. No matter what it takes find . . .' The words were cut off as the room shook slightly and a deep rumble came up from below. The doors leading to the stairs rattled and a draft of air could be felt flowing across the room.

Dayan looked ghastly. 'What . . . what was that?'

'I think,' Goldstein paused, gulped and continued, 'it was an explosion.'

'Get down there. Find out what's happened. Go on, man. Get on with it.'

Goldstein rushed out of the room. He was away long enough for Dayan to start yelling for him. Finally he reappeared. If it were possible he looked worse than before. 'The communications room has been blown to bits. We found the bodies of the operators in one of the cells.'

'My God. Is there no end to it? What's happened upstairs?'

'The two of them have got away.' Goldstein mentally cringed, though he kept his face straight and looked Dayan in the eye.

The expected explosion did not come. Instead Dayan spoke with an icy calmness that was even more frightening. 'Get after them. Now! Stop them! Kill them!' He spoke in staccato sentences. 'I want them dead. Go.'

Goldstein was about to argue then thought better of it. Once he was upstairs he would send Sheffield. A chase was more in his line. As he turned to leave Dayan stopped him. 'Wait. What about the armoury? Has that been checked?' The blank look on the other man's face was answer enough. 'You fool! Must I do all the thinking around here? Get somebody to check it. Carefully. It could be booby-trapped.'

Numbly Goldstein nodded and left. This was not why he had joined Dayan. He was a strategist, a thinker. He didn't go around killing people. He planned while others executed orders. He was there because of his belief and the fact that he had been able to deliver many names of American sympathisers to Dayan's cause. He wanted out but knew that he had to bide his time. He'd get an opportunity to escape. Dayan was like Hitler, caught like a rat in a trap giving superfluous orders to non-existent armies although in this case, to non-existent supporters.

He found Sheffield standing on top of a wall looking east, a pair of binoculars to his eyes.

'Do you see them?' Goldstein asked.

'Yes. About two kilometres away. I can give chase in about ten minutes.' He was as eager as a gun-dog that hears shooting.

'Good. He wants you to get them, dead or alive.'

Sheffield lowered the glasses and looked at Goldstein. 'I want him dead and her alive. We're just about ready. Luckily they hadn't attacked the ready-use armoury. I have one or two nasty surprises for them.' The ready-use armoury was a locked store room near the main gates. It contained missiles, heavy machine guns and other weapons. There was sufficient weaponry to hold off a small army while replenishments were brought up from below. In the compound below they watched as the three remaining vehicles were fitted with GPMGs and new Chinese Dragon Hawk missiles.

'Shouldn't you hurry?' Goldstein asked nervously. Sheffield terrified him and they both knew it.

'They won't get away,' said Sheffield calmly. 'I know what I'm doing. I heard the comms room is out.'

'Yes. It was blown to pieces.'

'A smart man, Hunter. I won't underestimate him again. What about the armoury?'

'It's being checked now. I sent Zarak and Belovski.'

'Good. They know what they're doing.' There was a yell from below and both men turned to look. 'I must go. I shall be back within six hours. Tell Mr Dayan.' Abruptly he turned and stalked away, Goldstein happy to see him go.

Goldstein sighed. He had better start taking stock. He needed to find out the full extent of the damage and to deploy the men around the compound. The last thing they needed right then was an attack by the Israelis. But having listened to the news broadcasts and the arguments that were going on from the United Nations to the Knesset an attack did not seem at all likely.

Zarak and Belovski stood outside the door of the armoury. They examined the door carefully. After a few minutes Zarak took a mirror on the end of a telescopic pointer, pulled it open and put the mirror through the door crack. The lights had been restored to the corridor and the lights in the armoury had been switched on from the control box outside the door. Zarak took his time. Finally he grunted.

'Anything?' Belovski was a short, squat, brute of a man whose finger dexterity and gentleness belied his appearance. He was an expert with explosives, a Russian émigré and a passionate Jew. Zarak on the other hand was nondescript, lost in a crowd of two, and a mercenary. He had learnt his trade in the Ukraine. When the Soviet Union had broken up he had left and sold his services to the highest bidder.

'Yes. Scissors will solve the problem. I think this man is an amateur,' Zarak contemptuously dismissed Hunter's ability and expertise.

A few moments later he pushed open the door and removed the explosives. 'Like I said, an amateur. I don't think we'll have many problems here.'

The two men meticulously checked the periphery of the room, working inwards. Ten minutes after they had begun they found the trap in the safe. It was quickly dealt with. Within an hour they had found the trap in the machine gun racks and were beginning to feel safer. It was a full three hours before they found the trap in the desk drawer and announced that the armoury was clear of explosives. Both men heaved sighs of relief. They left to report to Dayan.

Hunter and Ruth dived down the slope, hitting the ground hard, bruising hands and knees as they tried to avoid the bullets. Hunter slid a few metres and came to a stop, the wind jarred from his body.

After a second to regain his wits he said, 'Are you all right?' There was silence and he looked around for Ruth. She was lying nearby, not moving. For a fearful second he thought she had been killed but then she raised her head and turned it towards him.

'I'm not hit,' she said in a strained voice. 'But I've got a problem. I dislodged that stone,' she nodded her head at a white painted stone. 'And I heard a click,' she added.

Hunter swallowed and moved quickly towards her. 'Let's see what we can do,' he spoke lightly, for her sake.

'What can we do? Just go. I'll stay here. I'll feign unconsciousness and when they arrive I'll move. It'll be quick and . . . and painless.'

'Alternatively,' said Hunter, taking out his knife and probing

323

gently under Ruth's elbow which was resting where the stone had been, 'I can give you a kiss, you sit up and we go to Paradise together. I'll die a happy man. Or,' he scraped at the sand, 'you keep your weight down while I get a thumb to the plunger and get you out of there. Luckily we're out of sight for a moment. But they'll be galloping over the hill any second so we've no time to lose. Unless of course,' he stopped as an explosion erupted behind them and then he grinned, 'they find the mine field. That'll keep them busy for a while.' As he inched his thumb over the mine casing there was a movement of Ruth's elbow more imagined than real. Then, as his thumb touched the edge of the plunger the movement was real not imagined. He just managed to push down with his thumb as the plunger came up to meet it. 'Ah, got it.' Hunter slid his thumb over the plunger and shoved it back down the fraction it had moved. 'Take your elbow away and give me some room,' he ordered.

Ruth rolled away, flopped back with relief and twisted onto her stomach. Dry, retching heaves followed and then she stopped. 'Sorry. I've never done that before.'

'Don't apologise.' Hunter found a flat rock and placed it on the mine, holding the plunger down. He looked at it pensively for a moment but then shrugged. 'I can't think how to rig a booby trap so we'd better get going.'

He helped Ruth to her feet and they moved quickly down the slope. Hunter broke into a jog, Ruth right behind him. 'Follow me. I'll watch where we put our feet while you glance back and tell me if you see anything. Okay?'

'Okay.'

Hunter easily fell into the mile-eating lope he was used to, aware that he could keep going for hours. Although he knew that Ruth was fit he doubted she had trained for stamina like he had, a requisite for all clearance divers. The sun was now well over the horizon and the day was heating up quickly. In the distance Hunter could see the hills of Syria and nearer, the dark lush vegetation of the forest he knew lined that side of the border. The white rocks were easily avoided and Hunter risked a glance behind him. Ruth gave him a twisted smile and also looked behind. There was nobody in sight. The slope in the ground levelled out and now there were bigger rocks and boulders to contend with. As he jigged past them, keeping up the pace, Hunter suddenly had a fear of catching his foot and spraining an ankle or something worse.

'Ruth,' he called, 'don't bother looking back. Look where you're putting your feet. We daren't risk either of us tripping and doing ourselves any damage. We need to outrun them and that's all there is to it.' The words were barely out of his mouth when a shot was fired and a bullet hit the ground far to their right. 'Ignore it. It's a difficult shot to fire downhill at a running target and don't forget each time they shoot they have to stop and aim.'

Ruth gulped, the feeling between her shoulder blades like an itch she wanted to scratch but she kept running, her eyes fixed on the ground.

Hunter could feel the sweat trickling down his back. As he ran, a plan to slow down the opposition formed in his mind. He risked a glance behind. They had increased the distance and were at the very edge of gun shot range. He slowed down, conserving energy, wondering what the enemy were up to. They weren't taking any notice of Hunter and Ruth but were doing something to the ground. It took a second to realise that they were lifting mines. They intended bringing their transport with them. Hunter looked and counted eight, no nine, men at work. Another two were driving and Sheffield made twelve. It made sense. With nine of them lifting and shifting, the vehicles could follow quickly and once past the minefield would easily catch up. After all, the field would not go on forever. It would be a fixed width, maybe as much as a kilometre but more likely somewhere between half and three-quarters of a kilometre.

The land dipped again and they were out of sight. Hunter stopped. 'They're bringing the Jeeps with them. Look, that's the edge of the field. Damnation, I'd hoped it went further. We can run like hell but we won't be able to out run them.'

'So what do we do?'

'We try and slow them down. That gully will serve our purpose.

Come on.' He led the way to the edge of the mine-field and a deep gully that meandered across the landscape in the general direction that they wanted to go. 'Dig up some of the mines and bring them here and throw the rocks into the gully out of sight.'

'Why? Why not leave the rocks. It'll delay them for a few seconds as they feel around for the mine.'

'It'll also tell them that the mine has been lifted and make them wary of a trap. I recognised Sheffield back there and one thing he isn't is a fool.'

Ruth asked no more questions and went to dig up some of the mines. She was careful to press the ground back into place in an attempt to hide the fact that it had been disturbed. A shot rang out so close that she jumped. She looked across at Hunter as he put away his pistol. She was about to ask him what he was doing when he disappeared into the gully. A few seconds later he climbed back out carrying a large green lizard.

He placed it carefully on the ground where it lay, dead. He stripped off the jacket and trousers he was wearing until he stood in only shorts and tee-shirt. Quickly he stuffed the legs and arms with stones and earth and laid them out on the ground. Hanging the arms and torso over the edge of the gully, he picked up the lizard, cut its head off and squeezed blood out of the body onto the leg bottoms. He stood back to appraise his handiwork. Not great but not bad, he thought.

'Bring the mines here,' he indicated a spot about ten metres from the "body".

'What are you doing?'

'Setting a trap.'

'That won't fool anybody,' she said dismissing the idea. 'Let's just keep running.'

'Ruth, the gully will help but they can drive along the top and head us off. I can lay a few mines but they won't necessarily drive over them. We need to tempt them in this direction. They'll see this and hopefully will take a closer look. One thing for certain is that this points the way we've gone. We need to destroy their Jeeps if we're to stand a chance. One mine under any wheel will be sufficient. Now, I'll bury the mines while you get some more.'

He quickly dug into the ground and covered a mine. He set them half a metre apart and staggered them by the same amount. Ruth brought another six and Hunter ended up with a zig-zag pattern of twelve mines stretching about six metres across an obvious route to the dummy.

'Right. Let's get a few more mines and get out of here.' Hurriedly they dug up a further five. Hunter took one of them and stopped at the edge of the gully. 'Duck down,' he said, throwing the mine upside down over the edge. It landed and exploded simultaneously. Earth and rocks shot into the air and a dust cloud wafted over them. 'They'll hear the explosion, see the clothes and think one of us has had it. Now let's go.'

'You think of everything,' Ruth said. 'Any more tricks?'

He ignored the question. 'Once we're down,' he climbed into the gully, 'I'll remove the detonators from the mines so they won't be dangerous.' The gully was about three metres deep, steeply sided but easy to scramble down. Where they stood it was four or five metres wide but they could see that it narrowed to half that a short distance behind them. Hunter walked along, unscrewing a plunger and detonator as he did. As he made each mine safe he put it into a bag and took another from Ruth. Within minutes he was finished.

'Let's get going,' he smiled at her. 'It's time we took our training for the marathon seriously.'

She managed a tentative smile back. Somehow he instilled confidence in her which made her believe they would make it. They broke into a run but almost immediately had to slow down. The gully was strewn with rocks and boulders of all shapes and sizes, worse than the open country. The fear of injury was uppermost in their minds. The gully narrowed and twisted. At one point it closed over their heads, both sides almost touching in the middle. They were protected from the sun at first but it suddenly burst over the edge and the gully began to heat up like an oven. There was no breeze and the air was already becoming stifling.

Half a kilometre along Hunter scrambled carefully up the side. He looked over the edge and back along the way they had come.

He took a pair of field glasses from a bag and focused them. He saw the two Jeeps carefully driving down the slope, one behind the other, the men walking, stopping and kneeling in front of the lead Jeep. They stopped and someone shouted and pointed. The Jeeps had been heading at right angles to the gully, away from the trap, when the dummy was spotted. The lead Jeep turned and drove towards the trap. It stopped short and a man stood up through the sun-roof. Hunter recognised Sheffield. He looked carefully at the dummy, binoculars glued to his eyes. He gestured behind him and said something. The second Jeep inched forward towards the dummy. It was less than a metre in front of Sheffield when it ran over one of the mines. The front bucked, the Jeep slewed around and landed on another mine. This time it was thrown to one side. It tottered and slowly continued past the point of no return. As it hit the ground a third mine was set off and the Jeep was blown to smithereens. Sheffield had ducked down as the windscreen in his Jeep shattered, spraying him with glass and causing tiny nicks and scratches all over his hands and face. One tyre of his vehicle blew and the force of the explosion shoved the Jeep bodily back a metre or more. At the first explosion the men had thrown themselves flat but pieces of metal and debris rained down on them, killing one and injuring another two. The fuel tank remained intact for a second or two after the third explosion but then erupted. As the burning petrol seeped along the ground towards the second Jeep, Sheffield rammed the gears into reverse and accelerated backwards out of the way of the flowing flames. The men who could, stood up, dazed and disorientated. Sheffield yelled at them and they knelt or lay down, weapons ready.

As the flames crackled and died with no further incident, the men began to climb to their feet again. Sheffield climbed down from the Jeep and knelt on the ground. Hunter watched as he removed a knife and began to probe the ground. He worked his way towards the dummy, crawling along the ground. When he reached it he stood up, anger and disgust on his face. Hunter's binoculars were so powerful he felt he could reach out and touch Sheffield even at that distance. He watched as the men argued, Sheffield gesticulating and pointing, the men shrugging, sheepish. Two of their number made no effort to get up; one in obvious distress propped himself up on an elbow. One of the men went over to him, knelt next to him and then felt the injured man's leg, shaking his head. The man sank back down. Another man approached the burnt-out and shattered wreck, looked inside and said something with a shake of his head. Hunter counted the men. There were nine including Sheffield. The odds had changed in their favour but not by much. Nine men could do the job as efficiently as twelve.

Some of them were scrambling down into the gully while two of them turned their attention to changing the wheel on the Jeep. Hunter slid back into the gully. 'Time to go,' he said. As they walked Hunter told Ruth what he had seen.

'Good. It should slow them down.' She looked at her watch. 'It's not even zero eight hundred hours and we have the whole day to survive.'

'Ruth, I've been thinking. Dayan's organisation is badly wounded. If we stop him now he's gone once and for all. If we let him re-group and re-build his movement again somebody may have to stop him again. And the next time it might not be possible. TIFAT is attacking tonight and I want to be there to help them. You can go on if you like. I don't mind. You've done more than your fair share.'

Ruth sighed. 'I guess not. To be honest I've been thinking much the same thing. This is my fight, not yours. We've come this far so I guess we ought to see it through to the end. One way or another. Can we go a little faster? I'm getting a prickly feeling in my neck.'

Nick felt a surge of admiration and something else. Right then he would have given half his fortune to kiss her.

29

Macnair was satisfied that he had done all that he could. His conversation with Admiral Charles M. Myer of the American Sixth Fleet had been highly satisfactory. A Sikorsky S-80 Super Stallion helicopter had delivered a net full of wire rope and spars and Macnair's men were busy building tripods and fixing blocks and tackle. When he was told the objective of the mission, Charles Myer didn't hesitate to give his full co-operation and promised Macnair that the helicopters he needed would be ready when called for. In the meantime Macnair stood on the bridge of the ship and looked at the coastline through long base binoculars, designed so that the glare from the sea did not interfere with the view.

Jim Carter stood next to him, also studying the coastline. 'I guess this is as good a spot as any,' said Macnair.

'It looks it, sir. It's deserted. The beach is narrow and the water gets deep very quickly. We can get in close, drop the anchors in a Mediterranean moor and back in.'

'What's a Mediterranean moor?' Macnair asked. His knowledge of nautical matters was strictly limited.

'It's where a ship or boat drops one or two anchors and backs up to a jetty. It enables many more boats to have direct access to the land. I suppose,' Carter shrugged, 'it's called that because this is where it was first done.'

'Are they ready to break the cable?'

'Yes, sir. Hiram is down there now.'

'Good. I know we have plenty of time, but I'd like everything

330

finished so we can move quickly when we have to. Has every-body eaten?'

'Just about. The last few are going through now. Mainly the morning watchmen. If you want to go below and get some rest I can take over up here. I'll call you when we're ready.'

Macnair stretched and stifled a yawn. 'I think I will. We've a long twenty-four hours ahead of us.'

Walsh stood on the fo'castle. The two anchors had been securely stropped off using a screw slip. The screw slip was shackled at one end to a deck clench and the other was secured around the shackle next to the anchor ring. The screw slip was turned tightly until the weight of the anchor was taken off the cable and transferred to the slip. One of the men broke apart the lugless joining shackle connecting the cable to the anchor. Two men took hold of the cable while Walsh operated the capstan. They dragged the cable along the deck and down aft. The first shackle of cable lay on the deck, all 27.5 metres of it. They dropped the end and walked back to the bow.

'Is that enough?' Sam McReady asked.

Walsh shrugged. 'I guess so. If we break the cable here and fix it back to the anchor we can do the same to the other one.'

An hour after starting the evolution they had two shackles of cable laid out each side of the ship and the anchors reconnected. Walsh went up to the bridge and said to Carter, 'That's it, Jim. The inboard end of the cable has been shackled to deck clenches in each corner of the aft deck and the cable is ready to pass out. I've rigged two inch manila rope to haul on so I guess we're ready to go.'

'Thanks, Hiram. I had a word with the General. We'll start operations at fourteen hundred hours. That'll give us plenty of time. In the meantime as soon as all the equipment is ready the men can take it easy. Tell them to get some sleep, if they can.'

Walsh nodded agreement. He could use a few hours himself, ready for the night ahead.

It was mid-morning and Hunter and Ruth found the going slow.

The gully was becoming more difficult to walk along, attempting to jog out of the question. Already both of them had slipped a number of times and pulled a muscle or two but luckily nothing that was a full blown sprain. Suddenly they heard the Jeep. It was coming up fast behind them. Both stopped under a rock overhang and listened intently. The Jeep roared past out of sight and faded into the distance.

'What's going on?' Ruth asked.

'It's what I'd do,' said Hunter. 'Get far ahead and come back slowly. That way Sheffield knows he has us in a pincer.' He grinned. 'Which is all to our advantage.'

'How?'

'It means they've split their forces. Us two against four or five of them, why that's almost even odds,' he bantered.

'I wish I shared your optimism,' said Ruth sourly but, in spite of herself, could not help being enthused by Hunter's brand of cheery optimism. It was now stifling hot and they both took healthy swigs of their water. When she stoppered her bottle and hung it on her belt, Ruth observed, 'At least by drinking it we don't have to carry it.'

Hunter unwrapped a chocolate bar, specially manufactured to contain extra glucose and raisins. It was a soggy mess, half melted. He broke it and handed half to her. 'Eat this. The energy surge will make you feel better.' He dropped the paper on the ground.

'Are you mad?' Ruth was aghast, bending down to pick up the tell-tale sign that they had been there.

Hunter grabbed her arm and pulled her upright. 'I want them to know. I want them to feel cocky and sure of themselves as we carelessly let them know we've passed this way. I want them lulled into a false sense of security so that they'll think us so stupid that we drop paper. That way they'll be more likely to walk into my trap.'

'What trap?'

'I don't know yet, I haven't thought of one,' he replied casually, much to her exasperation. 'Come on, let's go.'

Hunter started walking again, Ruth right behind him. Then he stopped. 'I think,' he said, 'that it would be a better idea for you to walk in front.'

Ruth didn't question it but did so, assuming Hunter had his own reasons. He did, but omitted to tell her that if he had underestimated the speed of the men chasing them then the first indication of trouble could well be a bullet in the back. Or, Hunter listened carefully, his ears tuned in to the sounds around him, he might just hear the snick of a rifle being cocked early enough for him to warn Ruth and dive for cover.

The sun was now beating straight down into the gully and Hunter felt as though he was being grilled alive. He felt his skin prickling where it was exposed to the sun and, in spite of his tan, becoming burnt. They were now clambering over rocks and the going was getting decidedly harder. Hunter was beginning to wonder whether they should climb out of the gully and head across the easier flat ground. The problem was, if they were spotted and Sheffield's men were in radio contact, which was a reasonable assumption, the heavily armed Jeep would easily catch them. In the open they wouldn't stand a chance.

By the middle of the afternoon Hunter was beginning to worry. He had not found what they needed and it was fair to assume that Sheffield and his men were beginning to get nearer. At best Hunter knew that they were walking into a trap. A couple of grenades dropped into the gully would soon finish them.

The sides of the gully suddenly became higher and they found themselves in shade. The sides closed over leaving only a narrow gap and the bed of the gully flattened out, becoming easier to walk on. It was at that point Hunter saw the dark shadow at waist height in the side of the wall.

'That could be just what we need,' he said. 'If that's a recess, we might be able to hide there.' He walked towards it.

'Wait!' Ruth said harshly.

Hunter stopped and looked at her questioningly. Ruth picked up a handful of small stones and dirt, approached the opening and flung them into the opening. She stepped back as angry hissing could be heard and two black and grey snakes slithered angrily over the edge of the opening.

'Ugh,' said Hunter, 'I hate snakes.'

Ruth raised a quizzical eyebrow, glanced at him and then returned her attention to watch the snakes slide into the gully. 'You mean there's something you're scared of?'

'Not scared. I just don't like them. Thanks. I would have put my hand in there and got a nasty surprise.'

'They won't kill you,' Ruth began.

'I know,' Hunter interrupted her. 'They're vipers. A nasty bite that'll leave you ill and weak but not life-threatening to a normal healthy man or woman. Deadly to a child, though.'

'How do you know so much?'

'It's part of the desert survival training course we do. I ate snake once. It was like chicken, only more tender.' They had spoken in whispers, eyes glued to the snakes. The two reptiles had slithered away from them and then stopped on a shaded flat stone, coiled up, raised their heads to listen and then sank down to sleep.

Ruth repeated throwing the stones into the recess but its occupants had fled. Hunter stepped warily up to look. The side of the gully had been scraped away and a rock fall had made a partially walled enclave a metre wide by half a metre deep. The wall was about a metre high. He stood looking at it thoughtfully for a second and then looked back at the snakes.

'Ruth, can you stack some rocks over here and build up the wall?' As he spoke Hunter was shucking off his webbing. Taking one of the shoulder belts, he used his knife to cut it into thin strips. When he tied them together he had a length of strong material about nine metres long. He did the same again with another piece of webbing, added it to the first piece but kept a separate length of about three metres. He retraced their steps to find the dried-up branch of an olive tree he had noticed that had obviously been swept down the gully by a previous storm or more likely a flash-flood. Tying a slip knot in one end of the short length of material, he knotted it to the end of the three metre long branch.

Cautiously and slowly he approached the two snakes. He surmised that they must have eaten recently as they hardly took any notice of him. Normally they would have been away like lightning if they had felt in the least bit threatened. Stretching forward as far as he could, he dangled the noose over one of the snakes. He was about four maybe five metres away and the snakes suddenly stretched up to look at him, taking fright. Deftly he dropped the noose over the nearest one and as it whipped around he jerked the line tight. The other snake slithered away at great speed while his reptilian captive arched back and forth in a frenzy.

'What are you doing?' Ruth asked. She had added a number of rocks to the wall and, without being told, had taken up a position to guard their backs.

'Preparing our defence.' The snake wriggled and thrashed but was gradually slowing down as its airway became blocked. 'Rip out one of your jacket pockets,' he said.

The snake was about a metre long and as thick as a man's thumb. Ruth used a knife to cut the pocket out and handed it to Hunter. Dropping the branch, he held the webbing material, feeding the snake into the pocket. It just fitted. He put his thumb and forefinger around the neck of the snake and squeezed gently. As its mouth hung open he loosened the noose and removed it from the snake. Letting go of the snake, he clamped the pocket shut using the material to hold it in place. He was gratified to feel the snake move as it regained full consciousness. Placing the snake on the wall, he smiled at Ruth.

'Now we set the trap,' he said. He took two of the mines and placed them where the gully narrowed above them. Next he cut two one metre lengths off the branch. Finding a large flat rock, he held it against the gully wall. He jammed it in place using the two pieces of the branch. Next, he swept them away and watched with satisfaction as the rock landed squarely on top of the mines. He tied the end of the longest length of material to the bottom of the wood, looping it around both pieces and led it to the recess.

'Ruth, can you cover the webbing with dust and small stones? Nothing too heavy that'll jam it when I pull on it.'

'Sure.' Ruth got to work.

He reset the rock and then replaced the detonators and plungers in the mines. Finally he got handfuls of dust and sand and scattered it lightly over them, hiding them from sight.

'Right, now it's time to get out of sight. Get behind the wall and let me see if I can spot you.' Ruth gingerly climbed into the recess, careful not to dislodge any of the rocks she had stacked there. Hunter added a few more rocks and was finally satisfied. He climbed in beside her and lifted the snake off the wall. He was gratified to feel it moving restlessly in the pocket.

It had been thirsty work and they both took a satisfying drink of water and settled down to wait.

'Ruth, I wanted to ask you . . . What happened in Switzerland? Why didn't you just kill me?'

'Orders. Dayan was desperate to discover who you were and what you knew. At all costs we were to take you alive. When we knew which direction you were taking we were dropped off to meet you. If we had tried to take you the chances were you would have died keeping out of our clutches. Hence the subterfuge by us.'

'Your idea?' Hunter could not keep the smile out of his voice.

'Naturally.'

Hunter stifled a laugh. 'In that case I'm glad the operational brains are no longer working for them.'

Ruth smiled.

There was no wind and the gully was like an oven. It was stupefying and Ruth found herself nodding off, her head falling forward and lifting with a jerk. Hunter closed his eyes and meditated knowing that it helped to increase his awareness of his surroundings. It was late in the afternoon when he raised his hand.

'They're coming,' he whispered.

Ruth frowned, hearing nothing. Then . . . a scuff, a jingle of metal on metal, then silence.

Suddenly someone spoke. 'Over there. The cave. Somebody could be in there.' They heard the snick of a safety catch being flicked off. 'Don't forget what Sheffield said. Only shoot if we're sure. He doesn't want them to know where we are.'

'Are you going to walk over there and put your head in? You could get your face blown off. Alternatively a few bullets will settle the matter. Of course, we could walk past and get a bullet in the back. But then, if they are there, they'll sneak out and escape. What's it to be?'

'We fire a few shots and then radio Sheffield and tell him what we've done. Movement!'

Hunter had cut the pocket open and placed it on the wall. He gave a nudge and the viper uncoiled itself and moved angrily into the gully.

'Don't shoot! It's a snake. Ugly creatures. At least we won't give our position away. Wait until it's gone then we'll head off.' There was silence and then, 'Let's go.'

The two men passed the recess and Hunter risked a glance at their retreating backs. They moved carefully, slowly, examining the way ahead. They were abreast of the trap when Hunter pulled hard on the makeshift rope. The pieces of branch collapsed, the rock dropped and both Hunter and Ruth crouched low with their hands over their ears and their eyes tightly shut. Both mines exploded with a huge bang that reverberated along the gully. As the dust settled and wafted towards them there came a rumbling noise and then the sides of the gully caved in.

Hunter looked up and saw that the walls had collapsed creating a solid barrier across the gully. 'Come on, it's time to go.' He helped Ruth climb over the wall. There was no sign of the two men who had passed and Hunter knew that even if they had not been killed immediately by the explosion they were now buried under tons of rocks and would die soon.

They hurried back the way they had come, chased by a dust cloud that hung in the air like a nuclear mushroom cloud. They jogged for a few hundred metres before the ground became too rocky and they were forced to slow down. Already the day was beginning to cool as the sun passed over the hills and cast a deep shadow in the gully and across the land. After about a kilometre Hunter stopped and climbed up the side and onto the flat. He used his binoculars to scan the area they had just left. He had the patience of a cat and lay still, watching. After a while he was gratified to see movement. Two men appeared, one either side of the gully and close to the explosion. He saw two black balls fly through the air followed by the shattering bang of hand grenades exploding. The two approached the gully slowly. One he recognised as Sheffield. Hunter slid down into the gully and grinned at Ruth.

'That should keep them guessing. Were we caught in the explosion? Are we dead and if not where are we? Did we escape ahead or are we back here? Sheffield has some hard choices to make and he's running out of manpower. So let's put as much distance between them and us as we can. Once it's dark we can climb up out of here and run on the easier ground.'

They set off, the gully becoming gloomier by the minute and the way underfoot more difficult. It was perhaps inevitable that as night fell Ruth should stand on a rock which instantly slid from under her. Her foot twisted and she fell with a bone-jarring crash.

Macnair was on the bridge. The ship was a mile off shore and he was practising going astern in a straight line. The problem was, everytime the ship started to go backwards it veered to one side. Finally, in disgust, the General said, 'Jim, do we have any ship handlers on board?'

'No, sir. But Napier is RM and will have had a lot of experience in boats. He might be able to help.'

'Ask Mr Napier to join us. Let's see if he has any more joy than me. I just don't understand it. There's no reason why we go shooting off to one side and if we can't drive backwards in a straight line we'll have problems lining up on the shore.'

A few minutes later Napier appeared. 'You sent for me, sir?'

'Lieutenant Napier, have you handled a ship before?'

'Eh, no, sir. Why?'

'I'm trying to get the ship to go backwards and it keeps veering off to one side. Damn it, Hunter made driving this thing look easy.'

'With all due respect, sir, Lieutenant Commander Hunter is used to driving ships and has spent years practising. However,

I do have a lot of experience with twin engined boats. Let me see what I can do.'

'Please,' Macnair waved his hand in front of him.

'Midships,' he ordered. 'Half astern both engines.'

The helmsman repeated the order and Napier stood looking aft, watching how the ship performed. As soon as stern way was on the ship veered to starboard.

'Stop both engines. Half ahead both.' He watched until the ship was no longer going backwards and said, 'Stop both engines. Hard a port. Half astern starboard.' The ship took longer to respond but slowly she picked up speed and went astern in a straight line. 'That's your problem, sir.'

Macnair was frowning, looking at the sea and the straight line the ship was travelling. 'What is?'

'Unfortunately both shafts are turning in the same direction when they should be going clockwise and anti-clockwise to reduce paddle wheel effect.'

'What's that?'

'As the screws turn not only do they push the ship ahead or pull us backwards but they also pull the ship to one side. You probably noticed that you had to keep a few degrees of wheel on to hold a steady course.'

'Yes, I did. About five degrees.'

Napier nodded. 'Paddle wheel effect is far more pronounced when going astern. Get her into position, sir and do as I just did and you'll drive her straight onto the beach.'

'I have a better idea, Lieutenant. You drive her onto the beach. Are we ready, Major Carter?'

'Yes, sir. All the gear is ready to go. The boats are turned out and ready to launch.'

'All right, Mr Napier, take her in.'

'Aye, aye, sir.' Napier headed towards the beach and when they were about two hundred metres away with the echo sounder showing ten metres of water beneath the keel he turned the ship hard to port and took the way off. The boats were launched and they hovered a hundred metres away either side of the ship. He lined the ship up at right angles to the beach and drove her slowly straight in. At about fifty metres he ordered the starboard anchor to be dropped. The ship sailed parallel to the coast paying out the cable as she went. After two cables Napier ordered the port anchor to be dropped. The starboard cable was hauled in and the port cable veered out until the ship was sitting equi-distant between the two anchors. He lined the ship up with the beach and steamed slowly astern and at the shore. When the yell from the stern was that the screws were churning up the sand he stopped both engines.

The boats were signalled alongside and the two inch manila rope passed down to the crews. They headed onto the beach and men from both boats leapt ashore dragging the ropes with them. They ran up the beach and six men on each rope began heaving. The manila quickly gave way to the heavy cable and soon they were sweating and pulling on the iron links of the anchor cable. When they had pulled the cable all the way out the ship rested on the weight of the two cables, close into the shore, her stern lined up with the beach.

Four jackstays had been wishful thinking. Two tall metal tripods were handed down and carried up the beach. They were jammed into the sand and steadying guys were fixed from the top of the tripods and secured to long spikes hammered into the ground. Extra flexible steel wire rope was shackled to the top of the tripods and led back onto the ship. There the wire rope was passed through a snatch block shackled either side of the superstructure three metres above the deck and then fed through another snatch block shackled to the deck. The two jackstays were rigged. Onto both wire ropes was hooked a further snatch block with a strop and hook hanging from it. Another line fed from the block and hung to the deck.

The equipment had been broken down into bundles held in strong nylon netting. The netting was clipped onto the hooks hanging under the snatch blocks, the jackstays were hauled tight and the bundles lifted off the deck. They were fed over the stern and ran smoothly down to the beach, controlled by the line fed from the block. As each bundle was unhooked the snatch block was quickly hauled back inboard and another bundle hooked on. It took less than thirty minutes to get all the equipment ashore.

The men followed, carrying their personal gear with them. By sunset they were finished. All equipment and men were in teams of eight and ready to be picked up. Five helicopters would be used, with three as back-up.

02:00 hours was departure time.

Hunter was instantly by her side. 'Are you all right?' he helped her to sit up.

She let out a heavy sigh. 'I think so. Just tired I guess. Ouch,' she exclaimed as she moved her legs. 'It's my ankle.' She sat forward, flexing her shoulders and arms, stretching to touch her foot.

Hunter gently felt around her left ankle. Already it was swollen to twice its normal size. 'Sprained, I'm afraid. Sorry, I shouldn't have pushed you so hard.'

'Nonsense,' Ruth retorted. 'There was no choice. Let me try and stand and we'll see if I can walk.'

Hunter helped her to her feet and kept one hand under her arm as she took a pace. It was just as well that he was ready as her leg collapsed under her and he only just managed to prevent her from falling. Instead, she stumbled against him and he was aware of her lithe firm body against his. He looked into her eyes and saw an invitation. He kissed her gently and then more passionately. After a minute or two they broke apart.

'I've wanted to do that practically since I first saw you,' he said.

Ruth smiled shyly. 'What do we do now?'

'Keep going.'

'No. Nick, I think you should leave me here. I'll try and hide while you go and do what you have to do. I'll be all right.'

'No, you won't,' Hunter retorted. 'If Sheffield finds you I hate to think what he'd do to you. We'll rest here for a while until it's pitch dark and then we'll climb out of here. It'll be easier up there.'

'Nick, I'll be a hindrance. I can barely hobble.'

'You won't be hobbling, I'll be carrying you.'

'But . . .'

'But me no buts,' he put a finger to her lips. 'We'll ditch the gear and travel light. Finish the water and the food. I'll put a compress on your foot to keep it from dangling and jarring too much.'

Ruth smiled. In spite of their predicament she felt calm, at ease. Hunter had an incredible way about him that made everything seem simple and matter of fact. If he said he was going to do something he did. There was no argument, no discussion. And, she thought happily, no fear.

They finished their water and food. Hunter strapped up her ankle and they shucked their webbing and extraneous equipment. Hunter kept his gun and knife. He helped Ruth to her feet and put her onto his back, piggy-back style. He tucked his hands under her legs and nudged her up to a more comfortable position.

'Okay?'

'Yes. Only the gun is digging into me.'

Hunter slid Ruth to the ground, undid the belt, adjusted it and strapped it around her waist. He put her on his back again. 'Okay?'

'No problem. Are you sure you can manage?'

'Easily. You're as light as a feather.'

Ruth chuckled. 'Liar. Whatever I am, I'm not that. Giddup, boy,' she gently squeezed her knees together.

'I take it you ride horses,' Hunter said.

'No. Only men,' Ruth replied mischievously.

'Hold tight.' Hunter scrambled up the side of the gully. He paused to look and listen but the night was silent. The moon had not yet risen and the stars shone down from a cloudless sky. It was a beautiful, breathtaking night, a myriad stars illuminating the sky like fairy-lights. A breeze had picked up, blowing towards the coast as the land cooled faster than the sea and the heavier, denser air over the land moved west to the Mediterranean.

He tried running for about a hundred metres. It was hopeless. He couldn't get into a rhythm as he was having to use his hands to hold Ruth on his back. Stopping, he gently lowered her to the ground. 'Wait here. I've got an idea.' He ran back to the gully, climbed down and found the webbing they had discarded.

Returning to Ruth, she asked, 'What are you doing?'

'Making a harness. It was your comment about riding that set me thinking. If I now loop these two shoulder belts like this, and let them hang down, we might give you a better ride and I might be able to move faster.' Putting the belt on around his waist, he slung two straps over his shoulders. 'Up you come.' He lifted her on to his back. 'Now put your feet in the shoulder straps either side of my knees.' He helped her find them. 'Try pushing down and putting your weight onto the straps.'

Ruth did as she was told. 'Aah, that hurts but the other one's okay.'

'Can you use one leg and your arms to hold on?'

Ruth experimented, shifting her weight on his back. 'How's that?'

'I can cope if you can. I've now got my arms free and can run better. Let's go.' Hunter started to jog. Ruth was a solid one hundred and thirty pounds dead weight on his back but Hunter ran as though she wasn't there. He concentrated on where he put his feet, careful not to fall, ignoring her presence. For her part Ruth kept her arms tightly around Hunter's shoulders and tried to ignore the pain in her injured ankle as it jogged against the strap. She could feel the heat and sweat pouring out of Hunter, although it was curious that initially it was only on the front of his tee-shirt.

Soon Hunter was running like an automaton, only his superb stamina and strength keeping him going. Searing pain in his shoulders had been relegated to the deepest recess of his mind as he kept running. After fifty minutes his vision became blurred and he stumbled but recovered. Ruth had been nodding off and jerking awake as fatigue settled in. She lifted a hand to wipe her face and gasped. In the starlight her hand was black.

'Nick, stop. Stop now.'

Hunter stumbled again, slowed, stopped and sank to his knees, his head between his arms, panting. Pain shot up his legs and back and as Ruth climbed off he rolled onto his back, gasping.

343

Excruciating pain shot across his chest and the tops of his arms as he lay there, unable to move.

Ruth kneeled by his side and lifted the webbing off his shoulders. He flinched. The rough webbing had rubbed away layers of skin and was caked in blood. The front of his tee-shirt was sodden, blood having soaked down into his shorts.

'Nick, this is a mess.'

'What is?' he mumbled.

'The webbing has rubbed away the skin on your shoulders and front. I need to put some antibiotic powder on and cover it up.' Ruth opened the first aid kit, found the plastic container with the powder and shook liberal quantities over Hunter's wounds. Next she taped field dressings to both shoulders and across his front. 'Take these,' she put two powerful painkillers into his mouth which he managed to swallow with difficulty.

'Thanks.' Hunter looked up at the stars feeling his strength return, the pain receding. He sat up. 'That's better. Come on, time to go.' He dreaded the thought of lifting Ruth onto his back once more.

'Take a rest for a bit longer,' she said. 'Let the tablets work.'

He smiled at her and didn't argue. 'Once we're out of this do you fancy coming sailing with me?'

'Where to?'

'Around the west coast of Scotland. Maybe down to Wales and Cornwall.'

There was no hesitation. 'Yes.'

He leant forward and kissed her. He looked her in the eyes and said, 'Now it's time to go. I feel invigorated at the idea of sailing away with you.'

'I'd better warn you, you'll need all your strength for what I've got in mind.'

'In that case,' he said, 'I'd better start building up my stamina.' He stood up, willpower alone ensuring he didn't wince.

'Wait a moment. This jacket I'm wearing is too small for you but cut off the sleeves and put them between the dressings and the straps. It might help.'

Hunter used his knife to hack the sleeves off and did as Ruth suggested. He picked her up and gritted his teeth as fresh waves of pain swept across his chest. 'Okay?'

'Okay,' she answered in a small voice, aware of what he must be suffering but awed by his indifference and determination.

Hunter broke into a jog, his strength renewed, the pain not as bad as it had been. However, the effort was taking its toll and he quickly tired, falling once more into a shambling gait. Sweat dripped down his face and stung his eyes, his breath became laboured and soon he was on auto-pilot, thinking of only putting one foot in front of the next. Then again. And again. He stumbled, recovered, stumbled again and fell. Ruth had been jerking in and out of consciousness and gave a little scream as Hunter hit the ground heavily. She rolled off him and sat up. Next to her was a white rock.

30

'Nick, we've got a problem,' Ruth said softly.

Hunter groaned. 'I know. The Champagne's gone warm and the ice has melted.'

'There's no time for jokes, Nick. I think we're in the middle of the minefield.'

'What?' He sat up quickly and looked around him. In every direction he could see the white stone markers. As the enormity of their position sunk in he broke into a cold sweat. How on earth had he missed stepping on a mine? 'The gods,' he announced, 'are on our side.'

'No, they aren't,' said Ruth. 'Listen.'

They both heard the faint sound of an engine in the distance and as they looked back the way they had come the loom of headlights appeared and faded as they dipped up and down.

'Sheffield,' said Hunter.

'Well done, Sherlock Holmes. What'll we do?'

'We'll do nothing,' said Hunter, struggling to his feet. 'But I've got an idea. Stay here until I come back for you.'

'Why?' Ruth asked with alarm. 'What can you do against seven armed men?'

'You'll see,' was the short reply. 'Now, stay here.' Hunter shed the harness he had made and was left standing with the gun wrapped around his waist and the knife in its scabbard. 'I'll be back,' he leant down and kissed her.

Ruth flung her arms around him and pressed her lips tightly to his. 'Be careful, please,' she whispered.

'Aye, aye, madam.' He gave a mock salute and turned away before he saw the tears in her eyes. Without Ruth on his back he ran as though he had wings. He ate up the distance and was almost past the place he was looking for. As he ran, dodging the white stones, he kept sweeping his gaze left and right. Finally, on his right he saw the path that Sheffield and his men had made through the minefield. It was the one piece of ground Hunter could be positive the Jeep would traverse.

Stopping, he darted up the slope until he could see the limit of the minefield. Quickly he knelt down and began to scrape away the top soil with his knife. He loosened the hard-packed sand and stone before scraping a shallow hollow right across the path with his hands. Standing up, he looked for the Jeep. The loom of the lights was still fifteen maybe twenty minutes away as the vehicle came carefully across the desert.

Hunter dug up nine mines and placed them one after the other across the road, each one touching the next. He scattered sand and small stones over the top to disguise their presence. When he stepped back to look at his handiwork it was obvious something was wrong. The ground over the mines did not blend in with the surrounding land. Or maybe it was because he knew what he was looking for. He shook his head; the reality was anybody driving carefully over the path would see it. Unless . . .

He looked back. The lights were much clearer now and Hunter guessed the Jeep would be on him within the next five minutes or so. Quickly threading his way through the minefield, he dropped down behind a large boulder. The car drew nearer. As the lights passed his position he bent double and ran back towards the path. The Jeep was thirty metres away and driving slowly when he reached the pathway. He sprinted after the Jeep and quickly closed on it. There were no yells and no shots were fired at him. When he was ten metres away he stopped, drew his pistol, took careful aim and fired rapidly.

He emptied the gun into the back of the Jeep. Every bullet smashed into the rear window, hitting some of the men. There were screams and yells and suddenly the Jeep took off as the accelerator was hit to the floor. Seconds later the front wheels went over the mines and set off two of them. The sympathetic detonation set off the remainder in the line and the Jeep was blown sky-high, its back broken. Bodies were thrown everywhere, the diesel burst into fire, and rocks and sand rained down into the huge crater created by the explosion.

Hunter waited for the thunder to subside and the debris to stop falling. Walking slowly forward, senses alert, he was ready for any trouble. He stood looking down on the broken Jeep and the scattered inert bodies. The occupants were obviously dead. He tried to find Sheffield. For a long moment he couldn't see him but then he spotted the body. It had been thrown clear, almost at Hunter's feet. He could see an arm was broken and the back was covered in blood. Looking down at the body without pity, he turned to go. He had taken only a pace when a clamp wrapped itself around his right foot and he went down heavily and awkwardly onto the ground.

Dazedly he twisted round to see the grotesque features of Sheffield looming over him. One eye socket was bloodied and empty, his face covered in deep cuts and gashes, and the jaw hung to one side, broken. The automaton ignored his injuries as he pulled Hunter inexorably towards him. Hunter kicked and thrashed like a landed salmon, but to no avail. The one eye glared hatefully at him. The words uttered through the broken face were unintelligible.

Hunter kicked at Sheffield's face and incredibly the man brushed the foot aside with his broken arm. It was as though Sheffield was indestructible and felt no pain. Fear welled up in Hunter's throat. Logic told him that the man was neither indestructible nor immune to pain so this time he aimed his foot at Sheffield's broken arm. He was rewarded with a grunt of anguish and more high-pitched nonsensical words. But still Sheffield didn't let him go.

Sheffield suddenly gave a massive heave and Hunter was dragged under Sheffield's body. He dropped on top of Hunter, knocking the wind out of him. They lay face to face. Before Hunter could recover, Sheffield got his broken arm behind Hunter's neck, clamped his good arm across Hunter's throat, grabbed his broken arm and began to squeeze inexorably. Hunter desperately tried to bend his head, to keep the weight off his throat as breathing became harder and harsher. He looked up into Sheffield's leering face and good eye and then did the unexpected. He lifted his chin and tensed his neck muscles. As Sheffield dropped forward Hunter put his hands behind the other man's head and pulled him down. He opened his mouth and clamped his teeth into Sheffield's neck and bit as hard as he could, sawing his mouth back and forth.

Sheffield screamed and tried to pull away but Hunter hung on for grim death. Suddenly his teeth shut tight and Hunter spat out a lump of flesh, feeling blood spurt over him. He had bitten through Sheffield's carotid artery but he was too late. The pressure on Hunter's throat did not let up and Hunter began to die from asphyxiation. He was at the beginning of the long black tunnel that led to oblivion, sliding down it fast, dropping into that warm place where there was no more pain and anguish. He saw bright stars up ahead and rushed to embrace them. His last conscious thought was that Sheffield's strength had beaten him in the end.

The lights faded and the tunnel went from black to grey. His breathing was ragged in his ears, painful in his throat. He groaned and pushed at whatever was holding him to the ground. It was soft and yielded to his touch.

'Nick! Nick! Are you all right?'

'What? What? I . . . I guess so. Christ. What happened?' Painfully Hunter tried to sit up, his hand to his throat, massaging it.

'Sheffield nearly strangled you.'

Hunter looked at the body lying nearby and saw the bayonet sticking out of Sheffield's back, the spinal cord severed.

'What happened?' he croaked.

'I followed you. I was scared. So I hobbled and crawled after you. Then I saw the explosion. I saw Sheffield on top of you. I tried to pull him off but couldn't. I grabbed the bayonet from one of the others and cut his spine in half. You weren't breathing.' Her voice choked at the memory. 'I was terrified. I was sure I'd lost you. I started to give you mouth to mouth. It seemed like forever but it could only have been for a minute or two. You groaned and suddenly came to.'

Hunter groaned again, remembered what he had done, rolled over and was promptly sick. After a few minutes he stopped, a foul taste in his mouth. Wiping his face and hands, he rubbed his hair. He was covered in blood. Coated with the stuff. Awkwardly and stiffly he walked into the crater and to the Jeep. He located the front and opened the bonnet, found the hose pipe to the radiator and pulled it off. Warm water gushed out and he held his hands and face in it. It tasted metallic but Hunter did not care. A pint of real ale had never tasted better. Energy seeped slowly into him, exhaustion and pain ebbing slowly away. The doors of the Jeep were hanging open. Looking inside, he dragged a corpse from the back seat, dropping it onto the ground. He pulled a second and then found what he was looking for. A water bottle. It was empty. Walking back to Ruth, he found her sitting, quietly, exhausted on the ground.

'I'll get us some cold water,' he announced.

'Where from?'

'The other Jeep. I'll fill up this water bottle. Will you be all right?'

Ruth managed a wan smile. 'I guess so. Surely nothing more can happen now?'

'I don't know but just in case take this.' He handed her an Uzi machine gun he had found near the Jeep. In his other hand he hefted a Kalashnikov. 'I won't be long. He had no strength to run but he walked briskly enough. Ten minutes later he reached the other Jeep and located the bottom hose to the radiator. Cutting the hose, he filled the water bottle. He used the water to wash more of the blood away, took a bellyful of water and refilled the bottle. His strength was returning fast and he hurried back to Ruth. He found her where he had left her, only she was fast asleep. Looking at his watch, he saw that there were two and a half hours to go before the attack. How was he going to get Ruth and himself back to the compound? He knew he didn't have the strength to carry her.

Gazing at the wrecked Jeep, an idea percolated into existence.

He searched the wreckage for rope but found none. Instead he stripped the bodies of their webbing and belts and tied them together. Lifting the rear door off its hinges, he placed it on the ground. Next he tied the ends of the webbing to a corner of the door and dragged it up onto the flat surface of the path. Picking Ruth up gently in his arms, he was aware for the first time of her scraped knees and bloodied hands. She moaned unintelligibly but didn't wake up. He placed her on the door. Stripping some of the bodies of their jackets, he used one for a pillow and the others to tie Ruth to the door, her legs tucked clear of the ground.

Hunter picked up the makeshift harness and pulled. The smooth metal slid easily over the hard packed ground and he walked steadily towards their destination. From time to time the makeshift sledge would jam on a rock or screech loudly as it was dragged over a sharp edge, but on the whole they made good time. An hour later Hunter could make out the walls of the compound. He stopped for the first time since he started and took a drink of water.

'Can I have some?' Ruth asked.

'What? Yes, of course.' He knelt beside her and undid the cloth holding her down.

She took the bottle and drank greedily. 'I needed that,' she sighed and handed it back to him. 'Thanks for the ride.'

'Have you been awake long?'

'Not long. Maybe ten minutes. I couldn't understand what was happening at first so I lay still until I was fully aware. I saw you walking ahead and felt the bumps as we slid over the rocks. I was about to call out when I sort of dozed again. Not really under, just unable to move or speak. Odd really.'

'Reaction as well as exhaustion,' said Hunter.

'I guess so, doctor. Now what?'

'The compound's about half a kilometre away. There's a copse of trees over to the right. I'm going to put you there until after the attack. I'll come back for you later.'

Hunter picked her up and carried her towards the trees. Ruth snuggled closely against him, nuzzling his neck. 'Why not stay? We can while away the next hour or two until after the

351

battle. If there is one.' She looked up in alarm. 'What if they don't come?'

'The General said he'll be here so he'll come. If not personally then he'll send in the team. I need to be there to help. I guess they'll come by helicopter and I can do a lot of damage before they arrive.'

He stopped beneath a stunted tree. The undergrowth was fairly dense and he placed Ruth onto a large rock. Gazing about him, he said, 'That's odd. Look at that wall over there.' He went to take a closer look. 'There's some sort of door.' Try as he might he couldn't find a way to open it and so gave up. 'Not to worry. You stay here and this time I mean it.' Smiling at her, he added, 'I didn't say thanks.'

'What for?'

'For saving my life. If you hadn't disobeyed me I'd be dead now. Only,' he added, 'don't make a habit of it.'

'Of what? Disobeying you or saving your life?' She was laughing at him and he grinned back.

Leaning down, he kissed her nose, her eyes and then her mouth.

'Take care,' she said. 'I don't think I could bear it if something were to happen to you after all we've been through.'

'Don't worry, nothing will. I'll be back before you know it.' He brought her the clothes off the sledge and made her comfortable. 'Now rest. I'll be back soon.' He paused and then added, 'Before I go I've been meaning to ask you something. A life time ago when you laid me out when I was fighting Sheffield I heard you saying something about *ka-shi*. Somebody being dead yet killing someone?'

She nodded. 'Yes. It happened four, nearly five, years ago. We'd received information that a Chinese triad gang was using the Sudan to distribute heroin into the west, targeting mainly America and Britain. Using black women as carriers. You know the sort of thing. Condoms carried internally. Cheap and expendable couriers.'

Hunter nodded. 'Sure. It happens all the time.'

'Well this was a big operation. We paid off a local warlord

in the Sudan and passed the information to the DEA.' Ruth was referring to the American Drugs Enforcement Agency. She paused in thought, remembering.

'Go on.'

'We were asked by Washington to take care of the problem. You know us. We planned to the nth degree and carried out a text book attack. Going in three times stronger than the opposition with our special forces, we wiped them out. We took care of a particularly nasty Sudanese warlord along with about fifty of his men. In the process we destroyed tens of millions of dollars worth of heroin and trapped the triads in a building. Surrounding the building, we smashed it to smithereens. Yet somehow three of them got out. We still don't know how. Anyway, we were mopping up when we came across them trying to escape. Two old men and a scrawny individual who didn't look strong enough to stir his own tea. We knew who the old men were. They were the two big bosses of the triad and wanted by half the agencies in the western world. Our instructions had been explicit. No prisoners. We shot them both from close quarters. The scrawny one just stood there with his head bowed and his eyes closed. He looked defenceless and was obviously not carrying a weapon. The two old men died immediately but somehow the other one was unscratched. He remained standing there with his head bowed. We stopped shooting and approached him. We just didn't know what to do. Not knowing who he was, he could so easily have been an innocent who had been caught up in it all. Heck, anything. There were nine of us, three Mossad and six paratroopers.' She paused again.

'What happened?' Hunter prompted her.

'We walked up to this guy and he suddenly erupted. That's the only word to describe what happened next. He yelled "*ka-shi*" and went berserk. One blow each and four men dropped dead. It was so quick I swear they were dead before they hit the ground. Another was badly injured and I grabbed my bayonet and rammed it into the man's back, dragging the blade through his heart. His heart must have stopped but before he dropped he kicked two of the men from Mossad in their throats and killed them. It was awesome. He had actually turned to look at me and taken a step towards me when he collapsed. In my estimation his heart had been stopped for five maybe seven seconds before it was over. I learnt a lesson that night, I can tell you. No more second chances. Shoot first and ask questions afterwards. You don't bring back the dead, that's for sure.' Ruth sighed. 'Who am I kidding? If a little old man stood defenceless before me I'd still give him the benefit of the doubt. It's what our humanity demands of us.'

Hunter kissed her again and said, 'True. Only don't get close to little old men and remember the most dangerous animal in the world is the cuddly looking polar bear.'

'I'll remember that the next time I come across a polar bear in the desert. Now you'd better go.'

Hunter headed towards the compound, his senses alert, the Kalashnikov ready to fire. Moving silently, he was a ghost in the night. He stopped about three hundred metres from the buildings. There was plenty of activity with men coming and going around the tops of the walls. Checking his watch, he saw that it was 02:44 hours.

At 01:00 hours precisely, eight American USN helicopters had landed on the beach near the ship. Five were to be used in the operation; the other three were for back up in the event of failure. The memory of the débâcle when the Americans had tried to rescue the hostages in Iran still rankled. Not enough back-up· helicopters and aircraft failure on the night of the operation had resulted in the rescue attempt being abandoned. The ridicule of the world still brought blushes of shame to some American leaders' cheeks especially when it was pointed out that the Israelis had told the Americans not to proceed with too few helicopters. The Israelis had been proven right and the American operation had become a textbook study on how not to conduct an operation. So now, in typical American fashion, they went for over-kill instead. Macnair thoroughly approved of the American viewpoint.

The five helicopters were quickly filled with equipment and men. A final briefing took place standing on the beach, the quiet lapping of the Mediterranean at odds with the discussion.

'Ready to go?' Macnair asked Walsh.

'Yes, sir. All set. The two helos going high will arrive on station ten minutes before the rest. I've computed drop times and we'll be arriving two minutes after the attack begins. That should give Dayan and his men a nasty surprise.'

'Good. I'll keep in touch. Now I need to go back on board the ship. It's time to report in to our political masters.'

'I don't envy you, sir,' said Walsh. Already he was gripped with a pre-op fever, an adrenaline high that carried men into battle and danger. Mentally he was already dropping through the night sky, attacking the enemy.

Ten minutes later the first two helicopters were airborne and clawing for height. Inside the fuselages the men sat quietly, each immersed in his thoughts, the primary one being whether he would survive the night or not. The flight seemed to be over before it had began. Unlike Dayan's nocturnal journey, they flew openly with the blessing of the Israeli military who had been told that five helicopters belonging to the United States Navy were flying night exercises over Israeli territory as a sign of solidarity with Israel. The only Israelis who knew the truth were a handful of politicians within the Knesset.

At fifteen thousand feet the helicopters could not be heard from the ground. They passed ominously in the night, eerily blotting out the stars to anyone who happened to be looking up at the moment of their passing. No lights were flashing and radio silence was strictly maintained.

'You have amber,' the navigator of the lead helicopter announced to Walsh. It meant they had ten minutes to go to the drop. The time ticked quickly away as the men prepared to jump. The door was rolled back and the men checked each other's gear one last time. 'You have green.'

Walsh threw himself out through the door.

Dayan was pacing the room in his quarters. They had heard the faint sound of an explosion earlier on and he was worried where

Sheffield and his men had got to. Not that he cared one jot for their safety but he wanted their fire-power as well as Sheffield's special skills. Not that he expected any trouble. He would be leaving the compound in less than twelve hours now that he had a safe haven lined up. His business empire would collapse but he had other assets salted away for dire emergencies. Grinning wolfishly, he had no doubt that he would be back within two years. He would increase the pressure on his friends and enemies alike. It was time to up the ante and he knew precisely what he would do. Israel would become a powerful, rich and safe country three times the size it now was.

His mood turned to white-hot rage when he thought about Hunter and the damage that had been wreaked in the compound. In particular he felt lost without world-wide communications, manipulating and ordering his vast army of cohorts to do his bidding. His pacing became more agitated until finally he could stand it no longer and he decided to go upstairs and into the fresh air. He might discover that Sheffield was back.

On the rooftop, standing by the battlements, he looked east towards Syria. His hatred of the country rose up like bile in his throat and he clenched his fists. The warbling of his mobile phone was a surprise. It was an ordinary digital phone and usually he did not bother carrying it around the compound as the reception was so bad. This had proved to be the case earlier on when he had tried to use it. He had left it in his pocket and forgotten to switch it off. Now, by a helpful quirk of attenuation, somebody was able to get through.

Flipping open the lid, he said, 'Dayan.'

He was greeted with crackling and a faint voice. More imagined than real he heard somebody say, 'Samuel?'

Grinding the phone against his ear, he cupped his hand over the other one. He paced the roof trying to get a better reception. Hearing his name again, he thought he recognised the voice.

'Abdullah?'

'Yes,' crackle, 'attack.'

'What? What was that?'

'Attack. Attack,' the word was repeated clearly.

Suddenly Dayan felt a gripping pain in his guts as he bent over, sweat forming on his brow as he tried to hear what his contact in Saudi had to say.

'Just learnt . . . any minute . . . Tif . . .' he faded away.

An attack at any minute? Tif? What was Tif? TIFAT, the acronym exploded in his brain. TIFAT was attacking any minute? Where ? Here? It wasn't possible. Few people knew where he was. 'What was that? Is TIFAT attacking here? When?

There was silence, crackling and then clearly Dayan heard, 'Zero three hundred. Helicopters. Get ready,' and then the connection faded completely.

Dayan looked at his watch. It was 02:48 hours. There was hardly any time. He needed to get down to his escape route and hide. He would take Goldstein with him.

'Zarak!' He recognised one of the men walking across the compound. 'Is there any sign of Sheffield yet?'

'No, sir. Nothing.'

'Right! Get ready for an attack. I have it that we will be attacked in less than ten minutes. Get the heavy weapons and missiles ready.'

'They are, sir. I just need to warn the others. Half the men are sleeping.'

'Then get them up. Now. And then get more ammunition and weapons out of the armoury.'

Zarak was about to protest that they had all they could handle but thought better of it. There was no arguing with Dayan when he gave an order. It was simpler and safer to do as he said. Zarak ran yelling through one of the doors rousing the men. Next, he ordered three of them along with Belovski to follow him down to the armoury. They ran down the stairs and along the corridor. The door was open and they began to grab weapons and ammunition from the racks and stack them outside the door. Zarak looked at his watch. 02:56 hours.

Belovski grabbed a French FAMAS automatic rifle and froze. He goggled at the block of plastic explosive that lay hidden in the bottom of the rack. He was suddenly aware of the fact that he and Zarak had underestimated Hunter.

'Hsst,' he warned Zarak and pointed.

'My God! What is this?' Zarak asked. He quickly and nimbly felt along the detonating cord. Satisfied he took out a knife and cut the block free. 'Quickly, either find the timer and detonators or remove the blocks.'

They worked feverishly not knowing when or how the explosives would erupt. While Zarak reduced the risk by removing the blocks, Belovski followed the hidden detonating cord. It was awkward and laborious, and twice when he thought the cord ran straight on, it turned away at an angle and he lost precious seconds re-locating it. Suddenly he broke into a cold sweat as he realised that Hunter had taken them for a ride. The other traps had been easy at first but more difficult as each one was found. But this! This was special. The others they had contemptuously dismissed as the work of an amateur. This was expert. Seriously expert. What time would it explode or was there a different firing mechanism? Like a booby trap? Relief flooded through him as he reached the end and found the small plastic timer. He looked at it and balked. The second hand was sweeping towards 03:00 hours. He didn't even have time to run away. He had to cut the electric connections. The wire slipped in his hands. In desperation he grabbed the timer in one hand and the wire in the other and pulled them apart. The countdown to the explosion stopped with only seconds to go.

'Got it!' he cried ecstatically. 'I've stopped it.' It was precisely at that moment he knew that he had been had. It was, in fact, his last thought as a second timer, five seconds slower than the first, reached 03:00 hours. The explosion was devastating, ripping apart the armoury and shaking the foundations of the whole edifice like a jelly. The ammunition and explosives erupted as a result of sympathetic detonation which followed one another like Chinese fire-crackers. The missiles and guns stacked in the corridor blew – a blow too many. Cracks appeared along the walls and ceiling, fanned outwards and ever widening and then the building collapsed in on itself.

Dayan and Goldstein had, only moments before, closed the door on the specially constructed room hidden in the bowels of the building. They each carried a bag containing important papers and Goldstein was armed with an Uzi machine gun. As the building collapsed around them Dayan opened the secret door to the corridor that led away into the desert. He did not look back as he followed the torch light and plunged headlong down the corridor. The cat slinked after them.

31

Hunter was in the shadow of one of the walls, his senses alert, as he looked for a way in. The hole he and Ruth had blown in the gate was blocked again and there appeared to be a guard standing nearby. Hearing Dayan yelling orders, and men calling and running around, he took advantage to climb the outer wall. It was rough and dilapidated and he easily climbed to the top. He got his fingers curled over the edge and carefully raised his head to look. Nobody. Slithering over the wall, he lay in the shadows regaining his breath and looking about him. Glancing up for a few seconds, he grinned. The stars were winking on and off in a clear sky. At that moment he heard the clatter of helicopters, the noise seeming to come from all directions. The men in the compound rushed to take up their positions around the walls of the roofs and the night was torn asunder with the sound of heavy machine guns opening fire.

Hunter saw two men, less than twenty metres away, manning a General Purpose Machine Gun, firing towards the south. Bringing his own gun to bear, he flicked the safety to single shot and killed both men with a bullet in the back. He darted forward, grabbed the GPMG and turned it inwards. Across the compound, about a hundred metres away he saw a man standing with a missile launcher at his shoulder. Even as Hunter pulled the trigger and sent a hail of lethal lead pouring in the man's direction the missile was fired. The Chinese Dragon Hawk locked onto its target. In the throes of landing it was impossible to avoid and even as the men of TIFAT were leaping out of the hovering machine and onto the ground the missile slammed into the side of the helicopter. The machine blew apart, spilling men and equipment onto the ground, killing and wounding indiscriminately.

The heavy rounds of Hunter's GPMG cut the man in half before he traversed along the top of the walls finding other targets. Suddenly another heavy machine gun opened up and this time Hunter was the target. As the bullets swept along the wall towards him Hunter did the only thing he could; he dived head first into the compound. He somersaulted in the air, got his feet under him and landed with a breath-expelling thud onto the sand and gravel. He pitched onto his back and lay where he had landed for a few seconds, regaining his breath. At that moment the parachutists began to land, shooting as they did, cutting down targets left and right. The compound was thrown into a frenzy. The attack from outside had distracted them. Hunter had confused them and the parachutists rained death down on the defenders. At that moment the explosives in the armoury went off and it seemed as though a silence fell over the compound. Abruptly the firing began again, more concentrated, more deadly than ever.

Men trying to escape from their 'chutes were cut down while others rolled on the ground and out of sight. A man landing four metres from Hunter released his parachute a good two metres above the ground and landed unencumbered.

'Hiram! Drop!' Hunter yelled. Unquestioningly Walsh fell to the ground. Hunter shot the man who had stepped out of the shadows to shoot Walsh in the back.

The Lieutenant Colonel crabbed across the compound with a big grin on his face. 'Listen up,' he said into his throat mike, 'I've found Lieutenant Commander Hunter well and kicking.' The message was heard by the force and relayed to Macnair. As if in happy response the men of TIFAT attacked with an added ferocity and as missiles rained down on the walls of the compound, fired by the attackers outside, the opposition crumbled. Weapons were thrown down and hands raised. As suddenly as it had started it was over. The silence was a ringing endorsement of success as men came forward carefully, warily, alert for any double-crosses. They began to round up the enemy. There were only eleven survivors uninjured, two wounded and the remainder dead. There was no sign of Dayan.

Hunter and Walsh picked their way around the compound and the buildings. The explosion in the armoury had devastated the inside of the building and there was no way down to the lower floors.

'If Dayan was in there he's either dead or as good as,' Walsh announced.

'If he's in there,' Hunter repeated bleakly. 'I don't trust him. He could have sneaked away before you got here or during the fight. I know he was here just before you arrived because I heard him yelling orders but after that I heard nothing.'

'Sir.' David Hughes joined them, threw a salute at Walsh and grinned at Hunter. Then he wiped the smile away and said, 'Sir, we've six dead and five wounded. The wounded are on their way out now.' As he spoke a helicopter lifted into the night and clattered away, this time with the tail rotor lights flashing. 'They're being taken to the Sixth Fleet. I've been told by the General that the doctors there are equipped for full surgical operations.'

'Who died?' Hunter asked.

'Lieutenant Napier has the names sir, he'll be along shortly.'

'Thanks,' said Hunter. 'Now . . .' he broke off as the unmistakable sound of machine-gun fire came from the distance, a faint popping in the night. The unmistakable sound of an Uzi.

'Christ! Ruth!' Hunter took off at a run, yelling for backup.

Ruth was sitting where Hunter had left her. Her head drooped with fatigue and as she nodded off she would jerk awake, her heart hammering wildly. She saw the explosions and heard the gunfire as clearly as though she was in a cinema watching a film. Feeling the tremor of the ground under her bottom, she saw the helicopter explode. She was wide awake looking towards the compound hoping and praying that Hunter was safe. She smiled. She was looking forward to getting to know him better. He had

362

an inner strength that was . . . what? Awe inspiring. Yes, that was the word. He was, she thought, the most interesting man she had ever met. She spent the next few minutes pleasantly dreaming about Hunter and a possible future. Shaking herself out of it she thought, there can be no future. She was Mossad and he was TIFAT. After this operation never the twain should meet. Sailing in Scotland was merely wishful thinking.

The sound of rock grating on rock brought her back to reality. She sat still, senses alert, heart hammering. Was it Hunter coming back for her? But if it was, why didn't he call out?

'Nick? Nick? Is that you?' Ruth spoke in a stage whisper.

As the door opened slowly Dayan listened intently. The sounds of battle were in the distance. He had switched off the torch and stood quietly, allowing his eyes to become accustomed to the dark. Goldstein stood behind Dayan, his Uzi cocked and ready to fire.

At the sound of her voice Dayan froze. Goldstein lifted the Uzi, bringing it to bear in the direction of her voice. Goldstein stepped forward, dry leaves and twigs crackling underfoot. Ruth held her gun on her lap, her finger curled round the trigger, her left hand clamped tightly on the barrel holding it down.

'Goldstein!' she said loudly.

'Yes, me, you bitch!'

Ruth remembered the story she had told Hunter earlier about the ambush of the triads and did not hesitate. She pulled the trigger and kept her finger squeezed tight. As the gun kicked up to the right the bullets stitched a line across Goldstein's chest, from his bottom right hand side, through his heart and past the left side of his neck. Two bullets hit Dayan, one in the mouth and the other in the shoulder. As he staggered backwards, his finger coiled around the trigger. The Uzi fired a continuous stream of bullets that followed a line across the ground towards Ruth as Dayan fell. Ruth sat frozen to the spot watching the hail of death draw nearer. Seconds passed like an eternity, as her tired mind screamed at her to move. She couldn't. Her body refused to obey orders. The cat slinked out of the opening and into the wilds.

* * *

363

Hunter ran as fast as he could. The firing had stopped abruptly and he was tormented by the idea that something dreadful had happened. Even so he did not rush headlong into a potential trap. As he got nearer, he signalled the four men with him. They carefully fanned out and approached the area with caution. Standing patiently in the shadows, they carefully examined the scene in front of them. Ruth was lying on her side and nearby they could make out a body. Satisfied that it wasn't a trap, Hunter rushed over to her while two of the others approached the bodies and the remaining two covered them.

Hunter knelt by Ruth, trepidation in his voice and fear in his heart. 'Ruth? Ruth are you okay?' He gently put his hand down to her shoulder.

'Nick? Oh, Nick? Thank goodness.' She put her arms around him and Hunter drew her gently to him.

'Are you okay?' he repeated.

'What? Oh, yes. It was Dayan and Goldstein. Over there. Careful. I think I killed Goldstein but I'm not sure about Dayan.'

'Stay here,' he said to Ruth and then turned to the men with him. 'Cover me. Nice and slow now.'

They spread out, senses alert, listening, ready for anything. The night was quiet. Hunter stopped a few metres away from Goldstein and patiently waited. It was obvious that Goldstein was dead but of Dayan there was no sign. Slowly Hunter moved forward, stopping frequently to listen. He thought he heard a chink up ahead but couldn't be sure. He paused at Goldstein's body and checked for a pulse. Nothing. There it was again. A slither, a faint sound, from behind the rock. It could be anything from a wild cat to a bird roosting. But somehow, Hunter doubted it. Looking about him he signalled one of the men. It was David Hughes.

Hughes crept alongside Hunter who put his mouth to the other's ear. 'Any grenades?' he whispered.

'No. I've checked. None of us have any.'

'Okay. I'll go in. Cover me.' Hunter crawled up to the rock, stopped, listened, heard nothing and dived in. Rolling into a corner, he was ready to fire at anything that moved. He saw that he was in a tunnel and that ahead of him was a yellow glow, like the loom of a torch.

Hearing a faint noise, he climbed carefully to his feet. He stepped very slowly along the tunnel, making no sound. The tunnel curved to the left and as he approached the light he saw a figure sitting on the ground. It was Dayan. He sat with his back against the far wall; his eyes seeming to be closed. Blood coursed down his body. Hunter stood and watched him for a few minutes. He was in no hurry. Finally, satisfied that Dayan did not represent a threat, Hunter went forward.

The Uzi lay on the ground, still clasped in Dayan's fingers. Hunter put his foot on Dayan's hand and pressed hard. Dayan flinched and opened his eyes. In the light from the torch, lying on the ground, Dayan could see Hunter's face.

'Swine,' he croaked and passed out.

Wearily, Hunter bent down, uncurled Dayan's fingers from the gun, grabbed Dayan by the jacket and dragged him to his feet. Slinging him over his shoulders, Hunter picked up the torch and walked back down the tunnel. Halfway along he found the other four who had followed him in as backup.

'Is he dead?' Hughes asked.

'No. Although I don't know if he's going to live or not.'

'What'll we do with him?' asked Masters.

'That's for the General to decide,' said Hunter. 'Come on. Let's get out of here.'

Outside, Ruth was standing next to the rock. She looked in surprise when Hunter arrived with Dayan. 'We'll take him with us,' said Hunter. 'It's over. It's time to go. The helicopters will be waiting for us. Peter, Dave, give Miss Golightly a lift, please.'

Weir and Hughes joined hands in a chair-lift and Ruth sat on them. They picked her up and easily followed Hunter towards the compound.

'Boss,' said Masters, 'I've found two briefcases.'

'Good. Bring them. They might prove useful. In the morning we'll take a look behind the stone and see if we can get into the building and find anything else.' Hunter trudged away, each step harder than the last, determined not to show the others how much he was struggling. At last they reached the compound and he unceremoniously dropped Dayan to the floor. Dayan groaned but did not move.

A medic came across, examined Dayan and applied a field dressing to his wounds. 'I think he'll live,' was the verdict.

'Pity,' said Hunter. 'I suppose we'd better get him back to the ship. The General can decide what to do.'

'Nick,' Walsh appeared. 'General Macnair rang a few minutes ago. You and Ruth are on the first helicopter out of here. We'll stay and tidy up.'

'But . . .'

'That's an order. You're all in. You'll be a hindrance, not a help. So go.'

'Aye, aye, sir,' Hunter smiled weakly. 'I'll take Dayan with us.'

Dayan was strapped to a stretcher and placed on board the helicopter. It lifted off with just Hunter, Ruth and Dayan as passengers. At five thousand feet the American pilot levelled off and turned towards the coast.

Hunter took the sat-nav phone he had borrowed from Masters and called Macnair.

'Sir? Hunter. I've got Dayan here. He's wounded and needs medical attention. Do we bring him to the ship or take him to a hospital somewhere?'

'What? Damnation! Neither, Commander. Dayan must not be brought in alive. That was the agreement we had with the front-line states. They want no come-backs. No hero for the Israelis to rally around. No trial. Do you understand?'

'Yes, sir,' Hunter replied and broke the connection. Somehow, he was not surprised.

He undid his seat belt and went forward. He tapped the pilot on the shoulder and said, 'Sorry. A slight change of plan. Where's the nearest water?'

'Right below. We're passing over the Sea of Galilee right now.'

'Good. Can you go as high as possible and slow down? I've got something I need to throw out.'

'Sure. No problem.' The pilot slowed the airspeed and took the helicopter higher. He looked back. 'Nine thousand feet. Will that do you?'

'Thanks. I won't be a moment.'

Hunter looked at Dayan, strapped helpless to the stretcher. He felt no pity. The man had been prepared to kill millions of men, women and children. Dayan opened his eyes and saw Hunter staring at him.

'I will succeed,' Dayan said, barely audible above the noise of the helicopter. 'My supporters will rally around. I will not spend one day in prison. You'll see.'

'I agree,' said Hunter. He took hold of the door, slid it open and picked up the end of the stretcher.

'What are you doing?' screamed Dayan. 'Stop! This is a blasphemy! I am the saviour of Israel. Stop!'

Dayan on his stretcher slid out of the helicopter into oblivion. He screamed all the way down.

Hunter closed the door. He let out a sigh. Now it was over.

Back at the compound it was clear that there was no way into Dayan's lair. The tunnel led to a door that was jammed solid. It had been decided that it would be too dangerous to blow open and instead they lay charges within the tunnel and collapsed the roof.

Twenty minutes later the helicopters were airborne. The bodies of their own dead, including the pilot and navigator of the helicopter hit by the missile were stowed on board the first helicopter out. Satisfaction at a job well done was tinged with the sadness of their loss. Dawn was breaking on another warm eastern Mediterranean day as they landed on the beach. The helicopters were off-loaded and flew onwards to the American ships taking their own dead with them.

The remaining gear was dragged back up the jackstays and onto the ship. The jackstays were dismantled and stowed and the men followed wearily. Macnair had already told David Golightly that his daughter was safe.

After a few hours sleep, by mid-morning Hunter was to be found on the bridge of the ship, a mug of coffee in his hand.

Macnair joined him. 'Well, my boy, how are you feeling?'

'Fine, sir. A bit stiff.' He eased his shoulders, feeling the fresh bandages and plasters pulling across the cuts and scrapes lacerating his torso. 'I'll mend. There's nothing so serious that a few days won't cure. What's happening?'

'We're ready to go. I thought it wiser to let the men have a rest. The Americans have kindly offered to ferry them back to Cyprus. I've accepted. From there they'll be picked up by Hercules and flown home.'

'What about you, sir?'

'I'm going as well. I need to be back in London as quickly as possible. There's a lot of political fallout to deal with. However, I need to talk to you and Jim before I go. Once we're ashore you get the ship underway and head for Toulon.'

'Toulon?'

'Yes. Sail to Toulon and sell her. I've been in touch with your cousin and he's arranged for a ship's agent to meet you. The agent will sort out the sale. We'll put the money back into our coffers. I've a few disbursements to make.'

Hunter nodded, thinking about the dead men. 'I'll have the boats take the men and their personal gear ashore. Should I just signal the Americans and ask them to come?'

'No need. I've already done so. They'll be here soon. I've asked the Admiral for the names and addresses of the next-of-kin of the two dead pilots. I told him it was to allow me to personally thank them and offer my condolences. I'll make sure they appreciate the necessity for privacy when it comes to receiving a donation from the trust. In the meantime I want to brief you and Major Carter on some serious matters.'

'Roger, sir. I'll hand the watch over to Napier. He can send the boats in and raise the anchor and get us under way.'

Macnair nodded. 'I need to speak to David Golightly again. Apparently there's serious blood-letting on the floor of the Knesset. Pandemonium has broken loose with accusations flowing thick and fast. It so happens I may be able to do something about David's problem.'

Macnair left the bridge while Hunter contacted Napier and passed him his orders. He then followed Macnair below to the stateroom.

Without preamble Macnair said to the two men seated opposite him, 'Isobel has now discovered the names of the men and women all over the world who were helping Dayan. It's a frightening list of individuals. Some were either coerced or bribed whilst others helped out of conviction. I've given some of the names to Golightly and he's using them to quieten things down in Israel. In the meantime I've had copies made of all the information we've amassed and told Isobel where to send it for safe keeping. One copy is to David Griffiths. He'll know what to do should the need arise.'

'That's a bit extreme, sir, isn't it?' asked Hunter.

'No, lieutenant commander, it's not. If you saw some of the names you'd understand. The power represented between them is awesome. They could easily shut down TIFAT if they wished and I'll fight tooth and nail to stop that happening. I also don't trust them not to take, shall we say, extreme action, in revenge. So I have made it known to many of those named that I have the information and what will happen should they try anything.' Macnair smiled with satisfaction. 'It was rather enjoyable making some of them squirm. For your own sakes I won't show either of you the names as I think it's better you don't know. Just know where the information is should anything happen to me.'

Hunter and Carter nodded.

'Once you get to Toulon hand over the ship to the agent and finish the arrangements for the sale. I'll leave you a skeleton crew to help you get there. The rest of us will fly back to the UK. Jim, you stay all the way to Toulon.'

'And Colonel Walsh, sir?' Carter asked.

'He's flying off with me. I'm sending him to the States. He has one or two personal messages to deliver. I want him to look certain men in the eyes and make a few facts of life clear to them.'

369

'What about Ms Golightly, sir?'

'I've spoken to her father who said she can stay here for a while and rest. After that it'll be up to her. Once you get to Toulon she can return to Israel if she wishes. Incidentally, you may be interested to know that from those two briefcases you brought with you we've found hidden assets worth in excess of twenty million dollars. I've passed the information to David Golightly. He's in the process of acquiring those assets for Israel. I've let him borrow Isobel as she appears to have a natural bent when it comes to grand larceny. Right, that's all except to say well done. We came close to one of the most frightening incidents of the last fifty years. Too close. Let's hope it doesn't happen again. That'll be all.'

The two men stood up and walked out as Macnair began to pack his holdall with his personal belongings, deep in thought.

A short while later, back on the bridge, Hunter sat alone, once more officer of the watch, his feet on the console, the ghostly hand of the auto-pilot keeping the ship on track. The boats used to deposit the men ashore had been recovered and the helicopters were already arriving to pick up the team and ferry them onwards. Hunter was contentedly scanning the sea using binoculars when he sensed that he was no longer alone. He looked over his shoulder and smiled at Ruth. She smiled back.

'You've heard the news?'

'Yes. General Macnair told me before he left,' she replied.

'Have you decided what you're going to do?'

'About what?'

'About what happens once we reach Toulon,' Hunter said.

'That depends.'

'On what?' He held his arm out to her. Self-consciously she crossed the deck and stood next to him, enjoying his touch.

'On what you have in mind.'

'I've been sitting here thinking about that very thing. What I have in mind is to hire a motor-sailer, say thirteen or fifteen metres long. We fill her up with provisions and we head down to Italy and maybe the Aegean. Or even go west to Gibraltar. Scotland we can do another time. What do you say?'

370

Ruth leant down and kissed him. 'I say that sounds just wonderful.'

A cough behind them made Ruth spring back. Major Carter stood in the doorway trying hard to keep the smile off his face.

A Million Tears

by Paul Henke

1890. Murder and intrigue have forced the Griffiths family to flee their native Wales. They leave behind a village devastated by a mine disaster and the oppression of the Victorian ruling classes.

Their subsequent adventures represent the American Dream. With bravado born of necessity, Evan Griffiths builds a business empire – retail, transport, banking, real estate – in the frontier town of St. Louis. With an inherent sense of justice, and the support of his beloved Meg, he forges a political career. But on his right hip, Evan carries a gun. No one will ever hurt his family again.

In Wales, David yearned to travel, dreamed of discoveries. Shipwrecked on a coral island in the South Seas, he discovers himself.

His brother, Sion, dreams of flying, craves freedom and adventure. But will his dream – and Sion himself – die in the lawless hinterlands of the Wild West?

Through meticulous research, author Paul Henke expertly braids together fact and fiction, recreating the Frontier of America. With consummate ease, he conveys a vivid sense of life at the turn of the century, weaving the thread of history – and the lessons it can teach us – through his narrative.

The vitality of Henke's fiction is mirrored in the energy of his vibrant characters. On his vast canvas he captures their triumphs and their tragedies. In 'A Million Tears' he unveils the portrait of the remarkable Griffiths Family. A gem to be treasured.

ISBN 1-902483-00-6

The Tears of War and Peace

by Paul Henke

It is 1911 and David Griffiths is in Wales, bored and lonely. He travels to London at the behest of their family friend, John Buchanan, to start a new business in banking. There he gets caught up in the suffragette movement and falls in love with Emily. Against the backdrop of women's fight for votes and the looming First World War, the Griffiths build a vast, sprawling company encompassing banking, aircraft manufacturing, farming and whisky distilling.

The enmity of a German family follows them tragically throughout this period, leading to murder and revenge. At the end of the war, thanks to a change in the Constitution, Evan is invited to run for President of the United States. The family rally round for the most important battle of Evan's life.

With the Brown-shirts running rampage across Germany, David and Sion are soon involved in a battle for survival.

Sir David Griffiths is a colossus of a figure, striding across the world and through the century, a man of integrity and bravery, passion and dedication. Determined to win, nothing comes before the family.

The story is as compelling as ever. Historical fact woven into the fictional characters makes a breathtaking tale of adventure you will not want to put down.

ISBN 1-902483-03-0

Débâcle

TIFAT File I

A Nick Hunter Adventure

Following a summit meeting in Paris an alliance of interested countries form an elite fighting force to combat terrorism throughout the world. Based in Britain and under the command of a British General, the team is made up of Western, Russian and other non-aligned countries' special forces.

Without warning the terrorists strike. A group of bankers, politicians and industrialists are taken prisoner off the coast of Scotland and the new, untried force is sent to search for them.

The Scene of Action Commander is Nick Hunter, Lieutenant Commander, Royal Navy, an underwater mine and bomb clearance expert with experience in clandestine operations.

The enemy is one of the world's most ruthless and wanted terrorists – Aziz Habib! Hunter leads the team against Habib, backed up by two computer experts: Sarah from GCHQ and Isobel, hired by the General to run the IT for the new force.

While stock markets take a pounding and exchange rates go mad, the state sponsoring the terrorism is making a fortune. It has to stop. At all costs.

This is non-stop adventure from beginning to end. A riveting story told by a master story teller. You are guaranteed not to want to put it down!

Débâcle mixes fact with fiction which will cause you to wonder, how true is this story? Did it really happen?

ISBN 1-902483-01-4

Chaos

TIFAT File III

A Nick Hunter Adventure

Ambitious Alleysia Raduyev has inherited the family business – the largest crime cartel in Eastern Europe. Operating on the classic theory of supply and demand, she caters for her customers' every desire – narcotics, arms, prostitution, illegal immigrants, slave labour. Known as the black widow, she has systematically woven a web of conspiracy and treachery across Europe.

Cash rich but morally bankrupt, Alleysia creates a shadowy network of contacts to distribute her invisible supplies, oblivious to the deaths caused by drugs and desperation. Her payroll now boasts Heads of Security, Eurocrats, judges and politicians. Her power base secure, she calls a summit in Colombia. The leader of every major crime cartel rallies to her banner. The widow plans global expansion of her terrible empire, aided by her latest acquisition – three nuclear warheads.

Desperate to prevent the chaos of a new, anarchic world order, the West declares World War III against Crime. As violence escalates, the battle-hardened troops of TIFAT are pitched against the massed forces of Evil. With two successful missions behind them, the members of the anti-terrorist force have honed their specialist skills. TIFAT's inventory of technological and military resources has grown, along with its influence.

Their major asset is Lt. Commander Nick Hunter, a bomb-disposal expert whose reserves of integrity and resourcefulness will be tested to the full. His mission is clear: Search and destroy.

His target: the black widow.

Author Paul Henke's explosive new thriller is a clarion call, a stand against the moral and political apathy gripping society. Grimly he highlights the insanity of protecting the rights of the criminal faction rather than their victims.

'Chaos' will be published in the Spring of 2001.

ISBN 1-902483-04-9

About Paul Henke

Paul spent nine years in the Royal Navy and qualified as a bomb and mine disposal expert, specialising in diving and handling explosives. As a Lieutenant, he survived a machine gun attack by IRA gun runners in Ireland in 1976. Using plastic explosives he was responsible for blowing-up a number of Second World War mines found off the coast of Britain. He was promoted to Lieutenant Commander in the Royal Naval Reserve where he had command of various minesweepers and minehunters.

In 1979 he spent fifteen months in Nigeria where he was in charge of a saturation diving system prior to moving to the American Midwest.

He has travelled extensively, researching material for his work and is now a full time writer. He lives with his family near Loch Lomond in Scotland.

Author's Note

Thank you for reading my novel. I hope you enjoyed it. At the beginning of the book you will find my web site *and* my e-mail. I mean it sincerely when I invite you to write and tell me what you think of my books. I have had plenty of replies which, as an author doing one of the loneliest jobs in the world, I have appreciated very much.

Thanks again, and all the very best,